Praise for Bob Host

"An absorbing sequel to *Northkill, The Return* concludes the story of the authors' Amish ancestors as each contends with Indian captivity and wrestles with issues of identity, family, and spiritual truth. Skillfully researched detail—both the 18th century Amish world and that of Native America—heart-wrenching emotional journeys, and profoundly rendered themes of grace and God's sovereignty combine to create a tale I couldn't read fast enough, yet didn't want to end."

—Lori Benton, Christy-award-winning author of *Burning Sky, A Flight of Arrows,* and other historical novels

"*The Return* is frontier fiction at its finest, made all the more remarkable given it is the authors' own family history. Compelling and heartbreaking yet always full of hope, with enduring spiritual truths woven by master wordsmiths, this story is not only difficult to put down, it has a timeless quality that leaves you pondering for days. Beautiful!"

—Laura Frantz, bestselling author of *A Moonbow Night*

"*The Return* is a marvel. With unflinching commitment to history and an artist's palette of imagery, the authors have offered a rare and important tale that will break your heart and piece it back together again. My life is richer for having experienced this novel."

—Jocelyn Green, award-winning author of the bestselling *The Mark of the King*

"*The Return* captures in terrible and poignant detail the emotional and spiritual tug of war between conflicting loves, loyalties, and beliefs born of the human will to survive. Even more beautifully, *The Return* reminds us that between life's deepest struggles, there is a divine integrity to reality that transcends our many cultures, creeds, failures and victories. I didn't want this story to end, it is that good. And, for me, a descendent of the family whose story is told here, it hasn't!"

—James Hostetler Brenneman, President, Goshen College

"J. M. Hochstetler and Bob Hostetler bring to life the tale of their common ancestor, Jakob Hochstetler, and how he and his sons braved Indian captivity and later returned to their own people to forge new lives in their Christian communities. I admire and appreciate that no blame is cast or bitterness is held against their Native American captors. The importance of such stories cannot be underestimated. We all need to know the past so we can make a better future."

—Louise M. Gouge, author of *A Family for the Rancher*

"Set against the backdrop of the French and Indian War, *The Return* weaves a harrowing and desperate tale of Jakob Hochstetler, a father whose life has been undone by brutality and war. Authors J. M. Hochstetler and Bob Hostetler vividly depict the sights, sounds, emotions and heart-rending struggle of a family trying to cope with their difficult new circumstances. Every page sets the reader right into the moment, capturing the details of a life that is hard for modern day Americans to even comprehend. This is a must-read."

—Rene Gutteridge, author of *Misery Loves Company*

"Filled with the life-changing events of a family legacy, the authors show us a story filled with emotion, adventure, and determination. Beautifully crafted and authentic, *The Return* takes us on a historical journey that allows us to not only know this family, but feel their plight."

—Cindy Sproles, award winning author of *Mercy's Rain*

"Working from known chronology and geography and extensive research on the life of Indians at that time, the authors have constructed a gripping, plausible narrative of the return of our ancestors from Indian captivity. The high drama will keep you eagerly reading and the ending will warm your heart. Descendants, whether biological or in faith, will gain a new appreciation of our heritage."

—Daniel Hochstetler, teacher, historian, and contributing editor
of the *Jacob Hochstetler Family Association Newsletter*

"In this engaging sequel to *Northkill,* readers will be drawn into Christian and Joseph's heart-rending dilemma: Should they remain with their Lenape family and friends or return to their birth family and their Christian faith? The authors' use of historic and authentic-to-the-period details make Christian and Joseph's relationship with their adoptive 18th century Lenape families come to life!"

—Beth Hostetler Mark, Librarian Emeritus, Messiah College

The Return

NORTHKILL ✦ AMISH
BOOK TWO

BOB HOSTETLER

J. M. HOCHSTETLER

x

Elkhart, Indiana 46514

The Return
Copyright © 2017 by J. M. Hochstetler and Bob Hostetler

Please address requests for information to:

Joan M. Shoup
Editorial Director
Sheaf House Publishers
1703 Atlantic Avenue
Elkhart, IN 46514
jmshoup@gmail.com

Library of Congress Control Number: 2017930788

ISBN: 978-1-936438-44-0 (softcover)

All scripture quotations in German are from Die Bibel nach der deutschen Übersetzung D. Martin Luthers. Quotations in English are from the King James Version of the Bible. The Lord's Prayer is taken from Matthew 6:9-13. The scripture verses quoted on p. 138 are Jeremiah 29:7, 14. The verse quoted on p. 301 is Zechariah 8:21. The verse quoted on p. 363 is Isaiah 43:6.

Cover design by Marisa Jackson.

Cover image from iStockphoto.

Map by Jim Brown of Jim Brown Illustration.

PRINTED IN THE UNITED STATES OF AMERICA.

"Fear not: for I have redeemed thee, I have called thee by thy name; thou art Mine. When thou passest through the waters, I will be with thee; and through the rivers, they shall not overflow thee: when thou walkest through the fire, thou shalt not be burned; neither shall the flame kindle upon thee. . . . I will bring thy seed from the east, and gather thee from the west; I will say to the north, 'Give up'; and to the south, 'Keep not back: bring My sons from far, and My daughters from the ends of the earth . . .' "

Isaiah 43:1*b*-2, 5*b*-6

"For thy waste and thy desolate places, and the land of thy destruction, shall even now be too narrow by reason of the inhabitants, and they that swallowed thee up shall be far away. The children of whom thou wast bereaved, shall say again in thine ears, 'The place is too strait for me: give place to me that I may dwell.' "

—Isaiah 49:19-20

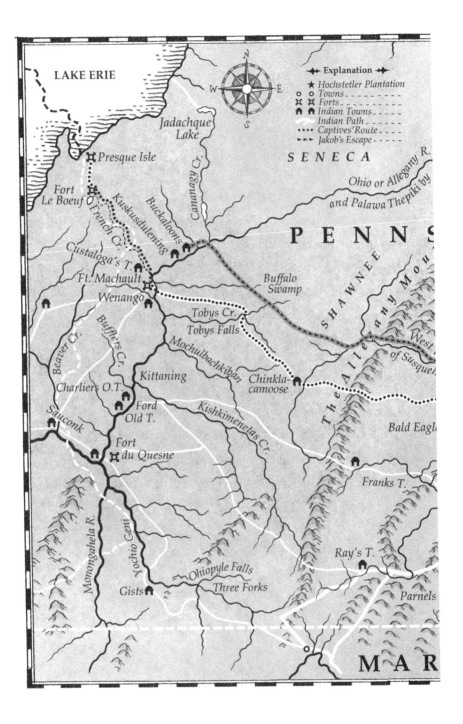

LAKE ERIE

Jadachque
Lake

Explanation
★ Hochstetler Plantation
○ ○ Towns
⛫ ⛫ Forts
🛖 🛖 Indian Towns
〰 Indian Path
•••• Captives' Route
▸▸▸ Jakob's Escape

SENECA

Presque Isle

Fort
Le Boeuf   French Cr.   Kuskusdulening   Buckaloons

Cananagy Cr.

Ohio or Allegany R.
and Palawa Thepiki by

PENNS

Custaloga's T.

Ft. Machault

Wenango

Buffalo
Swamp

SHAWNEE

Tobys Cr.

Tobys Falls

Mochulbachkiban

Beaver Cr.   Buffers Cr.

Kittaning

Charliers O.T.

Ford
Old T.

Chinkla-
camoose

The Allegany Mou

West
of Susque

Sauconk

Fort
du Quesne

Kishkimenetas Cr.

Bald Eagl

Franks T.

Monongahela R.   Yochio Genii

Ohiopyle Falls

Gists   Three Forks

Ray's T.

Parnels

M A R

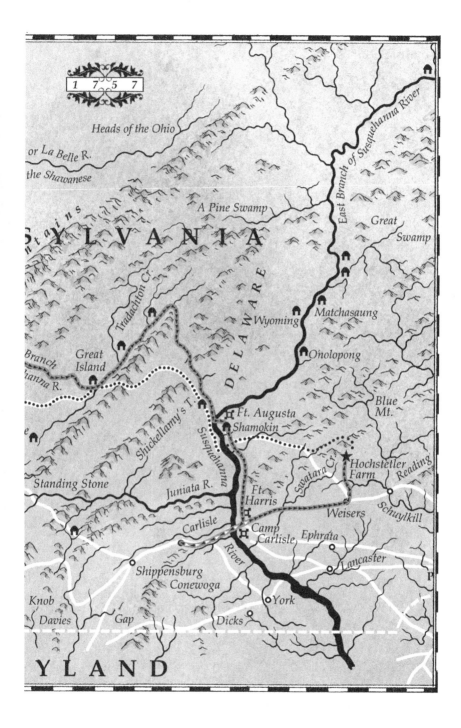

Chapter One

T HIS TIME THEY WOULD be given no reprieve as at Shikellamy's
Town.

Jakob Hochstetler looked fearfully around as a deafening roar
filled the air. The milling prisoners were being prodded between
two lines of jubilant tormentors.

He shoved his fingers through his sweat-drenched black hair,
three-weeks' growth since the morning his captors had shorn his
head and carried him and his two youngest sons far from Northkill
Creek and their ruined plantation, leaving behind the scalped bodies of his wife, older son, and baby daughter. Moments earlier, his
party had been driven across a small tributary that formed the
northwest boundary of a broad, arrow-shaped point of land. It
was bordered on the northeast by swift-flowing Buxotons Creek
and along the southeast by a wide waterway the Iroquois called
Ohi:'i:o`, the beautiful river.

The ancient Mingo-Seneca castle of Buckaloons sprawled
across this point, its weathered, palisaded walls rising nine feet
high. From its gates spilled a roiling tide composed of many tribes,
with French traders and trappers jostling among them. Brilliantly

painted men, women, and children danced in fierce anticipation to the pounding beat of drums, waving knotted clubs, thorny brambles, rocks, handfuls of stones and dirt, any weapon that came to hand. Already a double-rowed gauntlet was forming, winding from the gates between rows of bark-clad longhouses, wigewas, and log cabins all the way to the great council house at what appeared to be the town's center.

Jakob threw a despairing glance at his friend Hans Specht, who stumbled against him in the press of the panicked captives, sweat stinging his eyes in spite of the cool breeze. "Can you understand anything they say?"

Specht shook his head wearily and shouted back over the din. "The Seneca tongue is nothing like the Delaware's."

It was near sundown of that sunny day, the third since those brought to the French fort at Presque Isle by Indian raiders had been parceled out to representatives of the various tribes. Three days since fifteen-year-old Joseph and eleven-year-old Christian had been ripped from Jakob's arms. All along the bitter path angling southeast, the joyous autumn colors that set the woods to flame had silently mocked the mournful company to which Jakob belonged.

The surge of prisoners jolted another man into them. He muttered an apology, then added, eyes wild, "Run fast as you can! Our only chance is to make it to the council house. They'll kill any that fall. God help the young'uns!"

Anguished cries arose from the captives at the rear, where the company's guards had begun to beat those who hesitated. The man was thrust roughly past Jakob and Specht.

Fifteen were left of the nineteen who had begun that desperate journey. Those unable to keep up or who had fallen along the way had been summarily dispatched with a tomahawk blow, scalped, their bodies left sprawled along the path.

One had been the man who confided to Specht that he had seen Specht's young children, Franz and Hannah, in a party being taken away by a chief named Custaloga. And that one of Jakob's boys had been with them. That was all Specht had been able to learn before the man had met his end.

Jakob had determined to make it through whatever came, to escape and find a way to rescue his boys. All the way from Presque Isle, he had focused on putting one foot in front of the other. And as the company had continued to move southeast, he consoled himself with the knowledge that every mile brought him closer to home.

Now, however, courage failed. He reached out to clasp Specht's hand, but the mass of captives shifted and the two were borne away from each other.

Jakob watched the women and children of their company being separated from the men and herded off to the side. They clutched one another, sobbing, while the men were prodded into a tight knot, with the younger men forced to the head of the gauntlet.

"*Danke, Gott,* that at least the women and children are spared," he whispered.

The first man was thrust between the lines of villagers. Drums began to beat, and he ran, arms flailing, but within a few steps hunched over, covering his head as he tried to dodge the vicious blows directed at him. Each time a weapon connected, he howled, finally collapsed well short of the council house, his bloody form writhing. Wails rippled through the huddled captives when at last he lay motionless beneath the clubs.

One at a time, those ahead of Jakob were forced to run the gauntlet. Each made it to the end and collapsed inside the council house door, dazed and bleeding from multiple wounds.

When Jakob was dragged to the line's head, he thought fleetingly of Specht, somewhere behind him, who had suffered more than he from the rigors of their long journey. And of his and Specht's children, who might even now be facing their own torment.

Ach, lieber Herr, steh' uns bei! Ah, dear Lord, stay by us!

The drums began once more to throb, and the warrior at Jakob's side shoved him between the lines. He lowered his head and sprang forward, blotting all else from consciousness but the goal that lay before him.

Chapter Two

Friday, October 14, 1757

E LEVEN-YEAR-OLD CHRISTIAN squinted into the thin sheen of
the overcast October morning, chilled by the sibilance of
the water along the elm-bark canoe's side and the wind
rustling in the dry leaves that still clung to the trees. He concentrated on keeping the strokes of his oar as smooth as those of the
warriors seated before and behind him.

The four large canoes rode swiftly on the creek's current,
bearing their burdens of Lenape chiefs and warriors, along with
the captives and supplies acquired at the French fort of Presque
Isle four days earlier. Christian glanced toward the banks on either
side of the stream. The dark bulk of the forest had thinned out
early that day, and a pleasant, park-like vista of scattered trees and
greensward slipped steadily past.

Fort Machault can't be far off now, he told himself, remembering
the fearful journey that had brought him, his father, and older
brother to Presque Isle with several other captives. *They must be
taking me home now.*

He had heard the anxious talk of the adult captives in his
party, but Crouching Panther was his friend. He had saved

Christian's life and cared for him, even carrying him on his back when he became tired. Christian had silently repeated this hope to himself innumerable times while they followed the portage south again to Fort Le Boeuf, then rode in the canoes down French Creek toward Fort Machault—the reverse of the course they had taken to reach the place where he had been torn away from his father and older brother, all that remained to him of his shattered family.

His stomach lurched as he recalled Daati's anguished, bleeding face and Joseph struggling against the men who dragged him away.

Crouching Panther's voice broke his reverie. "You do well, little brother. You are strong and do a man's work."

Christian hastily pushed the memory aside. Forcing a smile, he answered in the Lenape tongue, "I like to row." The words came with increasing ease after almost a month of conversing with the young warrior who was his master, as the Lenape called those to whom each captive belonged.

The canoes swept around a gentle curve of the stream. Along the bank grazed a number of sturdy horses, shaggy with their winter coats, the bells around their necks making pleasant music with each movement. The closest raised their heads to watch the canoes pass, ears twitching as they chewed. Several children appeared among them and at sight of the bateaux raced for the village, a few dogs barking and leaping at their heels.

Christian let his oar dangle in the water and clutched the top edge of the canoe with his free hand as a cluster of grey, weathered wigewas emerged from behind the trees a short distance ahead. They had passed another village not far upriver but had not stopped. Here, however, the rapidly changing vista that stretched out of his sight through the trees revealed many more wigewas, a few log cabins, and two larger structures. Beyond the town he could make out a ripple of water flowing into the river from a smaller stream.

Christian started at a touch on his arm. Seeing Crouching Panther's frown, he smiled apologetically and plied his oar again.

Daati said to do what they tell me to. If I'm good, surely they'll take me home, and Daati and Joseph too.

As the town drew rapidly closer, Christian could see people running down to the bank. Most were Lenape, but some white adults and children mingled with them. The babble of voices reached him clearly along the water's channel as the crowd grew.

Crouching Panther leaned close to Christian's ear. "We are home now, Blue Eyes. This is Custaloga's Town where we live."

Christian nodded, though his chest tightened. "It is good."

He means this is his home, he assured himself. *I'm just going to stay here with him for a little while. It's a long way back to my home, and we have to rest and get supplies together.*

Crouching Panther laughed and ruffled Christian's hair, which had grown long enough to curl around his ears in the weeks since his head was shaved. The warriors began to fire their guns into the air and halloo loudly, their warbling cries echoed by the crowd on the river's bank. The canoes pulled up onto the muddy shore, and the warriors sprang out to receive the towns-people's greetings.

Each held aloft on poles the scalps they had taken, as they did at each place they stopped. Christian averted his eyes, not wanting to know whether the scalps of his mother, brother, and baby sister were among them.

A group of women and maidens rushed to unload supplies from the canoes, and Crouching Panther beckoned Christian to follow him. Other captives were already clambering reluctantly out of the vessels after the tall chief who led their party.

Christian had learned from Crouching Panther that the man's name was Packanke, and that he was also known as Custaloga. He was the sachem of the Lenape's Wolf division, to which Crouching Panther belonged. With his ribbon-bedecked blanket wrapped around his shoulders and held together in one hand, Custaloga moved with the instinctive dignity and majesty of a king. His dark eyes were mild, and a smile softened his seamed, tattooed face as he greeted the people who pressed close to him.

Christian stepped out of the canoe and started up the slope after Crouching Panther. He glanced back toward the canoes behind his, where eight-year-old Franz Specht and his six-year-old sister, Hannah, rode. They had been with another war party that joined Christian's near the Susquehanna and traveled with them the rest of the way to Presque Isle. The three of them had been kept apart since being separated from their fathers and taken from the French fort. Little Hannah had become even more wan and withdrawn than before, while Franz obeyed his master somberly, speaking little and showing no interest in his surroundings.

Crouching Panther clasped Christian's hand and pulled him away, leading him through the throng and up the slope into the town. Christian's eyes widened as he took in two imposing structures that faced each other across a broad yard. In front of the larger a vast array of food spread across boards set on trestles, and all across the yard copper kettles hung on iron tripods over numerous fires. The fragrance of their bubbling contents made Christian's mouth water and his stomach growl.

"We come at a good time, Blue Eyes." Crouching Panther motioned toward the bark-roofed log building at the yard's far end. "The gathering for the Big House Ceremony has ended, and today the people feast before those from other villages return home."

"I'm hungry!"

Crouching Panther laughed. "So am I, little brother. After the council meets, then we will eat."

Hoping the council meeting would be short, Christian followed him through the river of people now flowing into the nearest of the two structures. The council house was a long building with a rounded roof. Framed with poles and clad with bark, it was smaller than the Big House but still spacious enough to accommodate the throng.

Custaloga sat in the building's center, surrounded by grave men Christian assumed were the headmen of the town and the surrounding villages. Younger men and warriors took seats behind them, with the women at the rear, while a clutch of others waited in front of the gathering.

Crouching Panther led Christian to the other captives, who stood with their masters, silent, heads hanging. He rested his hand reassuringly on Christian's shoulder.

Christian chewed his lip as he surveyed the people taking seats around the perimeter of the building, then glanced down the line on either side of him. All the captives appeared as nervous as he felt. Some of the townspeople who waited before the council came over to look at each of them closely, and only his two small friends appeared indifferent. Nearest him, Hannah gazed at the ground, her expression blank, and at the far end Franz stared into the air as though seeing nothing.

When the throng hushed, a lengthy silence ensued, while fragrant tobacco rose into the air as the people smoked their pipes. At last Custaloga rose to speak.

Christian understood the substance of what the sachem said, but uncertainty and fear made it hard for him to concentrate. Custaloga's speech was succeeded by a series of impassioned pleas from the townspeople, whose glances and gestures made it clear that they asked for one or another of the captives, just as the tribal representatives had at Presque Isle. And one by one each captive was awarded to one of the petitioners.

Several townspeople showed interest in Christian, and he began to fear that he might be forced to stay here after all. But surely Crouching Panther meant to take him home.

At last a wizened, elderly man with a hooked nose and hunched shoulders began to speak, leaning heavily on a walking stick and waving toward Christian. The dry, thinning white hair that wreathed his wrinkled face and his yellowed, broken teeth made him appear ugly and frightening, and when Crouching Panther went forward to stand beside him and support his suit before Custaloga, Christian's heart plummeted.

Custaloga called the old man Nútemau—a name Christian interpreted as "He Watches." Nútemau explained that he had been the husband of White Crane, the sister of Crouching Panther and Deep Water's mother, and that only his nephew and niece were left alive to take care of him.

Christian listened with growing horror as Crouching Panther said that as a warrior, he was often gone, while Deep Water had a husband and children to care for. He had captured the blue-eyed boy to take the place of Nútemau and White Crane's son, Dark Forest, and perform the duties of a son for him.

The large room fell silent. There was no further debate. The claim of a captive's master could not be denied.

Custaloga beckoned Christian. Crouching Panther gave him a pleased, reassuring smile, but as he went to Custaloga with lagging steps, Christian fought back tears at the realization that he now belonged to Nútemau.

✦┄┄┄✦

CHRISTIAN HUDDLED beneath a musty blanket on the sleeping platform, cuddling the puppy Nútemau had given him. He gently stroked its fuzzy brown fur to still its muffled whines, while he took in the weathered wigewa's interior through a haze of grief.

Painted rush mats, so old that pieces were flecking off, decked the curved walls and covered the floor. Overhead, cooking implements and bundles of food hung from the bent poles that formed the rafters. Bark boxes and clay pots filled the space beneath the sleeping platform that ran along the walls' perimeter.

The past hours were as blurred as his sight, but one thing stood out in stark clarity: With Custaloga's words the past and future that had once belonged to the Amish boy Christian Hochstetler—his home, his family, his very identity—had been wiped away forever.

Even his name. During a strange, confusing ceremony he had become Dark Forest, the son of the old man who sat at the fire, stirring the cherry embers that did little to drive away the night's chill.

Along with the other captive boys, Christian had been made to run a gauntlet of children wielding switches. Praised for his fortitude, he was then washed in the river with all the captives being adopted and taken back to the council house, where his face and head were painted, ears pierced and earrings poked into them. Gifts had been presented to him and his tattered garments cast away. Then Crouching Panther and Deep Water had dressed him in new clothing, hung a belt of wampum around his neck, and draped a blanket over his shoulders. Deep Water's husband and children had looked on approvingly, and Nútemau nodded and smiled and muttered to himself.

Afterward, the townspeople gathered, all festively garbed, and Custaloga made another speech, this time assuring the adopted captives that they were now one with the Lenape people, members of the Wolf division, and that they held all the privileges and responsibilities of those whose names they had been given. At last they had been presented to their new families, and a great banquet followed.

When they finally left the council house, Christian noted that one of the younger couples led Hannah away, while Franz followed a stern-faced middle-aged woman out of sight. The children were Christian's last contact with . . . the time before. He wondered anxiously whether he would ever see them again.

The memory of Daati telling him that they were to be Indians for a while filtered into his consciousness. Daati had said it almost gaily, as though they embarked on a great adventure.

This is what he meant, Christian thought, fighting to gather courage. It's just for a while. If I do the very best I can, they'll let me go home again someday.

He did not know whether it was these people, Daati, or God who would allow it. But he clung to faith that a day would come when his lost family would welcome him home again.

As long as he was good. He had been bad before, and all this pain and horror had happened because of him. But he would be obedient now, and he would be forgiven. This much he knew, and he clung to it—and to the Lord's prayer, known from his earliest memory, that Daati had prayed with him and Joseph at Presque Isle.

Unser Vater in dem Himmel! Dein Name werde geheiligt. Dein Reich komme. Dein Wille geschehe auf Erden wie im Himmel. Unser täglich Brot gib uns heute. Und vergib uns unsere Schulden, wie wir unsern Schuldigern vergeben. Und führe uns nicht in Versuchung, sondern erlöse uns von dem Uebel. Denn dein ist das Reich und die Kraft und die Herrlichkeit in Ewigkeit. Amen.

The puppy had fallen asleep, its nose buried under Christian's arm. Nútemau came close and bent over him, and Christian shrank away, peering anxiously up at him. The old man brushed Christian's hair back from his forehead and caressed his cheek, his dark eyes warming with tenderness and affection.

He sat on the sleeping platform beside Christian and lightly patted the puppy. "Have you given him a name, Dark Forest?"

Christian shook his head. "Thank you for giving him to me."

Nútemau smiled. "Tomorrow maybe Crouching Panther and Crooked Legs will help you to name him."

Christian nodded. Crooked Legs was Deep Water's eldest boy. He was perhaps a couple of years older than Christian and had bowed legs, though that didn't seem to hinder him in any way. He had a friendly smile. They had eyed each other during the banquet, but Christian had been too shy to speak to him.

Nútemau spoke softly, his voice quavering. "You have nothing to fear, my son. I will help you, and you will help me. We will get on well. Together we will be strong."

Christian said nothing. But it occurred to him that this old man was like a grandfather. Christian had never known his own grandparents. Daati and Maami had often talked sadly about leaving them behind when they left the place called Alsace to sail across the sea. Christian had always felt their lack in his life and had longed to meet them.

Grandfathers are good. His eyelids drooped with the weariness of the long day. *He gave me this puppy. And Crouching Panther wouldn't make me stay with someone who isn't kind.*

Tears welled into his eyes, and he clutched the puppy tightly against his chest.

Chapter Three

Monday, October 17, 1757

FIFTEEN-YEAR-OLD JOSEPH stood in the line of captive youths and children, head down, expression blank. He drew a shaky breath, grimacing at the odor of close-packed bodies mingled with smoke from the central fire. Fighting back the heavy cloud of emotions that had hung over him ever since his party left Presque Isle, he glanced furtively at the Lenape people who crowded the great council house.

Most of the younger men of the town were tall. All held themselves proudly erect, their handsome features, long black hair, and sun-bronzed skin striking. Some wore their hair in a scalp lock, which Joseph knew meant that they were warriors, while the rest simply parted and tied theirs in a thick lock behind each ear.

Silver or copper nose and ear rings and amulets adorned all the men. They sported strange dark tattoos or had painted themselves with a layer of white clay over which they swirled curious snake-like designs in red and black. The effect was bizarre and intimidating.

In contrast, the women painted a spot of red on one cheek, black on the other, and the reverse on their eyelids. Their hair was pulled back and neatly wrapped behind their heads in a wide piece of cloth. Almost all of them wore numerous brooches and necklaces. Their modest, gracious manner surprised him as well as how shapely and attractive many of them were in their colorful stroud petticoats and hip-length shirts.

He shifted his attention to the older matrons and men. Like many of the elders he had seen at the villages where they stopped on their long march to Presque Isle, most were poorly clad, bent, and wizened. Some were crippled, others appeared weak and ill—a result of the rigors they endured, he reckoned. He felt no sympathy for them, however. Only a deep anger.

Late in the afternoon the previous day Joseph's party had arrived at the town they called Sauconk, a haphazard collection of bark wigewas and log cabins. It lay along the western bank of the stream they had followed south to its mouth on a much larger river flowing west across churning rapids.

Since then the captives had been held in the council house without food or water. In spite of terror and uncertainty about what lay before him, Joseph had done his best to help the adults comfort the younger children until they cried themselves to sleep that night. He had found it difficult to relax as the older ones whispered fearfully among themselves about what the morrow held.

The wails of one of the small children had jerked him awake, and with both relief and dread he saw faint light filtering through the roof's smoke holes. After what seemed an eternity, several elders had come in, their faces painted red and black. The captives were finally allowed to go outside under guard to relieve themselves, after which a woman brought a clay jar of water for them to drink. There was little more than a swallow each, which did little to slake anyone's thirst.

Shortly thereafter the warrior he knew as Shingas had entered, followed by a crowd of townspeople, all garbed in what appeared to be their finest regalia. Now, steadying his trembling knees, Joseph directed a baleful glance at his captor, the cruelest of his family's murderers.

The warrior was short and powerfully built, with a head that appeared too large for his body, and an intricately tattooed face and torso that intensified Joseph's revulsion. He cringed as Shingas strode toward him along the line of captives, his blanket wrapped around his shoulders and held together at his waist with one hand, as was the custom of the Indians.

Pausing before each one, the warrior touched a head or patted an arm reassuringly, and the children's muted sobs stilled. When he came to Joseph, Shingas laid his hand on Joseph's shoulder as he had often during their journey to the town.

Joseph avoided the warrior's gaze, struggling to make sense of what he said and wishing he had made more effort to learn his captors' language as his younger brother had on the journey to Presque Isle. It had finally sunk in that, if he was to survive, he had to know what they said. From the little he knew of it, however, he interpreted Shingas' words and signs as reassurance that he should not be afraid and that he had come to a good place among a kind people.

Joseph lowered his gaze to the earth floor, vivid images of his family's and home's destruction searing his mind. His mouth tightened as every fiber hotly rejected the warrior's fine words.

At last Shingas took his place among the leaders of the town. He sat on a bearskin before the central fire beside a somewhat younger man who resembled him closely, though he was taller, with features more open and kindly. He was evidently not a warrior; he wore his hair long and tied in two braids, rather than in a scalp lock as Shingas did. Joseph guessed the man to be Shingas's brother or at least a close relative.

For the next hour people took turns speaking. An older matron who sat at the women's head spoke infrequently, but when she did, Shingas and the others accorded her respectful attention. Because her features were similar to Shingas and his brother and she appeared to be near their age, Joseph concluded that she must be their sister.

The petitioners' glances and gestures toward the captives quickly made it clear to Joseph that he and the others were the subject of their negotiations. Anger and dismay that again, just as at Presque Isle, he would be given no voice in his own fate roiled in his gut. Teeth gritted, he fixed his gaze on the turkey totems that hung on each support post down the length of the council house. Hatred of them and everything about this place and these savages seized him.

By the time all the petitioners presented their cases, Joseph's stomach growled with hunger. Shingas gave yet another lengthy speech, and just when Joseph concluded that the meeting would never end, the warrior began to present the captives to the petitioners. The few adult captives were led out of the council house by their masters, clearly distraught.

Shingas now turned his attention to the children and youths. A couple whom Joseph judged to be in their early thirties appeared to have fixed their interest on him. They sat beside the matron Joseph took for Shingas's sister.

The woman's face, although pockmarked, seemed to reflect a kind nature, and when she spoke it was gently and with a pleasant smile. Her husband was strikingly handsome in spite of a scar that disfigured one cheek. Although his tattooed torso and shoulders bulged with hard muscles, his right leg was crooked and withered—due to some injury suffered in battle, Joseph guessed. The man leaned heavily on a staff and supported himself on his wife's arm when he walked.

Most of the children and other youths had been claimed by the time Shingas came to Joseph. Shingas spoke to the couple, who came forward eagerly. Then he took Joseph's hand and put it in the woman's.

As she and her husband beamed, Shingas said kindly, *"Quissis."* It was one of the Lenape words Joseph had learned: son.

Shingas turned to Joseph and indicated the woman. *"Gáhowees."* He signed the word *mother*, then gestured toward the man, signing "father." *"Wetochemend."*

Joseph remained silent but repeated the Lenape words to himself to fix them in his mind.

The man touched his own chest and said, "Menetopalis," then laid his hand on his wife's shoulder. "Wulachen."

Joseph glanced from one to the other, then to the ground, uncertain what they expected of him. That he was to be adopted

rather than made a slave offered a measure of reassurance, however.

It was short lived. The couple led him outside in the wake of
the other children and their new families and past a double file
of children from the town that extended from the council house
door to the far end of the yard surrounding it. Joseph tensed to
see that all of them held switches and called out to each other,
while eyeing the captives with gleeful anticipation.

Three young children ran up to them, calling out to the couple excitedly. Wulachen introduced the oldest girl, who carried a
bundle in her arms, as She Sings. Joseph guessed her to be
around eleven years old and the younger girl, whom Wulachen
called Moonflower, perhaps nine. The boy, Contrary Wind, could
not have been older than six.

All three greeted him shyly. As they crowded around with
upturned faces, he forced a smile in return. Anxiety returned in
full force when he was led to the far end of the line to take his
place among the other captive boys.

With smiles, gestures, and reassuring words, Menetopalis
indicated to Joseph that this was nothing for a boy as strong as
he, that when the drum beat his turn he had only to run between
the lines as fast as he could to the door of the council house.

Joseph watched those who went before him, quickly realizing that this test was not a fearsome one. The younger boys, terrified at first, soon began to laugh as their native counterparts
switched lightly at their legs, and although the youths who ran
ahead of him received harder blows, they did not appear to suffer unduly.

When the drum sounded his turn Joseph drew in his breath and leaped forward. The switches stung as they connected with his bare legs but only spurred him to a greater burst of speed. He flew down the last half of the line, moving so fast that the switches barely touched him.

Panting, he reached the council house door and turned to look toward Menetopalis, Wulachen, and their children. An unaccountable surge of pride swelled his chest to see them openly exult with their neighbors at his prowess. He felt an immediate wave of shame and gritted his teeth, determined never to allow any of these people to gain a hold on his heart.

When everyone had run the gauntlet the crowd surged through the town gates to the river. One at a time each of those to be adopted was stripped and led into the water by several young women, to the townspeople's laughter and applause, and scrubbed all over with handfuls of sand and small stones until their skin shone bright pink. No one appeared to note fact that the wind was icy and the water freezing.

When his turn came, Joseph cringed at having his nakedness exposed before the entire town, especially the young women. To have several of them actually bathe him was even more humiliating. It astounded him that none of the townspeople appeared to view this as anything out of the ordinary.

He endured the ordeal with as much stoicism as he could and, shaking in every limb, gratefully accepted the blanket Wulachen took from She Sings' bundle and wrapped around him. The ceremony reminded Joseph in a strange way of the baptism his Amish community practiced. From what he could understand of the people's talk, he and the other captives were apparently thus cleansed of their white lives and made Lenape.

They joined the other captives and their new families back at the council house, where Joseph's face was painted and his earlobes were pierced with an awl and studded with earrings, a procedure he suffered with eyes closed and teeth clenched, determined to make no sound. Then Wulachen and Menetopalis arrayed Joseph in a ruffled linen shirt with bright ribbons banding the sleeves; fringed leggings decorated with colorful beading and dyed porcupine quills, and woven garters to hold them at the knee; and moccasins also covered with bead- and quill-work. The shirt strained slightly across his frame but fit well otherwise.

Moisture glistened in Wulachen's eyes as she stood back to take him in. The children pressed around him, chattering and smoothing the shirt lovingly over Joseph's chest and shoulders with their hands. His heart contracted involuntarily as he noted how thin and frail they appeared in comparison to white children. The scattered pockmarks that disfigured their faces and arms made him wonder whether their older brother had died of the pox.

When Joseph glanced at Menetopalis, it dawned on him that this must be why the couple had chosen him—to provide food for their family since the crippled warrior was doubtless unable to hunt. Would they also expect him to become a warrior and fight against his own people? The thought brought a knot to Joseph's throat.

As though in confirmation, Menetopalis put a bow and beaded quiver of arrows in Joseph's hands, then took a beautifully fletched arrow with a sharp flint head from the quiver. He held it up for them all to see as he spoke, accompanying his words with gestures and signs.

Joseph slowly grasped Menetopalis's meaning: Wulachen had made the clothing for the couple's older son, Straight Arrow, not long before he died some months earlier. Joseph was now to take the boy's place. Menetopalis addressed him by the boy's name, and with nods of approval Wulachen and the children did the same.

Bile rose in Joseph's throat, but he gave a curt nod to indicate that he understood. He was given no time to ponder the matter. They draped a long belt of wampum around his neck, placed silver amulets on his arms, and presented him a fine pipe, tomahawk, and knife, and a pouch filled with tobacco along with another that held punk, flint, and steel for starting fires.

By the time they seated him on a bearskin in the midst of the other adopted youths, a large crowd of townspeople had come in, dressed and painted in their grandest manner. Everyone took their seats on bearskins as before and began to smoke.

Menetopalis showed Joseph how to pack the tobacco into his pipe, which Joseph managed clumsily. When Menetopalis lighted his own and Joseph's with a coal from the fire, Joseph followed his example and drew deeply on the pipe. Immediately he choked and coughed, his empty stomach turning over as he fought back a wave of nausea. He was relieved when Menetopalis grinned broadly and motioned with his free hand for Joseph to put the pipe down.

The smell of cooking food began to drift into the building from outside, and Joseph's stomach growled with increasing insistence. But more speeches followed. From what little he could make out, the gist was that he and the others who were adopted were now members of the great Lenape nation and the highly respected Turkey division, that he occupied the place and status of the person whose name he had been given with all the rights and privileges that included, and that he had nothing to fear, for the Lenape people would love and care for him in every way as fully one of them.

Joseph wrestled with a tumult of emotions. He would do what was required because he had no choice, he decided. But nothing more. Although these townspeople had not murdered Maam, Jake, and Annali, he would never forget that Shingas and the warriors with him had. And Menetopalis, who was now to be considered as Joseph's father, had been a warrior, too, and had surely slaughtered other white settlers along the frontier.

At length the speeches ended, cutting off his bitter reflections. Hope that he might finally be allowed to eat faded as the adopted captives were presented to their new relations.

A bewildering array of new grandparents, aunts, uncles, cousins, nieces, and nephews soon surrounded him. It appeared that he was now directly related to Shingas; his younger brother Tamaque, which Joseph interpreted as meaning Beaver; their sister, Bird's Nest, who was Wulachen's mother and now Joseph's grandmother; and their extended families.

Joseph struggled to mask his feelings as a wave of desolation washed over him. Inside he shouted, *Don't expect me to become one of you! I have a family, and I don't want anyone else!*

The horror he had striven so hard to deny now crushed him with agonizing force: All those he loved were utterly lost to him and he was alone in this alien land among these hostile people with little hope of rescue. And he had no idea how he was to navigate the days ahead.

✦┄┄┄✦

THE PUNGENT ODORS of sweat, bear grease, tanned hides, and wood smoke pervaded the small, two-room log cabin's shadowy interior. From his bed on the platform along one wall of the rear sleeping room, Joseph stared at the doorway into the front room where the banked embers in the fireplace still gave off a soft glow.

In spite of exhaustion, anxious thoughts kept him awake. He shifted cautiously into a more comfortable position beneath the coverings, careful not to wake Contrary Wind, who had insisted on curling up against Joseph. The unexpected memory of sharing a bed with Christian—and how he had resented it, had resented his little brother, whom he missed intensely now—pierced him. He would have given anything to be back in that bed with Christian cuddled against him.

He brooded over what the coming days would hold—and the weeks and months and years that would follow. Fear for Daat, worry about Christian, and about Johannes and Barbara and their families back home, mingled with bitterness that his father had refused to make any effort to stop their attackers. And anger at God for having allowed such horror to tear his family apart.

Would he ever see any of them again? Or his friends and the members of his church? Or Anna Blanck? It seemed horribly unfair that just when their relationship promised to mature into something deeper, they had been torn away from each other.

He had not valued any of them as he should have. And now that they were forever out of reach, each one had become incredibly precious.

That escape seemed to be out of the question caused the greatest anguish. He had no doubt that even if he could get away, he would never make it home, especially with winter coming on. Completely disoriented by the twists and turns of the month-long journey to this place, he only knew for certain that the Northkill lay somewhere to the east, hundreds of miles distant across daunting terrain thickly settled by Indians and controlled by the French. Unless he was rescued, a hope he had largely given up, he had to somehow become reconciled to the fact that this was now his life and he had no choice but to make the best of it.

The memory of that last moment at Presque Isle with Daat and Christian before they had been separated from one another filtered into Joseph's consciousness, and he felt as though he had fallen into a pit where light would never reach. He had angrily refused to pray the Lord's Prayer with Daat then. But now he had no other comfort, and he gathered those ancient words around him like a blanket.

Deliver us from evil. For thine is the kingdom and the power and the glory.

The words calmed him, easing the tension in his muscles and the knot of despair in his chest. He recalled stories of the biblical patriarch Joseph and the prophet Daniel, who also had been carried away into exile as young men. Forced to live amid a strange people in a hostile culture, they had determined to gain the favor of their captors and to prosper. And they had done so, with God's help.

Could he do the same? He tried to picture it. He'd have to forgive these people's brutal slaughter of his family. But he could never do that!

Silently he vowed that he would never become one of these savage people or give them his love and allegiance, no matter how kindly they treated him. Instead he would hope with each breath and with every beat of his heart that the British would do to Shingas and to all the Lenape what they had done to his family and free him to return to what remained of his real home and kindred.

At his side Contrary Wind turned in his sleep, his thin arm curving across Joseph's chest as he burrowed his head against Joseph's shoulder. Joseph lay still, considering that the child must have loved his older brother dearly and must still be grieving Straight Arrow's loss. Perhaps he now hoped that Joseph would fill that empty place.

Could this be the means by which God intended to give Joseph favor in this alien country? He clamped his free hand over his face, tears trickling through his fingers.

No! Don't ask that of me! I can't do it—I won't! He choked back sobs.

Gradually the need to urinate intruded into his consciousness. But that would mean going outside. If he tried to leave the cabin, would Wulachen and Menetopalis think he was trying to escape? Would they beat him? Or worse?

Hunger had driven him to eat and drink as much as he could hold at the feast. Now he regretted it as he squirmed, trying to find a more comfortable position on the rigid sleeping platform.

It was impossible. Sweat slicked his skin, and he knew the pain would only get worse. He carefully disengaged himself from Contrary Wind's grasp and sat upright.

He peered around the room. When no one moved, he pushed back the blanket and deerskin, pivoted, and swung his legs cautiously over the side of the sleeping platform, shivering as the cold air struck his naked flesh.

Menetopalis raised his head off the sleeping platform on the opposite side of the narrow room. A moment later Wulachen sat up, then rose and came to him. Threading her fingers through Joseph's sweaty hair, she peered down at him with concern and whispered something. He heard the question in her voice but, unable to understand her words, could only shake his head helplessly.

Menetopalis sat up and his gaze dropped to the arm Joseph held pressed against his lower abdomen. A broad smile softened his stern features.

Grasping his walking stick, he pushed awkwardly to his feet, draped his blanket around his shoulders with his free hand, and hobbled over to Joseph. He gestured toward the door and said in English, "Make water?"

Flushing, Joseph nodded. Menetopalis exchanged a smile with Wulachen, and she motioned for Joseph to wrap his blanket around him.

With Menetopalis leaning heavily on Joseph's shoulder, they went outside. When both had relieved themselves, Menetopalis did not seem in a hurry to go back inside despite the frosty wind. He threw back his head and swept one arm along the great arc of the heavens from east to west.

Speaking in a hushed, reverent tone, he pointed out stars and constellations twinkling high overhead. From the cadence of his voice it seemed that he told stories about them, and Joseph wished he could understand the words.

Menetopalis rested his hand on Joseph's shoulder, while he gazed into the black, moonless sky spangled with countless points of light. Joseph didn't flinch from the touch, for he felt good will radiating from this man. From Wulachen too. And eager affection from the children.

And as they turned to go back inside, Joseph allowed himself to hope that maybe things wouldn't go so badly for him after all.

Chapter Four

B ARBARA STUTZMAN hastily wiped a tear from her cheek as the *Küche* door banged open, and Anna Blanck burst inside.

The fourteen-year-old had come to live with Barbara and her husband Crist to help with the children soon after the attack on Barbara's parents' plantation.

Anna carried a limp rooster, and behind her trailed Barbara's small daughters Mattie and Annali. All three looked stricken, and tears streaked the little girls' cheeks.

"It's Rudy!" Anna laid the gold, black, and white Hamburg cockerel on the table. Its eyes were closed, and its tongue dangled from its beak.

Barbara laid her hand on her belly, rounded with her pregnancy, and pushed to her feet.

"What happened?"

Five-year-old Mattie's eyes filled with tears. "Goldy did it while I was feeding the chickens. Rudy got too close, and Goldy pecked him so hard on the head I think it killed him!"

Her younger sister began to wail, quickly echoed by Barbara's toddler, Mary, who had been playing on the settle by the hearth.

The little girl squirmed around until her legs dangled off the settle, and Anna rushed to catch her before she could fall backward.

Bouncing Mary in her arms, Anna pulled three-year-old Annali against her petticoats to hush her cries. "They've made a pet of him. We can't let him die!"

Barbara leaned over the rooster. "There's blood on his head." She ran her fingers up and down the bird's neck. "I suspect when Goldy pecked him so hard it bent his neck and stunned him."

"Is he dead?" Mattie asked in a small voice.

Barbara continued to gently rub the rooster's neck. "He's still alive. Put him on the hearth by the fire, Anna."

Anna set Mary down and obeyed. Straightening, she studied the rooster doubtfully. "He's not moving."

"Can we pray for Jesus to heal him?"

Smiling, Barbara gently placed her hand on the small white cap that covered her little daughter's head. "That's a *guud* idea, Annali. How about you say the prayer?"

Annali immediately folded her hands and bowed her head, while the others did the same. "Please, Jesus, heal our Rudy. Amen!"

Barbara exchanged a smile with Anna. "All we can do now is wait."

She set to work kneading the bread dough that had been rising on the warming shelf built into the side of the massive fireplace. Anna occupied the children with a game on the settle, then turned her attention to washing the breakfast dishes. Every few minutes, all of them glanced anxiously at the bird's motionless form.

As Barbara formed the dough into loaves, Anna asked softly, "Why were you crying when I came in with Rudy?"

Barbara raised her head to gaze out the window across from the worktable but made no reply.

"I'm sorry. I shouldn't have asked."

Hearing a clatter behind her as Anna put away the dishes, Barbara sighed and turned. "No, it's all right. I was just remembering. It's been a month. Today . . ."

"I know."

Barbara stiffened and whirled to glance toward the hearth. "Did you hear that?"

Anna knelt beside the rooster. The girls abandoned their game and joined her. A tiny croak, barely audible, made them jump.

"He moved!" Anna exclaimed. "Look, his beak opened!"

The cockerel's eyes fluttered open and he weakly moved his head.

Barbara reached for him. "Give him to me. Support his head carefully."

Anna gently lifted the rooster and handed him to Barbara, who began rubbing his neck again. Anna picked up Mary so she could watch, while the older girls stood on tiptoes.

The rooster twitched and jerked. When Barbara set him on the floor, he staggered and swayed. Suddenly he ruffled his feathers, flapped his wings, and strutted across the floor, letting out a loud crow that had all of them laughing.

"He is going to be all right, isn't he, Maami?" Mattie asked, her eyes round.

"Ach, *ya*. But we can't put him back with the other chickens until that wound on his head heals or they'll peck him to death."

Anna motioned to the girl's game on the settle. "Gather up your toys. Then you can help me build Rudy a cage."

The girls clapped their hands. As they rushed to obey, Barbara saw Anna's happy expression fade and her shoulders slump.

"What's wrong?"

Anna shook her head, looking down. "I don't understand."

"What don't you understand?"

"Why . . . why God would answer a prayer for a rooster . . . but not all our prayers to bring your Daat and the boys home!"

Barbara gathered Anna in her arms, her throat so tight it ached. "Ach, I don't know. Everyone says to keep on praying and wait on the Lord, but . . . there are times when that just doesn't seem like enough."

Chapter Five

FALLING LEAF MOON
Thursday, October 20, 1757

"STOP, BEAR!" Laughing, Christian caught the puppy and tried to drag him away from the vine net. "You're going to let all our pigeons get out."

Bear refused to let loose of the net's edge, weighted every few inches with a small stone. The tangled pigeons flapped their wings wildly, fighting to break free, the sound of their alarmed squawks deafening. Bear growled and shook his head fiercely from side to side.

"Bear?" Crooked Legs protested over the din. "Should you not call him Brown Bear?"

The net rippled across the ground, and a couple of pigeons tumbled out. They fluttered off before Crouching Panther and Crooked Legs's father, Standing Stone, could stomp the opening flat against the ground. Crooked Legs's dog suddenly darted in and grasped the puppy in her jaws by the nape of the neck.

"No." Christian rescued his yipping pup from the larger animal and held him up, stroking the soft, fuzzy coat that thickly covered his wriggling body. "Bear is enough. See? Does he not look like one?"

"And he is brown." Crouching Panther sprinkled an offering of tobacco on the ground to thank his guardian spirit, the panther, for success in the hunt. "Name him what you will, little brother. But before all our pigeons fly away and our hard work is for nothing, help us gather the net together so we can carry them home."

Christian deposited Bear between the larger dog's forepaws and joined the others in carefully drawing the net closed, with the captured pigeons inside. That done, Crouching Panther and Standing Stone wove a long pole through the top of the gathered vines that formed the net.

They had come upon the large flock of pigeons at the verge of a broad meadowland where the birds gathered to feed on fallen acorns. While Christian and Crooked Legs watched, Crouching Panther and Standing Stone had advanced so slowly they seemed hardly to move at all. They cast their net in a blur of expert motion, trapping a large number of the birds before they had time to escape.

Standing Stone helped Crouching Panther lift the pole and place it across their shoulders. "You have done well at setting traps and catching fish, Dark Forest. But the winter is almost upon us, and you must quickly learn all the ways of the hunt so you and your father will not starve while we are away at the hunting camp."

Christian hurried after his companions as they began to stride back in the direction from which they had come. "But why do you have to go to a camp when you can stay here and hunt, Standing Stone?"

The warrior explained that hunting in the region was poor because the soldiers killed or drove away all the game Manitou had given the Lenape for food. Many families went to the camps, while the elders and others unable to travel or hunt stayed behind, with several warriors to guard the town. Christian would have to care for Nútemau, tend his traps and fish weirs, and hunt alone until Standing Stone's family returned.

Anxiety welling up, Christian asked, "How long will you be gone?"

"Until the Cracking Tree Moon. But we do not go until the First Snow Moon. By then you have to learn not only to be a good hunter, but also to dress and cook the game for you and your father to eat."

"That's women's work!" Christian protested.

Crouching Panther exchanged an amused glance with Standing Stone. "A man must learn these skills as well if he is not to starve while on the hunt or warpath."

Standing Stone directed a pointed look at Crooked Legs. "It is also time you learned, my son, and I will suggest to your mother that she begin teaching you as well."

"Then we will have no time to practice shooting with our bows."

Crouching Panther laughed. "You will have all the time you need, my nephew."

Frowning, Crooked Legs put his hands on his hips. "But we must practice with muskets too. We're old enough to learn now."

"I can shoot a rifle," Christian volunteered.

Crouching Panther's eyebrows rose. "I have long wished to get one of those weapons."

Over his shoulder, Standing Stone said, "I hear they shoot more accurately than muskets, but they cost more skins—if one can even be gotten."

The two men led the way back to the path that bordered French Creek, then turned south, the boys and dogs trailing after. They retraced the route they had taken from Custaloga's Town that morning, first setting traps along nearby tributaries, then crossing broad French Creek in a canoe and walking some distance north through open woods.

Christian studied his companions' silent, stealthy movements and how they kept a keen lookout for traces left by the passage of animals or men, doing his best to imitate them as he followed. Shadows stretched long across the ground by the time they collected the game snared in their traps, gathered trout and salmon from the weirs along the creek, and again crossed French Creek in the canoe, heavily loaded with their bounty.

Custaloga's Town lay in the shadow of a high cliff that bordered the opposite bank, where North Deer Creek flowed into the broader stream, and they landed just below it. More than a hundred people inhabited its forty wigewas and log cabins, almost a third of them, like Christian, white captives.

A group of women hurried to the creek's bank to help unload the canoe. After the men distributed portions to several elders, they wound between the wigewas and cabins, Christian idly scanning the faces of the people they passed.

He glimpsed Hannah Specht sitting by her new mother in front of their wigewa. Her thin shoulders were hunched, her wan face downcast.

He caught up to Crouching Panther. "Where did my friend Franz go? I haven't seen him since . . . since the first day."

Crouching Panther looked at him for a moment, frowning, then his expression cleared. "Ah, you mean Bright Eyes. He has gone with his mother to her village. They live a day's walk from here."

"Oh." Christian glanced back toward Hannah, but she had disappeared.

◆━━━◆

"Eh. Eh. Eh." Christian chanted and stamped his feet, doing his best to imitate the rhythmic movements of the other boys.

Gathered at the edge of the broad council house yard around a great bonfire, they swayed to the beat of water drums and hiss of turtle shell rattles, while the inner circle of adult dancers moved in and out of light and shadow cast by the flames. Dancing was strictly forbidden in the Amish faith, and it felt strange to Christian. But so much about this great adventure seemed strange, and the custom of the people here was to dance. God wouldn't mind, he had decided.

It had been a long, exhausting day. After their return from the hunt, he had helped Deep Water and her daughters kill, pluck, and dress the pigeons, then salt some and set the rest on racks over low fires to smoke. He remembered helping Maami butcher chickens and game fowl but quickly thrust the memories away.

By the evening meal, which he and Nútemau shared with Crooked Leg's family, weariness had almost overtaken him. But large helpings of roasted pigeon breast, savory corn cakes, and beans sweetened with maple sugar had revived his energy for the nightly dances.

Crooked Legs deliberately bumped Christian's shoulder. He laughed, moved over a step, and concentrated on maintaining the dance's rhythm until the sound of the drumbeats and rattles faded away. Then he bent over and propped his hands on his knees, panting, more from excitement than exertion. It seemed to him that the windy night was filled with mysteries and wonder.

An older boy named Black Fox came over and put his hand on Christian's shoulder. "Though you have not walked among us long, my friend, you dance well."

Christian straightened, grinning as he noted admiration in some of the other boys' expressions, though a couple who were white like him seemed envious. "We already dance nearly as well as the older ones. Soon they will ask us to join with them!"

His companions met his boast with laughing agreement.

The drums began to beat again. Before Christian and his friends could move toward the larger circle of dancers, however, Nútemau beckoned them to join him and a cluster of elders at a smaller fire nearby.

Nútemau waited until Christian took a seat beside him with Crooked Legs on his other side. "It is time for my son to learn the ancient stories of our people. In former times under the great chief Shingas, Custaloga was made keeper of our tribe's wampum.

It was for him to recite the *Wallam Olum,* the Red Score of the creation of the Leni Lenape, the first people. That privilege has been given to another now, but this night I will recount a part of it so that all of you may know who our people are and where they have come from, and never forget our heritage."

Nútemau's thin, tremulous voice gathered majesty and power as he began to recite the ancient story. Christian leaned forward to hear better but soon had to stifle a yawn. He found it increasingly hard to keep his eyes open.

"In the beginning sea water covered all the land, and above the water was deep fog. All was made by the first being: He who is eternal, invisible, present everywhere, the great Creator God Manitou. He made much water, much land, many clouds, and a great heaven. He made the sun, moon, and stars and caused them to move as they do. The wind blew hard and cleared away the deep water. It ran off the land, revealing a bright island . . . "

It's like the story in the Bible, Christian thought sleepily. *They know about God too. They just call him Manitou.* He propped his chin in his hands as Nútemau told of Manitou forming the first man and woman and animals and all creatures.

Christian jerked awake, suddenly aware that Nútemau had stopped speaking and was looking down at him with a kindly smile. He thought he was expected to say something and blurted out, "That story's in the Bible."

Nútemau frowned and scanned the faces of the elders around the fire. One of them said, "It is the book from which the missionaries read when they tell us of the white man's religion."

Nútemau returned his attention to Christian. "Your white blood has been washed away, my son, and you have been made Lenape. It is our people's beliefs and traditions you must learn now. In his wisdom Manitou has given a different religion and way of life to white men than to us. It is not good for either to leave their way and try to take up that of the other."

Leaning on his walking stick, he pushed to his feet and held out his hand. Stricken by the old man's reproof, Christian sprang up and grasped it. They bade the others good night, and Christian led Nútemau back to their wigewa.

I'm a Lenape boy for now, he reminded himself. *If I do everything I'm told, someday they'll let me go home.*

When they reached the wigewa, Christian released Bear from the small pen he had made to keep him from wandering. He laughed as the puppy yipped excitedly and jumped up repeatedly to lick him. When Nútemau was settled on the sleeping platform, wrapped in his old bearskin, Christian brought his pipe, tobacco pouch, and a coal from the banked fire so he could smoke.

Nútemau drew Christian down beside him and gently stroked his cheek. "You are a good son. My nephew did well to bring you to me. Are you happy here?"

"Yes, *wetochemend.*"

Nútemau fumbled through the blankets and skins that covered his side of the sleeping platform. After a moment he pulled out a small buckskin pouch ornamented with dyed quills and closed with a rawhide string. He opened it and shook out a small wooden head onto his palm.

"I made this for you while you were away hunting. This is Wsinkhoalican, whose head is carved on the posts of the Big House where our ceremonies are held."

Christian studied the carving. "Why is the face painted that way—red on the right and black on the left? The women paint their faces that way too."

"Red represents those who are living. Black is for the dead. Through it we summon their ghosts."

Christian repressed a shudder and darted a fearful glance at the shadows on the walls.

Nútemau returned the carving to the pouch and tied it around Christian's neck. "You must always keep Wsinkhoalican with you, along with an object that represents your *manitowuk*."

"Man-ee-too-wuk?" Christian pronounced the word hesitantly, his voice trembling.

"The *manitowuks* are the lesser gods to whom Manitou has given charge of the elements." Nútemau waved his hand in the air. "Wind, lightning, thunder, fire, whirlwinds and rain, snow, and ice. Manitou is so vast that it is hard for mortals to speak to him or to hear his words, but the *manitowuks* are near to us. To them we can speak of our concerns and they will help us."

But we can speak to Jesus, and he's God. Christian pressed his lips together tightly and said nothing.

"Here is what you must do to gain the power and wisdom of a man. One night the *manitowuk* who is to be the guardian of your life will reveal himself to you in a dream. You must listen to what he tells you and thereafter always carry with you his symbol and pray to him."

Christian forced a nod, a knot forming in the pit of his stomach.

Nútemau patted Christian's shoulder. "The time comes near when I must travel beyond the western ocean to the land where Manitou lives. On that day, though you are still young, you must be strong and do the duty of a son for me."

Fear gripped Christian. All his friends would soon abandon him for the hunting camps, and he would be left alone with only the frail old man as a companion.

"You won't leave me, will you, *wetochemend?* Please don't leave me!"

Nútemau gathered Christian to his side. "Take courage, my son. It is the way of all men to die and for our sons to take our place after us. You are already stronger than you think, and you will never be alone, for the gods are all around us. Never neglect to make sacrifices to them so that they will protect you and give you power and wisdom. After I am gone you will grow to be a man of great respect and honor among our people."

Tears stung Christian's eyes. Nútemau's words made no sense to him, but he said nothing, fearing to arouse the old man's displeasure again.

Chapter Six

Tuesday, October 24, 1757

JOHANNES HOCHSTETLER held his hat in both hands, turning it around and around as he stood before the graves of his mother, brother, and baby sister, head bowed, moisture dripping from his hair. The autumn fog that shrouded the surrounding fields and hills, reflecting his emotions, showed no sign of lifting.

He shook his head as he stared at the mounded graves. No words came to his mind. It seemed to be empty, his heart leaden.

When a twig snapped behind him, he looked around with dull disinterest. His sister, Barbara, cloaked, black beaver-felt hat secured to her head with a woolen kerchief, walked toward him from the direction of her plantation, a mile away.

"This is no weather to walk so far in." He glanced at her midriff. "Especially not in your condition."

"Walking is good for me. And the baby too." She came to stand beside him. "I didn't expect anyone to be here. Do you want to be alone?"

Blinking back tears, he made no reply.

Barbara studied the fields around them, finally lifted her gaze to his. "It just feels wrong to do nothing."

He turned back to face the graves. "You know what Bishop Hertzler said. We must trust in God, not in man."

"I know he's Katie's Daat, but—"

"He's the *bishop!*"

"*Ya,* and Katie's Daat. I know."

"Katie's no more sure her father's right than I am, but he is the bishop."

"And our Daat is out there somewhere and our brothers too! And we're not supposed to do anything to find them? To bring them home?"

Johannes thrust his fingers through the wet hair plastered to his brow. "I know how you feel, and I feel the same way. I want to do something! But I keep coming back to what Bishop Hertzler said that night before the funeral. To try to go after them puts us in danger and Daat and the boys, too, and might tempt us to fight them. Nor can we ask soldiers to fight for us. Nay, we have to keep on praying. And hoping."

"*Ya,* but—"

He wheeled and faced her. "We also decided to stay here and trust God to protect us and our children instead of moving to Cumru Township like some did. You were the first to speak."

She flushed and stared at him. He couldn't tell if the tension in her face reflected sadness or anger. Or both.

"Barbara—" He reached out for her.

She stepped back, then whirled and stalked away. He watched until she disappeared among the trees bordering the lane. Then, feeling defeated, he bowed his head, jammed on his hat, and turned toward home.

Chapter Seven

FALLING LEAVES MOON
Tuesday, October 25, 1757

J AKOB SHUFFLED through the dry leaves along the path under the forest's thinning canopy. He ignored his back's ache as he pressed close on the heels of his master, the young widow, Sunshine, and her elder sister, Big Teeth.

Bent almost double beneath the large bundle of split wood strapped to his back, he stepped gingerly into the shallow stream at the ford, grimacing as cold water seeped into his moccasins and swirled around his ankles. The past fortnight's dry weather had greatly shrunk the creek that ran along Buckaloons' palisade wall, but he had to mind each foothold in the mud.

He winced with each tentative step, favoring his left leg. A savage blow as he ran the gauntlet had left a deep bruise below his hip. He thanked God that he had suffered nothing worse than bruises, scrapes, and cuts—by now mostly healed—and that the dizziness brought on by a staggering blow to the head had passed after several days. His hip, which still bothered him, had been slower to heal because the hard labor he was forced to do continually aggravated it.

As he slogged up the slope onto the opposite bank, one foot began to slide out from under him, threatening to pitch him headlong. He sucked in a breath and bit his lip hard at the pain that seared through back and hip. Big Teeth glared at him over her shoulder, her thin lips pulled tight over her protruding teeth, and he hastily regained his footing. Grasping the thick, woven hemp straps that crossed his chest, he wrenched the load back into balance.

Shoulders hunched, he fixed his gaze on Sunshine, who strode ahead of her sister without pausing, bent with her own load, secured by the tumpline that encircled her brow. Like most native women, she tied her hair in two long locks, one behind each ear, and her face bore spots of paint. She wore a hip-length shirt similar to the men's, made of trade goods without collar or sleeves, and beneath that a calf-length petticoat of stroud, brightly colored leggings, and moccasins. A trade blanket shielded her shoulders from the cold.

Big Teeth and the elder of her two daughters returned to the lead, each bearing her own bundle of wood, while at their heels a small brindled dog danced and yipped excitedly.

Ji:yäh. Dog.

Jakob silently rehearsed the way the Seneca pronounced the word to fix it more firmly in his mind. He blinked the trickling sweat out of his eyes and glanced over at Sunshine's little daughter, Red Bird, who had run up from behind to walk beside him. He returned her smile, his spirits lifting a little.

Her burden was of greater weight than he would have thought her slight body could bear, much less carry all the way back to

Buckaloons from the forest that bordered the extensive fields outside the town. Yet she bore it cheerfully and without complaint, as she did all things. And as he had many times over the past fortnight, Jakob resolved to follow her example.

By now the sun had descended toward the tops of the western trees behind a thin veil of grey clouds. He and the women of his longhouse had spent the greater part of the day in the forest with a large group of townswomen, splitting logs from the trees a party of the men had felled the previous day. Apparently this was customary work for women among the Seneca, Jakob concluded, shaking his head.

Approaching the town's gates, they passed Red Bird's twin brother, Little Raccoon, and his friends, who were shooting at targets with their bows. Among them was the youngest of the captives brought to Buckaloons with Jakob, a boy who, like the other captured children and youths, had been adopted into a family.

He slowed to watch. The other boys were showing him how to nock his arrow into the bowstring and aim at the target. When his arrow struck the target's edge, he turned to his new friends, laughing as they crowded around to join in his triumph.

Maybe Joseph and Christli also have new friends. The thought eased the ache in Jakob's chest. *Those who've been adopted seem to be accepted and well treated among these people.*

Sunshine called to her son. Little Raccoon responded quickly, waving to the other boys and hurrying to collect his arrows. The dog ran up to him, tail wagging, and the boy stroked her head before leading the way through the town's great gates, which during the day stood open to the constant traffic moving in and out.

Little Raccoon led the way through the maze of lanes that wound through the treeless town between large bark-sided long-houses and smaller wigewas and occasional log cabins. The boy and his twin sister were about nine years old, Jakob guessed. In spite of the chilly weather, Little Raccoon wore only a breech-cloth, leggings, and moccasins, and Red Bird a long sleeveless shirt over a coarse stroud petticoat and leggings. Like their elders, both wore around their neck a charm carved of antler or bone in the shape of some animal or bird—to provide protection or favor from one of their gods, Jakob had learned.

When they reached the wide yard that surrounded the council house at the town's center, he lowered to his knees beside the women, the weight of his burden and stiffness of his joints making his movements awkward. Red Bird quickly deposited her firewood beside her mother's, then jumped up to help Jakob loosen the straps that crossed his chest, ease his load onto the ground, and slip the straps off over his arms. He stifled a sigh of relief. The little girl patted him on the shoulder encouragingly.

A bustle of activity filled the area as it had for the past week. People from outlying villages were flooding into the town. From what Jakob could understand of the French traders' and children's chatter, the Seneca's harvest festival would begin the next day with rituals and dances of thanksgiving devoted to the Iroquois creator god, Nauwaneu, and to the sun and moon and spirits of nature for the abundant harvest that would sustain the people through the winter. *Gane'onwon,* they called it. Jakob tried to wrap his tongue around the Seneca word, but as usual his efforts prompted giggles from the children.

Over the past days, as he came and went, helping the women to lay up great stores of food at the council house, he had observed groups of townspeople preparing the building for the festival, sweeping it out and decorating it with symbols of the Seneca's gods. He shrank in dismay from their pagan practices, which he could only view as abominations in the eyes of the one true God.

He thanked God that he had not been ordered to participate in that work. If he had been, could he have done so with a clear conscience? Was he disobeying God's laws by even helping to stock food for a festival in honor of idols? Yet he was called to love and care for his enemies.

For almost twenty years Jakob had lived peacefully in his isolated Amish community along Northkill Creek in Pennsylvania. He had been free to live and serve God according to the stern faith that taught him that all creatures were divided between good and bad, believing and unbelieving, darkness and light, those in the world and those who had come out of it, the true God and vain idols. The Lord God called his children to separate themselves from worldly evils and have no part in them, the Bible taught, for they had been set free from fleshly bonds by Christ Jesus and fitted through his Spirit for God's holy service.

The memory of the intense persecution Anabaptists such as the Amish and Mennonites suffered in Europe had dimmed over the years. But now daily, even hourly, the question of how to live in the midst of this alien and hostile society while remaining faithful to God confronted him. He felt torn between what often seemed like conflicting commands.

Alone and completely dependent on the good will of his captors for his very life, he wrestled with God's command to love his enemies, to bless those who cursed him, to do good to those who hated him, and to pray for those who persecuted him. He struggled to plumb the depths of what it truly meant to love these people, not with human love, but with godly love, all while keeping himself separate from their pagan practices. He pondered this dilemma again, while he, Big Teeth, and Sunshine stacked their loads of split wood among the piles already gathered.

When they finished, they followed the children to the family's longhouse, and Jakob temporarily pushed his troubled thoughts aside. *Ganöhse:s,* he said to himself: longhouse. He despaired of ever getting the pronunciation right.

Big Teeth's husband, Falling Water, appeared on the flat-roofed porch at the weathered structure's front entrance. The long scalp lock dangling from the crown of his plucked head, ornamented with silver brooch, turkey feathers, and tuft of deerskin, designated him as a warrior. He wore the common dress of all Seneca men: sleeveless buckskin shirt, knee-length skirt of buckskin over breechcloth and leggings, and moccasins. Tattoos and various colors of paint adorned his arms and face.

Scowling, he gestured toward Jakob as he spoke to Sunshine, indicating that he wanted Jakob to be lent to him for some task. Jakob groaned inwardly. The day's labor had taken its toll. His muscles burned and his stomach pinched with hunger. He had eaten nothing since the morning meal, hours earlier, and then his ration had been meager, as usual, hardly enough to sustain him through the day.

With evening coming on he had hoped he would finally receive his late afternoon portion and be allowed to rest. But Sunshine motioned for him to go with her brother-in-law.

Jakob ducked through the longhouse's hide door flap after Falling Water and stepped into the front storage area immediately inside. Iroquois longhouses were all about twenty feet high, and equally wide, but varied in length according to the number of families who lived in them. Heavy strips of elm bark covered the exterior, which was held in place by a network of poles and lashed to a sturdy framework of larger poles that defined the structure's length and also divided the interior into spacious rooms. Rush mats and hides separated storage and living compartments from one another, with a central passageway running the building's length.

The longhouse, which belonged to East Wind, the elderly clan matron and mother of the two women, was relatively small. Only four families occupied it, though empty compartments at the rear suggested that at one time it had housed as many as four more.

Because of the rapidly cooling weather, the narrow openings in the building's walls were closed, leaving only the smoke holes open down the length of the roof. With the reduced ventilation, the pungent odors of cooking food, unwashed bodies, and animal grease hung in the air. Jakob hesitated, squinting as he waited for his eyes to stop smarting and adjust to the dim light in the thick, smoky atmosphere.

Always Anna kept our house clean—

He thrust the thought away and fixed his gaze on Falling Water, who squatted by a thick bundle of prime deer hides. Jakob guessed that he was to carry them to the French trader to buy needed supplies. They would undoubtedly fetch a good price.

He forced a cheerful expression and knelt to allow the warrior to strap the bundle of hides to his aching back, wondering whether he had any strength left to stand. A verse from the book of Colossians came to his mind: *Alles, was ihr tut, das tut von Hertzen, als dem Herrn und nicht den Menschen.* Whatsoever ye do, do it heartily, as to the Lord, and not unto men. He sucked in a deep breath, pushed to his feet, adjusted the load, and nodded respectfully to Falling Water, who surprised him with a grunt of approval.

Jakob staggered back through the doorway behind the warrior, who set a brisk pace along the path toward the town's gates. Jakob limped after him as rapidly as he could, gritting his teeth at the sharp pains that seared through every muscle. Little Raccoon skipped along in front of them, carrying a large basket to carry the trade goods. Along the way they met Big Teeth's youngest son, a boy a couple of years older than Little Raccoon, who joined their procession.

As they neared the trader's hut, Jakob saw Hans Specht coming toward him along the path behind the elderly woman who was his master. The two of them, along with a number of the other captives, had labored all day with the party splitting wood in the forest, tantalizingly close to each other, but too far away to speak. They had found no opportunity for conversation since being forced to run the gauntlet. Once separated for either adoption or servitude, captives were not allowed to spend any length of time together, and then never alone.

His friend was dirty, gaunt, and unkempt, his clothing so ragged it hardly covered his body, his skin livid from the cold. Bruises stained his face and arms, and he kept his head and eyes down, avoiding Jakob's gaze.

Jakob's heart sank. Specht appeared to have given up all hope. When the old woman turned and struck him with her walking stick to hurry him forward, Jakob shook his head and averted his own eyes as his friend brushed past.

Jakob wanted desperately to encourage Specht to endure and caution him that they dared not attempt an escape yet, for they could have no hope of surviving with winter swiftly approaching. As difficult as it was, they had to bide their time until the spring, when the weather warmed sufficiently and most of the warriors would be away from the town on renewed raids. But he had begun to fear he would never be allowed to get close enough to speak to him.

Chapter Eight

S HADOWS STRETCHED across the ground in the chill twilight by the time they returned to the longhouse, Jakob lugging the basket full of trade goods. The two boys ran ahead, while Falling Water stumbled along, cradling a bottle of rum with one arm while taking long drinks from the bottle in his other hand.

Following them inside, Jakob passed through the front storage area into the first living compartment, grateful for its warmth. Hot coals seethed in the fire pit at the passage's center, brightening the space where Big Teeth and Falling Water lived with their younger children, to Jakob's left. Their eldest daughter and her husband occupied the space on his right, and the two women squatted together beside the fire, preparing the evening meal.

As in all the living compartments, a wide sleeping platform extended the length of the exterior wall on each side, with a second platform at head height above it for additional sleeping space and storage. At night bearskins and deerskins were spread across the platforms to serve as bedding. During the day, covered with brightly painted rush mats, they provided both seats and tables. Additional mats covered the floors and decorated the walls, helping to keep out drafts.

Without a glance toward his wife and children, Falling Water sprawled, bleary-eyed, onto the lower platform where his sons lounged with several large dogs, a couple of which raised their heads to bare their teeth at Jakob. The warrior took another long drink and with a grunt rolled onto his side, his back to the room.

Big Teeth stopped stirring the contents of the brass kettle hanging from a tripod over the fire and glared at him. Her pregnant daughter shifted into a more comfortable position as she glanced apprehensively from one to the other.

It had been hours since the morning meal, and Jakob's mouth watered at the rich aroma of the corn stew simmering in the kettle. He allowed no sign of his hunger to show, however, and, keeping his distance from the dogs, set the basket beside Big Teeth, waiting while she rummaged through it. He could hear the low voice of their younger daughter speaking with her grandmother, East Wind, in the next compartment, but could make nothing of their conversation. In spite of Red Bird's and Little Raccoon's best efforts, Jakob had yet to fathom the names of the couple's four children, much less learn to pronounce them. The other names had been difficult enough to decipher.

His master's name was O`dän'kot in the Seneca tongue, and after querying the children repeatedly, he felt reasonably confident that it meant Sunshine. Her brother-in-law's name remained a guess, and, still uncertain of her older sister's name, Jakob had settled on mentally calling her by her most notable feature.

Scowling, Big Teeth handed him a small pouch of salt, a slender packet of steel needles, and a thicker one of brightly colored ribbons before impatiently waving him away. He rose, teeth clenched against the pain that lanced through his back, detoured around the fire pit, and padded into the second compartment.

Sunshine's frail, hunchbacked mother bent over the sleeping platform to Jakob's right, where her invalid husband, Broken Feather, lay. Although Jakob reckoned they could be no more than ten years older than he, the Indians' arduous life had left its mark, making them appear much older. Their granddaughter was with them, and all three looked around as Jakob entered.

"*Sgëno,*" Broken Feather said in a thin, reedy voice, the greeting quickly echoed by East Wind.

Jakob bowed respectfully. "*Sgëno.*"

The granddaughter rose and passed by Jakob without a glance, disappearing behind him into the front compartment.

He turned to the fire pit at the compartment's center, where Sunshine knelt, laying flat stones to heat in the hot ashes on the edge of the fire's seething embers. Red Bird sat cross-legged across from her, while on their sleeping platform Little Raccoon sprawled against the large white dog with brown spots that reminded Jakob of his dog, Blitz, who had been killed in the attack.

Forcibly suppressing the emotions that welled up, Jakob returned the children's smiles. He stowed the trade items on the upper shelf, then sat tentatively on the edge of the lower platform at the opposite end from Little Raccoon.

As usual the bedding in the longhouse teemed with lice and fleas, which tormented the inhabitants. He had noticed the boy and girl repeatedly darting shy glances at him, and now the boy, seeing that he scratched, quickly drew a small clay pot of bear grease mixed with mashed plantain from beneath the platform. He brought it to Jakob and helped him to rub the ointment on the itchy places. It gave off a pungent odor but instantly soothed the insect bites.

Jakob patted the boy's slender shoulder in gratitude. *"Niyawë."*

Both children immediately began to chatter at him like a pair of blue jays. Jakob made a comical face and shook his head.

"Dë'ëh o'si'?" What did you say?

They giggled behind their hands. When they repeated the phrase correctly, he grimaced and spread his hands, drawing more laughter. His playfulness seemed to gain him favor with Sunshine, whose face softened as she glanced at him.

Seeing that the fire's embers were settling, he jumped up to fetch a piece of split wood, which he laid across the cherry coals beneath the kettle. She gave him an approving look as thin blue flames licked along it, bringing the stew back to a slow bubble.

He returned to his seat, absently rubbing his chin and cheeks. When the town's sachem had given him to Sunshine, he had been forced to undergo the painful process of having his beard plucked. She had provided him with bear grease to smear on his face to ease the sting, and the soreness had abated after a few days. But he had worn a beard since his marriage many years earlier, as dictated by Amish tradition, and the smooth skin was a constant, painful reminder of how much his life had changed.

Clenching his teeth, he focused his attention on the children. He had observed that young Seneca boys spent most of their days playing games and practicing shooting, while girls were expected to help their mothers with their daily tasks. Boys and girls both seemed content, however, and there appeared to be few constraints on any of the children. The Seneca often turned work into play, and as a result most of the children joined happily in the activities of their elders.

Jakob felt a stab of regret for the strict discipline he had imposed on his own children, as his father had on him and his brothers and sisters. As he had repeatedly since his capture, he found himself wondering whose way was the better.

"*O:ne:ka'.*"

Jakob jumped to his feet. Sunshine's command was one of the first Seneca words he had learned: water.

He brought the large clay water jar and dried-gourd scoop to her. She dipped some water into a bowlful of ground corn seasoned with salt and chopped wild onion and kneaded the mixture, while he returned the water jar to its place and withdrew to his seat. Pinching off pieces, she flattened them and laid them on the hot stones. The cakes sizzled, releasing a savory cloud of steam that made Jakob's stomach growl.

A few days earlier he had taken it on himself to help the children carry food to East Wind and her husband at mealtimes, and when the food was ready they did so. Jakob gently helped Broken Feather to eat as much as the elderly man was able to swallow and received his and East Wind's grateful thanks.

When he returned to the other side of the compartment, he saw that Sunshine had been watching. She handed him a brimming bowl and gestured toward the sleeping platform where the children sat cross-legged.

Slowly and distinctly, she said, *"Sedékoní.'"* You come eat.

Jakob hesitated, wanting to make sure he understood. She seemed to be giving him permission to sit on the platform and eat with her and the children. When he did not move, she again motioned to him sit.

This was new. She had initially been gruff in her dealings with him, and until now he had been offered only a small portion of food before being shooed outside to eat alone, regardless of the weather. During the past fortnight he had often despaired of enduring the ill treatment to which he had been subjected. Energy sapped by relentless labor, he had often been so weak with hunger that he eagerly devoured any leftover scraps thrown out by the townspeople, along with half-rotted nuts, withered tubers, and overripe squash foraged from the fields and woods during the last of the harvest.

But perhaps his efforts to humble himself and give up all thought of vengeance—to learn to communicate in the Seneca language, to do Sunshine's bidding without protest and even seek ways to help, and to appear happy and content among them—were bearing fruit. He had seen other enslaved captives treated cruelly, but he realized now that his circumspect behavior had spared him the worst abuse. For the past few days, Sunshine's voice had lacked its previous sharpness, and even the harsh attitude of Buck Teeth and her family toward him had begun to ease.

Lieber Gott, danke! Dear God, thank you!

He settled gingerly on the opposite end of the platform from her and the twins, careful to spill not a drop of the stew. *"Nïyawë."* The inflection wasn't quite right, and he repeated it more slowly. Sunshine smiled.

The stew tasted strange to him, with pieces of dried pumpkin and fragments of bear meat mixed with parched corn and sweetened with maple sugar. But he eagerly devoured it and the corn cakes Sunshine gave him, savoring each mouthful, so hungry that the meal seemed like a banquet.

Between bites he surreptitiously watched Sunshine. Like many of the native women, she was tall, slender, and well-built and moved with a natural, easy grace. Her face, although plain, reflected a gracious and good-humored nature.

He was not certain that she was a widow; he thought of her as such since no man lived with her. He had observed that some children had fathers who did not live with their mothers and concluded that divorce must be acceptable among the Seneca. If Sunshine had divorced the children's father, he reasoned, they would still have a relationship with him. Yet the only men who appeared to be close to the twins were Falling Water and Broken Feather, which made Jakob think that their father must no longer be living.

Jakob had won the boy and girl over with little effort. The friendship they offered did much to comfort and reassure him as he struggled to navigate this alien society. They seemed fascinated by his blue eyes and curly black hair, which had grown enough over the past month to curl onto his forehead and around his ears. And to his surprise they were eager to help him and to teach him their language.

He had begun to make a game of it by often asking them in an exaggerated tone, *"Dë'ëh hi:gë:h?"*—What is that?—when he did not understand something they said. Each time he drew out the syllables and varied the pronunciation to make it more comical, which never failed to delight the children.

They had taught him their names and those of the others in their family—at least as far as he was able to decipher their meanings—and also that they called him something like One Who Carries Burdens, which he mentally shortened to Burden Carrier. Although they spoke the term innocently, Jakob had winced at the realization that being named according to the women's work he was forced to do was meant to emphasize his inferiority. But he resolved to welcome the gift of sharing in the humiliation his Savior had suffered for his sake.

Though his affection for the children continued to grow, he carefully guarded his emotions when he was with them. The twins' childish play often reminded him of his own children, which aroused unbearable grief and, worse, accusing memories of his strictness, even harshness, with them.

He struggled to choke down mouthfuls of food past the lump in his throat. He knew he had to eat to gain strength, and so with great effort he forced himself to swallow one bite, and then another until his bowl was empty.

✦ ⸺ ✦

THE HARVEST CELEBRATION would take place the next day. That night the longhouse filled with people from the town and new arrivals from one of the outlying villages who had been invited to take shelter in the empty rear compartments during the festival. Jakob tended the fires, while the adults sat in groups, visiting, and the children played, a hubbub of conversation filling the building.

Soon one of the men began to pound on a water drum, producing a deep, resonant rhythm. When the assembly quieted, the drummer started to sing and was quickly joined by other men, who came to sit beside him, shaking rattles made of gourd or turtle shells as they chanted.

The younger women were the first to dance, moving back and forth along the wide passageway down the length of the longhouse, with everyone joining in the alternating choruses of the song. Many of the older women and men, however, clustered in the rear living compartment to gamble.

From what Jakob had observed, the townspeople were avid gamblers who would wager any of their possessions on the turn of the dice. Sunshine, Big Teeth, and Falling Water joined this group, and each time Jakob passed into the storage area at the back of the longhouse and returned, carrying armloads of wood for the fires, they were bent over a wooden bowl.

Jakob had often watched the townspeople play this game. The pits from six wild plums blackened with charcoal on one side served as dice. Each player lifted the bowl in turn, then rapidly brought it down onto a folded hide to make the pits inside it bounce. Two teams took turns betting on how many of the dice would turn up their black side, keeping score with beans.

That night Sunshine's luck was good. She won back a number of items she had lost previous nights, along with a shirt, leggings, and moccasins from one of the older men that were little worn and relatively clean. After the townspeople had gone and the visitors had withdrawn to the rear compartments for the night, she presented the clothing to Jakob, motioning for him to replace the filthy rags he had worn since his capture.

When he thanked her again and again, she and the children beamed. She dug a worn trade blanket out of a bark box under the platform and gave this to him as well.

It was late when he finally settled on the upper platform where he was made to sleep each night. He knew this was done so that he could not leave the longhouse without rousing his master or the dogs, but he thanked God nonetheless for the mercies he had been shown.

When all was quiet, he pulled out one of two sticks he kept secreted beneath the hides on the platform. With a sharp stone he carried in the buckskin pouch on his belt, he cut a notch to represent the day that had just passed. At the end of seven days, he would notch the longer stick, by which he kept count of the weeks since he had been taken captive, and replace the short stick with a new one.

The nightly ritual never failed to bring back sharp memories of his home's burning ruin, the dead bodies of his wife and two children, and the forced separation from Joseph and Christian. But if he was to survive, he had to focus his thoughts on the path before him: To remain faithful to God. To work hard. To gain his captors' favor. To find a way of escape and make it back to his older children in the Northkill settlement. And then to bring Joseph and Christian home.

That was all that mattered now. All that kept him alive.

He removed a peach pit from the small bag hanging around his neck as he also did each night. It had come from a pouch of fruit he hurriedly plucked from his orchard the morning of his capture to sustain him and his boys on the journey he knew lay before them. At the first Indian town they had come to, he had presented the last of the peaches to the sachem, a gift that had spared him and his boys from the gauntlet. When they left the town, he had retrieved this single pit from the refuse pile. It was his only remaining physical connection to home.

He squeezed the pit tightly in his fist and prayed, beginning with the Lords Prayer. He prayed for each of his children and grandchildren by name and for his church family. He pled for the salvation of the inhabitants of the longhouse and the town and ended by requesting that God's will, not his own, be done.

Then he opened his hand and rubbed the grooved pit between his fingers. As had become his habit, he mentally traced the long pathways over which he had been brought to this place, fighting a growing dismay that the details were blurring with time, that weariness clouded some parts of the journey. But the need for sleep increasingly pressed down on him, and before he could finish, consciousness gave way to the deep slumber of exhaustion.

Chapter Nine

Wednesday, October 26, 1757

J AKOB ROUSED with a start. Even after the passage of weeks, he was still momentarily disoriented on awakening, expecting to be in his bed at home, with Anna already tending to baby Annali and the boys asleep in their beds upstairs.

He sat up slowly and peered around the longhouse. Its inhabitants were beginning to stir—unusually early for these people. Then he remembered that the festival began this day.

He rose hastily to rake out the banked coals in the compartment's fire pit and add kindling and split wood until the flames began to leap and crackle. Although the garments Sunshine had given him hung loosely on his shrunken frame, they provided much needed warmth and covering for his body.

Danke, Gott. He gave thanks for life and strength and clothing. And work to do, even if it was forced labor.

The first faint light of day illumined the eastern sky as he hurried to the town well, carrying two heavy elm-bark buckets dangling from a wooden yoke across his shoulders. He filled them with water and bore them back to the longhouse. Twice more he made the trip, each time emptying the buckets into large clay jars to supply the needs of the day for the longhouse's occupants.

Excited chatter filled the building, while the people put on their finest dress, oiled and ornamented their hair, and painted themselves in brilliant colors. Jakob received scant attention, and when everyone began to go outside, uncertain what was expected of him, he decided to stay behind with East Wind and Broken Feather. The elderly couple waved him away, however, indicating that he should accompany the others to the festival. So he hurried after Sunshine and the children, his blanket wound around his shoulders in the manner of the Indians.

To be warmly and decently clad after so many weeks was a great luxury he could hardly wrap his mind around. For the first time he did not feel ashamed when the townspeople looked at him. He praised God for giving him favor before his captors and added a prayer that his boys were also being treated kindly wherever they were.

The sky had grown distinctly brighter by the time they reached the council house yard, where a number of fires already blazed. Over them vast quantities of corn, beans, and squash simmered in huge kettles and haunches of venison and bear, turkey, fish, and other meats roasted. The smoky aroma of cooking food made Jakob's stomach growl.

Little Raccoon, Red Bird, and the other children ran ahead to join their friends among the throng gathering in orderly procession at the broad yard's center, with the French traders and trappers hovering on its fringes.

Jakob edged forward until he found a place where he could watch and listen without attracting notice. He looked anxiously around, his gaze at last finding Specht, but his friend kept his distance, face averted.

By angling his body, Jakob caught a glimpse of the sachems and shamans standing around the central fire at the front of the closely packed mass. An expectant hush fell, and just as the golden edge of the sun cast long bars of light through the trees surrounding the town, one of the sachems stepped forward to give a solemn speech, followed in turn by others.

A number of times Jakob heard the name Nauwaneu, the Seneca's Master of Life. When the first series of speeches ended, all the people prayed, arms lifted to the heavens. Then the leaders spoke again, more briefly, and laid sacrifices of tobacco, herbs, and each of the fall crops on the great fire.

Jakob observed the rituals with a mixture of wonder and horror. The native people's instinctive desire to thank God impressed him deeply, but dismay filled him at their worship of idols and demons. The sun, moon, and spirits of nature they prayed to had neither life nor power to save anyone from their sins or to change lives. He saw the sad evidence of this all around him, and a wrenching conviction fell on him.

How could he bring a word of salvation to these lost sheep when he could barely communicate about matters of daily life? He had been taught that a life faithful to Jesus' teachings bore the most powerful witness to God, and he believed it.

Yet without the ability to testify to his faith, if asked, how could he make anyone understand where this life-changing power came from? How could he ever direct them to the great Source?

His concern for Joseph and Christian deepened. Certainly they were exposed to the same pagan influences. As young as they were, how long would they be able to hold on to the faith? Would they be led astray?

As he searched his memory for scriptures of comfort, encouragement, and admonition to stand fast, the stories of Joseph and Daniel filtered into Jakob's mind. It was because of their obedience to the Lord's leading that both men had been elevated to high positions in the lands where they were held in exile, not in spite of it. Joseph and Daniel had acted with great wisdom and discretion, while continuing to worship God in the sight of the pagan rulers they were forced to serve. And the Lord had given them favor and allowed them to exercise enormous influence over those under whose earthly authority they had been placed.

You are yet with me, Lord. Give me such wisdom to act as pleases You. And give me favor with these people so they may see You through my life.

Jakob continued silently praying that the Lord would also guide his boys through the pressures and temptations of this alien culture and keep them faithful. And as he pled for their lives, the certainty that he must escape and find a way to bring them home intensified.

By the time the morning rituals were completed, hunger gnawed at his stomach. A few other captives timidly pressed into the lines of celebrants at the fires, Specht among them, and no one hindered them. Jakob edged into the nearest line, prepared to quickly duck out if driven away. But he received generous portions of food and drink without any apparent objection, and for once he ate his fill.

He had just finished when Sunshine brought a large bowl of stew to him with orders to take it back to the longhouse for her parents. He did so gladly, with Red Bird and Little Raccoon hurrying alongside, carrying bark plates heaped with bread and roasted trout.

All afternoon and evening, Jakob hovered along the border of the council house yard, watching teams of youth and adults engage in races, shoot at targets, and play a ball game. As the sun sank below the treetops, he again carried food back to East Wind and Broken Feather, grateful to be given some useful work to keep him occupied.

With nightfall, clusters of townspeople began to circle around the bonfires. Watching their rhythmic movements, Jakob repeated to himself, *Oä'no`*, a word the children had recently taught him: dance. This custom of the Indians, completely alien to his Amish way of life, simultaneously fascinated and repelled him.

The people's habit was to gather at the council house for the nightly dances, or if the weather was bad, in individual longhouses. Many, including the Frenchmen, gathered inside to drink and while away the hours—and their treasure—at various games of chance, as the children raced around, shrieking with glee.

It was invariably midnight or later before the participants finally wandered off to their own habitations for sleep. They then got up late in the morning and took their time in attending to necessary tasks—when they worked at all. Jakob, used to rising early to tend to the work of the day, found this custom a source of intense frustration.

◆┄┄┄◆

THE STARS GLITTERED from the indigo heavens overhead in twinkling, distant points of light above the blacker silhouettes of the surrounding trees. For the third day in a row, the throb of drums and chatter of rattles pulsed on the air, underlaid by the chants of the dancers and the multiplied stomp of feet.

Jakob had received little attention and no instructions from Sunshine, who was now dancing around the central bonfire with a large group of women. It was the last day of the festival, and he hoped that tomorrow the townspeople would finally return to their normal routines.

He had not managed to exchange even a brief word with Specht, catching only occasional glimpses of his friend, and then at a distance. As he wandered along the fringes of the crowds, he wrestled with deepening anxiety and doubt. All that he had depended on for sustenance—family, church, *Freundschaft,* the most essential necessities of life—had been torn away. And the overwhelming sense of his vulnerability before his captors, of being abandoned and desperately alone, which he held at bay most of the time, now struck him forcefully.

He turned and strode through the shadows along the side of the council house, intending to seek sanctuary back at the longhouse, where East Wind and Broken Feather would by now be asleep. He had taken only a few steps, however, when a darker shadow moved hastily out of his way. He started and grasped the man's arm, bending forward to study him intently.

"Hans!"

Specht shifted and glanced around uneasily.

"*Wie geht's, mein Freund?*" How are you doing, my friend?

Specht shrugged, his dirt-streaked face blank.

Jakob leaned closer. He made out the shadow of a bruise across Specht's cheek and a raw scrape along his arm.

"I saw the old woman beat you the other day."

Specht shrank back. "They think I'm lazy."

"You do everything they tell you to?"

Specht shrugged, apparently determined not to meet Jakob's gaze. "What difference does it make?"

"If you do your best to get along, to learn their language and help them, they'll treat you better. We need to gain these people's trust."

"Why?" Specht finally lifted his gaze to Jakob's. "We've both lost everything, Jake. Our children are gone, most likely dead." He waved his arm, indicating their surroundings. "None of this matters!"

"It does matter! We have to live as best we can—according to the way *Gott* leads us. You see how kindly the Seneca treat the children they've taken into their families? They make them their own. Ours are yet alive! And they're being treated as well as these, wherever they are. We have to pray for them to keep the favor of their captors. *Gott* will protect our little ones when we cannot."

Specht turned his face away.

"We've survived so much, and will you give up now? *Gott* has not forgotten us. He has yet a purpose. We have to go on.

We will—we *must!* If only we can endure until the spring when the warriors go back to their raiding, *Gott* will open up a chance for us to get away from here."

"Even if we made it, even if somehow we found the children, what good would it do? We could never get them away from the Indians and bring them all the way back home."

"But we can get home ourselves. This war can't last forever, and if the English win it, they can force the Indians to give their captives back." Jakob gripped Specht's shoulders. "When we get home, we'll petition the governor to make the Indians give them up. We're the only hope they have. We can't fail them!"

Specht's lower lip trembled, and Jakob continued urgently. "Do your best to gain your masters' favor and trust so you can move around more freely. Learn all you can. We're not alone! We have *Gott* to help us. No matter what happens, as long as we have breath, we have hope."

Chapter Ten

FALLING LEAF MOON
Saturday, October 29, 1757

JOSEPH GRUNTED, fighting to break the grip of the older, heavier youth who pinned him against the ground. Again.

Three times before, he had determined that Mehíttuk would not overcome him. Each time he had suffered numerous bruises and scrapes to prove his defeat.

It was bad enough that their audience included all the other youths and children of the town, both white and native, the majority of whom voiced loud support for Mehíttuk. A smaller number—many who had also been bested by the tall, lean youth currently sprawling across Joseph's torso as they writhed in the dirt—shouted encouragement to Joseph.

Among them he could hear little Contrary Wind's voice. But worse was the large group of young women who had gathered to jeer and laugh. Several had caught Joseph's eye in recent weeks and returned equally admiring glances. The thought of yet another public defeat before them caused his stomach to churn.

Sweat-blinded, he hastily reviewed the clandestine wrestling matches he and his friends had engaged in behind one or another's barn out of view of the adults, contests he had most often won. But little he had learned then helped him now since, like most of the Lenape youths, Mehíttuk was bigger, stronger, and more skilled than any of Joseph's previous opponents.

He remembered a hold Menetopalis had shown him after his last losing battle. He had made it a habit to listen and watch silently when given instructions, keeping his expression blank to show his indifference. But he was learning that it was always a mistake to ignore Menetopalis's counsel, not because Menetopalis punished him for it—he never even admonished him—but because Joseph invariably benefitted from following the older man's advice.

If he could just gain some leverage and reverse positions with Mehíttuk.

He gritted his teeth, summoning all his strength to break his adversary's hold. His effort forced Mehíttuk to shift and arch slightly upward, his hands slipping on Joseph's sweaty flesh as he did so. Joseph rocked violently to the side, opening enough space between them to jerk his knee upward in a savage thrust that knocked Mehíttuk sideways and dropped him to his stomach on the ground.

Before he could regain breath and spring to his feet, Joseph rolled onto hands and knees and pounced onto Mehíttuk's back, pinning him securely. He grasped his adversary's chin in both hands and pulled his head back with all his strength, forcing Mehíttuk's body into a backward curve.

Mehíttuk slapped the ground with one hand. "I concede!"

His hoarse croak brought a flurry of cheers from the surrounding crowd. Joseph released his hold and sprang to his feet as many of the onlookers pressed around to pound him on the back and others shouted their congratulations. He darted a quick glance at the young women clapping and cheering at the circle's edge before turning back to Mehíttuk.

The older youth rolled slowly onto his back, face contorted and dripping sweat. He propped himself on his elbows and scowled up at Joseph through slitted eyes.

For a moment they glared at each other, then Joseph extended his hand and waited. Finally a smile spread across Mehíttuk's face. He grasped Joseph's hand and allowed him to heave him to his feet.

"You are strong, my friend! And you learn quickly."

Joseph lowered his head in response to the compliment.

Without warning, Contrary Wind bowled into him, almost knocking him down. He wound his arms around Joseph's waist, looking up at him in adoration. Laughing, Joseph ruffled the child's hair and drew him close.

On Joseph's other side, Red Squirrel said, "You will soon be one of the best among us."

Joseph wiped the sweat from his eyes with the back of his free hand as he met Red Squirrel's gaze. He had liked the look of this sturdily-built Shawnee youth from their first encounter. About Joseph's height and age, with regular features and an open, friendly expression, he seemed to go out of his way to make Joseph feel accepted.

He turned and searched above the heads of those who thronged around them for a glimpse of Menetopalis and found him sitting on a log nearby with Tamaque and several other elders, who all seemed to exult in his victory. Menetopalis's dark eyes reflected such pride and approval that Joseph nodded an acknowledgement of the older man's strategy, which had won the match.

The day was clear and sunny, but a light breeze chilled Joseph's sweaty body. He brushed off as much dirt as he could before drawing on leggings and shirt and stepping into his moccasins.

By now the maidens and most of the youths had drifted away, and Contrary Wind ran off toward their cabin. A few of the onlookers had gathered around the elders, talking. Joseph wrapped his blanket around his shoulders and went to stand near Menetopalis, but slightly outside the circle.

It helped that Shingas had left Sauconk a couple of weeks earlier to travel north along Beaver Creek to a scattering of towns collectively called Kuskuskies, where his and Tamaque's eldest brother, Pisquetomen, lived. From conversations between Bird's Nest and his new parents, Joseph gathered that, although Sauconk was Shingas's principal residence, he was often absent. Joseph was glad for it.

Menetopalis reached for Joseph's arm and drew him closer. He turned to Tamaque. "Do I not have reason to be proud of this son of mine?"

"You do indeed." The sachem assessed Joseph. "One day, my nephew, you will be a man of great renown in the Turtle division and among the Lenape people."

Joseph felt warmth rise into his face as approving murmurs rose from the others. Still, he fought to conceal his pleasure.

The sun hung low near the leafless treetops. Menetopalis levered to his feet with his walking stick and drew his blanket more closely around him. Joseph quickly moved into position on the side of the older man's crippled leg. He had grown used to walking with Menetopalis leaning on his shoulder and fell instinctively into the rhythm of his halting stride as they turned onto the path toward their cabin.

The town occupied a point of tree-dotted bottomland where Beaver Creek flowed into the Ohio River. It was composed mainly of one- and two-room log cabins, with a number of wigewas scattered among them. The structures appeared dilapidated and poor to Joseph in comparison to the larger, well-kept log houses of the Northkill community where he had grown up.

At the far end of the broad central yard they passed the imposing building the people called the Big House. Joseph had learned that it was used for the tribe's religious ceremonies and that the town's official business was transacted in the long, wide council house opposite, which also accommodated visitors when needed.

Nearby lay the town's burial ground, where a post marked the head of each grave. Menetopalis turned aside to it. When he and Wulachen had brought Joseph to their oldest son's grave a couple of days after his adoption, they had explained that the posts left undecorated denoted the graves of the town's head-men. The graves of captains—the war chiefs—were painted red and decorated with scalps and weapons. Those displaying a small turtle shell indicated the graves of shamans, and small tokens of the deceased's life marked some of the other graves as well.

Joseph guessed that Menetopalis and Wulachen's oldest son had most likely died the previous summer, for the earth around the grave was not yet fully settled and an uneven growth of weeds and grass sparsely covered it. The post was decorated only with an arrow the boy had made. Tears filling her eyes, Wulachen had lightly run her fingers down the graceful, weathering shaft fletched with neatly trimmed turkey feathers to its sharp flint tip. Menetopalis had placed his arm around her shoulders, and for some moments they had stood motionless and silent, heads bowed, as he and Joseph did now.

They lost a son, as I lost my family. And they hurt like I do.

Menetopalis turned away without speaking, and Joseph steadied him as they returned to the path. Before they reached their cabin, however, the older man again veered off, this time into a broad clearing.

Several large trees sprawled across the forest floor there, uprooted, their lichen-covered trunks falling into decay. All around them undergrowth had sprung up, with small saplings rising above the lower growth, slender branches stretching upward to the hazy sunbeams that slanted through the break in the forest's overarching canopy.

Menetopalis raised his walking stick and swept it in a slow, graceful motion from one side of the clearing to the other. "When the Whirlwind passes through the forest, he uproots many great trees. Men may say this is a bad thing, yet when the trees fall many insects find a home and food in them. As the trees decay they nourish the soil, and all around them young trees and other plants grow up and stretch their arms to the sky."

The look he directed at Joseph was piercing. "The tall trees are beautiful to see, my son. But if they had not fallen, the sun would not reach the ground. The soil would not be replenished. And the young trees would never reach their full height and bear their fruit and seed in season to give life to others." He paused before adding, "But these must choose to grow and not be downcast."

Joseph dropped his gaze to the nearby trunk of a dead tree. The bark was falling away in many places, and he could see ants and beetles scurrying about in the spongy fibers underneath. Then he looked across the clearing to where slender saplings and underbrush, now bare of leaves, had crowded into the gaps left by the fallen trees.

Already they were pushing more roots deep into the soil. And in the spring, after the melting of the winter snows, they would send out new growth and reach ever higher.

He's saying that I'm like those saplings.

Tears blurred Joseph's sight. He bit his lip, unable to speak for the knot in his throat and unwilling to meet Menetopalis's gaze. Yet the knowledge that this man understood and cared softened the sharp edges of Joseph's grief.

At last he looked up and lowered his head in acknowledgement. Menetopalis's arm tightened around his shoulders, and for the first time Joseph found himself leaning into his adoptive father's side.

No one except Barbara and little Annali had embraced him since he was a small child. He had known, of course, that Maam and Daat and the others loved him, for they showed it in many ways by their actions. But these people were different. Wulachen and the children freely expressed their emotions toward him by touch and words as well as by actions.

As did Menetopalis. Joseph was not used to this from a man, and it moved him. In spite of every effort to hold Menetopalis at a distance, Joseph was coming to admire him deeply and to welcome his gentle touch.

"It will be well, my son." Menetopalis drew in a breath, straightened, and relaxed his embrace. "Your mother will be cooking our evening meal and I grow hungry."

"I grow hungry too," Joseph repeated carefully.

Menetopalis chuckled. "She and your sisters will rejoice to hear how you overcame Mehíttuk."

"You are the one who showed me how. I thank you."

"And you are the one who overcame Mehíttuk, not I."

✦┄┄┄✦

THE WIND HAD COOLED even more with the sun's descent below the treetops, and Joseph was shivering by the time they reached the cabin. Wulachen and the children had gathered at the fire pit outside, where hot coals seethed beneath a brass kettle covered with a large pumpkin-vine leaf.

Near the cabin's porch, Moonflower was pounding dry corn kernels into flour in a mortar carved from a hollowed length of tree trunk. She Sings sat cross-legged on a deerskin beside her mother at the fire, skillfully weaving a new mat of supple reeds, while beside her Contrary Wind lay on his stomach, playing the scatter game with a bundle of slender sticks dropped onto the ground.

At Joseph's and Menetopalis's approach, Wulachen and the children turned expectant faces to them, and Wulachen exclaimed, "Your brother told us that you overcame Mehíttuk, my son! We are eager to hear how you did it."

Joseph helped Menetopalis settle comfortably on a stump near the fire pit. The children ran over and threw their arms around Joseph, laughing and chattering so rapidly that he understood little of what they said other than that they shared in his triumph.

Menetopalis winked at Joseph and, speaking slowly and distinctly, related a detailed account of the match, while using his knife to smooth the handle of a ladle he was carving from a length of hickory wood. Joseph took a seat at the fire beside Contrary Wind as Menetopalis told the story, with Wulachen and the children breaking in with questions and admiring comments.

He was watching every move I made. This time Joseph did not try to stifle the pleasure that stole through him.

His stomach growled as he watched Wulachen make corn cakes and place them atop the clean, hot ashes at the fire's edge. When she lifted the pumpkin leaf off the pot to stir its contents, the rich fragrance of stewing pumpkin mixed with corn and venison caused Joseph's mouth to water.

He was becoming accustomed to the difference between the rich, varied German dishes Maam used to cook and the corn, squash, and beans that were the staples of the Lenape's diet. The Lenape custom of eating only twice daily, however, was a more difficult adjustment, and as usual he was ravenous. He tried to distract himself by turning his attention to the game Contrary

Wind was playing, using a stick carved into a hook to tease another stick out of the pile.

When it collapsed, he groaned and handed the hook to Joseph. "It is your turn, my brother."

Wulachen had already begun to ladle stew into bowls, however, and Joseph set the hook aside with alacrity. "First we eat."

The boy sat up quickly, pressing close to Joseph. The girls also vied to sit beside him, with She Sings capturing a seat on Joseph's other side before Moonflower could do so. When Wulachen put an end to their argument with a calm, but firm reprimand, Moonflower pouted, but obediently carried food to her father before taking her seat.

Joseph's chest clenched. The children's easy acceptance of him as their brother touched him but at the same time aroused aching memories of his older brother, Jake, and his little sister, Annali, both killed during the raid. And of Franz and Hannah Specht, captured on the same day and wrenched away along with Christian at Presque Isle.

Wulachen handed him a bowl of stew, and he set aside the painful memories. While they ate, she reminded the children to teach Joseph new words. Between mouthfuls, they took turns pointing to objects and calling out their names, while Menetopalis interjected suggestions.

Joseph listened carefully and repeated the words to himself, striving to fix each one in his mind. As had become his habit, however, he refused to speak any aloud until he had mastered it. He caught the worried look Wulachen cast Menetopalis, who responded with a casual shake of his head.

Despite his hunger, Joseph forced himself to eat slowly, waiting for the others to eat all they wanted. But Wulachen was watching, as usual, and as soon as he mopped out his bowl with a remnant of corn cake, she spooned the last of the stew into his bowl and handed him the two remaining corn cakes. He ducked his head in silent thanks.

Menetopalis's crippled leg made hunting impossible, and Joseph knew their supply of meat was almost gone, though the hunters always shared a portion of the game they took with those in need. He suspected that Wulachen, Menetopalis, and the children ate less so that he could have more.

Several of his new friends had taught him how to make and set traps along the streams a little distance outside the town, and he had caught some small game for meat and pelts. But Tamaque had not allowed Joseph to accompany the hunting parties, undoubtedly fearing he might attempt an escape. Daily practice had considerably improved his accuracy with bow and musket, however, and he determined that when he could finally go out with a hunting party he would bring back a large kill that would sustain his family for some time.

Suddenly Contrary Wind sprang to his feet and playfully ran his fingers through Joseph's hair, which had grown out enough by now that it curled around his ears. *"Nilàxk!"*

Joseph already knew the word for hair, and he repeated it, pleased that he had mastered the correct inflection. Giggling, the girls also scrambled to their feet and began twining strands of his rich mahogany waves around their fingers and tugging at it as though it fascinated them. Joseph couldn't help laughing.

They took turns pointing to different parts of their bodies, and Joseph easily recited the Lenape name for each. From the corner of his eye saw that Wulachen glowed, and her pleasure warmed him.

His stubborn resistance was slowly softening, melted by fleeting moments of happiness, even contentment, as now. Much in the Lenape way of life engaged him and drew him in. There were no chores like those he had chafed at back home, the endless work that consumed both daylight and evening hours and left little time for fun.

In contrast, Lenape boys appeared to have few responsibilities. Those of Joseph's age practiced shooting at targets with bow and musket, accompanied the men to learn the skills of the hunt, wrestled, ran races, and played all sorts of games. Even when they were expected to help the men in tasks such as building canoes, making household items, or felling trees and clearing new fields, it seemed more like play than work.

A surge of guilt and shame unexpectedly tightened his throat until he found it hard to breathe. Such treacherous emotions felt like disloyalty to his own family. Worse, it felt as though to accept this new life and grow to love these people was to take the part of those who had brutally attacked his people, killed Maam and Jake and Annali, and carried him and Daat and Christian away into captivity.

Worst of all was the fear that this new life betrayed God. He had long ago lost track of the days and no longer knew when Sunday came when he ought to worship as his Amish community did. Though he had often been bored by the lengthy church services, he now missed the prayers, the Scripture readings, and even the sober sermons—all the rituals and traditions that had formed his identity.

He fingered the small pouch tied around his neck, feeling the tiny carved image of the Lenape's idol Wsinkhoalican inside. He did not want to wear it, but Menetopalis and Wulachen insisted, and he shrank from displeasing them.

What would he do when he was expected to engage in their religious rites and participate in worshiping their gods? How could he possibly reconcile all the precious things that lay behind him with the strange and uncertain future that lay ahead?

"It's your turn now." Contrary Wind's voice interrupted Joseph's thoughts.

The girls had already collected the wooden bowls and spoons and were rinsing them out in a bucket of water. Contrary Wind had returned to his game and now held out the hook to Joseph.

Wulachen extended a water bucket to each of them. "First I need my sons to bring water for us."

Joseph sprang to his feet and gestured toward the path to the town well. "Come, let us hurry, little brother. When we get back we will play."

Chapter Eleven

First Snow Moon
Monday, November 14, 1757

JOSEPH TOOK ANOTHER BITE of bean pudding, keeping his gaze fixed on his bowl. He studiously ignored the young women clustered on the far side of the council house, particularly the occasional casual glance of a slender young woman with dark, shining eyes and pleasing features.

He forced his wandering thoughts to focus on Mehíttuk as he reviewed the rules of the hunt with the boys Joseph's age, a traditional part of the feast held the night before a hunting party went out.

"It is disgraceful to desert your party to hunt on your own. When we leave the town, we must stay together until we return." He surveyed the youths seated around him. "What else, Red Squirrel?"

"If one of us wounds a deer, and it is later killed or found dead by another, the skin belongs to the one who wounded it, and the meat to the one who finds it. And each of us must share his first kill with one who is old or in need."

Mehíttuk nodded gravely. "We must never neglect to supply meat and pelts to the elders and others who are weak or ill. Only Straight Arrow is excused because his father is crippled and his family depends on the game he can provide."

Joseph felt himself flush. This was only the second time he had been allowed to accompany the hunters. Embarrassed by his failure to bring in any game, he concentrated on wiping his bowl clean with the last of his bread and hastily devoured the morsel.

He set the bowl down and fingered the pouch hanging from his neck. Like those worn by all the hunters, it contained roots, herbs, and seeds supposed to ensure success. He told himself he had no faith in such things and had only added the charm to his pouch in deference to Wulachen and Menetopalis.

He winced when he met their sympathetic gazes from across the council house. *Even my traps have remained empty. If I come back with nothing again, the others will have to give my family some of the meat they need for their own.*

That afternoon, the hunters had purified themselves in the sweating ovens, pouring water on the heated rocks around which they crouched naked and perspiring profusely in the searing, humid heat. When they could endure no more, they crawled out into the still, icy air. This was repeated several times, a ritual Joseph found as strange and discomforting as the lengthy prayers the sachems and shamans offered at the feast to invoke the spirits' aid on the hunters' behalf.

"What else, Wildcat?" Mehíttuk asked another of the captives.

The boy, slightly younger than Joseph, colored and shifted his position. "If several hunters shoot at the same time and it cannot be determined who brought the animal down . . . "

When Wildcat hesitated and gave him a sidelong look, Joseph said, "The eldest receives the skin, and the meat is divided among all the hunters."

Wildcat added quickly, "And when the animal is killed, we must leave a gift of tobacco and thank the animal's spirit for its sacrifice that we may eat."

Mehíttuk regarded both of them with approval. "Your understanding is good."

From the corner of his eye Joseph saw the slender young woman rise from her seat. He had learned by eavesdropping on her companions that her name was Many Leaves. She was about Joseph's age and as tall as he, and she wore her gleaming, straight black hair pulled back into a single braid that reached to her hips. The confident grace of an athlete distinguished her, but what attracted him most was her open, happy demeanor and apparent kindness and generosity.

He risked a quick glance at her. How different she was from delicate, fair Anna Blanck, to whom he had pledged his heart what seemed like a lifetime ago. The two young women were nothing alike, and even as he vowed never to forget Anna he found it impossible to ignore the Lenape girl.

Red Squirrel's voice pierced Joseph's musings. "And before we enter the home of one who is to receive our gift, we must first face the place of the sun's rising and give thanks to Manitou, who made the animals to sustain us."

Mehíttuk regarded them all with a pleased smile. "Gather here at first light, and do not be late or we leave without you. We travel a day's journey toward the sun's setting to where the game is more abundant."

Just then Many Leaves reached their circle. Although Joseph had pretended to pay no attention, he had been very aware that she moved from one group to another, offering a basket of bread. She handed the basket to Mehíttuk, who broke a piece from one of the loaves and passed it around.

Joseph felt a pang at the fond look Mehíttuk directed at her. She smiled but did not let her gaze linger on the older youth. As she moved around the circle, greeting each of the young men while offering them bread, it seemed to Joseph that her gaze rested on him the longest.

"There is yet much food. Please do not hold back. You must eat well so you are strong for the hunt." Her voice was melodious as birdsong, and he judged by his companions' expressions that they equally affected by it.

He went with them to refill his bowl from the steaming kettles, knowing that they would eat little while on the chase. Before returning to the circle of the hunters, he stopped briefly to talk with Wulachen, Menetopalis, and Bird's Nest, each wrapped in a striking turkey cape, and the children and others of their extended family. Their obvious confidence and pride in Joseph buoyed him, and his nerves thrilled at the prospect of exploring the mysterious lands that stretched a vast distance to the west.

When the feast was finally over, Tamaque came to Joseph and placed his hand on his shoulder. "When we are on the chase, my nephew, be sure to stay at my side."

Pleased at being singled out by the notable sachem, Joseph said quickly, "Yes, grandfather," using the Lenape term of respect.

He lingered with Red Squirrel, Wildcat, and several of the other young men of his age, while the townspeople dispersed and his family returned to their cabin.

Red Squirrel's admiring gaze followed Many Leaves out of the council house. "Is she not pleasing to look at?"

Joseph shrugged. "Indeed, but I know nothing about her."

"She is a member of the Turtle division. Members of each division can marry only someone from another. Thus we of the Turkey division must take a Turtle or Wolf woman."

Wildcat punched him on the arm. "Do you think of marrying, Red Squirrel? Are you not too young?"

Red Squirrel grinned. "It is well to make plans before they are needed, my friend."

Joseph lowered his voice. "Mehíttuk is already making plans, it seems."

"But I think hers do not include Mehíttuk," Red Squirrel returned, grinning, then continued, "Many Leaves excels at playing *pahsahëman,* and we have opposed each other many times already. She has often beaten me too."

Joseph frowned. *"Pah-sa-hë-man?"*

"It is a ball game we play in the summer. Everyone who is old enough joins in. It is great fun!"

"The women play too—against the men?"

"They are given special rules that make it more difficult for us to overcome them. You will see in the summer." Red Squirrel clamped a hand on Joseph's shoulder. "You are fast and strong, my friend. You will do well at this game, without a doubt, and will make it much harder for the women to win. I am glad you are one of us now!"

❖ ⸺ ❖

MORNING DAWNED with lowering clouds and a chilling wind— the cold, dreary weather the hunters preferred. At the first faint light they had set foot upon the Great Path, following it far to the west, and now a drizzling, icy rain numbed Joseph's limbs. In spite of physical discomfort and the bleak November landscape, however, he marveled at the beauty of the dense forest, rocky promontories, winding streams, and broad rivers through which they rapidly passed.

They made camp at nightfall in a sheltered glen far west of Sauconk, and the next day was given over to the chase. They covered many miles, the most experienced hunters moving with a swift stealth and felling game with a skill that awed Joseph.

As he had promised, he shadowed Tamaque. He was soon glad the sachem led the hunt this time. Because of Tamaque's guidance and generosity, everyone in their large party made at least one kill. Joseph took two plump turkeys with his bow and arrow and a large panther with his musket, swelling with pride at the admiration of his companions.

They returned to the outskirts of Sauconk at late afternoon on the third day, hauling their butchered game, exhausted and frozen through, stomachs pinched with hunger. As they approached the scattered wigewas, Runs Free, a boy a few years younger than Joseph, came running toward them along the path.

Despite the cold weather, Runs Free wore only breechcloth and moccasins. His hair was disheveled, his face painted black. With every other step he looked fearfully back over his shoulder at his mother, who followed, red-faced and shouting imprecations, while vehemently shooing him away. He gave Joseph's party a wide berth, avoiding their gazes, and dodged into the woods and out of sight.

Taken aback, Joseph stared after the boy. In the weeks he had been with the Lenape, he had never seen parents treat their children unkindly. When he turned around, he saw that the older ones in his party exchanged grins and amused glances, while the younger ones appeared as startled and puzzled as he.

"Why did Runs Free's mother drive him away, Red Squirrel? Surely he did something very bad."

Red Squirrel shook his head, chuckling. "How many winters do you have?"

"This winter will make sixteen."

Red Squirrel looked Joseph up and down. "Ah, then you will likely discover the reason soon. It is our custom for this to be done before a boy's fifteenth winter."

"To be driven away by their families? But why? For how long?"

Wildcat's brow furrowed. "This will be my fifteenth winter."

Tamaque came to join them, his expression grave. "You must become men, and so you must also endure this trial. But you have been with us only a short time. Your testing may not take place until the trees bud and the grass grows green again. Do not think of it now, but learn all you can of our people's ways and of the spirits who hold sway over us so that you may gain their favor when your time comes."

THAT NIGHT JOSEPH PONDERED Tamaque's words, while lying on the sleeping platform with the children curled up around him. He had questioned Wulachen and Menetopalis after his return to the cabin, but they had merely exchanged knowing glances before changing the subject to Joseph's success on the hunt.

Wulachen had exclaimed repeatedly over the large turkeys he brought her, though more for their feathers than for the meat. "These will give me enough to make a cape to keep you warm this winter, my son. I will begin weaving it tomorrow, as soon as I have set the meat to smoke."

"We must have a turkey feast before you smoke the rest," Menetopalis said to her before turning to Joseph. "And I will show you how to tan the panther's pelt. It will bring you a good price from the trader."

Joseph had protested that the pelt should be traded for supplies for the family, but Wulachen and Menetopalis insisted that it belonged to the one who killed the panther. Seeing they would not be moved, he had acquiesced, but determined to trade for something the children would like—perhaps a real doll for the girls to replace their crude ones made of cornhusks and a small knife for Contrary Wind so he could teach the boy how to carve as Menetopalis was teaching Joseph.

A couple of weeks earlier, he had volunteered to help Menetopalis carve bowls and other items out of the burl of trees to trade for supplies needed by their family. For the first time he had addressed Menetopalis as father, and seeing a sheen of moisture come into the older man's eyes, his heart had swelled.

The murmur of voices filtered into his consciousness, and he strained to hear what Wulachen and Menetopalis were saying in low tones, while they sat before the fire in the cabin's shadowy front room.

"See, you have worried for nothing."

"You are right, my husband. Our son may speak but little, yet his words are well chosen for one who has been among us for so short a time."

"It is because he listens and watches carefully. He strives always to do well."

"He is kind and good as well as brave. He is a fine example for his younger brother and sisters, and he is already a good hunter."

"*Bischi!*" Menetopalis responded. Yes indeed! "I am proud of this son Manitou has brought to us."

Joseph rolled over and closed his eyes, warmed by their good opinion of him and even more determined to live up to it.

FIVE DAYS LATER Joseph was watching Contrary Wind race some of the other boys his age, when Runs Free staggered into the town, gaunt, dirty, and disheveled from wandering through the forest for days. He showed the gathered crowd a bear's claw and told of seeing a vision in which a bear had revealed itself to him as the guardian of his life.

The townspeople insisted that he tell his vision repeatedly, after which Runs Free made a sacrifice of tobacco to the spirit of the bear and took the adult name Bear Claw. He was given a small stone carved in the image of a bear to carry in the pouch he wore around his neck.

Joseph watched and listened with trepidation. Clearly this trial involved a dream sent by the Lenape gods. And soon he would be expected to seek one too.

What if he didn't have such a dream? What would he do? Would he be disgraced? Should he invent a spirit animal? But that would be a lie. And what would happen if such a lie was discovered?

Then a worse thought occurred to him: What if he had such a dream? The possibility squeezed the air from his lungs.

Would that mean that the God he had been taught to worship was not real? That the Lenape religion was the true one? He had already heard other men and women of the town relate visions they had received from their gods. Where had they come from?

Joseph hoped Tamaque was right and that he would not have to face the trial until at least spring. Maybe longer. But it hung over his head like a dark cloud.

He raised his questions and fears with no one. Nor could he admit the anger that welled up whenever he thought of how his own God had failed his family when they most needed Him, how He had not spared them from destruction in spite of Daat's obedience to His laws.

Chapter Twelve

LONG NIGHT MOON
Friday, December 23, 1757

SITTING CROSS-LEGGED in the sweat lodge beside Nútemau, Christian wiped away the sweat that poured down his face.

"Why can't the shaman give you a *beson* to make you feel better?"

"We have nothing to pay him, my son." Nútemau calmly resumed the low, rhythmic chant of thanksgiving to Manitou.

Hunger turned Christian's thoughts to how members of his Amish community always helped each other in times of need without demanding pay. "But you're sick. He should give you medicine anyway."

Crouching Panther, with Crooked Legs and his family and most of the able-bodied villagers, had left Custaloga's Town for the hunting camps little more than a moon earlier. Only a few warriors, widows with young children, those who were too old or sick to travel, and several other white captives remained. Though it was now only the Long Night Moon, it seemed to Christian that an eternity had passed since their leaving.

The nightly dances, now sparsely attended, included fervent

prayers to the *manitowuck* of the hunt to give success to the hunters so they would return with enough meat to last until the Frog Moon and the return of spring. In the meantime Christian's traps snared little game, and on his lengthy hunting forays he had seen few deer and killed none. He had only occasionally taken a hare, squirrel, or other small animal, which he and Nútemau quickly devoured.

Just after the sun reached its zenith he had returned from a two-days' absence, stiff with cold, weak with hunger, and empty-handed once again. They'd had no meat for more than a week. Only a few roots and nuts and a small quantity of ground corn remained of their carefully hoarded stores.

Nothing was left that he could trade for the services of the village shaman—although what Christian had observed of the man's rituals and medicines did not inspire confidence in his healing powers. Yet to do nothing for his ailing father seemed worse.

He had been grateful when Nútemau insisted on going to the sweat lodge. At least there they could get warm for a little while.

He rubbed Nútemau's inflamed, swollen joints with oil he had skimmed from the surface of a nearby oil spring and boiled according to Deep Water's directions. He wished that she and her family and Crouching Panther would return soon. He missed their company sorely, and since Nútemau's health had worsened, Christian longed for Deep Water's advice and help in tending him. But the hunters were not expected to return before the Cracking Tree Moon, still many sleeps away.

The stifling heat and humidity in the cramped sweat lodge made it difficult to breathe. When Nútemau shakily poured more water onto the red-hot rocks, the erupting steam increased Christian's lightheadedness.

Abruptly, Nútemau stiffened. His chant ceased, and he stared upward as though enraptured. Christian's timid attempts to rouse him had no effect.

After an anxious interval Nútemau slumped and looked around. He dragged himself through the lodge's low entrance on his belly and collapsed on the frozen ground. Swirling snow struck Christian's naked, overheated body like the blow of a knife as he crawled out of the lodge on Nútemau's heels.

Christian grabbed the clothes they had draped across a log, shook the snow off the old man's blanket and covered him. Shivering uncontrollably, he donned his clothing as rapidly as he could and wrapped his blanket around his shoulders before helping Nútemau to dress.

He decided that the old man's strange behavior in the sweat lodge was only another symptom of his poor health. Nútemau's weakness and lack of appetite had become a constant worry in recent weeks. As the temperature dropped his joints and abdomen were becoming increasingly swollen. Every exertion left him short of breath, and he had developed a cough that often brought up pink-tinged foamy mucus.

Eager to get back into shelter, Christian grabbed the bark bucket he had brought along and hurried to fill it at the well. Sloshing freezing water with every step, he carried the heavy bucket in one hand, while supporting Nútemau with his other arm. They staggered along the snow-drifted path, bent into the wind, and by the time they pushed through the wigewa's door flap, Christian's limbs shook.

He settled the old man on the sleeping platform and stirred up the fire. As he placed a couple of the few remaining split logs on it, he reminded himself to cut more firewood in the morning before leaving on another hunt, at the same time shrinking from the prospect of another fruitless foray alone through the bleak forest.

With his last strength he filled the kettle with water, hung it on the tripod over the low flames to heat, then released Bear from his pen. He cuddled the rapidly growing puppy as he curled up beside Nútemau to share the warmth of his bearskin.

"When the water is hot, I'll make that tea for you that makes you feel better, my father. I'm sorry I didn't find any game again this time, but surely there'll be something in the traps tomorrow. I'll check them before I go out to hunt again."

"Early this morning I prayed to Wsinkhoalican. He directed me into the woods to where a fat hare waited for me." Raising his arms, Nútemau motioned as though he shot with a bow.

Christian stared at him, openmouthed. "You went hunting?"

"Wsinkhoalican gave me strength like a warrior. And a steady aim." A smile spread across Nútemau's wizened face, and he nodded toward a hide bundle lying on the sleeping platform on the other side of the wigewa. "I made a sacrifice to the spirit of the hare, then dressed him and brought him back for you to cook. After I scrape and dry his pelt, I will use it to line your moccasins so your feet stay warm and dry this winter."

Christian set Bear down with alacrity and soon had the pieces of the hare simmering in the kettle along with several handfuls of pulverized corn. When it was finally tender enough to eat, the hearty meal brought the strength back into Christian's limbs and seemed to strengthen Nútemau as well. Even after feeding a small portion to the puppy, there was enough left over for them to share the next day.

Christian set the kettle by the doorway where the draft would keep its contents cold, then lit Nútemau's pipe for him. As the light outside the door flap faded to full darkness, they sat in silent contentment, watching the seething embers slowly dying in the fire pit.

Silence and stillness always aroused a flood of painful memories. Christian wondered whether Daat and Joseph were safe and warm, whether they had enough to eat and were being kindly treated, as he was.

Nútemau's voice broke his reverie. "My son, while we prayed in the sweat lodge, Manitou gave me a vision."

Startled, Christian stared at him. "Yes, my father?"

"Manitou showed me the place you must go to hunt, where there is much game that will provide us food enough to last the winter."

The old man described the route Christian was to take in exact detail, and Christian made him repeat the directions so he could fix them in his mind. The path followed the same general direction Crouching Panther and Standing Stone had taken when they caught the pigeons, he reckoned, but angled farther to the west.

"You must set out alone at first light but before the sun rises. Do not eat anything, and do not awaken me or anyone in the town. Walk stealthily so the spirits of the animals do not see you nor hear your passing. Take only your bow and arrow, your knife and tomahawk, and a tumpline to carry back the animal if it is large. You must keep perfectly silent while you hunt, and do not forget to offer a sacrifice to the spirit of the animal you kill.

"Afterward, bleed and gut it, taking care to make no sound that might attract the notice of any demons. Then return in the same manner before the sun's setting. Greet no one when you arrive, but come directly to me."

Christian nodded, wide-eyed. He didn't know what to make of Nútemau's vision, and he had little hope that the strange directions would do any good. But nothing else he had tried worked, and he determined to follow them to the best of his ability.

"Sleep now," Nútemau told him, "for you must rise at first light and be gone from here before the sun lifts over the edge of the earth."

✦━━━━━✦

CHRISTIAN HELD HIS BREATH as he crouched in heavy undergrowth. Seventy-five yards away a young buck had pawed through the snow to graze on the moss covering the dank ground beneath the trees. Christian eased into position, raised his bow, and drew the taut bowstring to his cheek, aiming at a point slightly above the buck's shoulder to allow for the arrow's upward spring.

He had followed Nútemau's directions exactly, taking care not to wake him when he left the wigewa at first light and creeping through the forest as softly as wind across a grassy field. The air was still and cold, with an icy layer of snow blanketing the ground, yet it seemed to him that the path opened before his steps as though he moved in a waking dream.

Still astounded that he had crept so close without alerting the animal, he released the bowstring with a steady hand. The arrow streaked through the air in a perfect, soundless arc, curving downward from its zenith to drive deep into the buck's side right behind its shoulder. The animal leaped upward, kicking convulsively, and then bounded off through the underbrush.

Christian's first instinct was to immediately push his way into the clear and run after it. But the total silence that lay over the forest held him spellbound. The buck had crashed through the dense, tangled undergrowth, yet Christian heard nothing of its passing.

Remembering Nútemau's directions, he stole from his hiding place and cautiously followed in the direction the deer had taken. He had not gone two hundred yards when he found it, fallen but still quivering.

He stood motionless, staring down at the buck in wonder, his mouth dry. It had happened just as Nútemau had told him.

He took a pinch of tobacco from his pouch, sprinkled it on the ground by the dead buck as he had seen Crouching Panther and Standing Stone do, and muttered a perfunctory prayer thanking the buck's spirit. Then he knelt and slit open its abdomen with his knife, gutted, and bled it.

He secured the carcass to his tumpline, which he bound around his chest as the men did. The buck was full-grown, though, judging by its rack of antlers, not more than two years old, and he feared that he would not have the strength to drag it all the way back to the town. But he moved with unexpected ease back along the path and passed into the town's boundaries just as the sun dropped below the horizon.

A couple of elderly matrons and one of the warriors fell into step with him, loudly praising his skill as a hunter. Christian took care not to speak until he reached the wigewa, however. He, Nútemau, and the warrior made quick work of butchering the buck, while Bear danced around them, yipping eagerly.

After distributing portions to those who gathered and they had gone, Christian built a fire and set the venison over it to smoke. Then he made the haunch he had set aside into a fine meal for him and the old man. While they ate in companionable silence, Christian pondered all that had happened that day.

Who had given Nútemau the vision? Who had led Christian to the buck? Was it Manitou? Or Jesus?

Was the God of his ancestors the same as the god of the Lenape? Or was one a false god?

And if so, which one?

Chapter Thirteen

Monday, January 9, 1758

SEATED IN THE DEEP WING CHAIR in the *Kammer's* warmest corner, Barbara stroked the downy cheek of the newborn at her breast. "Welcome, Christian."

The infant's mouth went slack. His head fell back against her arm, and he looked up at her with eyes as blue as the sky. Smiling down at his tiny face, she tucked the edge of her bodice back over her breast as her mother-in-law, Maudlin Stutzman, bent over her.

"Ach, it'll be such a comfort to have your own Christli now."

"No child can replace another." *Or a father,* Barbara added silently.

"I didn't mean—"

Barbara realized she had spoken more sharply than she had intended. "I know what you meant, and you're right. This one will be a comfort to me."

Anna came to her side and scooped the baby into her arms. "Ach, now that your tummy's full, you're a happy boy, aren't you?"

Barbara pinned the front of her bodice closed and accepted Maudlin's help in settling her triangular *Halsduch* back in place over her shoulders and bosom. Rising, she wrapped her black shawl tightly around her shoulders against the draft that crept in around the shuttered window's frame.

Hearing the sounds of jingling harness, muffled hoofbeats on packed snow, and hiss of sleigh runners, she exclaimed with surprise. With Maudlin and Anna on her heels, she hurried out into the *Stube*, then into the large front room.

Barbara's husband, stocky, blond-haired Christian Stutzman, looked up, eyebrows raised, from the settle on the near end of the immense hearth, where two blazing fires held the cold at bay. On his lap, sixteen-month-old Mary bounced and waved her arms in excitement, while Mattie and little Annali ran to the door as someone pounded vigorously on it.

Familiar voices hailed them from outside. Crist handed Mary to his mother and hurried to admit the visitors, letting in an icy draft.

"It's *Onkel* Johannes and *Tante* Katie!" Mattie clapped her hands as Johannes's heavily bundled family rushed inside.

They stomped the caked snow from their shoes as Crist slammed the door shut. "Nobody with any sense would be out on a day like this!"

Barbara reclaimed the baby from Anna. "Ach, a little cold isn't going to stop my brother."

"That wind cuts like a knife!" Johannes pulled off his gloves and blew on his reddened fingers.

Katie shooed the children to the hearth that spanned most of the kitchen's long interior wall. Johannes began to unwrap the little ones as Katie unwound her thick woolen scarf from around her nose and chin with her free hand, while balancing baby Frany on her other arm.

Anna smiled mischievously. "Cold, is it?"

"You could say so," Johannes said with a grimace. "Maybe this wasn't such a good idea. We about froze coming just a mile. The drifts were so high in places I wasn't sure even the Belgians could make it through."

Barbara patted the baby's back as his head wobbled against her neck. "You could have stayed home, but we're sure glad you came. You heard our news then?"

Katie beamed. "We did! And I wasn't about to stay home with a new baby in the neighborhood."

Little Mattie eyed her cousins, five-year-old Jake and three-year-old John. "Can we play, Maami—please?"

"You can be quiet for a few minutes yet. The boys need to warm up after being out in this cold." Barbara waved the children to the settle.

Annali and the boys obediently lined up on the seat in the sheltered nook, but Mattie scowled as she joined them with lagging steps, arms crossed, lower lip protruding. Anna went to draw the five-year-old onto her lap and proceeded to tease and tickle her until her reluctant giggles turned into happy squeals.

Crist grabbed his heavy greatcoat from the pegboard by the door. "I'm going to drive your sleigh into the barn so the horses don't freeze." He motioned for Johannes to stay by the hearth and headed outside.

Katie handed Frany to Johannes, and reached out to Barbara, who laid her newborn son in her sister-in-law's arms.

Johannes leaned in to inspect his new nephew. "Hans told us yesterday at worship that the baby was on the way, but it was snowing hard by the time we got home. We debated on it, and this morning when the weather cleared we decided we had to get over here today yet."

"I'm so glad you made it through. Though for sure it was foolish to go out in that cold wind!"

He answered Barbara's teasing jab with a grin. "It's not the first foolish thing I've ever done and probably won't be the last either."

Katie looked up from the baby. "We better not stay too long, though, with this wind blowing up more drifts. And you need to rest yet."

Barbara lowered onto a chair at the table. "I'm doing good. And with Maudlin and Anna here to help, there isn't much I need to do except feed the baby."

Katie returned baby Christian to Barbara and took Frany back from Johannes. Sitting next to Maudlin, she laid her free hand on the older woman's arm.

"I know Maudlin's been a great help to you. I don't know what we'd have done without Anna over the past couple of months."

"Ach, she's been a jewel for us, too, that's for sure." Barbara laughed. "I just wish there were two of her so she wouldn't have to go back and forth."

Anna blushed. "I don't mind at all. You know I love taking care of the children."

"Well, the little ones love you too." Barbara gave Anna a warm smile before turning back to Katie. "I hate to see you take the children back out in that cold this evening. We can put you all up for the night. Why don't you stay?"

"We don't have so far to go, but that sure would be fun."

Johannes pulled out the chair beside Katie and sat. "*Ya,* but then who'd do the milking and feed the livestock?"

"That's the trouble with farming: always more chores to be done." Barbara sighed as she wrapped the baby more snugly.

"What's this about chores?" Crist came back inside, stamping his snowy boots. He shrugged out of his coat and hung it on the peg. "Are you and Jacobli volunteering to help me with mine?"

Three-year-old Jacob jumped off the settle. "Ach, *ya!* Can we, Daati?"

Johannes's eyes narrowed playfully. "Sure, so long as Uncle Crist comes on back home with us to help do ours."

"That's likely to happen," Crist returned, his tone dry. When his nephew's face fell, he grinned at his daughters. "Why don't you go play with your cousins before they have to go home?"

The children squealed in unison and dashed through the opening in the waist-high partition that divided the *Küche* from the girls' small sleeping area. Anna joined the others at the table, and Crist came to sit beside Barbara, his face softening as he gathered his new son into his arms.

"I know you're glad to finally have that boy you've been wanting." Katie rubbed Frany's back, and the little girl laid her head on Katie's shoulder, her thumb in her mouth.

Maudlin beamed. "He looks just like his Daati when he was born."

"I've been the only man in the house for too long." Crist chuckled. "He'll be helping me with the chores before you know it."

"Don't count on that too soon," Barbara objected. "He's hardly over a day old yet. Give him time to grow."

Anna shook her head. "It's not that far off. Little ones grow real quick."

"You named him Christian?" Johannes asked.

"*Ya*," Barbara answered softly. "For his Daati. And for our Christli too."

Anna pushed back her chair and left the room.

Barbara exchanged a sober glance with the others. They had all been aware of the budding relationship between Joseph and Anna that had been cut short on that terrible late-September morning. Barbara's heart ached for her. For all of them.

✦ • ┄ • ✦

BARBARA LEANED on Crist's arm as they went into the dim *Stube*, her shoulders drooping from a weariness she knew came from more than giving birth the previous day. As she looked around the room she was struck by the thought that on the surface things seemed as they always had.

Everything was in its place. They all went about their daily chores, cared for the children, attended church services as usual. But underneath the pain never eased or even lessened.

A heaviness hung over their family gatherings, most noticeable in the brief spaces when silence fell between them and every face settled into lines of grief and worry. Then, as though by some secret agreement, they began to talk of everyday matters as if nothing was wrong.

But everything was wrong. And she knew that nothing in their lives would ever be the same again.

As had become her habit, however, she put on a cheerful face, as did the others, and took the seat next to Crist's, close to the glowing five-plate stove connected by a flue through the wall to the *Küche* fireplace. Anna soon came quietly to sit beside Barbara, her composure recovered, while Maudlin lit the candles, dispelling some of the gloom the shrouded windows cast over the small parlor.

Crist leaned back in his chair, cradling the baby against his shoulder. "I'm sorry I wasn't able to go with you men to Reading to deliver Loudoun's levy for the British army."

Johannes waved his apology away. "We all knew the baby was coming any day. None of us thought you'd be much use anyhow."

"When he came, he came quick," Barbara said with a chuckle.

Anna brightened. "It was a good thing I came back over from Johannes and Katie's Saturday."

Barbara studied Anna, thinking of how suited the slight, blonde young woman was to tame her younger brother Joseph's impetuous nature. But her green eyes had lost the sparkle they once held, and a pang stabbed through Barbara at the thought that Joseph might never come home.

Where did the Indians take him? Is he even yet alive—and Daat and Christli?

The children ran into the *Stube*, each carrying one of the wooden toys Crist had carved for his daughters. The boys settled on the floor between their elders and the stove to play, but the girls gathered at Crist's knee. He leaned forward, holding the baby so they could see him. They crowded around, cooing and touching little Christian's soft blond hair and kissing his tiny cheek.

When the girls joined the boys on the floor to play, Crist returned the baby to his shoulder and glanced at Johannes. "So you got everything delivered to Colonel Weiser's safely Friday."

"Five wagons full of flour, salt pork, cheese, and bolts of woolen and linen cloth—not counting the hay and grain we had to give over for their animals too." Johannes shook his head. "I know we agreed to supply the British instead of serving in the militia, but it worries me whether we'll have enough to get us through the winter, particularly without Daat and the boys to help—" He broke off and his expression froze for a moment before he continued hastily, "But I know all our church families face the same hardships."

Barbara regarded him sorrowfully. She had felt a strain between them since their confrontation at the gravesite, but her conscience convicted her suddenly that it was on her part, not his. Her kind, patient brother had not changed. In fact, she had been holding a grudge against him for no reason, and she was sorry for it.

"Ach, we'll be all right. We'll help each other like we always have."

Johannes glanced over at her, and a look of understanding passed between them. "*Ya,* we'll get through this together."

It felt as if one burden, at least, had rolled off her shoulders. Barbara turned to Katie.

"I'm just thankful your Daat reminded us that we're called to care for all our neighbors, even if they're soldiers. And that he was willing for the church to pay a tax and send supplies to the army. It's the right thing to do."

"*Ya,* and it's a good thing your Daat made our case to Colonel Weiser so he could persuade the British captain to accept this compromise. To think what could have happened if our men had been arrested for not joining up to fight! If they were taken away—" Katie shuddered.

"God will provide for us under this testing, too, but we have to be careful to hold back enough seed for the spring planting, which means less to eat." Johannes turned back to Crist. "When we got to Weiser's, he didn't say much, but we could tell he wasn't happy about Loudoun's demanding so much from us farmers—or that every bit of it is going to the army and not to Weiser's militia."

"Loudoun's sent so many of Weiser's men away to the army that he doesn't need as much," Crist said, shrugging.

Maudlin waved her hand impatiently. "*Ya,* and the families of those who did sign up for the militia are angry that they've been left without their men's help and protection at home." Referring to her older sons, she added, "Hans and Jake called on several of the families a fortnight ago to find out whether they needed any help, and they told them their men are real upset about how they're going to get their spring planting done and what might happen if there are more raids hereabouts."

When the baby began to fuss, Barbara took him back from Crist. "Were the families willing to accept any help from us?"

"A couple did because they're in real need," Crist told her, "but they all had hard words to say about our refusing to fight. They blame us for their men being taken away."

"We can't expect them to see things the way we do," Johannes reminded them. "We just have to hold fast in obedience to God and trust He'll help us through whatever comes."

"And love our neighbors as ourselves in doing it," Barbara agreed.

"It seems so long since your Daat and Christli and Joseph were taken," Anna broke in, her voice muffled. "Three months, and we don't know any more now than we did then."

Judging from the others' expressions, they had all been thinking the same thing, but no one wanted to bring the subject up. "Ach, I know. I'm tired of feeling so helpless!" Barbara carefully avoided looking at Johannes or Katie. "There's nothing anybody can do this winter for sure, but I wonder whether we'll even hear anything once the weather warms up. So long as this war's going on, how is any news going to get to us from behind the French lines?"

Katie gave her a sympathetic look. "When we visited Baltzer Smith and his wife, they still hadn't heard a single thing about their daughter, and she was taken by the Indians last summer. Neither had Andrew Wolback's family gotten any news yet of their girl who was carried off the fall before that."

Seeing Anna's stricken expression, Barbara patted her arm with her free hand. "We have to keep praying that this war will soon be over. If the British win, we can petition the governor right away to make the Indians release their captives so they can come home."

The others exchanged worried glances. No one asked what would happen if the French won.

Anna stared down at her clenched hands. "Come spring there'll likely be more attacks along the border. The war will go on, and your Daat and Joseph and Christli will be forgotten just like the others. Nobody wants to talk about it anymore. They all just go on with their lives."

"We won't forget," Johannes said firmly. "We'll never stop trying to find them and bring them home."

Anna's eyes brimmed with tears. "Do you think they're all right? Do the Indians treat their captives well and make sure they have enough food and a place to stay and warm clothes?"

Silence hung over the room. At last Johannes said with a heartiness that sounded hollow, "Everybody we've talked to says most captives are adopted into families and they treat them the same as their own people. God promises to keep us safe in trial, and we can trust him to be with Daat and the boys wherever they are and whatever their circumstances."

"It won't be so long before spring when the tribes begin to raid again." Katie's voice quavered. "Do you think they'll come back here?"

"No way to know," Crist answered gruffly.

Maudlin stared down at the handkerchief balled up in her hand. "I heard a few more of our families from the church are moving back east to stay with family or friends until they see what happens this summer. Some of our English neighbors are too."

Again they all fell silent, not looking at one another.

Finally Barbara straightened her shoulders. "All of us agreed to stay as long as it doesn't get to be too dangerous for our children. And I mean to. This is our home. This is Daat and Joseph and Christli's home still. Unless we find out—" She stopped, swallowing around the lump in her throat. "I'm going to stay right here and trust God until they walk through that door."

Chapter Fourteen

JAKOB DREW IN a sharp breath and stepped back from the edge of the crowd that overflowed the council house yard. He jostled the French trader, Jacque, but was careful to give no indication that he knew the man.

Over the past weeks Jakob had deliberately—and discreetly—made a friend of the trader. With the townspeople occupied in preparations for their great midwinter festival, his frequent visits to the trader's hut had gone unnoticed. The previous day, using a mixture of signs, French, and broken English, Jacque had described *Gänä`yasta`*, the longest and most important of the Seneca's annual ceremonies.

Held after the second new moon following the winter solstice, it marked the beginning of the tribe's spiritual year and required that two dogs, white or with as few spots as possible, be sacrificed to their god Nauwaneu. The dogs must be strangled in front of the council house, with care taken to make no wound or spill any blood.

Although he had expected this, Jakob was nonetheless sickened as he watched Little Raccoon's white dog give a final convulsive shudder, its head lolling at an unnatural angle in the hands of the young man who held it by the neck. A short distance away Little Raccoon stood quietly by his mother, his face impassive in the soft light of dawn as he cuddled the puppy he had been given earlier that morning. Red Bird, however, looked anxiously up at Sunshine, who bent to smile at her and offer reassuring words.

Jakob winced as another of the young men who appeared to be in charge of the festival wrung the neck of the second dog they had chosen the previous day, this one spotted white and tan. The trader spoke without looking at Jakob, keeping his voice low and his gaze fixed on the men holding the lifeless dogs. Although Jakob could not understand all Jacque said, he gathered that the Seneca made this sacrifice at the beginning of their new year to purify themselves and to help the Master of Life bring back the spring before his evil brother could stop him.

Jakob raked back his chin-length hair. He drew some encouragement from this people's desire to worship their Creator but mourned that they had so little understanding of Him.

The keen wind kicked up the heavily drifted snow and blew a thin mist across the council house yard. Jakob shivered and pulled his blanket more tightly around his shoulders. By now the clothes Sunshine had provided were almost as tattered as the rags they had replaced. The frayed garments gave little protection against the piercing blast, and he despaired of ever being truly warm again.

Or clean. He had not bathed since winter set in with a vengeance. Before the creeks iced up, he had occasionally ventured to strip and wash. But now both skin and clothing felt greasy and foul, and he grimaced at his own rank odor and that of the people who pressed close around him.

He watched while a group of young women painted the sacrificed dogs' faces, the edges of their ears, and their feet red. This done, they tied feathers, beads, wampum strings, and ribbons around the animals' necks, legs, torsos, and tails. Then the delegation of young men in charge of the festival secured the carcasses to the top of two posts, one on each side of the council house door.

A sudden intense longing for his church's faithful worship pierced Jakob to the heart as prayers and speeches by the tribe's headmen ensued before the multitude dispersed to their lodges. Jakob followed Sunshine and the others to their longhouse, his feet and hands stiff from the icy wind. He admired how inured the native people seemed to be to the cold even as he despaired of ever growing used to it himself.

According to the notches on his makeshift calendar, it was mid February. Repeated blizzards had buried the surrounding hills and mountains in deep drifts. The creeks and river were blanketed in ice, and even the narrow channel at the Ohio's center where the water flowed most swiftly had finally frozen over.

Following the harvest festival, groups of hunters had left the town with their women and children—Buck Teeth's family among them—for hunting camps scattered throughout the region. Jakob had hoped he might be allowed to go, giving him an opportunity to scout out the area, but in this he had been disappointed.

Instead, as often as the weather allowed, he continued to go with Little Raccoon to tend the traps they set in the forest, although the quantity of small game they brought back had continued to diminish as cold and snow deepened. However, he had been able to gain a better idea of the terrain around the town with each foray through the woods, and in that he took satisfaction.

The people remaining in the town had eventually been forced to ration their dwindling stores and barter with the French traders for what little food they could afford to buy, and the nightly dances included petitions and sacrifices to the Seneca's gods for the hunters' success. By the time the hunters had finally returned a few days earlier, Jakob's stomach continually gnawed with hunger. But to his dismay, instead of laying up the precious meat the hunters brought in, the townspeople would consume a large quantity of it in the feasts that accompanied the festival.

The respite from hunger would be only temporary. It would be a couple of months yet before the weather warmed and planting could begin, then months more until the first crops could be harvested. Another thought struck Jakob: When spring returned the warriors would likely go off on raids again. His spirits rose at the realization that that might provide an opportunity for him and Specht to finally make their escape.

When they returned to East Wind's longhouse the found the fires reduced to embers. Piercing cold had settled in each compartment despite the snow drifted against the structure that helped to block drafts.

Each time a blizzard struck, the smoke holes in the roof were closed to keep out snow. Although the smoke at first gathered against the ceiling of the 20-foot-high structure, it soon lowered, choking the atmosphere with a miasma that included the stale odors of cooking food and the stink of unwashed bodies. The longhouse was again crowded with tribal members from outlying villages, and no one paid any attention as Jakob busied himself shoving open the narrow panels in the roof above each fire pit with a long pole to provide some relief.

He began to build up the fire in the front compartment but was soon distracted by a clamor outside. Excited shouts and the sound of shaking rattles grew rapidly louder, followed by loud blows against the bark cladding of the longhouse that startled him and brought everyone running to the door.

Several of the young men in charge of the festival burst inside, each one wearing only a breechcloth in spite of the weather. They carried wooden paddles, which they shook and beat on the platforms and lodge poles, while shouting for everyone to leave. A babble of laughter and chatter and the terrified cries of Buck Teeth's newborn granddaughter filled the longhouse as men, women, and children pushed their way outside.

Alarmed, Jakob began to follow them. But curiosity caused him to linger in the storeroom to watch as the young men scooped up the seething coals and ashes of each fire with their paddles and cast them into the air, scattering a rain of swirling ash and hot, sparkling embers throughout the longhouse. They proceeded to gather wood, light new fires in each fire pit, and sprinkle tobacco on the flames.

As soon as all the fires down the length of the structure blazed and the fragrant smoke of their sacrifice twined into the air, they left the longhouse, driving Jakob ahead of them. Back outside, they fired their rifles twice into the air. Jakob saw other groups running from one habitation to the next and heard shots resounding throughout the town.

Over the next two days, the young men roamed Buckaloons, their legs wrapped in bearskins, carrying baskets and shaking tortoise-shell rattles. They fired their guns and demanded from the townspeople contributions of tobacco, herbs, and other items to be used as incense during the ceremony.

Many of the adults, including Falling Water and Buck Teeth, wandered, as though crazed, from longhouse to longhouse, spending hours in each relating strange dreams. East Wind's longhouse was similarly—and repeatedly—invaded, to Jakob's growing astonishment.

Every time, the occupants were obligated to listen to lengthy tales, none of which Jakob could understand, and then to present the dreamers all manner of objects in an apparent attempt to guess their dreams' meaning, even to the point of impoverishing themselves. They also spent much time dancing in groups in the council house.

The fourth day the young men ran around the town, smeared with dirt, each wearing a fearsome mask made of cornhusks. Again they demanded contributions to their incense baskets, this time daubing dirt on anyone who refused.

Jakob caught only occasional glimpses of Specht, and then from a distance. Since their last meeting, Jakob had made numerous attempts to get close enough to speak to his friend again, but without success. By the fifth day Jakob feared the festival would end before he found an opportunity while everyone in the town was too occupied to notice.

That night he watched from outside the council house doorway as a large group of men and women danced, lumbering and waddling as though they were bears. People continued to stream in and out of the building, and he finally drifted away. Moving a short distance across the yard, he edged close to a smaller fire, where one of the elders was drawing figures in the dirt with a stick and exhorting a cluster of children, among them several adopted captives who watched and listened gravely.

As Jakob glanced furtively around, he spied Specht lingering in the shadows of a nearby longhouse, head down, back hunched against the cold wind. Jakob kept his movements casual as he strode toward him, but at his approach Specht turned and disappeared. Jakob walked all around the town searching for his friend without success, but dared not enter Specht's longhouse for fear of discovery.

The remaining days of the festival followed the same pattern as the previous ones. Jakob received little attention as he pursued his daily chores and cared for East Wind and Broken Feather, who were neglected by the others. With few duties to occupy him, he spent much time pondering Bible verses he had memorized and praying for his children and the lost sheep among which God had placed him.

On the eighth and final day, the young men removed the dogs' carcasses from the poles. After a lengthy ceremony these were placed on a large stack of wood and set ablaze as the people gathered around to throw tobacco and sweet herbs onto the flames.

Speeches and a great feast followed, and the people danced late into the night before the ceremony finally concluded. At last the townspeople dispersed to their dwellings.

Jakob followed Sunshine and the others back to their longhouse with lagging steps, shoulders bowed by a deep sense of abandonment as though he carried a leaden weight.

◆－－－－◆

HE STOOD BEFORE AN ALTAR in the greening spring, atop a high hill. The sun had just begun to cast long, golden fingers across the land and into the sky's cloudless blue. Jakob raised his face to the cool wind, breathing in the clean scent of coming rain.

Before him on the wood piled on the hard grey stones lay a lamb, its legs bound, its white fleece rippling softly. All was uncannily still. Neither wind nor lamb made a sound.

When he lifted his hand, he saw that he held a knife. The early morning light glittered along its keen blade.

He stepped forward as though drawn by a force outside himself and reached for the lamb with his empty hand. Movement off to his left stopped him, and he swung around to see a man striding toward him up the slope. Although Jakob did not recognize him, he yet knew him to be a brother.

He came to a halt at Jakob's side. In sudden, unreasoning anger Jakob turned and plunged the knife with all his strength into the man's breast.

Gouts of blood spurted from the gaping wound, and without making a sound his brother dropped to his knees, his eyes rolling back in his head. Jakob watched in breathless horror as he slumped forward onto his face.

Jakob bolted upright, his heartbeat thudding loudly in his ears, face and body slick with sweat. He gasped for breath, shuddering, staring into darkness illumined only faintly by a fire's banked embers.

By achingly slow degrees he became aware that he was in his usual bed on the upper platform of the longhouse. Yet the dream remained disturbingly real. It had come to him before, he knew suddenly—more than once. But always before its shadows had vanished by morning's light.

Still shaking, he lay down. Almost instantly sleep overwhelmed him, and he was back again before the altar. But this time when his brother approached, it was he who held the knife, he who struck Jakob down. And Jakob felt the terror of the blade, the searing agony of the killing blow, the sickening nausea and vertigo of his life's blood pulsing from his body.

He jerked awake to morning's faint light, unsure for a moment whether he still lived or had died.

Chapter Fifteen

MAPLE MOON

Tuesday, March 21, 1758

JAKOB CROUCHED, imitating Falling Water's movements as he kept to the thicket's shadows, the knife sheathed on his belt ready to hand. He had done much hunting, but he had to admire the warriors' cunning and stealth. Though the party of eleven and their dogs lurked in the woods, the only sound came from the wind sighing through bare branches overhead and the occasional scurry of small creatures across the sodden leaves and icy patches of snow.

His stomach growled with hunger. Food was so scarce in the village that every day the hunters went out to scour the area for game, usually with little success.

This was the third time he had been assigned to accompany them, although the only weapon he was permitted was a knife to help butcher their kills. He hoped to gain enough trust to be allowed a musket and eventually to hunt alone.

During two previous forays, they had gone eastward along the river about ten miles, Jakob figured, almost to the small Seneca village on the other side of the next creek. Since he and

Little Raccoon mostly went north and west to set and tend their traps, he had eagerly taken in every detail of the terrain.

They had found little game there, however, so early this morning they had retrieved two large canoes from the reeds where they were stowed along the river just east of Buckaloons and crossed to the plateau on the opposite shore. Jakob felt certain they had wandered ten miles or more during the day. With growing excitement he took careful note of the terrain as they stopped often to lie in concealment, watching for the game that was abundant on this side of the river. So far they had taken a number of turkeys, waterfowl, rabbits, and other small animals, but no deer.

That the weather was steadily warming in spite of occasional, lingering snowfalls pleased him, not only for the greater comfort it brought, but also because it signaled the arrival of spring. Sunny days with blue skies now regularly succeeded freezing nights, reviving Jakob's hopes of escape.

Falling Water abruptly raised his hand, and Jakob froze. He scanned the dense web of leafless underbrush and spied a great stag a hundred yards ahead, pawing through a melting snow bank to reach the small, tender saplings underneath.

Falling Water slowly raised his musket to his shoulder and took aim. The stag lifted his head at the same instant the warrior pulled the trigger, then leaped into the air, blood spurting from a wound in its chest. It crashed into the underbrush and fell, thrashing

Triumphant whoops rose from the men around them. The dogs ran, baying, to the fallen stag, with the hunters close behind. It was Falling Water's first kill of the day, and he received the congratulations of his friends with obvious pride.

Jakob hung back while the warrior pulled tobacco from his pouch, sprinkled it on the ground around the dead stag, then bowed his head to give thanks to the spirit of the stag for giving its life as food for his people. After he finished, Jakob joined the others in eviscerating the stag, throwing the entrails to the whining dogs before carving the meat from the bones.

The sun now hung halfway to the tops of the western trees in the lightly overcast sky. The men quickly wrapped the deer's meat in its hide, washed their knives in a nearby stream, and reloaded their muskets. They gathered the rest of the game they had taken, with Jakob bearing the heaviest burden on his back, and turned back north toward Buckaloons.

Falling Water led the way, but motioned the party to a halt after they had gone less than a mile. Two hundred yards ahead of them a black bear appeared from behind a rocky cliff and lumbered in their direction—roused from hibernation, Jakob reckoned. Shaking its head sleepily, it raised its snout in the air, then halted, its gaze fixed on their party, its hackles rising.

When the warrior at his side raised his musket, Falling Water laid a restraining hand on the man's arm. "We have all taken game this day." He extended his loaded musket to Jakob. "Except this one. Let us see whether he can shoot."

Jakob hesitated, looking from one to the other, taking in the warriors' haughty expressions. He lowered his pack to the ground, then took the proffered musket and turned to study the bear.

It had closed the distance between them to about 150 yards, moving deliberately. Jakob raised the musket to his shoulder, aimed at the center of the bear's head, and waited. When he estimated the animal had cut the distance to 120 yards, he squeezed the trigger with a smooth motion.

The sharp report reverberated from the cliffs and echoed through the forest aisles. The bear halted as though stunned, bared its yellowed teeth, and shook its head violently. Then it staggered and collapsed to the ground.

Falling Water's face darkened. Jakob lagged behind the hunters as they warily approached the bear, which sprawled motionless across the muddy path. One of them pointed to where the musket ball had passed straight through the animal's forehead. Jakob offered the musket to Falling Water, who snatched it back.

Another man kicked the bear's paw lightly with his foot. "He killed the bear with one shot. It is his."

They stared at Jakob, eyes narrowed, awaiting a response. He knew the tradition: Each hunter claimed the game he personally killed, and if that was uncertain, the meat was divided between those who had fired at the same time. Clearly none of them had reckoned on him making a kill, Falling Water least of all.

Hunger burned Jakob's stomach. The rigors of the past months had left him as lean as in his youth, and his mouth watered at the thought of the bear's meat. Smoked, it would sustain him for several weeks, and he would not be dependent on Sunshine's good graces for his daily portion.

He glanced at Falling Water, then away. The deer's meat would provide enough food to last the occupants of the longhouse hardly more than a fortnight, even with careful rationing. Could he refuse to share when God had provided such bounty?

He struggled to form the Seneca words. "It is for the people of our longhouse."

Falling Water's countenance darkened even more. His obvious displeasure could do Jakob no good.

One of the others laid his hand on Falling Water's shoulder and spoke rapidly. From what Jakob could understand, he said that it was good Burden Carrier would be able to supply East Wind's longhouse with meat since they had to leave for Fort Machault soon. Falling Water responded with a shrug, but the tension on his face eased.

They dressed the bear quickly. The animal was old, its fat stores depleted from long months of hibernation, but it provided a generous supply. When the meat was wrapped in the hide, they piled it on Jakob's back along with the venison, while the hunters carried the rest of the game they had taken.

Jakob groaned under the heavy load all the way back to the canoes, but what Falling Water's friend had said crowded his mind. When the warriors returned to raiding he would be expected to supply his master and her family with meat. And if Specht could also gain more freedom to move in and out of the town, escape would become a real possibility. New hope buoyed him all the way back to Buckaloons.

Upon learning of Jakob's kill, Sunshine smiled and signed for him to take the thick pelt for himself. Falling Water made no objection, but seeing his resentful expression, Jakob suspected that he had intended to take the bearskin for his own.

Jakob thanked Sunshine, then carried the pelt to East Wind. Since Broken Feather's death, Jakob had noted how the elderly woman continually shivered as she huddled under the worn buffalo robe that was her only cover.

With gestures and such words as he knew, he said he would cure the hide and give it to her. Gone almost blind, she fingered the luxurious fur and thanked him profusely, tears filling her eyes.

His kindness clearly pleased Sunshine and Buck Teeth and even seemed to impress Falling Water. But the warmth that filled Jakob's heart had nothing to do with any favor his generosity might gain him.

SINCE THE FIRST TIME he had been able to remember the dream, it had returned often during the darkest hours of the night. At times he was the one who killed, at others the one who was slain. He felt himself at first Cain, and then Abel.

Each time, as the vision unfolded, he viewed the act from different angles. But always he was on the same high hill before the same altar. Always he recoiled from the knife and the fatal blow.

And with that shocking act a wave of agony rolled over him and the crushing doubt: Should he have defended his family during the attack? Should he have killed to save them?

Each repetition, as he experienced the terror of the blade and the impact of the killing blow, felt it the next time from the other side—the rage of the slayer, and then the horror of the slain— drove home to him, however, the conviction that no man was to kill another, that no way of looking at this act could ever make it right. He became increasingly certain that he could never raise his hand against his brother, that regardless of what others might conclude, the witness and testimony given to him was never to take another's life no matter the circumstances.

Yet the consequences of his decision not to resist his family's attackers still haunted him. He had been faithful in refusing to kill. Then why hadn't God saved his wife and children? Hadn't He promised that He would protect and care for those who served Him?

Instead, God had allowed Jakob's family to be torn asunder. Overwhelming grief at the deaths of Anna, Jake, and Annali amid such violence, along with the ripping away of his younger sons, continued to torment him.

Was there purpose to their suffering? Could God yet turn it to their good? If he was never able to escape from this alien place and return home, how was he to live?

Portions of a passage from Jeremiah that his mother had read to him often as a child during his father's imprisonment for their faith returned to his mind: *Seek the peace of the city whither I have caused you to be carried away captives, and pray unto the Lord for it: for in the peace thereof shall ye have peace. . . . and I will turn away your captivity, and I will gather you from all the nations, and from all the places whither I have driven you, saith the Lord; and I will bring you again into the place whence I caused you to be carried away captive.*

He clung to those words. They brought calm and peace to his heart and the determination to continue to pray for the welfare of these people among whom he had been placed and do good to them as God led.

And he would trust his God to lead him—and his boys—home in His perfect time.

Chapter Sixteen

THUNDER MOON
Wednesday, March 29, 1758

J AKOB LEANED CASUALLY toward the men seated around a small fire at the edge of the council house yard, while keeping his head down, gaze fixed on the small peach pit he held. Since being trusted with a knife, he had begun carving a tiny cross on its grooved surface whenever he found opportunity, and now he pretended to delicately smooth its edge.

Among the men were the town's sachem and the most important of Buckaloons' elders and warriors. And two Delaware warriors who had arrived in the town early that afternoon.

Jakob had learned that they had come from the British stronghold of Fort Augusta on the Susquehanna River. Though he had to strain to hear their conversation, their postures and tones made it clear that they discussed a matter of great importance.

The Delaware warriors' voices rose. From what Jakob could make out, they were enraged because the fort's commandant had been suspicious of them and had taken away their weapons.

They were now on their way to Fort Machault to warn the French that the English were gathering an army.

Jakob caught the names Du Quesne, Conestoga, and Lancaster. The British were paying much money for cattle, the two men said, adding something about grass growing that Jakob did not fully catch. Gooseflesh rose on his arms.

A gust of wind stirred the smoke, and one of the warriors glanced idly in Jakob's direction. He made a show of holding up the peach pit, turning it around in the firelight as he pretended to study his carving.

The British plan to attack Fort Du Quesne and are probably gathering their army at either Conestoga or Lancaster. Maybe both. Likely they're waiting for the grass to grow so their horses and cattle have enough forage.

He scanned the crowd moving back and forth around the yard but saw no sign of Specht. He was anxious to relate the information to his friend as soon as possible, but they would have to be careful not to attract anyone's notice.

If the British move against Du Quesne, the French will take their Indians west to fight them. And that'll give us a chance to escape.

"Burden Carrier!"

Jakob looked up to see Red Bird approaching at a run. Her face was brightly painted, and she was dressed in her finest shirt, petticoat, and leggings, garments that were threadbare in many places. She beckoned him to come with her.

He slipped the peach pit back into the pouch around his neck, got up, and obeyed, careful to mask his reluctance. When she confidently placed her hand into his to lead him to the central fire where the dancing had begun, however, his heart lightened. He squeezed her small hand and smiled down at her with genuine affection, his heart catching at the thought that if he and Specht got away, he would greatly miss her and Little Raccoon.

◆━━━◆

JAKOB PONDERED what he had overheard for the rest of the night and the following days. It was the first news of the war that had reached Buckaloons since the fall, and his hopes soared.

March gave way to a sunny April, and he continued to carefully count the passage of days and weeks with his makeshift calendar. The weather was steadily warming, and although sheltered patches of ground in the forest remained frozen, snow no longer lingered even in small patches. The first delicate tints of spring tinged the trees and undergrowth.

The elders in the council repeatedly argued for peace, but Jakob had learned that Indian leaders did not hold the power to force their people to obey them. The men were free to fight or not as they chose. He had sensed the warriors' restlessness increasing as soon as the worst of the snows passed, and each night they performed the war dance around the great fire.

At last several large parties of warriors arrayed for war left for Fort Machault. Falling Water accompanied them, buoying Jakob's spirits.

With the town's population reduced to mainly the elderly, women, and children, life in the longhouse settled into a quiet pattern. Sunshine sent Jakob out to hunt several times a week, entrusting him with a musket in addition to a knife or tomahawk, though she measured out only enough bullets and gunpowder for one day. He was required to return before nightfall and was expected to bring with him game for every bullet missing from his supply or to account for the shortfall.

He was always careful to do as she ordered. Rarely did he fail to bring back game, and he also continued tending the traps with Little Raccoon. His cheerful obedience and success in hunting soon earned the full trust of the longhouse's inhabitants, which gave him much greater freedom of movement. He and Specht even stopped to talk occasionally as they passed in the course of their duties, and no one raised any objection.

The hope of escape lay constantly in the back of Jakob's mind as he worked. Certainly he and Specht would have to wait a few more weeks, for morning frost still often coated buildings and ground. The rivers also overflowed with snowmelt and regular rains, their currents racing so swiftly that Jakob knew safe fords would be hard to find. He reminded himself, however, that the Indians often secreted their canoes along riverbanks. With God's help he and Specht would find a way to cross.

His greatest concern was to determine the exact direction the Northkill lay from Buckaloons. Their chances of survival would improve if they did not waste time wandering through the wilderness in the wrong direction and end up still miles from home.

Jakob spent an evening patching the worn places in his moccasins and advised Specht to do the same. They would have to bring along enough supplies to sustain them on the long journey. Until they were far enough away that it was safe to hunt, they would need a stock of food. He carried flint and steel in the pouch on his belt for starting fires, and both he and Specht would have the blankets they wore. Thus they would be able to cook and keep warm.

One day he chanced upon a large, dead tree about two miles east of Buckaloons with a cavity in its trunk. The mouth was barely wide enough for him to squeeze through stooped over, but inside was a spacious hollow where he could stand upright. Dry and sheltered from the weather, it provided the perfect place for a hoard of bullets, gunpowder, and other supplies.

He never dared to save more than one bullet a day while hunting, and then was obliged to give an evasive account to Sunshine for the lack when he returned. His store grew with frustrating slowness, and he agonized over the sin of giving false witness. Could lying ever be justified? Would God forgive him? Would He bless an escape that was aided by deceit? Was it possible to escape by any other means?

One thing he knew: He had to get away and make his way back to the Northkill. Thus, praying for forgiveness, he doggedly continued in his course.

✦┈┈┈✦

WITH THE PASSING DAYS Jakob carefully noted the rise and fall of stars and moon and sun. He sensed the earth's inexorable tilting, more rapid now, toward the summer solstice still some weeks off and found himself frequently staring off to the east, where the dusky line of the eastern woods powerfully drew him.

The dogwoods flowered and new leaves the size of mouse ears thickened the trees' bare branches with delicate green. Each morning Jakob, Specht, and the other captives accompanied the women and maidens of the town to the surrounding fields to break the soil with mattocks and prepare it to receive seed.

The women took turns planting rows of corn, their gossip, laughter, and fellowship lightening the tedious work. It reminded Jakob of how his Amish community worked together to plant and harvest, deepening his longing for his own people and intensifying his concerns for Jakob and Christian.

After they finished planting all their fields, the people celebrated *Waano`'naogwa:'ciot,* the Corn Planting Ceremony, giving thanks for the budding of the plants and the warming of the earth to receive seed. They prayed to their gods for a good harvest and held a great dance to thank the sun and rain and to beseech the thunder to protect their crops against wind and lightning.

While watching the white children enter into the celebration as eagerly as the Seneca, Jakob couldn't help wondering if his boys had by now also learned to worship the native peoples' idols and forgotten the one true God. They were so young, and everything of the life they had known had been ripped away. How could they resist the constant pressure to fit in with new families and friends when they had no one to stand with them?

At the thought, the urgency to escape weighed ever more heavily on Jakob's heart, giving him no peace.

Chapter Seventeen

Shad Moon
Tuesday, April 25, 1758

"Quick, Crooked Legs! Help me!" Christian cried as the wide, woven hemp basket full of wriggling fish began to slip from his numb fingers.

Crooked Legs shoved through the men and youths gathered in the shallows of French Creek and hurried to Christian's side. Both boys were soaked and cold through from the chill water.

Black Fox lifted his vine net high above the river's surface. "You weaklings! You're going to spill all your fish!"

Crooked Legs shouted back. "Take care that you don't fall on your face in the mud!"

As if on command, Black Fox stumbled and almost fell, spilling half the fish out of his net. Hoots and taunts echoed across the water as everyone hurled playful jeers at each other while splashing back and forth to haul their loads onto the bank and return for more.

Standing Stone straightened, hands on hips. "This is no time for play! There are many more fish to bring in, and if you make the women wait too long, you will suffer for it."

He scowled, but Christian could tell that he struggled to suppress his laughter. Grinning, Christian set his bare heels in the cold mud and with Crooked Legs hefted the basket upward against the weight of fish and water. They staggered together up the slope and lugged their load between the trees to where the women waited.

Bear, now a half-grown ball of brown fur, ran after them, growling and leaping in the attempt to snatch a fish from the basket. Christian drove him away with shouts and gestures. The rest of the dogs crowded around them as other fishermen followed behind. When the matrons and young women darted forward, shouting and waving sticks, the pack retreated, whining, tails tucked between their legs, to crouch by the maidens who gutted and prepared the fish to hang on racks over low, smoky fires.

Christian and Crooked Legs poured their catches onto the ground for the women to sort and returned to the turbulent creek for another load. They found Standing Stone wading waist-deep along the weir, a net woven of supple vines secured between sturdy poles driven into the mud to trap the fish swarming upstream to spawn.

As Crouching Panther splashed toward him from the far shore, Standing Stone motioned toward the sun that hung low in the clear sky above the western treetops. "The women still have much work to do this night. The fish will run for several more sleeps, and we need food and rest before the sun wakes again."

Christian turned to Crooked Legs. "Let's go help the women. The sooner they finish their work, the sooner we will eat!"

They ran back up the slope, Bear and Crooked Legs' dog bounding after them. Many of their friends had left the stream, too, and they called to one another, chattering and laughing about the day's events.

Christian had eaten only a quick meal of corn cakes and duck eggs before leaving the town that morning, and the rich aromas already wafting on the chilly air made his mouth water. He eagerly followed Crooked Legs to the fire where his sisters and mother clustered, preparing fish for the drying racks. Fat perch roasted in the ashes along the edge of the seething embers, and thick slices of eel sizzled on flat rocks set among the hottest coals, their scent reminding Christian of frying bacon. A kettle of mussels gathered earlier in the day simmered above them.

Deep Water pushed smaller baskets of eel, trout, and perch toward Christian. "Prepare these for smoking. They are for you and your father."

"*Uleèwe!*" I thank you.

With Crooked Legs' help, Christian gutted the fish and eels, cut them up, and washed the pieces in the creek's shallows, while Bear watched sleepily, sated from the scraps he had already eaten. The boys carried the full baskets to the fires where Crooked Legs' sisters had arranged the day's catch on the drying racks. The maidens quickly set up another rack for Christian's portion.

He had stripped to his breechcloth for the day's work, with only the small pouch of charms around his neck and a woven sash around his waist from which hung his sheathed knife. The work had heated him, but now he shivered as the breeze grew keener with the sun's descent below the tree line. Crooked Legs led the way to where they had left their clothing lying on their blankets beneath a tree, and both of them quickly stepped into their moccasins and pulled on leggings and shirt.

Christian's clothing had grown dirty and threadbare over the past moons. He had added noticeable height and breadth as well. His shirt strained uncomfortably across his shoulders and the leggings no longer reached his ankles. When Crooked Legs' sisters teased him about bursting out of his clothes, his face heated.

"It is good that you took so many hides this winter," Deep Water broke in, casting a frown at her daughters. "Manitou gave you great success while we were off at the hunting camp."

Christian sat beside Crooked Legs. "The visions he gave my father never failed. I followed the instructions exactly, and they always led me to where the game waited."

Standing Stone and Crouching Panther approached out of the gathering shadows and took seats on either side of the two boys. "You tanned the hides as well as my wife and daughters could," Standing Stone approved.

Crouching Panther laid his hand on Christian's shoulder. "The trader will give you much cloth for them."

Deep Water began to portion out pieces of fish and eels onto wooden plates, adding a ladle of mussels and a piece of cornbread to each before she passed them around the fire. "Enough for two shirts and sets of leggings at least. I will teach you how to make them, Deep Forest, for soon you will no longer be able to wear these garments. Be sure to save some of the softest deerskin to make new moccasins."

"I'll do the beadwork for you," volunteered Good Road, her oldest daughter, as she handed him a loaded plate. Her younger sisters immediately echoed her.

Christian grinned. "My new clothes will be beautiful!"

Crooked Legs elbowed him. "The young women will swarm around you like hungry dogs."

"You'll have to drive them off with a stick."

Christian joined the others in laughing at Crouching Panther's jest before bending his head and concentrating on his meal. Between mouthfuls, he looked happily around him.

The forest was dotted with the sparkle of low fires that sent flickering light and shadow among the trees. The weather was pleasant, if cool, and the sky clear. With nightfall the breeze had subsided, and a thin, fragrant veil of grey woodsmoke drifted lazily upward to catch in the branches overhead, while above the treetops thousands of stars twinkled in the black bowl of the heavens. All around them other families gathered, eating and tending the drying racks, their muted voices filling the night.

He had never felt so content. But when his stomach was full, he thought of his father.

Most of the families would sleep beneath the trees for several days until the fish stopped running, but Nútemau remained at home. Although he was not alone—other elders had stayed behind too the winter had been hard on him. His health had improved since the snows ceased, but concern for his lack of appetite and lingering weakness continually nagged at Christian.

"May I take food to my father?" he asked Deep Water. "He has not been eating well."

Her youngest daughter, Cloud Dancer, sprang to her feet. "I will prepare it for you."

As Christian got up, Crouching Panther stretched and rose too. "I will go with you, little brother, and see how my uncle does."

"I'm not so little!"

Crouching Panther lifted his eyebrows. "Ah, it is so. Do you not have twelve winters now? It will not be long before you become a man."

Cloud Dancer handed Christian the bundle she had prepared, and he and Crouching Panther said good night to the others.

They walked in silence along the moonlit path back toward Custaloga's Town. After some moments Christian looked up to search Crouching Panther's face.

"I heard Standing Stone tell Deep Water that soon our warriors will go down to Fort Machault. I think she was not pleased."

Crouching Panther's expression sobered. "Parties from the other towns went out to attack the English settlements many sleeps ago. Our women demanded that we stay until the Planting Moon, but the French grow impatient. We must go as soon as the fishing is done."

"My father said that some of our people talk about deserting the French."

"It is so, little brother. We have lost many good warriors in this fight, with little benefit. The French give us gifts of food, clothing, and ammunition each year, it is true, but if they lose this war, that will cease. We cannot depend on them, and because we are at war with the British, their traders, who brought with them more goods at better prices than the French, stay away."

Crouching Panther shook his head, frowning. "Even so, Custaloga and our other Wolf leaders do not trust the British to keep out the settlers who steal our lands. They say it is better for us to stay with the French."

When they reached the town, the flickering light of a lantern shone in the windows of Custaloga's cabin, and two horses Christian did not recognize were tethered outside its door. Crouching Panther's eyes narrowed as he studied the unfamiliar horses.

"Who has come?" Christian asked.

"Someone who wishes to parlay with Custaloga." Thoughtfully Crouching Panther added, "The saddles are English."

NÚTEMAU ROSE AS EARLY as Christian the next morning and fried eggs for both of them to eat with the bread remaining from the night before. He seemed in unusually good humor and complimented Christian for working so hard with the fishing party.

"I'm glad I came back last night," Christian told him. "The food Deep Water sent did you much good."

He headed back toward the fishing camp with Crouching Panther. As they passed Custaloga's cabin, the sachem stepped out through the doorway, accompanied by two men. The first, older and taller, was Shawnee, judging by his dress. Christian could tell that the second man was not French, but neither did he appear to be English. He was well tanned, as though he spent much time outdoors, plainly dressed in black clothing, and wore his brown shoulder-length hair loose.

Christian felt inexplicably drawn to him. He read a kindness in the man's weathered face and a gentle power in his demeanor that stirred a vague memory of his white father and the other men of his lost home. Unsettled, he glanced from Custaloga to Crouching Panther and caught a look passing between them that Christian did not understand.

Crouching Panther gripped Christian's arm and pulled him forward. "We must go, little brother. It grows late and we still have much work to do."

The black-clothed stranger said something to Custaloga that Christian could not make out. As Crouching Panther urged him down the path, he looked back over his shoulder.

Custaloga's face had darkened, and he moved to block the two men's view of Christian.

Chapter Eighteen

SHAD MOON
Thursday, April 27, 1758

J OSEPH CRINGED as Wulachen swung the charred stick at his head.

"Away with you! Why do you laze around here like a baby, eating food we need for ourselves? Do you expect me to feed and clothe you forever? Let Gishela-mukaong and his helpers take care of you for I will not!"

She thrust a dish filled with a mixture of bear grease and pulverized charcoal at Menetopalis. Steadying himself with his walking stick, he lowered to the bench by the hearth and sternly beckoned Joseph to him.

Joseph obeyed. As Menetopalis smeared the black paint over Joseph's face, his chest constricted. The faint blush of dawn barely brightened the sky outside the cabin windows when Menetopalis finished, levered to his feet with his stick, and hobbled into the sleeping room.

Joseph bit his lip hard. There was to be no sympathy or comfort from his father either.

I'm dead to them now.

Contrary Wind said through tears, "*Gáhowees,* why are you so mean to Straight Arrow? He has done nothing wrong."

Wulachen silenced him with a stern look. She Sings and Moon-flower busied themselves with their usual chores, their expressions stunned and fearful.

Wulachen and Menetopalis had begun treating Joseph with uncharacteristic harshness several days earlier, feeding him only scraps left behind by the dogs, speaking sharply to him, and forcing him to sleep without cover on the floor by the hearth at night. He had dreaded what he knew was coming despite his older friends' reassurances that the purpose of this trial was for him to seek a vision so that he might become a man.

Now, although he felt no surprise that the day had come for him to be driven out, hurt and shame caused his stomach to clench painfully. He stood, already feeling like an outcast.

His stomach growled with hunger, but Wulachen gave him no food. Nor did she allow him to fetch his blanket or any weapon, though he wore only breechcloth and moccasins. She drove him out the door into the early morning chill.

The Shad Moon had begun a few days earlier, and the first delicate shades of green tinted the bare branches of trees and shrubs. That morning a light frost again whitened the roofs of cabins and wigewas, however, and he shivered in the cold breeze.

Wulachen lifted her face to the brightening sky. "I call upon you spirits of the Earth and Sun, the Four Winds and Thunder! This boy is without family or friend to care for him. See, we have nothing to do with him any longer! Bring to him a guardian to help him or he must die!"

She turned fiercely on Joseph. "Be gone now, and do not return until you have become a man!"

He drew a shaky breath and turned quickly away, determined not to look back or make any protest like some of the younger boys had when their time came. Several of his friends stepped outside their cabins as he strode down the path to the forest, but they looked through him as though he didn't exist, giving him no greeting, and turned their backs.

Head down, he plodded into the forest, sick at heart. In recent months the patterns of the Lenape way of life had crowded out memories of the family that once had been his and the grief and anger those memories aroused. He was becoming increasingly fluent in the Lenape tongue, and skilled in the dances, games, and hunting that filled most of his days. He had absorbed the complex religion, legends, and lore of the tribe through the stories related nightly by the town's elders, while Menetopalis imparted to him skill in carving, tanning hides, and the daily obligations of a Lenape man.

Joseph had come to fit comfortably into his new world, and tentative reconciliation to his new life had given way to the eager embracing of it. He had come to think of Wulachen and Menetopalis as mother and father, the children as brother and sisters. It seemed as though he had always been a part of their extended family, his circle of friends, and the life of the town. Now to be cast out from these bonds of love and fellowship brought flooding back all the anguish he had suffered at the loss of his first family and community.

He wandered up the river past the falls, then angled off into the forest with the sun's rising behind him. At length he began to take note of his surroundings, his training as a hunter taking over, and he moved between the trees as silently as a shadow.

He knew he was to fast until he received a vision of his spirit protector and guide. That often required four or five days, his friends had explained. But his stomach already grumbled, and the thought of enduring so long without food was daunting. Worse, all the anxious questions he had grappled with since witnessing Bear Claw's ordeal and that of several other boys after him beset Joseph now with sharper urgency.

He noted the gradual warming of the air as the sun climbed higher in the sky. Scanning the area, he glimpsed a creek winding through the trees ahead of him and decided to find shelter and a source of water.

He followed the stream's course for more than an hour, traveling ever farther west and north of Sauconk. At last, ahead of him along the opposite shore, misty sunbeams filtering through the trees outlined the wooded shoulder of a low ridge.

The creek had seemed familiar to him, and now he was certain that his hunting party had taken this same path a couple of moons earlier. The ridge stretched for some distance, he remembered, and farther along it he had seen the yawning mouths of caverns in its rocky flank.

He pressed on until he reached the first of the caverns. It lay steps from the creek's bank, deeply shaded by trees. Carrying his moccasins, he waded through the rushing, thigh-deep water, several times almost losing his footing on the creek's muddy bottom. He was shaking from the cold water and the deep forest's pervading chill by the time he clambered out onto the far bank.

He stepped into his moccasins and strode around vigorously, swinging his arms to warm his body.

When he went to the cave, he found that it stretched well back into the cliff, its interior above head height. Cautious exploration assured him that no beasts occupied it and that it was dry.

He could make the space secure from animals by piling fallen branches in front of the opening and arming himself with stones and a sturdy stick, he reckoned. He had no knife, but if he could strip a supply of tender branches from the underbrush, he could make a reasonably comfortable bed.

The cave's walls still held the night's cold, however, and he had no blanket or means to build a fire. He would make himself as comfortable as he could, he decided, then settle down to pray. And wait for his vision.

He didn't want to think about what he would do if none was granted.

◆━━━◆

JOSEPH JERKED AWAKE. Had he heard footfalls outside or had he been dreaming?

He pushed cautiously upright, every muscle protesting. He was stiff and sore from hunger and from lying for hours on the thin layer of branches that did little to cushion the rocks beneath.

The cavern's chill left him feeling sluggish. Over the past four days he had left its concealment only to relieve himself, to lap up a handful of water at the creek's edge when thirst overwhelmed him, and to walk the stiffness from his limbs. The rest of the time he had made every attempt to pray and summon up a vision, but in vain.

The painful cramping in his abdomen made it difficult to focus, and his thoughts kept drifting. Weak and lightheaded, he feared that even if a vision did appear, he would not have strength to make it back to Sauconk to tell about it.

He had tried to pray to the Lenape gods as his family had taught him, while fingering the small image of Wsinkhoalican he carried in the small pouch around his neck. But he could not shake off a stubborn skepticism, and his prayers remained only pretense. Their gods felt like a fantasy and prayers to them like a vain endeavor, like deception and idolatry.

In desperation, the previous night he had finally called out to Jesus, fighting through the anger and anguish he harbored toward God. And unexpectedly, the turmoil of emotions had fallen away, and he had felt himself enveloped in a Presence so real, a love so profound that he had wept.

He couldn't understand it. He could only cling to it as a child clings to its father in the darkest night, until at last he fell into a deep, healing sleep.

Now he shook his head to clear it and looked fearfully toward the cave's mouth. Outside, the deep edge of night had softened with the approach of dawn.

There it was again: the sound of rustling in the dry leaves outside the cave. Heart pounding, he grabbed the sturdy stick he kept for a weapon, scrambled to his feet, and slipped to the barricade of broken branches he had piled along one side of the opening, leaving only a narrow passage through which he could enter and exit.

He could see nothing. He pressed through the opening, brandishing his stick, on guard for any intruder.

All was silent and still. He could not hear even the creek's burble ten strides away down the slope.

A loud snort raised the hair on the back of his neck. At the same instant a dark shape burst from the deep shadows off to his right and barreled toward him, closing fast—a gigantic buck, the largest he had ever seen. Its huge rack of antlers was lowered, and Joseph could feel the ground tremble with the force of its charge. It closed on him so rapidly that he had time enough only to drop the stick and leap aside.

To his astonishment, the buck stopped abruptly an arm's length away. It raised its head and fixed its gaze on him, as if measuring him.

For a suspended moment he and the buck faced each other, motionless. At last, hardly knowing what he said, Joseph gasped, "Are you my spirit protector?"

The buck shook its head up and down and pawed the ground.

"You are my spirit protector?"

The buck regarded him with a look that seemed to hold great wisdom and kindness. It lowered its head until its antlers almost brushed Joseph's bare chest.

Tentatively he reached out and grasped one of the sharp tips. As soon as his fingers closed around it, a long piece broke off in his hand. The buck lifted its head. Stepping back, it turned and calmly trotted into the forest, a sound like soft laughter floating behind it on the light breeze.

Joseph stared after it, mouth hanging open, too stunned to move, until it disappeared from his sight. He stepped in the direction the buck had taken and scanned the moist ground for hoof prints. There were none. Nor any other sign of the buck's passage.

He looked down at the piece of antler in his hand. When he looked up again, the full light of dawn illumined the sky above the eastern trees, casting long, golden shadows down the forest aisles.

How much time had passed? It would have taken at least an hour for the sky to grow this bright since he had left the cave. But that was impossible. Only the faintest hint of dawn had been visible when he awoke, and the encounter with the buck couldn't have lasted ten minutes. Yet the sun's fiery edge was already lifting above the horizon.

His hand trembled as he took a pinch of tobacco from his pouch and sprinkled it on the ground so he could truthfully assure his family that he had made a sacrifice to the spirit of the buck. But he whispered. "I thank you, Jesus."

He stumbled down to the creek and laved cold water over his face until he had washed off the last of the black paint. After raking his wet fingers through his shoulder-length hair to comb out the tangles and dirt, he rose and began to retrace his path toward home.

Had God sent the buck to provide what he needed to gain his people's favor? He had no way of knowing. His only certainty was that strength for the journey radiated through his limbs, and a quiet assurance filled his heart.

❦ ⸺ ❦

"I COULD NOT THINK for fear, but I reached out and took hold of the buck's antlers. And this broke off in my hand." Joseph held the piece of the deer's antler up for his audience to see. It was the third time he had recounted his vision. Wulachen and Menetopalis sat on either side of him, both festively arrayed in their turkey feather capes, as was Joseph. Along with the children and their extended family, Joseph's friends, and many more of the townspeople, they had gathered in the council house, with only Tamaque and Shingas missing, as they were gone from the town.

Red Squirrel regarded him, eyebrows raised. "He gave you a piece of his antler?"

Mehíttuk leaned forward to examine the antler more closely, then sat back, smiling broadly. "You were brave to do this! And he nodded his head when you asked him to be your spirit protector?"

"It is so."

Joseph sensed Many Leaves' gaze on him. He cast a quick glance in her direction and was pleased to see that she listened closely, her eyes bright.

Mehíttuk continued, "Your prayers are powerful, Straight Arrow! You have been given great favor by Gishela-mukaong."

Joseph avoided his friend's gaze. On the way back to Sauconk he had tried to prepare himself to make a forthright answer if anyone questioned him about his vision, but trepidation filled him at the thought of the reaction this confession might elicit.

He opened his mouth to explain that he had prayed to the true God and not to their Great Spirit, but Wulachen cut him off.

"You have become a man, my son, and now you must choose a name worthy of a man."

Relieved at the interruption in spite of the proddings of conscience, Joseph bit his lip, wondering whether he ought to say what he had rehearsed. But Menetopalis laid his hand on Joseph's shoulder, nodding gravely, and although he did not smile, Joseph could tell that he was very pleased. He would tell them later, privately, he decided.

Red Squirrel said, "You heard the buck laughing as he left you, so why not Laughing Buck?"

Other voices called out suggestions, but Bird's Nest settled the matter. She rose stiffly and came to settle cross-legged before Joseph. Her wizened face grave, she took his hands, still cupping the piece of antler, between hers and bowed her head, eyes closed, lips moving while she muttered a prayer.

After a moment she raised her head and met Joseph's anxious gaze. "This great buck came to you in the darkness, but when he left you the sun was rising. Is it not so?"

"It is, *Nóhum*."

"Then you are no longer Straight Arrow, grandson. Your man-name is Brings Dawn."

Chapter Nineteen

PLANTING MOON
Monday, May 1, 1758

J AKOB CAREFULLY PRIED away several sections of the longhouse's elm bark cladding that had split and rotted over the
winter, exposing the framework of sturdy poles cut from
saplings. Curious, he studied the dwelling's construction.

The bases of the uprights that ran along each side of the
structure were buried in the ground, with flexible poles bent to
form curved rafters laid horizontally across them and, tied
securely in place with thick ropes of braided hickory bast. More
poles were lashed horizontally the length of the walls and roof
for strength and stability.

He had worked the previous week with one of the elders,
Pine Tree, to pry strips of bark from large elms in the forest,
smooth their deep groves with an adz, and then submerge them
in the creek, weighted by rocks to flatten them. Sunshine and
Buck Teeth had braided bast into rope, which Jakob also set to
soak. The wet ropes would be used to join the poles and bind
the bark strips to the framework and would shrink and tighten
as they dried.

On his way through the town gates with a supply of bark and rope, he passed a party of Delaware warriors entering with their women and children. Five white prisoners accompanied them, plodding wearily forward, prodded by their Indian captors. Jakob covertly took in the men's ragged clothing and the dust that coated everyone in the party. They had clearly traveled a long distance.

He worked diligently all day to repair the longhouse, making numerous trips to and from the creek for more bark and rope. Each time he passed the Delaware party's camp on the council house yard, he calculated how he could get close enough to the captives to talk to them.

With darkness falling he made a show of eating his portion of the late afternoon meal, while slipping as many corn cakes into his pouch as possible without attracting notice. Sunshine and the others soon headed to the council house for the nightly dances, but he lagged behind and quietly slipped into the shadows.

He found the captives at the edge of the yard, huddled outside the circle of firelight cast by the bonfire where the dancers had begun to gather. Only one guard attended them, and he appeared to pay them little attention.

The drummers took up a slow, deliberate beat, and a group of young men moved into the first dance. By the time the younger women were halfway through the second dance, the prisoners' guard had moved farther into the crowd for a better view.

His heartbeat thudding in his ears, Jakob slid forward to sit cross-legged at the dispirited group's center. They eyed him warily.

"Sprechen sie Deutsch?" Do you speak German?

Their faces brightened, and one man said in a low voice, "*Ya!* We'd given up ever hearing our native language again!"

Jakob repositioned himself to keep the guard in his line of sight. "I saw them bring you in earlier today. Where did you come from?"

The men leaned close to hear over the pounding of the drums and the hiss of the rattles.

One gestured toward the guard. "They brought us up from Fort Du Quesne."

"From what I hear, Du Quesne is a great stronghold."

A man to Jakob's left answered, "There are about 300 soldiers garrisoned there."

Jakob stroked his chin. "The British will have much difficulty capturing it then. The French must have many cannon."

Another man shrugged. "Not so many as you'd suppose. And they're all dismounted."

"Is that so?"

A man with a festering wound on his forehead said eagerly, "That's not all. While we were there, we met a Dutch baker held prisoner in the fort for the last three years. He pointed out a hill on the far bank of the Monongahela that the French never fortified. It overlooks the fort. He said if the English put a battery up there, they can take it with no more than two hundred men."

"If only we could get word to the British," the first man groaned, "they might have a chance of ending this war and freeing all us captives."

Jakob watched the guard, whose back was still turned. "Why did they bring you here?"

The man with the wound grimaced. "The Indians leave their women and children at Du Quesne through the winter and spring so the French will feed them. But provisions were scarce this year because of the hard winter and the French not bringing more supplies down, so they're taking their families upriver."

"We thought we were going to starve," another prisoner added. "They'd hunted through the area till there wasn't any more game left."

Jakob scanned their faces. In the flickering firelight, every one of the prisoners appeared to be hardly more than a skeleton. He pulled the corn cakes from his pouch and divided them among the men. They devoured them, nodding their gratitude with their mouths full.

The drums had briefly stopped. But now they suddenly began to pound again, this time in the savage rhythm of the war dance.

JAKOB WAS HEADING to the well at mid-morning later that week, carrying the yoke and the large bark water buckets when loud voices captured his attention. The Delaware party had stayed only a couple of days before leaving, and the council house yard was empty except for a group of elders seated around the large fire pit smoking their pipes.

Among them were Pine Tree and a couple of others Jakob had sometimes supplied with game. Little Raccoon and a few friends sat with them, listening raptly to the elders' conversation and from time to time pressing eager questions.

Jakob slowed. The men seemed to be explaining something of great importance to the boys, who responded gleefully. He hurried away, but returned as speedily as possible, the yoke digging painfully into his shoulders as he steadied the heavy buckets on each end with his hands.

He pretended to stagger slightly as he passed behind them, sloshing water from the swinging buckets. Stopping, he squatted and lowered them onto the ground, then slipped off the yoke as though to adjust it.

One of the elders turned and beckoned imperiously to Jakob with his tin cup. Jakob filled it from one of the buckets and returned it to him. He did the same for several of the others, surreptitiously watching Pine Tree scratch a rude map in the cold ashes in the fire pit.

Jakob studied the scratchings, while struggling to understand the old man's rapid speech. Parallel jagged lines appeared to define mountain ranges, and he reasoned that the longer lines winding along and between them must be rivers.

Unexpectedly Pine Tree gestured for him to join the circle. Jakob sat cross-legged, while Pine Tree continued talking, mentioning the British several times.

A chill went through Jakob. *They're showing the boys where the warriors are raiding.*

With feigned nonchalance, he asked, "You attack British?"

The men exchanged glances, eyes narrowing. Pine Tree frowned at Jakob, but his expression quickly cleared and he nodded vehemently, his grin exposing stumps of rotted teeth.

"Many, many tribes." He waved his arms in wide circles. *"Gagwe:'gon!"* Everyone!

He returned his attention to the boys, pointing to the left side of his map, and Jakob caught the word *hekœœhkwë's. West*, he thought, holding his breath. Then east lay opposite, north above, and south below.

Pine Tree scratched several crosses on the map with his stick. The first, below a curved line on the map's northwest side, he called Presque Isle.

That curved line shows Lake Erie, Jakob concluded, excitement building.

Pine Tree inscribed two more crosses, the second a short distance southeast of the first, which he identified as Buckaloons, pointing to the ground where he sat. It lay just above a thick, crooked line Jakob had taken for a river. The third cross, a short distance to the west, where the line angled south, Pine Tree called Venango.

Jakob's mouth went dry. He remembered the town very well— and the broad river he and the boys had crossed to reach Fort Machault before they took canoes north up its tributary, French Creek, to Presque Isle. The river that flowed past Buckaloons was that same broad river.

Pine Tree added another cross well below Venango, where the crooked line marking the river turned westward. "Du Quesne!"

Jakob looked away from the map as though he had lost interest. But exhilaration made him almost lightheaded. The river could be none other than the Ohio, which meant that another line Pine Tree had drawn southeast of it, running generally south but branching to east and west on its northern end, had to be the Susquehanna.

He gripped his knees to keep his hands from trembling. "Where do you attack, *ti'so:t?*" He knew he mangled the words, but hoped the old man would understand.

Pine Tree's face lit up at Jakob's use of the respectful term *grandfather.* The other elders were clearly pleased too.

Pine Tree pointed his stick. "We attack here." He scratched a cross where the two branching lines combined into one.

Jakob was now certain the map indicated the two branches of the Susquehanna. *Shamokin. The British are planning an attack on Fort Du Quesne and are only waiting until the grass grows so they'll be able to feed their cattle. But the French must have decided to beat them to it by attacking Fort Augusta.*

He looked up to meet Pine Tree's triumphant gaze, struggling to keep his expression noncommittal. *The Northkill is not so far from there. And Johannes and Barbara and their little ones, if they still live. If I can make it to the Susquehanna, I can find my way home.*

Chapter Twenty

J AKOB'S HAND TIGHTENED around the musket, heart thudding beneath his ribs like a caged bird fighting to break free.

Though it was only an hour after dawn, it was already warm, with a light breeze stirring puffy clouds in the azure sky.

He forced himself to meet Sunshine's gaze calmly, without flinching. "I return before sun go down."

Little Raccoon bounced up and down on his toes. "Let me go with you, Burden Carrier! See how big I've grown? My arrows always hit the target and—"

To Jakob's relief, Sunshine shook her head. "Falling Water will soon teach you to be a great hunter, but you're still too young. Until you learn the rules of the hunt, you must stay."

The boy's face fell. Jakob steadied his nerves and smiled at Little Raccoon, pained that he would never see him and Red Bird again. He would miss them, and also, he realized, Sunshine and East Wind, who had been kind to him.

He took the small rawhide bag filled with powder and another containing wadding and a few musket balls. He tucked the bags into the large pouch hanging from his worn sash, reassured by the feel of flint and steel against his fingers. A second pouch held several strips of pemmican hoarded over the past couple of weeks and a supply of fresh corn cakes Sunshine had given him to take along—to which he had surreptitiously added a few more.

He adjusted his blanket around his shoulders and headed toward the town gates. With every step he felt Sunshine's gaze following him and wondered if she sensed anything out of the ordinary. But he resisted the urge to look back, and she did not call after him.

He passed Specht's longhouse. As they'd agreed, his friend was standing outside, looking casually around as though taking the measure of the day. Jakob met his gaze and gave a firm nod. Specht turned and went inside.

It seemed an eternity before Jakob entered the wood's dappled shade and followed the path out of sight of the village. He took several strides before turning to look back.

He waited and watched, holding his breath, at last let it out. No one came after him.

He splashed across the ford of Buxotons Creek and headed northeast, walking briskly. When he had gone a little more than a mile, he circled to the southeast, back toward the Ohio, taking care to cover his tracks.

The urgency to warn the British of the coming attack had doubled his determination to escape. He had spent every idle moment of the last four days reviewing all he knew of the region along the Susquehanna and around Fort Augusta. He and Specht had consulted at every opportunity, calculating the direction they would have to go, the number of days it might take to get to the Susquehanna, and what supplies they would need to carry. Now, pushing through the thick undergrowth and detouring around rocky outcroppings, he again went over every detail to assure himself that he had forgotten nothing.

Soon he saw the bare, gnarled branches of the hollow tree through the greening canopy of a dense copse. He was gasping for air by the time he reached it—not so much from exertion, for the months of captivity had hardened him, but from fear that someone might come after him, that he might encounter other hunters, or that a band of returning warriors might intercept him.

Leaning against the dead tree, he waited for his heartbeat to steady and his breathing to return to normal. He surveyed his surroundings, listening intently, seeking any unusual sound that might indicate someone's approach. He heard the stirring of the trees and undergrowth in the breeze, the movement and song of birds in the treetops, and the rustle of small creatures through the damp leaves underfoot, but detected no sign of another human.

As his tension eased, he looked up through the overhanging branches. The sun stood high in the heavens. No time to waste.

He pushed into the tree's hollow, retrieved the worn length of rawhide in which his store of powder, ball, and wadding was wrapped, and unfolded it. What had previously seemed like a substantial quantity now appeared paltry. It had taken three weeks to reach Presque Isle, and then Buckaloons; it would take at least that long for him and Specht to find their way back through the wilderness to the Northkill.

It was still early spring, and there would be little, if anything, to forage along the way. With this small stock of ammunition they would have to supply their food for at least as long as it took to reach English-held territory.

But first they had to get away undetected.

Teeth gritted, he shoved his hoarded stores into the pouch on his belt, stepped out of the hollow tree, and again looked around. There was as yet no sign of Specht, but they had agreed that Jakob would wait for a couple of hours before making his escape. And so he squatted beside the tree in the concealment of the underbrush to wait.

THE SUN'S SLOW CLIMB had reached its zenith. And still there was no sign of Specht.

What if he can't get away from Buckaloons?

Sweat beaded Jakob's brow, and his heart pounded. If Specht didn't show up, should he leave his friend behind, not knowing whether his fears had overcome him and he had given up the attempt or whether some obstacle had prevented him from getting away?

As the sun began its decline, he decided that if Specht did not appear by mid-afternoon, he would go on alone. No matter what happened, he could not return to Buckaloons, to captivity.

When he calculated that almost an hour had dragged by, he heard a thrashing in the bushes that rapidly came closer. He shrank back into the tree's hollow and peered in the direction of the sound. Finally, he spied his friend crashing through the intertwined branches, panting and wild-eyed.

Relief washed over Jakob. He sprang into the clear, waving his arms.

"Here! Not so much noise, Hans!"

Specht collapsed to the ground at Jakob's feet. *"Gott sei dank!"* Praise God!

Jakob crouched and waited for him to catch his breath.

"Dull Knife would have to go to the trader's this morning!" Specht groaned at last. "And of course I had to go along to carry everything. By the time she decided on what she needed, I'd almost given up on ever getting away—"

"It doesn't matter. You're here now, and we can't waste any more time." Jakob stood, expecting Specht to get up too. "She didn't seem suspicious?"

Specht shook his head, then let it sink onto his crossed arms.

"Then by the time you're missed it'll be close to dusk, and we have to be as far from here as we can!"

Specht finally heaved to his feet. "If only we could go to this Custaloga's town and look for our children—"

"You know it's too dangerous to try. Even if we found them, we'd never get them loose. We'd only be caught again and maybe killed—maybe them too. Our only hope is to get home alive. Then we'll find out what we can and petition the governor to make the Indians give them back."

When Specht turned toward the west, Jakob gripped his arm. "This way is east, Hans."

"The ford's on the other side of Buckaloons."

"There are villages on both sides of the river there. If we go that way, we risk capture."

"But the warriors are gone. We can skirt around the villages without being seen and cross the Ohio, then follow their paths toward home. It's the quickest way."

"It's along their roads that they'll most likely hunt us."

"It could take days to find a ford east of here—"

"I've seen how the Indians hide their canoes along the riverbanks. We'll find one."

"What if we don't, Jake? Even if we do, who can find their way across such a wilderness as this without following a path? Even the Indians don't try it unless there's no choice."

Jakob sighed and turned his face to the sky. "The Indians use the sun and other marks. I learned how to find my way in the woods while hunting with them. And Pine Tree's map showed which direction the Susquehanna lies."

The muscles in Specht's jaw tightened. "We can stay alongside the paths and hide in the undergrowth whenever anyone comes along."

"Do you remember how many others crossed our path on the way to Presque Isle, and how suddenly they appeared at times?" Jakob demanded, fighting back frustration. "The Indians move stealthily; they'd be on us before we even see them."

Specht crossed his arms and glanced back toward the west.

"Hans, if we go southeast, we'll get to the Susquehanna and follow it to Harris's ford. It's the only way we'll make it without being captured again. And you know what they do to those who try to escape."

He gave his friend no time to make further objection. Waving Specht forward, Jakob led the way east, deeper into the forest.

＋ ------ ＋

JAKOB SQUINTED against the deepening twilight, assessing the overhanging cliff. The ceiling of the shallow cavity at its base was barely more than head high, but it was deep enough to provide concealment and a snug shelter for the night.

"We can't make it much farther tonight. It's almost too dark to see already." Specht tilted his head toward the east, where the rush of water indicated a fair-sized stream. "We'd have to ford the creek blind, and there's a village on the other side anyhow."

Jakob studied the circle of stones at the cave's entrance. It enclosed ashes and pieces of charred wood. The shelter had regularly harbored others.

The Ohio lay a quarter mile to the south. Because Indian canoes regularly traveled along it, he and Specht had kept to the forest's cover as much as possible, while following the river's winding course east, searching for either a ford or a canoe stowed along its bank. They had found neither.

Jakob reckoned that they had traveled nine miles at most, much less than he had hoped. They had pressed forward as rapidly as they could and had not stopped to rest during that strenuous afternoon.

It had been hard going to traverse the rocky, forested slopes barricaded with windfalls and vine-twined undergrowth, while taking precautions to conceal signs of their passing. Twice they had hurried farther back from the river to lie in cover, while canoes full of warriors swept by, and that had slowed them even more.

But Specht was right. They were both worn out, muscles burning and stomachs growling. They needed food, shelter, and rest for the morrow.

If he'd calculated correctly, the moon's slender crescent wouldn't rise until well after midnight. It was unlikely they would find a better place to camp by groping through the dark.

Specht had already entered the cavern, and Jakob followed, ducking beneath its overhang. Inside, sandy soil and drifts of withered leaves cushioned the rocky floor. He laid his musket along the back where it would stay dry but close at hand, removed both pouches from his belt for the night, and laid the one containing ammunition alongside the weapon.

The two men sat cross-legged at the cave's mouth, threadbare blankets wrapped around their shoulders to ward off the falling dew, and divided a corn cake and a piece of pemmican from Jakob's other pouch between them.

Specht eyed the remaining supply as he tore off a bite of the dried, finely pounded venison with his teeth. "This'd chew easier if we boiled it in some water."

"Pemmican's tough on the teeth and dry to swallow, *ya*. Sadly we've no pot for cooking."

Specht rose. "We still need a fire. With just these thin blankets to cover us, we'll freeze overnight."

Jakob shook his head. "Someone might smell or see the smoke."

"Nobody's going to see a little fire behind this hill." Specht strode to the edge of the clearing and began to collect sticks, bits of bark, and pinecones, piling them in the fire circle.

With reluctance Jakob pulled his flint and steel from the pouch. In minutes low flames danced within the circled stones.

Specht moved off into the darkness east of the cliff to look for larger branches. Jakob noticed a half-rotted branch protruding from the underbrush a few yards beyond the cave's mouth, dragged it free, and began to break it into pieces. Hearing footsteps behind him, he straightened and turned, expecting to see Specht.

His friend stepped into the firelight's soft glow, his taut face ashen. Close behind him loomed an imposing, powerfully built warrior clad in the dress of the Delaware, fully armed, seamed face streaked with red and black paint. He studied Jakob with a narrowed gaze.

Jakob's stomach roiled. He glanced from the warrior to Specht and back again before raising his hand in front of his forehead palm outward with index and second fingers pointing to the sky in the Delaware sign for friendship.

"Nchu—Nchutièstuk." he stammered. Friend.

The warrior lowered his head a fraction, while keeping his hostile gaze fixed on Jakob. Without speaking, he went to the fire and settled cross-legged before it, then motioned to Jakob and Specht to join him.

With forced cheerfulness Jakob took a seat opposite the warrior. Specht lowered to his side, noticeably shaking.

"Welcome," Jakob said in the Delaware tongue, one of the few words he could remember from trading with tribal members in his neighborhood before the war. He picked up the pouch that held their food supply, keeping his movements easy and methodical. Removing one of the corn cakes, he extended it to the warrior with a respectful nod.

The man considered the food with suspicion before accepting it. He chewed deliberately and swallowed, his unreadable gaze flicking between Jakob and Specht.

Turning to Specht, Jakob smiled, fighting to keep his manner matter of fact. "It isn't likely he's traveling by himself," he murmured in German. "We have to get away from here before anyone else shows up."

Specht swallowed, then smiled tightly, lips trembling as he tipped his chin toward the west. "I'll tell him we need firewood. You go that way. I'll wait a couple minutes so he doesn't get suspicious, then go the other direction."

"Meet me by the creek. We'll have to follow it to the river, and in the dark we shouldn't attract notice from the village."

Again Specht nodded. He turned to the warrior and spoke haltingly in the Seneca tongue, gesturing with his hands toward the fire and their small collection of sticks, then to Jakob and the woods. The warrior appeared to understand him and relaxed, grunting assent.

While Specht laid pieces of the rotted branch onto the fire with deliberate movements, Jakob stood and stretched. He directed a quick glance into the cave, where the leaping flames illuminated the rock walls. And his musket. And the pouch of carefully hoarded ammunition.

He could think of no pretext to retrieve them or his food pouch while the warrior sat at the fire. If they were to escape, they would have to leave behind all their provisions.

He nodded at the warrior before pushing through the surrounding underbrush in a confident manner, at each moment fearing a gunshot or the strike of a tomahawk. He took his time, making a show of searching around him as though he sought fuel for the fire. With every movement he felt the warrior's gaze boring into his back.

After a dozen steps he passed around a dense copse and glanced back, grateful that the trees and undergrowth screened him from sight of the fire and that there was no sign of the warrior. It was fully dark now, and moving as rapidly as possible, he felt his way along the slope of the hill around its northern side, and then back east, drawn by the bubble and hiss of flowing water. He stumbled repeatedly on roots, almost falling as he fought through tangles of vines and thorny branches, his eyes stinging from trickling sweat.

With every step the creek's rush became more distinct, then very close, the ground beneath his feet growing spongy and slick. He staggered into a tree, banging his head hard against the seamed bark, then gingerly felt his way around the thick trunk. It leaned out over a marsh.

Faint starlight glimmered on the swirling surface of the creek just beyond it. On the opposite shore, well back from the marshes on the far side, he discerned the dim bulk of clustered longhouses surrounding a blazing fire where black figures danced to the muted throb of drums.

There was no sign that anyone noted his presence. "*Bitte*, let Hans come through and both of us get from here safe!" he whispered.

Pressing into the rank growth along the bank, he settled down to wait anxiously for Specht.

◆┈┈◆

JAKOB ROUSED with a start and glanced fearfully around. The village across the creek lay silent and still beneath the silvery light of a waxing crescent moon. All he could hear was the sigh of wind and water.

Exhaustion, hunger, and panic fogged his mind. He crept far enough away from the tree's black bulk to study the constellations that revolved on their course high above him in the black, star-studded heavens.

It had to be past midnight. He thought he could not have dozed off for more than a few minutes, but the sky told a different story. At least five hours must have passed since he found concealment along the creek's bank.

Dread settled heavily over him with the cold dew and set his limbs shaking. Could Specht have somehow gotten turned around in the darkness and lost his bearings? Had he fallen and gotten hurt? Had the warrior's companions arrived and taken him captive—or worse?

On leaden limbs he crept back along the hill. It took the better part of an hour to stealthily work his way up its slope to a concealed vantage above the cavern.

He flattened to his stomach, fearing discovery with every movement, and stretched slowly forward to look down. Immediately the powerful reek of fresh blood assaulted his senses. He jerked back, a wave of nausea sweeping over him.

Teeth clenched, he edged forward again. Twenty feet below the fire had died to seething coals that cast faint, intermittent flickers of light over the darkly shadowed warrior. He was alone, his own musket and Jakob's at his side. He held a dark object over the fire that appeared to be stretched across a stick bent into a circle.

Jakob's gaze settled on a black, ragged bundle lying off to one side. He couldn't recall seeing it before. Then he realized that it was not black, but drenched in blood.

The breath left him. He pressed his hand hard over his mouth, stomach churning, pulse throbbing in his ears. Careful to make no sound, he slid back from the precipice.

It was all he could do not to cry out. And retch.

✦ · · · ✦

JAKOB STUMBLED out of the brush at the creek's mouth and sank up to his knees in mud amid the reeds that thickly cloaked the Ohio's bank. He drew breath in dry, searing pants, unable to control the shaking of his limbs.

If only he and Specht had run when the warrior first appeared, taking different directions, they might have escaped. But no matter what happened, he should never have left his friend behind.

He threw back his head and sought the heavens in anguish. *Ach,* Gott, *why? We were so close to escaping! And now what will happen to Hans's little children?*

He was back at his desolated plantation again, emptied and starkly alone, smoke clogging his throat, the stench of blood and death nauseating. So much blood. So much death.

He wiped tears from his eyes with the back of his hand and stared bleakly across the river's racing current to the shore on the far side. The river was too deep and swift to wade. He was a poor swimmer, and even if he could stay afloat as exhausted as he was, he would be borne far downstream before he could reach the opposite bank. If he was not discovered as he floated past Buckaloons and the lower towns.

He froze for a moment. That warrior might have been traveling by canoe, and knowing of the cave, had sought it out, only to come upon Jakob and Specht by accident.

Jakob followed the tributary's course the short distance south to the river, slogging through the overgrown brake as he desperately scanned his vicinity by the dim light of the moon's slender sickle, now high above the eastern trees. His ragged clothing, dirty when he began, was soon thickly mud caked, moccasins and leggings soaked through.

He had almost given up hope when he finally bumped into the prow of an elm-bark canoe concealed amid the chest-high rushes. He gripped it with one hand and waded alongside, sliding his other hand along the hull's interior. Inside lay a pair of oars, nothing else.

Cautiously he pushed the canoe ahead of him to where the water swirled around his waist. He fought to keep it level, while dragging himself over the side. After several failed attempts, he finally managed to sprawl awkwardly into the rocking vessel.

He scrambled to his knees and grabbed one of the oars, using it to push the canoe free of the reeds, while he watched for any movement along the shore. Then he paddled hard, fiercely

184 | Bob Hostetler and J. M. Hochstetler

fighting the river's current as it bore him downstream toward Buxoton's Creek and Buckaloons.

His arms and shoulders burned by the time he guided the craft into the quieter waters of the shadowy far bank and drove it into another cane brake. He tumbled out into the marshy shallows, almost overturning the canoe, and righted himself. Pulling it as far into the reeds as possible, he made sure it was well concealed before he fought through the tangled growth and clambered onto the grassy bank.

He crawled to a dense stand of undergrowth just inside the forest's verge. There he burrowed into a drift of sodden leaves and gnarled vines, pulling them over him, and collapsed, chest and shoulders heaving with harsh sobs.

Chapter Twenty-one

Tuesday, May 16, 1758

J AKOB FELL TO HIS KNEES in the overgrown field that bordered an abandoned Indian village, hunger gnawing at his stomach, his body aching with the unrelenting exertion of the past six days. The misty light of early dawn cast long shadows between the trees, lending an ethereal look to denuded field and forest.

All his careful planning had come to nothing after all, and he had ended up with no weapon or provisions. And alone.

Was God punishing him for his sin of bearing false witness about the ammunition so he could hoard it for his escape? For trusting in his own abilities instead of relying on God to provide all that was needed? If so, then he suffered just discipline.

But Specht! Had his friend been punished for Jakob's sins?

He pushed his fingers through the tangled hair that fell about his face. Loneliness and grief pierced him, robbing him of breath and almost of the will to go on.

He had left the Ohio behind, fleeing through what felt like endless miles across the gently rolling plateau between the river and the tantalizing, mist-shrouded bulk of the Allegheny Ridge, which sprawled from southwest to northeast along the horizon. Not knowing whether he was pursued, he traveled by night whenever moon and stars provided sufficient illumination, afraid to stop for rest until strength utterly failed him.

He gave a wide berth to native towns and fields and occasionally shadowed Indian paths at a cautious distance, seeking concealment whenever other travelers passed by. Often he had been forced to walk miles out of his way to find a ford across a swiftly flowing stream. At other times he deliberately waded down watercourses to conceal signs of his passing from pursuers and his scent from dogs. He had skirted the edge of a great, dismal swamp where vegetation grew so densely that no light filtered to the ground. But always he returned to a path that led south and east, mentally tracing the map Pine Tree had drawn in the dirt.

His passage roused little game, but even if he had possessed a weapon, the ever-present threat of discovery would have kept him from hunting. He staved off starvation with cattail shoots pulled from marshes, along with the sour shoots of sorrel, half-rotted nuts discarded by squirrels, minnows, and crawfish—scooped from a brook, torn apart, and devoured raw—and even handfuls of new grass when nothing else availed. The agonizing cramps, vomiting, and flux that often resulted had caused frustrating delays and weakened him further.

With what little strength remained he searched among the village's decaying wigewas for food or weapons, finding nothing but a discarded stone adz he used to claw at the field's muddy earth, through tangled weeds, vines, clumps of roots. Finally he uncovered what he had hoped to find, though it had not yet bloomed:

the knobby tuber of a yellow-flowered weed the Indians culti-
vated.

He knocked off as much dirt as he could and devoured it.
Nothing had ever tasted so sweet. Half an hour of dogged labor,
while repeatedly scanning the landscape around him, gained a
small store he could carry with him.

No longer able to control the trembling of his limbs, he clumsily gathered the tubers in the hem of his tattered shirt and
crawled to the bank of the shallow stream he had been following,
which ran along the field's eastern edge. He washed off most of
the mud, and then hastily ate another; hoping to gain some
strength from the nutrients in the root. The rest he folded back
into the hem of his shirt and secured the bundle with his ragged
sash.

Cramps were not long in coming, and he found concealment
in a stand of saplings and bushes until they passed. The sun was
high in the sky by then, and the day promised welcome warmth.

More than once on the journey rain had drenched him
through, leaving him shivering with alternating fever and chills.
In six days of agonizing effort he had covered eighty miles, as far
as he could reckon. And though here the creek flowed northeast,
he figured it had to be the western branch of the Susquehanna. If
so, it would take him all the way to Fort Augusta and south to
Harris's Ferry. And from there he would head overland to the
Northkill.

He dropped to his knees and covered his face with his raw,
bleeding hands, rocking back and forth, shoulders heaving. He
felt empty—physically, mentally, emotionally, even spiritually. He

lacked even the strength to pray—unless, he thought, God would accept his mute helplessness as a prayer, a wordless plea.

Gradually his heaving stopped and his rocking slowed. He became aware, slowly, of something—Someone—brooding over him, enclosing him, even. Strengthened, he pushed to his feet and stumbled forward to follow the stream that stretched through the woods before him, beckoning him on.

Hundreds of miles still lay between him and home. Or what remained of it and his family, if anything. And every mile carried him farther from his boys.

◆┄┄┄◆

A GIDDY CERTAINTY settled into Jakob's mind. In the four days he had followed the stream, it had grown deeper and wider as the weary miles passed and more tributaries flowed into it. According to Pine Tree's map, it had to be the Susquehanna, though it stubbornly continued its northeast heading.

The shades of twilight deepened along the aisles of the deep forest, and overhead small birds twittered companionably as they sought their nests. In the past hour the clouds had cleared and the incessant rain of the past days had blown off to the east.

He shivered in his wet clothing. His store of tubers was gone, and he had eaten only handfuls of grass for the past two days, which did nothing to satisfy his raging hunger. He could see his bones sticking out beneath his skin.

He collapsed on the riverbank, knowing he could not walk much farther. His mud-caked moccasins were in shreds, his feet blistered and bleeding. Only rags remained of shirt and leggings.

He would never make it home, not this way. His feet would not carry him another mile. His strength was gone, and he feared starvation would overtake him before any pursuers could.

As he looked around in weary desperation, he noted the thick vines of wild grapes and honeysuckle that twined around tree trunks and bushes, and his breathing quickened.

"If I can build a float . . . "

By now the shadows were steadily deepening beneath the trees. Fearing that both light and strength would soon completely fail, he levered doggedly to his feet, groaning, and shuffled through the undergrowth, searching for fallen branches. Those he deemed strong enough for his purpose, he dragged to the riverbank, then tore free lengths of supple vines and laid them beside the stacked branches.

Night settled over the forest as sight and strength gave out. He sagged into a drift of leaves beneath a bank of underbrush, turned his face toward heaven, and closed his eyes.

❖┄┄┄┄❖

HE AWOKE IN ANOTHER downpour as the first, tentative light of dawn filtered through the rain. Dragging himself upright, he began to lash together the waterlogged branches he had gathered, using his hoard of sodden vines. He set aside one long, slender branch to use for steering.

By midday he had fashioned a raft he thought would be large enough to bear his weight. He hauled it to the riverbank, legs trembling from exhaustion and emptiness, and knelt beside it.

"*Bitte, Gott,* bless this float. Bless me and keep me safe. Ach, *mein Herr,* bring me home for my boys' sake!"

He grabbed the pole, shoved the float ahead of him into the river, wading beside it. When the water reached his thighs, he heaved himself over the side and, using the pole, shoved the fragile craft out into the river's turbulent current.

✧┄┄┄✧

JAKOB POLED HIS MAKESHIFT raft into the smoother water along the shore and drove it into a tangle of half-submerged weeds. He clambered off into the swirling brown eddies and secured the vessel before fighting wearily to the shore.

Night approached. The ceaseless, driving rain had raised the river's level, dramatically increasing its turbulence and drowning bordering marshes and low-lying lands. It had heaved his small craft like so much flotsam on the crest of churning rapids, at times spinning him in dizzying circles until he had been forced to lash himself to the raft with vines. Even so it had been all he could do to keep from being swept away to his death.

The rain had also obscured him from view of the shore, however, allowing him to travel by day with little chance of discovery when he floated past Indian towns. Fearful of impaling his raft on some obstacle in the dark, he found shelter on shore at night until morning allowed him to continue his dangerous journey.

His only nourishment over the past three days had been grass, supplemented by a few cattail shoots. He was so light-headed with hunger, exhaustion, and fever that he could hardly hold himself erect or concentrate on the necessities of each moment. Threatening visions often crowded his mind: bands of brilliantly painted warriors pursuing him along the misty river, herds of deer and elk taunting him for his lack of weapons, his home obscured by smoke and flame as it collapsed in a rain of sparks over his lifeless wife and children.

He climbed the bank on hands and knees, scrabbling for the relative safety of the forest, away from the dangers of the river. Suddenly his hand plunged into a swarming mess in the mud-streaked grass.

He jerked back and saw the disemboweled remains of a dead possum. Hunger drove him to brush away maggots and ants, tear off a handful of rotting flesh, and stuff it into his mouth. Barely chewing, unmindful of the stench, blood, and insects, he gorged himself. When only pelt and bones remained, he crawled away and rolled onto his back, his stomach already protesting its contents.

For four days he had floated on the river, and still it maintained a northeasterly course. Surely if it was the Susquehanna, it would have turned southeast, and then south by now, he reasoned. His hope dwindled daily, and the fear that this was some other river, one that bore him away from the Northkill, sapped his will to endure.

It's enough, Gott. *I cannot go on. I commend my spirit to you.*

He closed his eyes and welcomed the blackness that engulfed him.

❧———❧

A STRANGE, WARM LIGHT suffused his surroundings. He turned his head and forced his eyes open, rubbing them to clear his vision.

"Anna," he whispered.

His wife knelt beside him, young and slender as she had been when he had taken her as his bride, that unforgettable smile wreathing her face and capturing his heart again as it had on that cherished day in their youth. When she gently touched his shoulder he rose effortlessly and stood staring at her in disbelief, his heartbeat thudding loudly in his ears.

He reached to take her into his arms for the assurance that she was flesh and blood, not spirit or dream. Yet his aching arms could not reach her.

Her well-remembered voice soothed away all fear. "Ach, don't be afraid, *Liebe*. You're going the right way. Keep on. Find our boys and bring them home."

He awoke abruptly to pelting rain and tentative daylight. Lifting his head, he wiped the muck from his cheek with the back of one hand, then pushed up onto his knees to look dazedly through the mist that enveloped him.

He saw no one. Yet he was not alone. The Presence again brooded over him.

He stood, surprised that he did so easily. Although he was still weak, something had changed.

That Anna had come to him, he could not doubt. Sent by God to guide him home. And by the Lord's grace, he would not falter again until he reached the Northkill.

He returned to his raft, pushed it into the river, and clambered aboard. He did not look back as he shoved it clear of the tangled weeds and into the river's raging current.

Chapter Twenty-two

Wednesday, May 24, 1758

J AKOB RAISED HIS HEAD from the raft, senses swimming. The rain had ceased overnight, and morning dawned a sun-drenched, cloudless blue.

He had not been surprised when the river's course turned sharply southwest the previous day, angled south, and then southeast. Ever since the vision he had rested in the certainty that it would be so.

Now he blinked and brushed his tangled hair out of his eyes. Was he dreaming again or was the palisade coming into view on the shore to his left real? Did his eyes really see a British flag fluttering above it and soldiers patrolling its walls?

As the river swept his raft closer, his heartbeat quickened. Fort Augusta. He recognized it instantly from the brief glimpses he had caught between the trees as his Indian captors skirted it on the way to Presque Isle. No sight had ever looked lovelier.

He released his grip on the raft and lifted his arm to wave. He tried to shout, but his voice came out as a hoarse croak, only to be snatched away by roaring water and wind. The current twirled the raft toward the opposite shore and swept it downstream but a strange, calm assurance flooded his breast nonetheless.

A short distance below the fort lay a ford, he remembered, though it was flooded now. A man in the uniform of a British officer stood there, holding the reins of a tall bay horse that drank from the rushing stream. Jakob waved again, and saw the officer's head snap up. He shaded his eyes with one hand and looked in Jakob's direction.

"You there—what are you doing?"

"*Hilfe!*" Jakob's cry sounded impossibly weak in his ears.

With a jerk that almost pitched him into the water, the raft collided with the partially submerged trunk of a large tree and stuck fast in its branches. When Jakob's head stopped spinning, he scanned the bank for the man and his horse, but they had disappeared.

He could hold up his head no longer and sagged back onto the raft. After an interval he again became aware of his surroundings and saw a small company of riders waiting at the ford, their mounts mud-splattered. One of them raised a spyglass in Jakob's direction.

At last a rowboat veered into sight, fighting the surging current. It came alongside, and several soldiers tore away the vines that bound Jakob to the raft. They wrestled him roughly into the boat, then fought through the seething water to the riverbank, yards below the company of riders, who quickly joined them.

They laid Jakob, all but senseless, on the muddy shore. Their commander spoke in English with the men around him. The words buzzed in Jakob's ears, and when the officer directed a question at him, he could make no sense of it.

He closed his eyes and tried to form his thoughts into English, but gave up the attempt. "Escape . . . Indians." he managed in German.

The officer consulted again with his companions. A man clothed in buckskin appeared, hardly more than a youth. He squatted beside Jakob.

"I'm Captain Samuel Weiser—Colonel Weiser's son, assigned here to Fort Augusta," he said in German, then indicated the tall officer. "Our commander is Colonel James Burd. What's your name?"

Jakob stared at the man, his thoughts floating away. "Name?" He moistened his cracked lips.

"You escaped from the Indians?"

"*Ya,*" Jakob managed. "My boys . . . held captive."

"Do you know where you were held?"

"Buckaloons . . . on the Ohio."

Weiser's eyebrows rose. He stood and consulted with the officer, then again squatted at Jakob's side.

"You were taken behind French lines?" When Jakob nodded weakly, Weiser asked, "Did you get inside any French forts?"

"*Ya* . . . three." Jakob let his eyes drift shut, surrendering to fever and exhaustion.

<hr>

THROUGH A FEVERISH HAZE Jakob took in the short, slender secretary seated at the camp table in front of him. "Jakob Hochstetler," he responded hoarsely in German, moistening his cracked lips.

"John Hochstattler, a Swiss by nation," muttered the scribe in heavily accented French as he scribbled on the paper in front of him. He dipped his pen in the inkpot and looked up expectantly.

Jakob transferred his blurred gaze from Colonel Burd, who sat beside him, to the swarthy, dark-haired officer about forty years of age who strode back and forth across the marquee, his burly form militarily erect. Colonel Henry Bouquet, second-in-command to Brigadier General John Forbes, was gathering a formidable British force for the coming campaign against Fort Du Quesne at the village of Carlisle, where Colonel Burd's two-hundred-man detachment had arrived with Jakob the previous day.

"Where are you from?" Bouquet snapped.

Jakob started, momentarily at a loss. "Berks County . . . Bern Township."

Tremors and renewed cramps seized him. An orderly at Fort Augusta had provided him with clean, dry clothing and soldiers' rations, but his pleas to be allowed to return home were ignored and he had been forced to accompany Burd's detachment.

Four days of being miserably jarred in a rattling wagon on the way south had been torture for Jakob. A fortnight of drenching rains had turned the ground into knee-deep mud that required herculean efforts for horses and supply wagons to navigate. And when they finally reached Harris's Ferry, the detachment had crossed the Susquehanna and traveled twenty miles west to the small town of Carlisle. Another day farther from the Northkill.

He became aware that Bouquet was again speaking, his German saturated with a French accent. Jakob struggled to filter the question through the Seneca tongue he had heard daily during the months of captivity and his own Pfälzisch dialect before finally realizing he was being asked how many Indians and what tribes had taken him captive.

"Delaware and Shawnee . . . fifteen in the whole."

While the secretary wrote, Bouquet repeated Jakob's reply to Burd in English. The two officers exchanged meaningful glances.

"Which way did you pass before you came into the enemy's country?"

Jakob considered, feeling as though he fought through a fog. "We marched three days . . . before we arrived at the Susquehanna . . . twenty miles from Shamokin, where it can be forded. From there, we kept entirely west all along the west branch. After seventeen days' journey we arrived on the Ohio."

"In what place on the Ohio did you arrive?"

Jakob rubbed his hand over his face. "Where the French Creek empties into the Ohio. There upon the corner . . . a small fort established lately . . . built of logs framed together."

While the young secretary scribbled, Bouquet said sharply, "How many did you observe in the garrison? Did they have artillery?"

"Twenty-five men. No artillery. We passed the Ohio to come by it . . . a place called Venango."

Bouquet's expression reflected satisfaction. "Fort Machault. How did you proceed further?"

Jakob rubbed his burning eyes, struggling to remember, wanting nothing more than to lie down. "Up the French Creek . . . three days traveling on bateaux. At the end of it we came to a fort built the same as the other . . . also with twenty-five men."

When Bouquet translated, Burd exclaimed, "Fort Le Boeuf!" The two men turned eagerly back to Jakob.

He drew a shaky breath and forced himself to go on. "From there, the French Creek . . . then on a road to Presque Isle . . . a day's journey from it distant."

All three men stared at him for a moment, open mouthed, then Bouquet quickly asked, "What became of you after that?"

Jakob stared blankly at him, unable to give voice to that agonizing day his boys had been torn from his arms. Burd motioned to the secretary to refill Jakob's cup.

The rum warmed and steadied him, and he continued haltingly, "After three days travel east southeast, I was brought to Buxotons Creek where it empties in the Ohio. We came to an Indian castle that lies on the corner of it. . . . There I was kept prisoner all that time."

Another conference between the two colonels followed before Bouquet demanded, "Did you ever hear anything about Fort Du Quesne?"

Jakob clenched his hands on the table in front of him, struggling to concentrate. "Ten days before I escaped, five Dutch prisoners were brought up by the Indians from there . . . they told me three hundred men were garrisoned in Fort Du Quesne . . . provisions so scarce the Indians were obliged to bring away the women and children they left there to be fed in their absence."

"Are there any works about, besides the fort you heard of?"

"The same people told me that there was a Dutchman held prisoner for three years in the fort . . . baker by trade . . . who showed them a hill opposite the fort . . . over the Monongahela."

Gritting his teeth, Jakob pressed his hand to his throbbing brow. "He told them that if the English came, they could certainly take the fort with two hundred men because the French had nothing upon it."

Bouquet paced the marquee. "Did they tell you how many cannons the French had there?"

"*Ya.* . . . I heard several but all dismounted."

"Did you learn whether the Indians received orders to march against us?"

Jakob sighed, wishing mightily that the interrogation would be done, that he could finally go home. "Five days before I escaped an old Indian was telling to me . . . showing against all parts of the area . . . where Indians were coming from . . . and then he showed about east southeast of where we were and told that they would attack the English there. I imagined it was meant to be Shamokin."

Bouquet translated, and Burd's eyes widened. "Fort Augusta!"

An animated conversation between the two officers ensued. Jakob gathered that Burd pressed for reinforcements to relieve his garrison at Fort Augusta, and Bouquet appeared to agree.

Bouquet turned back to Jakob. "Did you learn how the French got intelligence of our plan?"

Jakob hesitated for a moment, confused, finally answered slowly, "Six weeks before my departing there came two Delaware Indians who said they came from Shamokin . . . that the commandant was suspicious and took their arms from them . . . and that the British were drawing together about Conestoga or Lancaster, buying up a great deal of cattle. They said you designed to attack the great Fort Du Quesne and were waiting till the grass was grown."

Bouquet grunted, clearly displeased. "How did you escape from there, how long and in what manner did you travel, and where did you arrive?"

"I got the liberty for hunting. One morning very soon I took my gun . . . "

He let the words trail off and stared vacantly into the air. Specht's image rose before him, then the blood-soaked form lying in the shadows at their camp. He lowered his head, eyes closed, swallowing the bile that rose in his throat. The room fell silent.

After a moment he raised his head without opening his eyes. "I found a bark canoe on the river, in which I crossed it. . . . Traveling east for six days from there, I arrived at the source of the Susquehanna's west branch. From there I marched for four days further till I was sure of it. . . . Then I took several blocks, tying them together to make a float. I floated down the river for five days, when I arrived at Shamokin, living all that time upon grass." He paused. "I passed in the whole fifteen days."

He opened his eyes and spread his hands in supplication. "The Indians still hold my boys. One of them is with a chief called Custaloga, but I don't know where the other is. Help me to find them and bring them home!"

Bouquet translated his words without inflection. Although Burd regarded Jakob with sympathy, Bouquet shrugged and answered in an indifferent tone, "There are many such captives. When the enemy is defeated, then we will make what efforts we can to free them."

He turned to Burd and spoke in English in a contemptuous tone that reminded Jakob of the British captain who had tried to force the members of his church to enlist at Fort Northkill a year and a half earlier. Jakob caught the words, "stupid German peasant," along with something about not taking up arms to defend his family.

The colonel gestured toward Jakob in dismissal and moved to the secretary's side. Burd steadied Jakob as he got to his feet, then ushered him to the door.

Before stepping outside, Jakob glanced back. Bouquet bent over the secretary's notes, taking no further notice of him.

Chapter Twenty-three

Wednesday, June 7, 1758

IT WAS MID AFTERNOON when the wagon turned onto the rutted track that curved into a narrow valley and out of Jakob's sight.

He laid his hand on Conrad Weiser's arm. "I'll walk the rest of the way."

Weiser pulled on the reins and studied him with concern. Jakob met his steady gaze, thinking how much the sturdily-built soldier had aged since they had met at Fort Northkill a year-and-a-half earlier. Weiser's bright blue eyes had faded, the furrows on his weathered face deepened., and his shoulders stooped with weariness.

He had confided to Jakob that early in the year he had resigned his commission as a colonel in the Pennsylvania militia. Jakob sensed that the demands of serving as messenger and negotiator with the Indians and soldier for the colony since his youth had taken a harsh toll on the older man's health and strength.

"You're sure you can make it from here?"

"*Ya.* It's not so far now. I thank you for taking so much trouble for me and for my children."

Weiser nodded and tugged the brim of his hat in farewell. "God be with you."

Jakob clambered down from the wagon and squinted up at him, eyes watering in the bright sunlight. "And with you."

Weiser shook the reins and turned the horses. As the rattle of the wagon and the clop of the horse's hooves faded down the road, Jakob turned to gaze down the well-remembered path that wound between wooded hills.

Weak and ill, he had accompanied a detachment returning from Carlisle to Harris's Ferry the day following his interrogation. At Mrs. Harris's insistence, he briefly stayed with her and her husband to regain strength to go on. The urgency to reach home had grown too great, however, and after two days he had ridden in a farmer's wagon to Lebanon, where he stayed with the farmer and his family that night.

The next day he had walked as far as the end of the Shamokin Path at Tulpehocken Creek, taking all day to reach it. Too weary to continue, he had hobbled up the lane of Weisers' homestead at nightfall and had been welcomed and cared for until he was strong enough to bear the final journey home.

Now he stumbled down the beckoning lane and around its bend beneath the trees. He began to fear he would not make it all the way after all, but although his steps faltered, he continued shuffling forward.

All seemed the same here. He could see no signs of change, and the strange impression possessed him that he had been dreaming all along, and that he had finally awakened. Surely he had only been gone a little while, and Anna and the children would be there after all, unharmed, to welcome him home.

It took a quarter of an hour to cover the short distance to the fork where the lane branched to his own plantation on the left and Johannes's on the right. He stopped, powerless to force his feet to take another step.

The branch to the left had grown over. The wagon ruts were hardly visible, eroded over the winter by snow and rain. A profusion of weeds, bushes, and vines had sprung into the opening, partially blocking passage and making it clear that the land beyond lay abandoned. Some distance below where the barn had once stood, he could see that a new lane had been cut through the hedgerow into the lower fields, the ground leveled to allow horses and wagon to pass.

It was bitter confirmation that he had not dreamed, that no one would be there to greet him.

He did not know how long he stood there, overcome by the turmoil of memory and grief before he heard children's voices, playfully calling to one another. As Jakob turned in their direction, to his right, they were answered by a man's voice, one that he knew well.

Letting out a low groan, he moved unsteadily to the bend, where the trees gave way to a clearing. He looked down the greening valley that spread before him and saw Johannes's unmistakable form striding toward the house from the barn. He carried a small girl in his arms, and around him danced two laughing boys, both taller than Jakob remembered.

These, at least, had been spared.

He sank to his knees, trembling too hard to go farther. One of the boys glanced in his direction, then gestured toward him, looking up to say something to his father.

Jakob was too far away to make out the child's words, but Johannes looked his way, then set the little girl down on the ground and started toward him, hesitantly at first, then running, the boys racing after him, while the girl wailed indignantly.

"Daat! Is it you?" Johannes stooped to lift Jakob to his feet, their tears mingling. "Ach, *Gott sei Dank!* You made it home!"

◆┄┄◆

JAKOB HELD FIVE-MONTH-OLD Christian on his lap, his head resting against the back of the rocking chair. Shaking with chills in spite of the day's warmth, he struggled to keep his eyes open.

Katie tucked a blanket around him. "We tried to make him lie down in our bed, but he insisted on sitting out here until you came."

"I still can't believe he made it all the way back." Barbara bent over Jakob, her brow creased with worry. "Daat, you need to lie down now. You're sick and all worn out."

"Nay." Tears streaming down his face, Jakob reached out to touch the heads of Johannes's boys Jacob and John, and Barbara's girls Mattie and Annali, who crowded around his rocking chair. "Let me just sit here and look at you and *die Kinder.* All this time I didn't know if any of you were still alive."

"We did everything we could to find out where you were taken," Johannes said, his voice choked with emotion. "But no one could tell us anything."

Anna slid over on the bench to let Barbara sit. "I still can't believe it. We'd almost given up hope. But we prayed all this time, and now God answered and you're here. And I can't believe it!"

As Anna wiped her tears with her apron, Jakob studied her quizzically.

Katie leaned toward him. "You remember Anna Blanck, Hans and Mattie's oldest? She's been back and forth between us and Barbara and Crist since the . . . after the funeral . . . to help with the children."

Jakob wrestled with a jumble of emotions until he thought he could trust his voice not to tremble or crack. "You're . . . Joseph's girl."

A warm blush rose to Anna's cheeks. Smiling, she jumped to her feet.

"Here, let me take little Christli. Frany and Mary are down for a nap, and this little one is just about asleep."

Jakob relinquished the baby, and she whisked him away upstairs.

Katie stood up. "When did you eat last? Anna and I were just starting supper when you got here, and with everything Barbara brought over we have plenty."

"Ach, what are we thinking?" Barbara exclaimed. "I'll help you get the table ready."

Anna returned downstairs, and while the three young women bustled around the *Küche,* Crist said tentatively, "What of Joseph and Christli?"

It took Jakob a moment to answer. "We were carried away to a French fort at Presque Isle on Lake Erie, where we were separated.

All I know is that one of the boys may be with a chief named Custaloga."

"Where did they take you, Daat?" Johannes asked. "And how did you get away?"

Jakob gave a brief, halting account of his stay at Buckaloons, his escape and journey home, avoiding any mention of Specht and the warrior who had intercepted them.

Barbara stopped cutting a loaf of bread and stared into space, a far-away look in her eyes. "Christli's twelve by now. And Joseph will turn sixteen in a couple of months."

The room fell silent. Finally four-year-old John said timidly, "*Grossdaati?* Where's your beard?"

Jakob rubbed his chin, smiling down at him. "The Indians pulled it out. They think beards look silly."

He winked, prompting the children to cover their mouths with their hands. Their giggles lightened the heavy mood that hung over the room.

In moments Jakob was seated with the others at the table, fragrant, buttered bread and a steaming cup of broth before him. Together they bowed their heads, while Johannes thanked the Lord for the food and for His mercy in bringing Jakob safely home.

As they ate Barbara cocked her head, frowning. "What's that around your neck, Daat? Did you get it from the Indians?"

Jakob put his hand over the small rawhide pouch, then fumbled with the knotted cord and pulled it free. Opening it, he spilled the carved peach pit onto the palm of his hand and held it up in trembling fingers for them all to see.

"That day . . ." He drew in a shaky breath and started again. "The Indians let me and the boys pick peaches from the orchard to take with us to eat. At the first town we came to, they were making all the captives run the gauntlet. I gave the peaches as a gift to their sachem and he spared us."

He looked around at his children and grandchildren, resolutely blinking back the tears that welled into his eyes. "The next morning when we left, I found this and took it with me. Those peaches were all I had left of our home. They saved our lives. I carved this cross so I'd never forget that *Gott* was with us every step of the way. And I pray He'll bring my boys back too."

Chapter Twenty-four

Thursday, June 22, 1758

"Hans, danke for stopping by. It's *guud* to see you. Next time bring Mattie along."

"I'll do that." Blanck smiled at his daughter, Anna, seated on the settle by the fireplace, cuddling Barbara's baby. Returning his attention to Jakob, he said, "Looks like you're getting your strength back."

Katie patted Jakob's shoulder. "He's able to be up more now, but in spite of these warm days, he still feels cold so much of the time. We've made him a bed in the *Stube* close by the stove."

Jakob forced a smile. His fever had lingered for a fortnight, leaving him still frustratingly weak. Although the emotional reunions with extended family and church community had buoyed him, they had also been draining—especially the tearful visits of his brothers-in-law, Crist and Jakob Buerki, and their families, whose fears for Joseph and Christian only sharpened Jakob's own.

This was the first time he had been out of bed for most of the day, and he hoped he would be strong enough by the coming Sunday to attend church services for the first time since his return.

He was hungry for worship. It seemed as though he saw his world, his church, his children and grandchildren—really saw them—for the first time. Every one was immeasurably beautiful and precious, and God's great mercy in bringing him back home overwhelmed him.

He cleared the emotion from his throat. "An Indian longhouse never really gets warm in winter, and I often had to work outside even in the coldest weather." He looked around at the others. "The Indians live a hard life."

"They made ours hard enough," Barbara snapped, arms folded tightly across her bosom. "Don't ask me to feel sorry for them. All of us miss Maam and Jake and Annali every day. And Joseph and Christli. You didn't have an easy time of it either."

Crist laid his arm around her shoulders as she dabbed away tears with her apron.

"They don't all raid for the French," Johannes reminded her gently.

"Even some who've been involved in the war are changing their minds," Blanck added. "*Saner's Pennsylvanische Nachrichten* had a report several weeks ago that some emissaries from a Delaware chief named Teedyuscung showed up at Bethlehem back in April, seeking peace with the English. These people told the Moravian brethren there that even one of their cruelest warriors—Captain Shingas, they called him—wants to stop fighting and restore the Delaware's old friendship with the English."

Jakob started at the sound of the name. "Shingas? He was the worst of the party that took us. I'm sure that was his name. And he was Delaware, judging from his dress."

The others around the table exclaimed in surprise.

Stroking his beard, Crist leaned back in his chair. "Well, if he's looking for peace, then the Indians must be serious about it."

Katie shook her head. "That's all well and good, but as soon as the weather turned warm, the raids started up again as bad as ever. Michel Ditzeler's wife and Nicholas Geiger's wife and two of his children were all killed and scalped right here along the Northkill just weeks ago."

"What did any of us expect when they took the garrison away from Fort Northkill last summer?" Crist asked. "The county and the town of Reading both sent petitions to Governor Denny asking for more soldiers. The assembly finally did send some, but so far they haven't done much good."

Jakob stared down at his clasped hands. "I was afraid I'd get here only to find all of you gone. Or killed."

"Most of our church families decided to stay unless it got too dangerous." Katie got up and went to look anxiously out the window at the older children playing in the yard. "Nobody wants to abandon their homes and all they've worked for. But after these last attacks, more have given up and moved away down toward Morgantown."

Barbara covered Jakob's hand with hers. "We decided to stay because we kept hoping you and the boys would come back, Daat. If we left, how would you find us? Now that you're here, well, maybe the boys will get away too."

"That's not likely to be possible for young boys. After what I went through, I don't see how they'd keep from getting captured again or find their way home even if they survived in the wilderness. If we don't find a way to get them back . . . " Jakob let the words trail off.

Blanck pushed away from the table and stood, followed by the others. He went over to Anna. "The sun's halfway down the sky, and I need to get on the road home."

Anna handed the fussing baby to Barbara and embraced him. "Maam will be wondering where you are."

They all went outside into the bright sunshine, continuing their conversation, while the children played beneath the trees under the watchful eye of Johannes and Katie's eight-year-old Jacob. Blanck made his farewells, mounted his horse, and rode away down the lane.

Jakob stood silent, staring after his friend until he disappeared from sight behind the trees. Anna went to supervise the children's game, and Katie and Barbara headed back into the house to begin dinner. Crist followed Johannes to the pasture to drive the cows up for milking, with young Jacob running ahead of them.

Until now Jakob had spent no more than a few minutes outside. And although he nodded and responded to the others as they drifted away, he remained distracted.

The shadows pooling beneath the trees at the lane's end beckoned him powerfully, drawing him down it to stand in the cool greenness at the edge of the narrow, rutted dirt road. Sweat beaded on his forehead, clammy in spite of the lowering sun's warmth.

Heart pounding, he fixed his gaze on the densely woven hedgerow that choked the opposite bank of the road. In only the fortnight since his return, it had already grown so thick that he could not tell with certainty where he had once kept the entrance to his plantation neatly cleared.

As though compelled by a power outside himself, he strode to where he thought the opening had been and began to tear at the overgrowth, ignoring the burning sting of nettles and thorns that drew blood on his hands and forearms. At last he forced his way through, brambles tearing at shirt and breeches and stockings, and stumbled forward into the long, untrodden grass of the field on the other side.

He could see no sign of barn or other buildings. Only the misty green line of the orchard that curved along the slope of the hill rising at a distance before him gave any indication of where his home had once stood.

A faint trace of the wagon path remained. He followed it up the gradual rise until he saw the stone walls where the barn's lower level had been set into the earthen bank. The walls were partially broken down, fire-scorched, covered in a thick growth of vines and thistles, through which he caught glimpses of charred wood, clumps of ashes, a few weather-bleached bones.

A guttural sob escaped his lips. He turned his gaze quickly from the ruin, and forced his shaking legs to carry him forward, past the smaller scatterings of ashes and debris that marked the various outbuildings, all the way to the fire-blackened, overgrown shell of the cellar, all that remained of what had once been home. Here he came to a halt, unable to go farther.

Vivid, searing memories of that night surged and receded before his eyes: Jake clutched in Jakob's arms, groaning, blood soaking his nightshirt at his thigh where the bullet had struck. The jarring sound of gunshots and of bullets splintering windowpanes. Anna and baby Annali shrieking in terror.

Joseph and Christian standing before him, Joseph holding out the rifle, imploring him to take it. His refusal. Joseph's disbelieving, accusing look.

The hours of horror trapped in the cellar's stifling heat and choking smoke as the house went up in flames and rafters and walls came crashing down onto the planks over their heads. Their escape moments before the blazing ruins caved into the cellar, sending thick coils of black smoke and incandescent sparks into the brightening sky. The chilling war cry as the Indian warriors raced toward them from the orchard.

Jakob dropped to his knees and buried his face in his hands, weeping. "Why? Ach, *Gott,* why did you let this happen? Why did you take them from me and let me live?"

Grief crashed over him in waves, ebbing and flowing, a merciless sea. When he wiped the tears from his eyes, his blurred gaze fell on the small wooden markers of two graves a few steps away. Where Anna's garden had once been.

He pushed to his feet, stumbled to them, and sank to his knees again. Someone had recently plucked the weeds from the sunken, grass-covered earth. A handful of wilted wildflowers lay on each grave.

On the nearest was painted in small letters: *Anna Hochstetler and daughter Anna.* On the other: *Jacob Hochstetler.*

Again he broke down in wrenching sobs. Rocking back and forth, he whispered, "Forgive me . . . forgive me."

Gradually he became aware that arms encircled his shoulders and a soft cheek pressed against his. He straightened and looked up to meet Anna Blanck's sorrowful gaze.

"I'm so sorry."

He cleared his throat and glanced behind her. They were alone and fear tightened his chest.

"The children?"

She helped him to stand. "Hertzlers came by to visit and took them inside. I thought I knew where you'd gone, and I came to find you."

He leaned heavily on her arm. "They'll come home . . . Joseph and Christli."

She nodded, certainty in her green eyes. "*Ya.* They will. God is faithful."

⊹——⊹

A PALPABLE HEAVINESS had hung over the dinner table that evening, nor had it lifted afterward when they gathered with Katie's parents in the *Stube.* Though no one had asked about the night of the attack since his return, Jakob felt the weight of their unspoken questions.

For some time they sat in silence in the candlelit room, then Johannes asked hesitantly if he felt able to tell them about the attack. In halting words, Jakob recounted that fearful ordeal.

"Joseph said if we just fire, they'll know we have guns and go away. Your Maam and the boys all agreed, but . . . it was dark." He looked from one to another in appeal. "When we looked out, we could only see shadows moving, and I kept thinking if we shoot and kill even by accident, then we disobey *Gott's* commandment. So I told them, nay, we can't—" His voice broke. "I was responsible to keep them safe . . . and I didn't."

The women clutched the littlest ones against their bosoms and dabbed away tears, while the older children stared anxiously up at him from their seats on the floor, wide-eyed. The men exchanged sober glances.

"You did what Jesus commanded, Daat." Johannes looked around at his family, shoulders bowed. "It seems to me like you did everything you could to keep them safe. I pray I can be as faithful."

Nodding, his expression strained, Crist put his arm around Barbara's shoulders.

"Then why did *Gott* let this happen?" Jakob cried. "Why did He take my Anna and my little ones from me?"

Bishop Hertzler leaned forward, his hands clasping his knees. "Going through persecution in the old country, we learned that our obedience doesn't necessarily mean that things will turn out good for us in this world according to the way we think. Jesus was *Gott* Himself, but evil men crucified Him. He allowed it for our sake."

"And that was good. But what good did this do? It didn't save anybody!"

"Maybe it did. Maybe it saved many."

Anna's murmured words drew Jakob's glance and evoked a chilling memory. "I asked my Indian guard what the war party would have done if we'd fired at them. He signed that . . . we all would have died."

For a long moment they all sat silent. At length Bishop Hertzler said, "We're only human. We can't understand *Gott's* mind and the working out of His purposes. They're bigger than ours. *Gott* sees more than we do, knows what we can't grasp with our little minds. Does He mean for us to suffer? *Nay!* Evil is man's doing! But *Gott* works out His will for us even if we have to endure the worst man can do. It may take some time for His perfect plan to come to pass, but nothing can stop it."

Jakob bowed his head. "A man named . . . Hans Specht . . . and his little son and daughter were taken that day too. Their party joined ours before we got to the Susquehanna." His voice trembled as he briefly related how Specht's children had also been taken away and how his friend had died during their escape. "I made up my mind that I'd find Hans's relations and let them know what happened."

"We heard about him and his children," Barbara broke in, "and we tried to find family members that were left. But we never were able to learn anything about them. Either he didn't have any other relations or they all moved away after the attack."

Jakob's shoulders slumped. "Then there's nobody left to look for them except me." Looking around at the others, he straightened. "If *Gott* will let me find Joseph and Christli, maybe He'll let me find them, too, and take care of them. Maybe that's part of His plan. They were all Hans had left in the world, and I can't just abandon them."

Chapter Twenty-five

CORN MOON
Sunday, August 20, 1758

B RINGS DAWN WATCHED a large party of horsemen followed by others on foot enter Sauconk to a din of enraged shouts, pulsing drums, and the echoing reports of rifles fired into the air. At the procession's head rode Shingas, Tamaque, and other headmen of the Lenape and Shawnee.

Brings Dawn was startled to see a man who appeared to be English riding freely in their midst. But it was the French officer pressing close behind him, clad in an ornate blue uniform and with face and eyes hard as steel, who drew his greatest interest.

The memory of his first life and his white name, Joseph, had receded from Brings Dawn's consciousness until he rarely thought of them. But now broken memories tumbled through his mind: the savage warble of war whoops, fearfully painted warriors racing out of a red dawn, their muscular forms illumined by long spars of golden light, his terrified family scrambling for escape, the horrifying carnage that followed.

The French scouts who commanded the warriors.

Beneath the blinding afternoon sun, the motionless air hung heavy over the parched ground, wilting vegetation, animals, and people alike. But it was not the heat that made Brings Dawn feel lightheaded, sick to his stomach.

He wore only a breechcloth, as did all the men and youths pressing around him, and the dust raised by the milling crowd coated his sweat-slicked skin. He clenched his jaw, grit grinding in his teeth.

Turning to his companions, he waved his arm to indicate the raucous crowd. "Why does Brother Onas send an Englishman to us when we are at war with them?" he demanded, using the Lenape name for the governor of Pennsylvania. "You hear how this man Post is received. Would it not be better if one of our own people or our northern brothers or uncles was sent to talk of peace?"

Red Squirrel raised his voice to be heard over the tumult. "Brother Onas must trust him. According to the message he sent ahead of him, his name is Post and he is one of the people called Moravian."

Brings Dawn crossed his arms, frowning. "If he comes from Brother Onas, why is this French officer with his party?"

Smoke in Sky, a tall youth about Brings Dawn's age, shrugged. "Perhaps he is jealous that Post will turn our hearts against the French."

Brings Dawn searched for Menetopalis over the heads of the crowd and found him leaning on his walking stick outside the council house door. With him were the other headmen of the town, and like them he regarded Post with cold disapproval.

From behind Red Squirrel, Wildcat craned his head toward Brings Dawn. "It is said these Moravians seek to persuade our people to worship the white man's God."

"Some of our northern brothers among the Wolf division do so, including Teedyuscung himself," Smoke in Sky said. "Even some of our own Turkey division approve of this God."

Brings Dawn kept his expression neutral. Since returning from his quest several moons earlier, he had not told the whole story of his vision of the great buck. His shame had only grown since then and, with the delay, the difficulty of confession.

"I don't think he has come to speak of his God," he said hastily. "My father says Teedyuscung and the headmen of our Shawnee and Seneca uncles in the Wyoming Valley have made a treaty to forsake the French and live in friendship with the English. They wish us to do so as well."

Smoke in Sky's eyes narrowed. "The message sent by this man Post said he has been counseling with our headmen at Kuskuskies for some days to that end."

Brings Dawn returned his attention to the slender Moravian. His weathered face was clean shaven, but his unbound, shoulder-length grey hair; plain white shirt; and black coat and breeches reminded Brings Dawn of the people he had lived among in his first life. His heart constricted, and he shook the unsettling memories from his thoughts.

Post, the man at the center of the crowd's attention, dismounted. He was immediately surrounded by a large number of Sauconk's warriors, the captains Killbuck and White Eyes in the forefront. Their faces distorted with rage, the men pressed their naked chests against Post, jostling him roughly, while they waved their unsheathed knives and screamed into his face, daring him to strike them.

Brings Dawn could not bear to watch, nor could he turn away his sickened gaze. The noise from the gathered villagers had by now grown deafening, the majority demanding that the Moravian be put to death, with only a few voices raised in protest.

Although Post's face was ashen, he did not shrink from those who pressed in on him, nor did he drop his gaze. He shouldered past the warriors in the wake of Tamaque and Shingas, who tried with little success to quiet the crowd and clear a path to the council house yard. The hard-eyed French officer pressed closely on their heels, head high, face fixed in a sneer.

Just when Brings Dawn felt certain the warriors would carry out their threatened violence, several Shawnee men who had recently arrived in the town shoved their way through to Post's side and surrounded him like a wall. They clasped his hand and greeted him with expressions of joy and welcome. Then, turning to Killbuck, White Eyes, and the others, they announced loudly that Post was a good man deserving of respect and that he brought a message of great importance from Brother Onas to which they would be wise to listen.

At that, Shingas had rounded on the two captains and told them sternly that their behavior was unworthy of warriors and leaders of the people. His rebuke had an immediate effect. Killbuck's and White Eyes' demeanor changed, the crowd quieted, and the French officer's face fell.

Brings Dawn watched Shingas, his emotions in turmoil. The warrior was often absent from Sauconk, but whenever he stayed there Brings Dawn observed him warily, keeping his distance.

Grudgingly he conceded that the townspeople were right to praise Shingas's character. He displayed the mild, unassuming demeanor of all the sachems, going out of his way to be kind and helpful and to provide for everyone in need. Nor did he favor those born of the Lenape over those like Brings Dawn who had been born among the whites.

But while Shingas seemed to be a better man in peaceful circumstances, Brings Dawn could not help thinking that his white father had been the same in war and in peace. It was the violent passions of war that caused a man to act in ways ordinarily foreign to his nature, he concluded. The warrior had not had the teachings of Brings Dawn's first life to temper his actions—teachings Brings Dawn had once denied, but whose truth he was increasingly coming to feel deep in his heart.

The captains were now meekly clearing a way for Post through the throng. They conducted him unmolested to a large cabin near the council house reserved for lodging guests, and all the leaders disappeared inside.

Mehíttuk came to join them as Smoke in Sky said, "It is true the French drove the English back from Fort Carillon with many casualties, but only a moon ago the great fortress at Louisbourg fell to the English." Using the Lenape name for the French governor of Canada, he continued, "It was from that place that Father Onontio brought supplies down the river they call the Saint Lawrence for those allied with him, If the English now control those waters—"

"Then who will stop them?" Mehíttuk finished Smoke in Sky's question. "Tamaque and Shingas and other leaders of our people hesitate to make peace because the British General Forbes has brought a great army into our country. Brother Onas says it is only to attack Du Quesne at the Forks of the Ohio, but they fear that the English mean to drive out the French only to take our lands for themselves."

Red Squirrel nodded, his expression grim. "We can deal with the French, for they live among us only to trade. But the English settlers build houses, bring in their cattle, kill or drive away the animals Manitou gave us for food, and steal our lands."

Mehíttuk's face darkened. "Manitou gave the land west of the Alleghenies to us forever. We must make both the French and the English understand that we will never allow any white men to settle here."

<hr />

THE THRONG BEGAN to disperse. As soon as the Moravian's message had arrived that morning with greetings and a request for escort into the town, the women had begun preparing the afternoon meal, and they hastened off to bring the food for their guest and the town's headmen. Brings Dawn's friends also drifted away.

Brings Dawn hesitated, wishing that he could join the meeting with Post. Unbidden memories of his first family aroused a longing to ask the Moravian whether he knew anything of them.

As he looked around for Menetopalis, his gaze fell on Many Leaves in a circle of young women gathered near the Big House. She glanced toward him at the same moment, and then quickly away, and all other thoughts fled from his mind.

She left her companions and moved down the path toward her family's dwelling. Her home was not far from Brings Dawn's, and after a brief wait, he casually strode along the path to his own cabin. After a short distance, he turned onto a cross path that intersected the one she had taken. He quickly found her standing beneath the boughs of a wild plum tree, gazing up into it as though arrested by the drowsy coo of a dove hidden in its foliage. At his approach, she glanced toward him.

Brings Dawn came to a halt before her, taking in her slender figure and coppery skin with admiration. He had at first been shocked when the women put off their shirts with the arrival of hot weather, only wearing loose, knee-length doeskin or trade-cloth skirts around their loins. At first he had blushed and averted his eyes from their bare bosoms, while sneaking quick, sidelong looks. But he had gradually grown used to this custom, and it now seemed natural and unremarkable to him.

Sometime during this Corn Moon he turned sixteen, he knew. He had grown taller and more muscular over the past moons and was by now an experienced tracker and hunter. He also excelled at games and was particularly skilled at *pahsahëman,* the rough-and-tumble ballgame the men played against the women from the earliest sign of spring until the beginning of the Strawberry Moon. The fastest and canniest player among the youths, he had enjoyed a fierce rivalry with Many Leaves, the women's champion, that he was sorry to see end with summer's arrival. But although was the first time he had found occasion to speak to her alone since then, he searched vainly for something to say, his mind gone blank.

She also at first seemed disinclined to speak, lowering her gaze to the ground at his feet. "There is much talk of making peace with the English. Do you think Tamaque and Shingas will indeed abandon the French and seek to end this war?"

Her question put him at ease, and he considered it thoughtfully. Remembering what Mehíttuk had said, he answered, "Now that Louisbourg has fallen, the English control the great river called Saint Lawrence. If the French cannot receive men and supplies from across the water, can they win this war—or supply our warriors that we may continue the fight?"

She looked up. "You speak wisely, Brings Dawn. Our people have gained nothing from this war. Indeed we have lost not only many warriors, but also elders, women, and children killed in reprisals by the British. And even some warriors who returned, like your father, suffer—" She broke off and looked away.

His mouth went dry and he stared at her, filled with a sickening fear. "No one speaks of his injuries to me. Was he . . . wounded in a raid against the Whites?"

She nodded warily, compassion in her eyes. "He was a captain, and his horse was shot and fell on him. It happened in the Strawberry Moon before you came to us."

"Where?"

"Far east of here. South of a river called Juniata at a place the Whites call Sherman's."

"What of their son whose place I received—Straight Arrow?"

Over their heads the dove cooed again. When they looked up, it took wing and fluttered away.

She lowered her gaze to meet his. "He was only a little older than you, too young to be a warrior. He died of the white man's pox before they carried your father back from the raid. Your mother and sisters were also stricken, but they lived."

Anger and grief washed over Brings Dawn—for his own suffering, for that of Menetopalis and Wulachen and the children. And all the others. Too many to count.

"Nothing good comes of war!" he burst out. "My white father would not let me and my brothers take up our guns against the warriors who attacked us, and he was right! No man should fight another." He swung away.

She stepped closer and gently drew him around to face her. "Was your white family called Moravian like this man Post?"

He shook his head. "They were called Amish. They also do not fight."

Her face softened. "Ah. You have come from people of good heart, and you are a man of good heart! But I am glad you are Lenape now. I am glad you are one of us."

Without thinking he reached for her, and she stepped into his embrace. For some moments they stood motionless, wrapped in each other's arms. Although painful emotions wracked him, he longed to hold her so forever.

"I am glad too," he said, voice choked.

She pressed her face against his shoulder. "I pray our sachems and captains sign this treaty with the British. Perhaps then we will all finally live together in peace."

Chapter Twenty-six

Monday, August 21, 1758

FRAGRANT TOBACCO SMOKE drifted lazily upward to form a dense blue-grey cloud beneath the council house roof. The humid air hung heavy and motionless.

A hush had reigned for some time, broken only by an occasional rustle of movement from the younger children at the rear with their mothers, where Wulachen sat with Brings Dawn's younger brother and sisters. His attention was momentarily distracted by Contrary Wind, who pressed through the crowd to squeeze in between him and Red Squirrel. Brings Dawn grinned but put a warning finger to his lips.

The entire town had gathered at the fire in front of the Moravian's cabin the previous night to dance until the waning moon reached its zenith in the heavens' star-studded bowl. Brings Dawn had obeyed Wulachen's gentle admonition not to approach Post, but even watching from a distance he was impressed by the missionary's kindness and his ease with the people, whose company he seemed genuinely to enjoy.

Brings Dawn suppressed a yawn and laid down his pipe. Rolling his shoulders, he turned his head back and forth, finally let his gaze settle on the far side of the council house, where Many Leaves sat with the younger women. When their eyes met her cheeks reddened, and she dropped her gaze.

The previous day's encounter still filled him with wonder and tentative hope. Not only had she filled in gaps in his knowledge about his parents, but she asked about his white life. She listened with compassion and, unlike Wulachen and Menetopalis, seemed to accept that his past would always be a part of who he was.

He returned his gaze to the building's center, where Menetopalis was seated in a large half-circle composed of the sachems, captains, and other headmen of the town, the sober Moravian amid them. The French officer sat with them, too, though he seemed chastened and reserved.

Tamaque rose and extended his arm to Post. "Brother, we are glad you have come to this fire to speak the good word from Brother Onas that you shared with us at Kuskuskies. As we told you then, we alone cannot make peace, for all the Indian peoples are united as one from the sunrise to the sunset. The peace made with Teedyuscung was for the Delaware on the Susquehanna only and did not include the Indians on the Ohio since they had no deputies at that conference.

"But we can assure you, brother, that all the Indians for a very great way, even beyond the Lakes, desire to establish peace with the English. As we are nearest of kin, they told us that if we see the English incline to peace, we are to hold it fast. Accordingly, this morning we sent runners to the Forks to announce your coming to the nations gathered before Fort Du Quesne and to invite them to this council fire. And now we ask you to read to this council all the messages you have brought from Brother Onas."

Tamaque sat down, and the slender Moravian rose to face the council. His manner was humble and conveyed good will, but his voice held quiet authority. He thanked Tamaque and greeted everyone in the assembly before beginning to read the letters sent by the governor of Pennsylvania.

"Brethren, we have for a long time desired to see and hear from you. You know the road was quite stopped, and we did not know how to come through. We have sent many messengers to you, but we did not hear of you. Now we are very glad we have found an opening to come and see you and to speak with you and to hear your true mind and resolution. We salute you very heartily."

Post laid a string of wampum on the low table before him as a record of the message. He continued, saying that he wished to remove every bad thing that the evil spirit had brought between the governor and the Lenape and to join both parties in the love and friendship their grandfathers had once shared, and presented another belt of wampum.

Brings Dawn straightened, hope and excitement growing in his breast. He cast a covert glance at Many Leaves, but her attention appeared to be fully engaged on Post.

Post related each of the messages from Brother Onas in turn, speaking slowly and distinctly and offering a belt of the richly colored beads at the conclusion of each one. He described the conference with the Susquehanna Indian nations at Easton the previous year. The war hatchet had been buried and belts of peace exchanged, he told the council. Then the representatives had prayed to God to take the bones of the dead and hide them where they would never be found again and to remove the remembrance of them from both sides.

Post called on the Allegheny nations to also lay hold of the belt of peace and to keep open the road to the council fire of the English. Acknowledging that the king of England had sent a great number of warriors into their country, he assured the council that their intent was only to fight the French and revenge the blood they had shed. Offering the large peace belt, he said he would take their whole nation by the hand and lead them and as many of their friends as would follow a distance from the French for their own safety so that their legs would not be stained with blood and that they and their women and children might live without fear or danger.

Brings Dawn noted that the French captain listened silently, his clenched jaw making plain his discomfort and displeasure with the Moravian's words—the more so as the crowd responded with approval. Post appeared to take no notice of the officer, however, addressing his speech only to the council and townspeople and assuring them that Brother Onas would readily hear their grievances and act justly toward them.

Appearing to choose his words carefully, Post concluded, "You know if anybody loves a little child or somebody takes it from him, he cannot forget it. He will think on his child by day and night. Since our flesh and blood is in captivity in the Indian towns, we desire you will rejoice the country's heart and bring them to me. I shall stretch out my arms to receive you kindly."

He laid down the last string of wampum as an uneasy stir rippled across the council house. As he bowed and turned, his glance alighted briefly on Brings Dawn.

He was uncomfortably aware of his friends' surreptitious glances at him, Wildcat, and the other white youths seated among them, and of Wulachen and Many Leaves behind him. Menetopalis's face had gone pale and hard as stone. Contrary Wind seemed to be the only one oblivious to the tension on every face around him.

Tamaque rose with great dignity and spoke graciously to the Moravian, thanking him for bringing the message of peace from Brother Onas and telling him that they would lay it before all the nations now gathered at the Forks of the Ohio. Shingas echoed his words, and a few headmen murmured their agreement.

As soon as Shingas finished speaking, Menetopalis levered clumsily to his feet with his walking stick. He drew himself to his full height and gave Post a curt nod.

"The messages you bring are indeed good, and we receive them with pleasure. I do not know why we went to war with the English. I did not begin it, therefore I have little to say." Turning to the Shawnee headmen seated among the rest, he continued stiffly, "You brought the hatchet to us, brothers, and persuaded us to strike our brothers the English. You may consider wherefore you have done this."

The Shawnee men were clearly taken aback. They acknowledged that they had received the war hatchet from the French and were sorry for it, and they swore to set Brother Onas's messages before their people.

Appearing satisfied at this, Menetopalis returned his attention to Post, a frown darkening his brow. "It seems to me very odd and unreasonable that you should demand prisoners before there is an established peace. Such a demand makes you appear as though you lacked brains." He looked from Shingas to Tamaque. "Let us hold all these words carefully in our hearts so we may determine how to make a peace with our English brothers that is indeed just and good—for the Indian as well as for the white man."

✦┄┄┄┄✦

BRINGS DAWN SAT OUTSIDE the circle of firelight, watching Tamaque and Shingas from the shadows as they and the other adults silently smoked their pipes. The night was cloudy, and the loud chirp of crickets, croak of frogs, and beat of drums throbbed on the humid air, pierced intermittently by the occasional hoot of an owl and eerie cry of a loon.

More than a dozen men had arrived from Kuskuskies shortly before the sun's setting an hour earlier, swelling the number of warriors in the town to well more than a hundred. They and the majority of the people were dancing before Post's cabin at the town's center.

Only the families with an adopted white family member, the two headmen, and Bird's Nest had gathered at Wulachen's fire, with the younger children shooed away to play or watch the dancers. Anxiety, even anger, etched the faces of many parents, and like Brings Dawn, their eyes were fixed on Tamaque and Shingas.

Brings Dawn had insisted on being allowed to stay. He was glad Wildcat had come and also Evening Rain, the oldest of the adopted maidens. They sat on either side of him, and he did not have to look at either one to know that they shared the emotions that caused his stomach to churn.

"I will never go back," Wildcat muttered, loud enough for only Brings Dawn and Evening Rain to hear. "The man who called himself my father was always drunk. He beat me and my brothers and sister and even our mother without mercy. I was glad when our people took me! If the English try to force me to go back, I will run far away to the Twightwee."

Evening Rain bowed her head, her sleek brown hair, unbound from its usual braid, curtaining her face. "I do not wish to go back either," she whispered, despair in her voice. "Everyone in my white family was killed. There is nothing for me to return to, and my mother and father are good to me."

Before Brings Dawn could speak, Tamaque removed his pipe from his mouth. "Brother Onas's messages are good to hear. Our people have suffered greatly from this war. It seems that only the French have benefited, and they now run before the English armies."

Wulachen's glance flickered across Brings Dawn before she said to Menetopalis, "You spoke well before the council, my husband! If the English will indeed hear our grievances and do justice as they say, then how can they snatch from us the children who take the place of those we lost?"

"I also have white children who are dear to me." Tamaque reminded her.

Shingas nodded. "As do I. They are my flesh and blood as much as those born to me, and I'd not give them up any more than you'd give up your son."

"It's well for us to make peace with the English," Menetopalis said, "but we must remember that no treaty has yet been concluded. We should only take up Brother Onas's peace belt and mark our names on his paper if every one of the terms is acceptable to all our people."

Bird's Nest regarded him with a shrewd smile. "There is always more than one path, my son."

"The British General Forbes is gathering a great army to attack Du Quesne—or so they tell us." Tamaque shrugged. "It remains to be seen whether this is true or whether they mean to wrest the Ohio lands from us. In either case Brother Onas would have us remove far from this place so that no harm may come to our women and children. This is wise counsel should it be that we cannot accept the peace belt—"

"Or adhere to all the treaty's terms." Bird's Nest's eyes narrowed.

Shingas looked from one to the other, his dark eyes glittering. "During the Bee Moon Tamaque and I visited the party who went before us to the Muskingum. We admired the cabins they built and the fields they cleared and planted. Many of our brothers and uncles are building towns along that river near the great town of Tuscarawas. It is a fertile land, well watered and pleasant . . . and far away from here. Fish and game are abundant, and even many English traders come there bringing all manner of desirable goods."

Evening Rain's mother leaned forward, her face taut in the flickering light and shadow cast by the fire's dying embers. "Our fields are almost worn out, and the harvest will be small this year. I will join our people on the Muskingum."

Wulachen seemed relieved. She and Menetopalis exchanged glances before she answered, "We also will go."

The decision was quickly made to leave as soon as the upcoming Green Corn Festival ended. A small party would stay behind to harvest the last of the crops before joining them, and those who went ahead would build cabins for the latecomers.

LATER THAT EVENING, with his little sisters and brother asleep in the cabin, Brings Dawn sat in the shadows of the cabin's porch, listening to Wulachen's and Menetopalis's low voices as they planned their move to the Muskingum. When they fell silent, he gathered the courage to speak.

"Brother Onas's messenger, this man Post, seems a good and thoughtful man. Is it possible that one might speak to him?"

Even in the darkness he could feel Wulachen tense, though she said nothing.

Menetopalis answered, "It is the time to talk of ending this war and making peace with the English, my son. Such an important messenger from Brother Onas must counsel only with our kings and sachems until a treaty can be concluded."

Brings Dawn scanned the clouded heavens, his throat painfully tight. A cool breeze stirred the trees, bringing with it the mingled scents of wood smoke and approaching rain, but it brought him no relief.

"You heard his words," Wulachen said, her voice shaking. "Do you wish, then, to return to the English?"

Menetopalis sat silent, a shadow in the darkness, head bowed, shoulders hunched.

They love me, as I love them.

It occurred to Brings Dawn that his parents could not bear to speak of his white life because they feared that doing so would reawaken the desire he had harbored when he first came to them: to leave them.

How would they suffer the pain of another loss? How would he? They and his sisters and younger brother were truly his family now, and he ached at the possibility that he might be separated from them and from the others who had come to hold such a large part of his heart.

He got up and went to squat beside Wulachen, laying his arm across her shoulders.

"Am I not fortunate to have a kind mother such as you, one who cares for me so well—and cooks such tasty food?"

She would not look at him, but he saw the hint of a smile. He glanced at Menetopalis.

"How could I leave such a one, or a wise and good father who teaches me many skills and to be a strong and faithful man among our people? Would I leave my sisters and my little brother without an elder brother to guide them? No, *gáhowees, wetochemend,* when it is time to go to the Muskingum, I will put my foot upon the path with gladness."

Chapter Twenty-seven

Friday, September 1, 1758

IT WAS THE LAST DAY of the Green Corn Festival. Brings
Dawn had feasted on the first roasted harvest of tender, milky
ears until his stomach groaned. Even so, his mouth watered at
the savory aroma wafting from bubbling pots of the green corn
soup the townspeople would soon share.

A company of twenty Shawnee and Mingo men had arrived
the day after Post read his messages to the council and insisted
that he read the letters to them as well. They had seemed pleased
at Brother Onas's words, and that same evening the messenger
returned from Fort Du Quesne to report that eight Indian nations
were gathered outside the fort, eager to hear the Moravian's message. The council, headed by Tamaque and Shingas, decided that
since there were so many, they would conduct Post to the Forks
so both the Indians and the French could hear what the English
had to say.

For the first time Brings Dawn had seen Post's self-posses-
sion fail. He protested that he was sent to speak to the Indians,
not to the French, and that as England was at war with France it
was not proper for a messenger from Brother Onas to go to the

French stronghold. Tamaque and Shingas remained unmoved, however, assuring the Moravian that they would carry him there and back safely. And early the following day, a large party including Tamaque, Shingas, and many other headmen and warriors, had ridden off along the path to the Forks with Post in their midst, his face pale but resolute.

Four sleeps later they had returned to Sauconk to a welcome very much the opposite of the Moravian's first, hostile reception. The captains Killbuck and White Eyes had taken Post by the hand and publicly apologized for their former behavior. And when the council gathered, Tamaque reported that their Shawnee brothers called the Lenape to be strong, saying that they were glad to hear the good news from the English and pledging to honor whatever contracts the Lenape made with them. He added that all the nations had resolved not to fight with the French to defend Du Quesne against the coming English attack.

His words had prompted joyful celebration throughout the town. When Tamaque's party set out to take Post back to Kuskuskies the next morning, they were given a cheerful send-off, with pleas for the Moravian to return and to keep open the road to Brother Onas.

The festival began the next day, giving Brings Dawn scant time to ponder the news or consider how it might affect him. A series of furiously contested games held his attention, including one in which teams of youths and maidens vied to hit a target set on a pole.

He managed to outmaneuver Mehíttuk in the line of the young men so that he opposed Many Leaves in the opposite line.

As usual she proved to be a fierce and skilled contender, and he outscored her only with luck and by one point.

He was troubled, however, that she avoided his gaze during the game and afterward seemed to cling to her friends, mother, and younger sisters. And Mehíttuk always seemed to be in the vicinity as well, his manner implying that she belonged to him.

Was she deliberately avoiding him? Brings Dawn wondered. Had he done something to offend her? Or had he misread her feelings? Was it Mehíttuk she preferred after all, and their tender exchange of affection had meant nothing to her?

Finally, as the festival concluded that evening and everyone dispersed to their homes, he saw her walking alone down the path to her mother's cabin. He ran to catch up, not caring who might see them.

Before he reached her, she swung to face him, her eyes dark and fathomless in the gathering twilight. Slowing, he closed the distance between them and came to a halt.

To his dismay the words he had meant to say eluded him. She waited, hands folded, expression unreadable.

"I . . . I have wanted . . . to ask you . . . " He started over. "A large party is leaving for . . . for the Muskingum tomorrow, and—"

"I have heard this." Half turned away, she looked back down the path as though impatient to leave.

He shifted from one foot to the other. "My family goes with them. Do you . . is your family . . are you going?"

She pressed her lips into a straight line and shook her head. "A message came from my uncle, my mother's brother. He is very ill. His wife died two winters ago, and he has no one to care for him, so my mother must do so. He lives in a town called Cussewago far north on the French River beyond Fort Machault."

"You must go too?"

She studied him, one eyebrow raised. "I must help my mother with my little sisters and my uncle."

Her tone brought heat into his face. "Will you make your home there?"

"I cannot say. Perhaps. Perhaps not."

"Of course. It's only that . . . I shall miss . . ." *you,* he thought. But the words he blurted were: "I shall miss playing *pahsahëman* with you."

Stiffening, she regarded him as though he had a loathsome disease. Without giving him the courtesy of a reply, she tilted her chin, whirled on her heel, and stalked away, not looking back.

THE SUN'S FIRST GOLDEN RAYS had just begun to spill between the trees the next morning when Brings Dawn relieved She Sings and Sunshine of their last armloads of green corn. "Thank you, my sisters! You and our mother are working hard though the sun has hardly awakened yet. You provide us much to eat on the way to our new home."

Both girls beamed as they helped him secure baskets of the unshucked ears behind the bulging pouches filled with blankets, clothing, and household goods that already burdened the pack horse.

He knew that Many Leaves and her family were preparing to travel far to the north. Would they ever meet again? That seemed unlikely, and it pained him to think that now he would never have opportunity to tell her what he had meant to say.

Unexpectedly the image of another maiden took form in his mind, one with green eyes and golden hair. It had been several moons since her face had last come to him, and he was pierced by a sharp sense of guilt.

Their relationship had been broken by circumstances beyond their control. As had his with Many Leaves now. And he did not know whether he betrayed Anna by desiring Many Leaves—or Many Leaves by the love for Anna that his heart refused to relinquish.

His reverie was broken by Wulachen, who crossed the clearing, brow furrowed, to the fire circle where Menetopalis waited, sitting on a log. Bird's Nest followed, leading her horse, equally loaded with her possessions, while Contrary Wind trailed after them, dancing on his toes.

Wulachen clapped her hands. "Hurry! Our party is already gathering on the path." She indicated the line of people and horses moving through the trees to where the Great Path continued its western course after passing through Sauconk.

Contrary Wind bounced up and down on his toes. "It is good of my uncle to send a horse for you from Kuskuskies, my father."

Menetopalis drew the boy into his arms. "It is so, my son." Beneath his smile, however, Brings Dawn sensed his father's concern.

Just then Red Squirrel and his father, Long Mountain, hurried between the trees to them. Long Mountain took in the packed horses with a glance.

"Come, my friend, let us help you to mount. We must hurry if we are to reach the Muskingum within four sleeps."

With Long Mountain's help Menetopalis got to his feet, his jaw set. While Wulachen and Bird's Nest held the mare's bridle and murmured reassurances to her, Menetopalis dragged himself up by the pommel, the powerful muscles of his arms bulging. Brings Dawn stood on the opposite stirrup to pull him forward by the shoulders, while Long Mountain pushed from behind. Red Squirrel carefully maneuvered Menetopalis's crippled leg over the saddle, then placed his foot in the stirrup.

Menetopalis settled in the saddle and gathered the reins, regarding them all with a triumphant smile. "I have not sat upon a horse since the time I fell. It is good!"

Everyone exclaimed with admiration, then Brings Dawn hurried to secure the remaining packs behind Menetopalis's saddle and patted the beast's rump. Taking the reins of the pack horse, he shooed his little sisters and brother after Bird's Nest and Wulachen, who were leading their horses toward where the rest of their party waited.

Brings Dawn looked once more in the direction of the sun's rising, other long-buried memories suddenly swirling around him like dry leaves in the wind: driving the cows up from the pasture with Jake and Christian early on a fresh summer morning like this one, when the dew lay heavy on the long golden grasses and the lazy wind was still cool; milking the cows with Daat and Jake in the large barn's shadowy interior; Maam's laughter and the mouth-watering fragrance of the hearty breakfast spread on the *Küche* table; baby Annali's sweet giggles; the promise in a girl's fathomless green eyes. Anna's smile, her fragrance, the firmness of her small hand in his larger one were suddenly so vivid that for an instant they seemed as real as the horse he led.

The memories faded as quickly as they had come, and he was overcome by the sense that, for all their intensity, those fleeting images were nothing more than a long-ago dream—that his life here among the Lenape was the only reality that had ever existed. Or ever would.

He had told Many Leaves that he was glad to be Lenape. He was.

I am one of this people now. Looking down at his clenched hand, he opened it. *I let go of all that is past.*

He started around as Red Squirrel grabbed his arm, laughing. "We're leaving, my friend, and here you stand like a post. Hurry! We have many miles to travel today!"

Brings Dawn chuckled apologetically and hurried after Red Squirrel to where his people waited on the path that led toward the place of the sun's setting.

Chapter Twenty-eight

FALLING LEAF MOON

Thursday, October 19, 1758

CHILLS CRAWLED DOWN Christian's spine as the huge bear-like figure leaped from the shadows into the center of the Big House. He suppressed a gasp but could not help shrinking back when it drew near to where he sat with Nútemau, Raven Eye, Standing Stone and other men of the Wolf division.

The creature walked upright, and except for the enormous wooden mask it wore over its face, it was entirely covered with fur like that of a bear. It carried a bag made of the same fur, a bent stick, and a turtle-shell rattle, which it shook rhythmically while it lumbered along the dancing path. The pounding of drums and chants of the singers that kept time to its clumsy dance reverberated across the enclosed space.

Terror and fascination kept Christian's gaze fixed on the Being's mask. The eye holes and misshapen mouth closely resembled the two carved faces hung on opposite sides of the enormous central post that held up the building's roof, the smaller ones that decorated each of the side and door posts, and the miniature Christian kept in the bag hung around his neck. Like them, it was painted red on the right side and black on the left.

He pressed his hands over his mouth. *Misinghalikun! It's real!*

It was near midnight on the fourth of the twelve days devoted to the Big House Ceremony. The effect created by the Mask Being was both startling and mesmerizing in the heavy, smoky atmosphere inside the huge structure, with the fires casting spars of light over the festively garbed people and deepening the shadows in the corners.

He jumped when Raven Eye jabbed him with his elbow. His friend put his mouth to Christian's ear and hissed, "It is a man wearing a bearskin. He plays the part of the Mask Being for the ceremony."

Christian eyed his friend. Both of them had added height and muscle during the past moons. But Crooked Legs, who had taken Raven Eye as his man name after his vision, now stood a head taller than Christian.

He turned back to the Mask Being. Even the creature's feet, paws, and the back of its head were covered with bear fur, making it look frighteningly realistic. But as it circled past them again Christian could see that Raven Eye was right.

"I knew that," he answered, earning frowns from Nútemau and Standing Stone, who sat with them in the men's section.

Christian pressed his lips tightly together, remembering his father's admonition that only children old enough to remain quiet were allowed to attend this annual ceremony, the most important of the Lenape religion.

His surroundings still awed him as much as when he had entered the building on the ceremony's first night. His first family had worshipped in homes, not in churches, and he had never been in a building so large. The imposing structure was built like an enormous longhouse, about twenty-four feet wide and, he guessed, close to twice that long.

As he looked around, Christian unaccountably found it difficult to breathe. It felt as though a faint tremor shook the earth beneath him as the Mask Being continued on its course along the dancing path. A mysterious power seemed to fill the building on the swirling smoke, and the flickering light and throb of drums raised gooseflesh on Christian's arms.

Nútemau had told him that the Big House represented the universe, which consisted of twelve houses stacked atop each other. Manitou lived in the highest house, and on coming into the Big House the people passed through each of them to stand before the great deity. Thus no impure person or thing was allowed to enter there.

The building's front door faced the direction of the rising sun and moon and the beginning of everything, Nútemau explained. The rear door faced the setting of the sun and moon, where everything ends. The hard-tamped floor represented the lesser manitou of Mother Earth and the underworld; the dancing path that circled the central post and the two fires symbolized the Good White Path, which each person traveled from birth to death; the four walls signified the four cardinal directions; and the high ceiling corresponded to the sky, the domain of the Elder Brothers, the sun and the moon.

When the Mask Being moved to the building's far end, Christian glanced furtively toward Deep Water and her oldest daughter, seated nearest the eastern door among the women of the Wolf division. The sorrow reflected in Deep Water's eyes brought Christian's own grief welling back.

That spring the warriors had returned from one of their raids bringing new captives . . . and the body of one who had been killed: Crouching Panther.

The waxing and waning of six moons since had done little to heal the gaping wound in Christian's heart. Nútemau did everything he could to comfort him, as did Deep Water and her family. But Crouching Panther alone had been the bridge between Christian's white life and his present one, and he felt adrift again on a sea of loneliness and pain.

Nútemau's declining strength added to Christian's worries. His father had seemed to grow stronger with spring's arrival, but now, as another winter approached, he seemed weaker and increasingly withdrawn. Christian's first thought each morning was whether he would be able to awaken Nútemau. His relief each time the old man opened his eyes only sharpened the reminder that the dreaded day would inevitably come.

Where would Christian belong then? If he even belonged here now.

When the Mask Being finally lumbered out the eastern door, a man rose and took a turtle-shell rattle from beside the central post. Shaking it, he moved in rhythmic steps along the dancing path, chanting his vision. A line of men and women soon followed, dancing and chanting along with him.

Christian stifled a yawn. It was becoming increasingly difficult to stay awake until the morning. The main event of the twelve-day ceremony seemed to be the men reciting their visions. On the final night, Raven Eye had told him, the women would be allowed to recite theirs too. But the ninth night would be different: a sacred rite of consecration in which the carved images on the posts would be given a fresh coat of paint, and the cheeks and foreheads of all the worshipers would be painted red.

Christian roused briefly in the middle of the night when the attendants passed baskets of boiled meat and cornbread. In spite of his hunger he was careful to take only one small serving like the others so there would be enough for everyone.

After devouring the food he dozed intermittently until sunrise, when the entire assembly filed out the eastern door to stand in a row facing east. Together they called out "Ho-o-o" in prayer six times while standing, then six times while kneeling.

✦ ⸱⸱⸱ ✦

BY THE TIME THE CEREMONY's Bringer-in dismissed the gathering, Christian couldn't tell whether he was more sleepy or hungry. It was all he could do to support Nútemau, while Raven Eye and his family hurried them along, laughing, through the crowd.

They wove between the huge kettles of hominy steaming over the fires and found a place in the line rapidly forming in front of the large table on the yard's north side. The mingled aromas of corn mush, smoked and roasted meat and fish, squash, beans, and other foods made Christian's mouth water.

The Falling Leaf Moon had brought with it brilliantly colored leaves on trees and bushes and cool, crisp air. Days earlier the town's population had begun to swell dramatically as people from Cussewago upriver and other outlying villages flooded in for the ceremony. Everyone camped along the edge of the Big House yard in their tribal divisions, the women's tents on the south side and the men's encampment on the north.

While Christian stood in the slowly moving line, stomach growling, he noticed one of the visitors and her white son in the line ahead of them. The boy was a few years younger than Christian, and he had the sense that he had once known him, an impression that was reinforced when the boy glanced back at him with what appeared to be recognition.

The mother and son got their food and moved away. Raven Eye's family filled their plates and went to find seats, with Nútemau leaning on Standing Stone's arm.

Christian stepped up to the table and returned the smile of the slender young woman helping to serve. She piled food on a bark plate and handed it to him along with a bark spoon.

Suddenly Raven Eye appeared beside him. "I've not seen you before. Are you visiting from far away?"

She shook her head. "My family moved to my uncle's home in Cussewago a moon ago."

"You are of the Wolf division?"

She arched her eyebrow and nodded as she held out a filled plate.

He took it. "I am Raven Eye, and this is my young friend Dark Forest."

Christian's embarrassment must have shown on his face because the maiden laughed.

"He does not look so young to me, nor you so old. I am called Many Leaves. It is good to meet both of you, and I wish you a good day."

Her words brought heat into Raven Eye's face. Christian stalked away from the table, carefully balancing the food on his plate, and went to join Standing Stone and Nútemau on the men's side of the yard, with Raven Eye trailing behind. Christian sat on the ground and concentrated on eating, not looking up when Raven Eye took a seat beside him.

"I am sorry I spoke of you as a child."

"You have only two winters more than I, and I will soon be a man too." Scowling, Christian tossed a piece of venison to Bear, who snapped it up and swallowed it whole.

Raven Eye remained silent for several moments, then said soberly, "I think you will seek your spirit guardian before the warm weather returns."

Something in his tone caused Christian to look up. Raven Eye was watching Nútemau with an expression that caused Christian's throat to tighten.

He means my father will want to see me become a man before . . . He concentrated on shoving the food around on his plate with his spoon.

The conversation of the men around him gradually drew his attention. They were discussing the council currently taking place between Brother Onas, the Lenape, and other tribes allied with the French at a town called Easton. Christian had heard that Custaloga was becoming increasingly disposed toward peace, but he had paid little attention to the talk until now. When one man pointed out that the English might demand back their captives, his stomach lurched.

After the feast ended they watched the afternoon games, while waiting for the evening's ceremony to begin. Christian stood on the sidelines, watching Raven Eye running races with the older youths and maidens, feeling as though a chasm separated him from them. When the sun hovered at the western treetops, he turned away . . . and came face-to-face with the boy he had seen earlier.

He was tanned and had grown during the past moons. And his well-fed appearance and fine clothing decorated with intricate beading and ribbons indicated that he had a mother who doted on him.

"I know you," the boy said. "My name is Bright Eyes."

Franz. The name sprang suddenly into Christian's memory. *Franz Spelt . . . Spet . . . no, Specht.*

The name evoked a welter of images: Franz and his little sister and father shivering with hunger and fear on the path to the Susquehanna, the terrifying gauntlet at Shikellamy's Town, the gift of peaches that saved them, the grueling journey to Presque Isle, and then to Custaloga's Town.

"I am Dark Forest, but I was once called Chri—Christian. Your white name was Franz."

The boy nodded and glanced over his shoulder at his mother, who stood a short distance away chattering with several others. When he turned back, he puffed out his chest.

"My mother and I are going far away before the First Snow Moon. Her sister lives among the Ottawa with her husband.

There are many rivers and lakes there, and the fishing and hunting are much better than here. She says we will never again have to fear that white men will steal our lands."

Or you, Christian thought.

The boy's expression sobered. "Have you seen my little sister? I do not know what they named her, but she was once called Hannah. I've looked everywhere, but I cannot find her. I want to know that she is happy and well and tell her goodbye before we go away."

Christian's chest tightened. "She . . . became ill during the winter . . . " The words stuck in his throat at the memory of the little girl's perfunctory burial, lacking ceremony of any kind. *I cannot even show him where her grave is.*

Bright Eyes stared at Christian, then his face crumpled. He opened his mouth, but before he could speak, his mother hurried over, glaring at Christian.

"It's almost time for the ceremony, my son. Stay beside me now. Don't wander away."

Bright Eyes returned her smile, but his expression had gone blank.

Just then Nútemau shambled over to them, steadying each step with his stick. He nodded to Bright Eyes and his mother before bending over Christian.

"It is time to make ready for the ceremony, my son."

But Christian couldn't tear his eyes away from Bright Eyes as the boy took his mother's outstretched hand and without a backward glance walked away.

Chapter Twenty-nine

First Snow Moon

Tuesday, November 21, 1758

CHRISTIAN AWOKE with a start. He was stiff and cold from lying by the rocky shore of a small lake, where he had collapsed in a drift of leaves some hours earlier, his stomach gnawing with hunger, too exhausted to go farther. Clad only in a breechcloth, he shivered uncontrollably in the frosty air.

Something loomed out of the twilight near at hand. He lifted his head and saw a tall, imposing creature standing against the fading blush of sunset, its radiant form wrapped in mist, the details of its face obscured by the glow that emanated from it. The Being moved closer, and Christian shrank away, rubbing his eyes.

"Are you my spirit protector?" His voice quivered.

He had asked the question of several creatures over the past days, but they had all scurried into the brush or flown away. This Being began to turn away as well. Then unexpectedly it paused to glance over its shoulder at Christian and beckoned him to follow before striding silently into the deep shades of the forest.

He rose and ran after it, simultaneously terrified and reassured, the pounding of his heart making him feel lightheaded.

The Being had gone only a short distance, however, when it suddenly disappeared into a thick copse of trees.

Racing forward, Christian pushed through the trees—and came to an abrupt halt at the edge of a broad clearing. An immense elm tree stood in solitary glory in its center, its seamed trunk much broader and taller and the spread of its branches wider than any tree he had ever seen.

Its top seemed to pierce the shrouded heavens. Surely it was visible from a long distance, Christian thought, yet he had wandered the forest for the past five days without glimpsing it.

The Being hovered directly in front of the great elm, its form glimmering. Again it turned and beckoned, and Christian immediately found himself standing within its glow in the shelter of the tree's boughs. Beneath him the earth trembled subtly as it had in the Big House.

He felt as though he stood inside an enormous chimney and that a strong draught threatened to suck him upward. Although his feet remained on the ground, the mysterious Being rose rapidly from beside him and vanished into the thick streamers of fog that wrapped the tree's uppermost branches.

Christian watched, breathless, as the draught continued to swirl the mist, unwinding a channel higher and higher until he could see the night's first star in the indigo heavens. Its light swelled until it seemed to stand directly over his head. Filled with wonder, hardly knowing what he did, he reached out his hand to touch it.

The star blinked out. The earth ceased its trembling, and night enclosed him again.

When he lifted his head, he was lying on the lake's shore, shivering in the icy blast that stirred the black, surging waves. Tears of disappointment sprang into his eyes.

He became aware that he clenched something hard in his hand. Looking down, he sucked in a sharp breath. A faint glow shone through his fingers, and he slowly opened his hand, almost afraid of what he would find.

In his palm lay a small cluster of pointed spikes as clear as glass that radiated from a thin crust of rock. Entranced by its beauty, he turned the cluster back and forth, admiring the changing colors that shot through the spikes even in the darkness, as though they held starlight.

A surge of relief engulfed him. He had feared that he would never find a spirit protector and would be forced to return home in disgrace. He could hardly grasp that his prayers had been answered in such an astounding way.

He pushed upright on shaking legs and took a bit of tobacco from the pouch that hung around his neck. As he sprinkled it on the ground where he had lain, he whispered, "I thank you, Star Spirit, for choosing to become my protector!"

CHRISTIAN SAT AT THE CENTER of the townspeople who gathered in the council house the morning after he finally stumbled back into the town footsore, fainting from hunger, and well-nigh frozen. The food prepared by Deep Water and a few hours of sleep had strengthened him, but he struggled to maintain the dignified posture and stoic expression fitting for a man.

Well before Nútemau had driven him out of the town, he had learned from his friends that he would have to find a personal *manitowuk*, one of the lesser gods who would serve as his lifelong protector. Indeed he had deeply envied Raven Eye's vision and the token of the small black stone that evoked his man-name, and had longed to endure this trial successfully to gain everyone's admiration and approval. What Christian had not expected was the wrenching sense of rejection and abandonment that pierced him to the heart when not only by his father, but also his friends and all the townspeople treated him as invisible.

After enduring days of wandering fearfully through the forest all alone, the familiar space, mingled scents of tobacco and wood smoke, sour tang of unwashed bodies, and darker tones of tanned hides and weathered bark and beaten earth that filled the large building drew him in like a loving embrace. He basked in the proud gazes of his father and Raven Eye and his family and the sense of acceptance and love that surrounded him.

An undercurrent he did not understand gradually impressed itself on his consciousness. He caught an occasional surreptitious glance darting between those seated around him, along with the subtle tension of a face here or there and the muted rustle as one or another of the people shifted uneasily. Some turned their eyes away from Custaloga, who sat beyond Standing Stone; even Nútemau avoided the sachem's gaze. And seated behind Christian, Raven Eye, who had welcomed him back with obvious pride, now appeared strangely downcast.

Did I do something wrong? Is the vision a bad omen?

The unsettling impression briefly dispelled when Custaloga asked him to recite his vision again. Christian held up the star-stones so they flashed in the firelight while he spoke. Everyone listened raptly, and as before murmurs of amazement rippled through the crowd.

When he finished, Custaloga set down his pipe. "I have seen such stones before that hold the heavens' light in them. Their medicine is very powerful, and they are given only to those who counsel wisely."

Nútemau leaned forward to scrutinize the crystals, then sat back, his wizened face wreathed in a smile. "I am glad I have lived long enough to see my son become a man who will walk the Good White Road with wisdom and honor. What name will you take, my son?"

Christian dropped his gaze to the star-stones. "I have not yet thought of it."

Custaloga scanned the faces of the townspeople. "The Star Spirit revealed his star to this one, and he took it in his hand. Is he not, then, one who catches stars?"

"Star Catcher!" Standing Stone exclaimed. "Does this name not hold strong medicine?"

"*Gachene wullet,*" Nútemau said. It is surely good.

Christian drew himself up proudly. "Indeed it is good! I take the name Star Catcher."

❧—❧

STAR CATCHER WATCHED the dancers circle the great fire from the shadow of the Big House, where he stood with Fire Keeper. She was a couple of years older than he, and, like his, her eyes were blue, her skin paler than that of her Lenape kindred. His hair had darkened to a warm brown, while hers, pulled back and wrapped in a red cloth trimmed with bright ribbons, was the color of ripe corn.

"It seems a wind rose to trouble our people while I sought my vision," he said, unable to hold in his emotions any longer. "I overheard Deep Water and Standing Stone speak of the treaty between our people and Brother Onas, but they fell silent when I came near. Everyone seems to know of this thing, yet not even my father will speak of it! It burns in my heart."

She met his troubled gaze with a sympathetic one. "This will only be your second winter among us, and they fear for you to know of this matter."

Could more than a year have passed since his first life ended? Star Catcher wondered. It must have happened near the beginning of the Hunting Moon, but he had not taken note of it. Indeed, the memory of that night of terror and all that followed had dimmed until it seldom came to mind.

"There are many like us here," Fire Keeper continued, "and though we are all Lenape now, our families are greatly concerned. My parents will not talk of it to me either, though I was adopted many winters ago at the beginning of this war."

She looked down and sighed. "While you were away, messengers arrived with news of the peace treaty concluded a moon ago. When my parents talked of it I pretended to be busy at my work. But I heard them say that our people have restored the friendship we formerly held with the English, along with many of our brothers and uncles who also fought for Father Onontio."

"But this is good!"

"It *is* good. But my father also said that to establish this peace our sachems had to agree . . . " She bit her lip, then said in a muffled voice, "They had to agree that all those born to the Whites must be given back to them."

Christian stiffened. "Custaloga did not attend the conference or sign the treaty."

"It is true, but in the summer he met with several sachems of the Turkey division about this matter. And afterward he went to Venango, where he counseled with a messenger from Brother Onas named Post and agreed to make peace with the English." She raised her shoulders in a slight shrug. "The Wolf division cannot stand against the English alone, and our people have lost much because of this war. We will lose even more if we continue to fight."

"*We?* It seems that *we* are not to be considered Lenape after all."

"Among our people we are, but it is not so to the English and they demand that we be returned to them. My parents whisper of it in the night when they think I am sleeping, and my mother cries herself to sleep. Custaloga also has children he is unwilling to send back to the Whites. Everyone is angry and fearful about this matter even though they wish to make peace."

❖ ┄┄ ❖

LATER THAT NIGHT Star Catcher lay on his bed with Bear burrowed against him, anxiously straining to hear Nútemau's uneven breaths. He wondered again where he truly belonged.

Other than fleeting, blurred images of a few faces and that long-ago night of horror, he could summon up little memory of his first life.

As he struggled to capture even a small part of it, he recalled that his white father had charged him to always remember something—a prayer, in the tongue that belonged to that world.

Unser . . . Vater . . .

Brief phrases formed slowly in his mind: *Unser Vater in Himmel . . . täglich Brot gib uns. Vergib uns . . . wie wir vergeben. Dein ist Reich . . . Ewigkeit. Amen.* Our Father in heaven . . . give us bread daily. Forgive us . . . as we forgive. Yours is the kingdom . . . forever. Amen.

Tears streamed down his face, and he clutched Bear so fiercely that the dog yelped. Through blurred eyes Star Catcher peered across the wigewa at Nútemau's still form, dimly outlined in the fading light of the fire's embers.

When he dies, what will I do? Where will I belong?

Bear licked the tears from his cheek, and Star Catcher clung more tightly to the young dog. And to the few words that were all that was left to him of the ones he had once loved, and lost in flames and anguish.

Chapter Thirty

Tuesday, November 28, 1758

"WETOCHEMEND. WETOCHEMEND!" Star Catcher repeated anxiously, patting Nútemau's face. His father's with-red skin felt cold, and he did not respond or open his eyes.

Star Catcher sucked in a deep breath and let it slowly out, forcing his breathing to calm. He was under the Star Spirit's protection, he reminded himself. One who caught stars in his hand could never give in to fear. He was entering his thirteenth winter and had become a man. He resolved to act like one.

Using the edge of his blanket, he dabbed away the blood-flecked moisture on the old man's lips, then held his hand over Nútemau's nose and mouth. Feeling a faint breath, he laid his ear on Nútemau's chest until he heard a heartbeat—weak and irregular, but reassuring.

After murmuring a prayer to the Star Spirit, he wrapped his own heavy bearskin over Nútemau. Then he built up the fire and rubbed the old man's cold hands and arms until faint color returned to them. At last, with great relief, he saw Nútemau's eyelids flicker.

Star Catcher hung the kettle of water on the tripod over the flames and soon had a tea of man-root steeping. By then Nútemau had awakened, though he remained too weak to sit up. Star Catcher raised him gently so he could sip some of the hot tea, and Nútemau's eyes brightened as color slowly returned to his cheeks.

Raven Eye ducked into the wigewa, letting in a cold draught. His family had not gone to the camps with the other hunters because of their concern for Nútemau, and he helped Star Catcher coax his father into eating a few bites of corn mush. When the old man drifted to sleep, the two youths went out into the cloudy morning together to tell Deep Water what had happened.

She set aside the moccasin she was mending. "He has been to the sweating house?"

"He goes when he is strong enough to walk, but it does no good. Indeed, it seems only to make him weaker."

Her face grave, she directed Good Road to pound dried corn into meal in the mortar outside the cabin and sent Cloud Dancer to the well with the water bucket. When they had gone, she said, "The shaman came last week?"

"I paid him my last deer hide." Star Catcher's shoulders slumped. "He turned up his nose, but he took it. Then he danced, made fierce faces, and blew smoke from his pipe into my father's face. He seemed no better, so I paid a fox fur, which was all I had left, for the shaman to give him some *beson,* which put him to sleep. I have brewed many teas for him and keep him as warm as possible, but he grows worse."

Deep Water regarded him with sadness. "All of us must travel the Good White Path to the sun's setting."

Commotion sounded from outside. All three of them turned toward the door as Standing Stone burst in. He looked from one to the other while Deep Water explained what had happened. Although he seemed distracted, his stern expression softened and he turned a compassionate gaze on Star Catcher.

"Your father has lived many winters and his spirit grows heavy from the sorrows he has borne. You have been a great comfort to him, but you must accept that the time will come for him to enter into the wigewas of Manitou. He will find peace and rest there. Is this not good?"

Star Catcher bit his lip hard. "It is good, and I would not hold his spirit back. But I will miss him very much. What will I do without my father? Where will I go?"

Raven Eye put his arm around Star Catcher's shoulders. "When he is gone you must take an elder brother to care for you. You will never be left alone, my friend. Are you not one of us? There will always be a place for you among our people."

Their reassurances were interrupted by voices from outside and footfalls moving hurriedly past the cabin.

Deep Water rose in alarm. "What has happened, my husband?"

Standing Stone glanced at Star Catcher, then quickly away. "Messengers have come from Du Quesne in a great hurry. Everyone gathers at the council house to hear the news they bring."

Fire Keeper's words rang in Star Catcher's mind, and his chest tightened. While Deep Water and Standing Stone hurried to the council house, trailed by their daughters, he and Raven Eye ran to Nútemau's wigewa.

They found him sitting up and looking stronger, softly chanting a prayer to Manitou. When they told him of the messengers, he insisted on going despite their protests. They got the old man to his feet, wrapped warmly in a bearskin, and supported him between them on the way to the council house. Entering with the last of the townspeople, they hurriedly found seats.

Three warriors had come, their clothing dusty and worn, rent in places from a long, swift journey. Their faces reflected weariness and anger. Custaloga took no time for the customary speeches, instead motioning to the eldest of the three, who rose to speak.

"We cannot stay, for we must bear this news to all our people." the warrior said, his tone laced with disgust. "We have come from the Forks of the Ohio, but not to tell you of a great battle. Four sleeps ago, while the English General Forbes approached with his army, the French abandoned Du Quesne in terror. They threw their cannon into the river, packed all the possessions they could carry on horses and wagons, and set fire to the fort. While it burned, they fled before the English like beaten dogs. Some of them come close behind us, seeking safety at Fort Machault or Fort Le Boeuf."

He raised his voice and his fist. "Our warriors stood aside and watched them run, for why should we spill our blood on behalf of cowards? The next day the English army took possession of the Forks."

Consternation rippled through the assembly; Star Catcher heard angry murmurs on every side. The warriors tarried only long enough to answer a few questions before striding out of the council house to resume their journey north.

Custaloga stood up. Eyes narrowed, he held up his hand to still the cries of outrage.

"It is well for us to make peace with the English, but can any of us doubt now that they will drive the French back across the sea? Many leaders of our people and our brothers and uncles have taken the peace belt from Brother Onas and pledged to live again in that old friendship we once held with the English. But if the French no longer oppose them, what then will stand between us and their ambitions?"

Star Catcher felt a chill go through him. He looked around and met Fire Keeper's gaze. Her somber expression told him that she also wondered what effect Du Quesne's fall would have on those who in their first life had been White.

<hr/>

THE NEXT MORNING dawned bitterly cold, with the wind driving before it a fitful snow. As the day wore on, Star Catcher watched small parties of French soldiers straggle miserably along the path north on the east bank of ice-rimmed French Creek. None crossed to the town.

That evening more Lenape messengers arrived, this time to meet privately with Custaloga and the other headmen. They were still conferring when darkness fell.

Star Catcher wrapped himself and Nútemau together in blankets and bearskins to share the warmth of their bodies.

"You will not leave me, my son?" Nútemau's words were barely audible.

"No, my father, I will not leave you. I will not forget the duty of a son."

Silence enveloped them. After several moments Nútemau said, "You will not leave our people when I am gone?"

Star Catcher blinked back tears. "No, my father," he said, struggling to keep his voice steady. "I will never leave our people."

⟡————⟡

WHILE STAR CATCHER and Nútemau were chanting their morning prayers, Raven Eye slipped into the wigewa. He waited quietly until they finished, then joined them at the fire.

Star Catcher glanced questioningly at him while offering the old man a bite of corn cake.

"My father says the messengers brought belts of wampum and an invitation to a conference with an English colonel named Bouquet," Raven Eye said. "He is second in command of Forbes's army."

Nútemau coughed, choking on the corn cake. Star Catcher held a cup of tea to his lips, but he waved it away and closed his eyes.

Star Catcher caught Raven Eye's gaze and tipped his head toward the door. Raven Eye slipped outside without speaking. After settling Nútemau back on the sleeping platform and pulling the bearskin up to his chin, Star Catcher joined his friend outside.

"This news disturbs him."

Raven Eye regarded him with a concerned look. "It disturbs all of us. The tribes are summoned to meet with Bouquet in the town the English call Pittsburgh at the Forks of the Ohio by Du Quesne's ruins."

"When?"

"Five sleeps from today." Raven Eye added that Standing Stone, along with Custaloga and the other headmen of the town, would leave that morning.

"Five sleeps," Star Catcher said hoarsely, wondering whether the fate of those born among the Whites would be decided at this conference.

"It is so." The tightness of Raven Eye's voice made it clear that he was thinking the same thing.

They stared at each other in taut silence.

If he and the others were to be taken away, Star Catcher knew, the grief of that loss would tear his people apart. And to be carried away from home and family yet again would surely rend his own heart past healing.

Chapter Thirty-one

LONG NIGHT MOON
Thursday, January 4, 1759

S TAR CATCHER DROVE his spear through the trap and into the
raccoon's neck, pinning it to the ground. Teeth clenched, he
held it there until the animal's writhing ceased.

Raven Eye stamped through the snow-dusted bushes, quiver
over his shoulder and bow in hand, and bent over Star Catcher's
kill. "It's hardly more than a skeleton." He straightened. "The
wild animals have no more to eat then we do."

The hunger time had come early on the heels of bitter cold
and repeated onslaughts of sleet, rain, and snow. With almost no
food left in the town, Star Catcher and Raven Eye, along with a
small party of their friends, had finally braved the weather to
check their traps and hunt for any game they could find.

Star Catcher pulled his spear free. "The hunters who returned
from the camps brought hardly any meat back with them." He
took the dead animal from the trap, laying it on the snow to let
the blood drain. "They said they went out much farther on their
hunts than before but still found little game."

While Raven Eye waited silently, head bowed, Star Catcher sprinkled an offering of tobacco on the ground and murmured a prayer thanking the spirit of the raccoon for giving its life so they could eat.

When he finished, Raven Eye said, "My traps held nothing, but I saw the tracks of three deer going from there to the French Creek. I followed them. They crossed on the ice."

Star Catcher regarded him dubiously. "Your mother says it's too dangerous to try to cross the creek. The water flows swiftly, and the ice is not thick enough to bear a man's weight."

Raven Eye shrugged. "The deer crossed."

"Big ones?"

"They were full grown, I think."

Star Catcher frowned and shook his head.

"We are starving! I'm going to the other side of the creek to see whether I can find game there."

"The others have gone that way." Star Catcher waved his arm toward the northwest. "Let us go after them or wait until they come back."

"Stay here or go after them if you are afraid."

Star Catcher watched Raven Eye stalk off toward the creek. When his friend disappeared through the snowy underbrush, he hastily slung his quiver over his shoulder. Taking his bow and spear in one hand, he grabbed the raccoon with the other and ran after him. He reached the creek's bank to find Raven Eye already well out toward the center of the wide stream, following the single file of deer tracks winding through the windblown snow on the ice.

They seek better forage across the creek. Star Catcher squatted to look more closely at the hoof prints. *They're hardly yearlings, and with little to eat, they can't weigh much. Yet they move cautiously.*

Raven Eye looked back. "See? The ice is strong. If we can take at least two of them, the meat will last for several days."

He was right. They needed food. Star Catcher straightened and stepped out onto the ice, moving gingerly after Raven Eye.

He had not gone far when he heard a sharp pop. Several long cracks snaked out from where Raven Eye stood thirty yards away at the creek's center. Raven Eye glanced back, wide-eyed, at Star Catcher. The ice broke with a loud crack, and Raven Eye dropped, flailing, into the icy, black water.

"Raven Eye!"

His friend broke the surface, gasping and churning the water as he battled the creek's swift current, struggling to haul himself to safety. Each time he caught the edge of the ice it splintered into jagged chunks and the hole yawned ever wider.

Star Catcher took a step, but another pop resounded through the frosty air. A crack ran through the ice almost to his foot. He backed onto the bank.

Raven Eye called to him, choking and coughing up water as he bobbed among the broken pieces of ice. His efforts were already becoming noticeably weaker, and dread clutched Star Catcher's chest;

"I'm coming!"

He looked around in desperation. Long-forgotten words sprang to mind: *Erlöse uns von dem Uebel.* Deliver us from evil. He repeated them with urgency.

A long branch lying on the ground beneath a tall sycamore drew his eye. He raced to the tree, dropped his weapons, quiver, and racoon, and seized the branch. Heart pounding, he dragged it behind him, moving a short distance upstream to where the cracks had not yet reached.

He slid down the bank. Easing out onto the ice on hands and knees, he dropped to his stomach and wormed his way toward Raven Eye, pulling the branch along. With each movement he could hear the low groan of the ice and the surge of water beneath.

"Hold on! I'm coming!"

"I . . . I can't . . . " Raven Eye's voice was barely audible and his movements had slowed.

Star Catcher slid the branch around in front of him, angling it toward Raven Eye's bobbing head. "Take hold of the branch!" He raised himself on his elbows. "Do you see it? Raven Eye, grab the branch!"

He watched Raven Eye fumble for the branch. Suddenly he disappeared.

"Raven Eye!"

His friend bobbed back up, gasping and shaking the water from his head. Star Catcher crawled closer and again shoved the branch toward him. This time Raven Eye clutched it and hung on as Star Catcher drew him out of the water.

Inch by agonizing inch, Star Catcher slid backward toward the bank, pulling the branch—and Raven Eye—with all the strength and speed he could muster. At last he drew his friend's limp body close enough to grab him under the arms and pull him up the bank to level ground. He laid him in the lee of a huge oak, where the wind had scoured the snow from around one side of the trunk, leaving sheltering drifts on either hand.

Raven Eye shook as though he would break into pieces. "T-t-thank you, S-star C-c-catch-er." His eyes drifted closed and his chin dropped to his chest.

Star Catcher shook him. "Stay awake!"

He stripped off his friend's wet clothing, then his own garments. Somehow he managed to pull his dry clothing onto Raven Eye's larger frame, shaking him repeatedly and talking all the while to keep him from losing consciousness. Finished, he wrapped Raven Eye in his blanket.

The icy wind seared his flesh like fire but he blocked the consciousness of it. He gathered firewood and lit a handful of damp, half-rotted bark and pinecones with his flint and steel. He fed sticks into the flames, then pieces of broken branches, and soon warmth spread beneath the sheltering tree.

As he spread Raven Eye's clothing on bushes around the fire to dry, Black Fox appeared. He took both of them in at a glance, peeled off his own blanket, and wrapped it around Star Catcher's shoulders before rushing off. In moments he returned with the rest of their hunting party.

As soon as Raven Eye had regained enough strength to walk supported between Black Fox and Star Catcher, the hunting party returned to the town. They brought little game with them, but Star Catcher received much praise for rescuing Raven Eye.

When they were finally alone in the wigewa, Star Catcher told Nútemau about the prayer he had recalled, and his belief that it had been answered. Nútemau asked Star Catcher to teach it to him in the Lenape tongue, and as they sat together, staring into the fire's seething embers, the old man repeatedly chanted the prayer to himself.

THE NEXT DAY, with snow driving at their heels, Standing Stone returned with several others who had accompanied Custaloga to the Forks of the Ohio. They led a number of pack horses laden with food and other supplies given as gifts by the English. When these had been distributed among the villagers, everyone gathered in the council house, eager to hear a report of the conference with the English Colonel Bouquet.

Standing Stone stood before the gathered townspeople, pride evident on his face. "All of our nation's greatest leaders and the leaders of our brothers and uncles gathered at the town the English call Pittsburgh, where the scorched ruins of Du Quesne lie. The English freely admitted that we did not cause the war, and that they should have respected our lands and not stained them with blood. Bouquet spoke of his love for us and the plans of the English to do us good. He advised us that as the French disturb our peace, we should send them out of our country in order to prove our sincerity toward the English."

Approving nods and murmurs of agreement met his words as he continued, "A man called Post also brought the message of peace from Brother Onas. Tamaque of the Turkey division told this man to tell the English General Forbes that we are glad to receive these messages, but that he advised the English to remove from the Ohio lands and go back across the Allegheny mountains. The English were unhappy with this answer and tried to get us to alter it, but Tamaque made it clear that we will never allow them to take these lands."

Standing Stone went on to relate that their party had stopped at Fort Machault the previous day. Custaloga boasted to the fort's commander of what had happened at the Pittsburgh conference, while saying nothing of his intention to remain at Venango and watch the movements of the French, as he had promised Bouquet. When Custaloga asked the French commander for additional food for his people, however, he was told that with the fall of Louisbourg and Du Quesne, the flow of supplies to the outlying forts had been cut off.

"The French will soon withdraw from this area," Standing Stone warned, his tone hardening. "Although we have taken up the English peace belt, we must never forget that they have broken previous treaties. Bouquet promised that the English will not build permanent dwellings on the Ohio lands, but all of us saw that they already prepare to replace Du Quesne with a greater stronghold."

Angry mutters rippled through the assembly. One of the men demanded, "What is to become of those we have taken as sons or daughters or wives? Was anything spoken of them?"

Star Catcher tensed as Nútemau shifted uneasily.

But Standing Stone's face relaxed into a smile. "Bouquet said he would not speak of those we took from the English settlers and adopted into our families. He said he only hoped that once peace is restored we will send back those who are old and of little use. He won't be angry if the young ones stay among us."

Chapter Thirty-two

HUNTING MOON
Sunday, October 7, 1759

F LANKED BY RAVEN EYE and Deep Water, Star Catcher stood
beside the bark-lined grave, staring into the shadowed forest that rimmed the burial ground.

That afternoon the rain had finally diminished long enough
for the grave to be prepared. The steady downpour of the past
days had brought many of the trees' brilliant leaves to the ground,
and the wet, black trunks and spreading branches stood out in
spectral silence against the gathering dusk.

A cold wind plastered Star Catcher's damp hair across his
face and knifed through the blanket around his shoulders and the
shirt beneath. The mournful death chant of the men and the wild
keening of the women clustered around him barely registered in
his mind.

He returned his gaze to Nútemau's withered form at the bottom of the grave. The women had garbed him in his richest cer-
emonial dress of beaded and quilled buckskin and painted his
face in bright colors. His arms, decorated with silver armlets,
were crossed over his chest, knees bent to bring his legs close to

his body. Beside him lay his weapons, the scalps he had taken in battle, and other marks of a renowned warrior, along with his pipe and tobacco pouch.

Above his head sat a clay pot filled with food to give his spirit strength to make the final journey to the end of the Great White Path. Deep Water had told Star Catcher that Nútemau's spirit would linger nearby for eleven days before traveling to the home of Gishela-mukaong, the Creator in highest heaven, where all those whose souls were good lived forever, free from pain, sickness, and sorrow and their spirit bodies were made perfect.

He took a handful of tobacco from his pouch as he had been instructed and, tears blurring his vision, walked around the grave, trailing the fragrant leaves through his fingers to waft down onto Nútemau's body. When he finished, Standing Stone and another man stepped forward and knelt to place a large sheet of bark atop the rude coffin, closing off Star Catcher's last sight of his father with painful finality. The wails and chants ceased, and the men filled in the grave with soil, pieces of bark, and leaves to erase any scent and keep wild animals from disturbing it.

Star Catcher drew in a shaky breath and brushed away his tears. He lifted his gaze upward, seeking the broad sweep of stars slowly emerging through the fading light of the sun's setting—the *Ane,* the Great White Path Gishela-mukaong had flung across the heavens at creation.

"Be well, my Father," he whispered. "I will keep my soul good as you have taught me. And one day I will come to you."

The mourners filed from the burial ground with measured tread, singing the death chant. Their voices roused in Star Catcher haunting echoes of another people's mournful, drawn-out singing, dimly remembered from long ago among the people of his first life. Head bent, he followed the procession blindly, heart aching even more at the knowledge that a person's name also died with him, thus Nútemau's name could never again be spoken.

When they returned to the town he caught a glimpse of Patterson and Hutchins, scouts for the English army who had sought refuge from the pouring rain a couple of days earlier. Ever since the tribes had made peace with Brother Onas, soldiers passed through the area with greater frequency.

Such visitors were formally welcomed, but with their increasing numbers in Lenape lands, resentment and suspicion were growing. They were kept well away from those who had been adopted into the tribe, but Star Catcher felt as though the eyes of the two scouts followed him from a distance. He gladly passed from their sight when he entered the council house with the other mourners.

No one spoke for a long time, while tobacco smoke mingled with that from the fires. At length Thunder on Mountain, a well-respected elder who had been close to Nútemau, stood.

"This one who has completed his journey on the Great White Path was a great warrior in his youth. Yet he became a man of peace in his latter years, a wise counselor, and a friend to all. He suffered many sorrows in this life, including the deaths of his wife and children. But Manitou blessed him with this youth who came among us to comfort him and carry out the duties of a son, and allowed him to see this son seek his vision and become a man."

He turned to Star Catcher. "It is our custom that a youth who is without mother or father or uncle take an elder brother to care for him until he is fully grown. Who will you chose as your elder brother?"

Star Catcher stared down at his folded hands. He had spent much time thinking of this since finding his father lifeless when he returned from hunting two days earlier.

After a moment he looked up, glancing from Raven Eye to Deep Water and Standing Stone. "I choose Raven Eye, if he and Deep Water are willing."

Thunder on Mountain frowned. "Raven Eye will have only sixteen winters and is himself not yet fully grown. It would be better to choose one who is older."

Star Catcher cast a look of appeal to Deep Water, who returned it with a smile.

"It is our custom as you say, yet this one has lost his father and needs a home. He is the closest to my son, and the bond between them is already like the bond between brothers. If my son chooses to take this one as his younger brother, then it is good."

"I choose it," Raven Eye said quickly.

Thus it was settled, and Deep Water took Star Catcher into her home.

Chapter Thirty-three

BEE MOON
Friday, August 15, 1760

SEATED BETWEEN Raven Eye and Black Fox at the rear of the council house, Star Catcher wiped the trickling sweat from his brow. Rays of hot sunlight slanted through the long building's smoke holes, dimly lighting the smoky interior.

He craned his neck to get a better view of the short, stocky Englishman clad in buckskins who stood before the half-circle of elders at the packed building's head. George Croghan, agent for the British Superintendent for Indian Affairs, Sir William Johnson, was unimposing in physical appearance, but he seemed not to know it.

He had arrived at Custaloga's Town two days earlier to a chorus of shouts and gunfire and immediately sent out messengers to call all the sachems and headmen of the area to a council. The day before, while they were still arriving, Colonel Bouquet had marched his troops past the town in an impressive display of English power. The council had begun early that afternoon, and now, near sunset, all the usual formalities had been completed and the speeches of the various sachems delivered.

Croghan's gruff voice carried to the back of the council house as he spoke in the Lenape tongue. "Brethren, His Majesty's general now at Pittsburgh has sent me to acquaint you that it is necessary for his majesty's service to open the communication from Pittsburgh to Presque Isle and establish a post there since the French have now removed from it. He desires that you and your brethren here may be assisting to any troops that may at any time be passing by your settlements that way."

Dark looks and low mutters of displeasure met the agent's words but gave way to approving nods as he went on to say that General Jeffrey Amherst gave his assurances that they would have the king's protection as long as they behaved well toward the English. The general would render any services in his power to them in order to establish a lasting peace and friendship.

Croghan held up a belt of wampum for all to see, then ceremoniously placed it on the low table in front of him. He straightened to scan the crowd. Star Catcher quickly bent his head, hoping the agent's eye would not light on him.

The French had surrendered Quebec the previous year, for all purposes ending the war. Since then Custaloga had urged his people to return all those captured in the raids, as he had promised the English. None at Custaloga's Town had yet done so, however. Star Catcher suspected that the English soldiers and other Whites who passed through the town looked for white captives, and he kept his distance.

"To assure you of his kind intentions, the general has sent gifts of clothing for all your women and children," Croghan concluded.

Custaloga rose and drew himself to his full height. "You know, Brother, that I am resolved to suffer none of my people to fight against the English any more. I have said I will do whatever Brother Onas desires of me anytime the French rise against you, and I will keep my word. We offer our thanks to the general for his gifts and will gladly supply meat to his soldiers and render any other assistance they may need."

The gathering ended and everyone filed outside to the laden wagons Amherst had sent. Croghan's men quickly distributed the goods, beginning with the sachems and headmen.

While Deep Water and her family went forward with the rest, Star Catcher slipped away to her cabin. He waited impatiently until they returned, bringing garments for him as well. Each received a white blanket striped in blue or red, moccasins, a brightly colored linen shirt, and stroud leggings, with knee-length stroud petticoats for the women and girls and breechcloths for the men.

Star Catcher fingered his shirt. "This cloth seems thin and poorly woven. Even the blanket is thin."

Raven Eye exchanged dubious glances with his parents. "I do not think these will last through the winter."

They arrayed themselves in their new clothes, nevertheless, and rejoined those gathered outside the council house. Star Catcher stayed at the back of the crowd while Croghan and his men joined in the feast the women had prepared.

Many Leaves brought Star Catcher a bowl of corn stew with a portion of fried bread. Her mother, First Snow, had become good friends with Deep Water, and their families often exchanged visits between Custaloga's Town and Cussewago. Star Catcher asked about the death of her ailing uncle several sleeps earlier.

She sat next to him. "My mother does not know what to do now. She talks about traveling southwest from here to the great Lenape towns far away on a river called Muskingum, where many of our people have gone. Many Shawnee, Mingoes, and others of our uncles and brothers live in those regions too. It is said that the land is fertile and the hunting very good, and no English soldiers come there, only traders."

"Do you think you really will go?"

"We have no male relatives to provide meat for us. All we have is my uncle's cabin, which is in poor repair. I fish and catch small game in my traps, but I have not yet the skill with a bow to provide meat or hides to trade. I do not know how we can buy a horse and provisions for such a journey, nor would it be safe for us to go alone."

"I hope you stay! We'll provide meat for your family."

Her eyes warmed. "Your family has done much already, my friend. We cannot depend on others forever."

He snorted. "The English soldiers would buy all the meat we kill if we sold it to them. And now their general sends more soldiers and asks us to supply even more. But our own families must eat, and game is becoming harder to find."

After thanking her for bringing him food, he joined Raven Eye and the other men in the shade of the trees bordering the council house yard, while Many Leaves went to sit with her mother and Fire Keeper. Star Catcher noted that the women were soon joined by Deep Water and a maiden named Clear Sunshine.

He quickly brushed the dust off his new shirt and leggings, then tried to appear absorbed in eating. His attention, however, drifted repeatedly to the beautiful, winsome maiden. They were close in age, she with almost fifteen winters, and he not quite fourteen. He had added height and grown lean and muscular. And he had gained much skill at tracking and hunting and moved through the forest with silent confidence. In everything he strove to emulate Raven Eye and the older youths and took pride in the respect they increasingly accorded him.

Raven Eye had taken a liking to Clear Sunshine as well, however, and she often looked his direction. Before Star Catcher and his friends finished eating, the young women drifted by to visit casually with them.

When Clear Sunshine spoke to him, his reply sounded awkward to his ears and brought heat to his face. He pretended not to care that she talked with Raven Eye for some minutes before leaving with Many Leaves and Fire Keeper.

Later, on his way to Deep Water's home, the low voices of several men drew him to Thunder on Mountain's cabin. Outside it stood Standing Stone, Thunder on Mountain, and Custaloga, along with several others. Star Catcher slipped into the shadow of a tall tree and knelt behind its trunk as Custaloga spoke.

"Tamaque and Shingas warned General Forbes at Pittsburgh that the English must return over the mountains and set no permanent settlement or fort on the Ohio lands. And yet they have built a great fort at the Forks. Nor is it the only one they have built. Fort Venango is just downriver, and they now hold Le Boeuf and Presque Isle too."

Standing Stone grunted. "They march their army in front of us, then ask us to supply their soldiers with more meat and to scout and carry for them more than we already do. Yet they sell little powder and ball to us, so how can we hunt? These clothes—" he flicked the sleeve of his new shirt "—are the first gifts sent us by this General Amherst, who took the place of Forbes when he died."

"Our women could weave finer goods than these had we the wool," Thunder on Mountain growled. "The French made us many fine gifts and supplied all the guns, ammunition, and other supplies we needed."

"Now that Brother Onontio is gone, the English traders pour in like a flood," a Shawnee warrior said. "But they bring mostly rum and whisky to keep our minds addled while their people wrest our lands from us. And now they demand the return of those born to them who have long been our children and wives!"

"I have given my word to fight for the English against the French. And I will keep it as long as I can." Custaloga paused before adding heavily, "Even if it means we must forcibly return the adopted ones."

Star Catcher's breath caught. Feeling sick, he craned as far forward as he dared in order to see the men's faces more clearly.

"If we give them up, they will suffer even more than we do!" another man protested. "What of my wife and my little son and daughter? They weep at the thought of being torn from my arms and from our people. My wife says that if she is forced to return to the Whites, she will run away. What is to become of them?"

As Custaloga looked away from his companions, Star Catcher caught the glint of moisture in his eyes. "Our people gain nothing from another war except death and destruction." His voice broke, but his face was set like iron.

"This will be the only course these English leave us if they continue to swarm over our lands like hornets," Standing Stone said bitterly. "We have made peace with them, but many of our people, along with those of our uncles and brothers, refuse to raise the hatchet against the French. It may yet be that Brother Onontio can be persuaded to return and help us to drive out these Englishmen before they devour us."

❖ ⋯ ❖

THAT NIGHT STAR CATCHER squatted before the dying embers of Deep Water's cooking fire. After the younger children withdrew inside the cabin to their beds, he said, "Many Leaves told me her mother considers moving to the great towns of our people on the Muskingum, where the English soldiers dare not come."

For some moments Deep Water made no reply, then she turned to Standing Stone. "First Snow has said this to me as well, my husband. The land is said to be very good there. I do not wish to leave our home and go so far, but—" She glanced at Star Catcher, then quickly away. "There our people are safe from the threat of war."

"Many Seneca already speak of taking up the war hatchet against the English." Standing Stone fixed his gaze on Star Catcher. "Custaloga says the English grow impatient to have those among us who were born to the Whites returned to them. He agreed to turn every one over, and his face is covered with shame to appear before the English again because so few have been brought back.

"I reminded him that your father no longer lives and that although my son has taken you as his younger brother, you are not the son of my wife. She has no authority to force you to go back." Staring into the fire's depths, he said softly, "Our hearts will bleed if you leave us, for you have become like a son to us. But only you can choose what you will do in this matter."

Star Catcher stared at the ground, fear giving way to a tentative hope for the first time in many moons. When he looked up, his gaze met Raven Eye's, who clearly awaited his answer with anxiety.

"You are my people, and my desire is to stay with you. If the English seek to take me, I will go to the Muskingum—alone if I must. Or farther west to the Shawnee or the Twightwee. My white blood was washed away, and I will never return to them! I made this promise to my father, and I will not betray it."

Raven Eye let out his breath in a loud gust. Grinning broadly, he threw his arm around Star Catcher's shoulders.

Chapter Thirty-four

FROG MOON
Thursday, April 8, 1762

B RINGS DAWN STEADIED Menetopalis as he lowered to his knees. They knelt side-by-side, bending strong, supple poles cut from slender white ash saplings and lashing them together with wet elm bark bast to form the ribs and frame of a new canoe. When they finished, Menetopalis placed one hand on Brings Dawn's shoulder, grasped his walking stick with the other, and pushed to his feet.

"Your leg has grown much stronger since we came to this place, my father. I remember how you hesitated to mount the horse, but you rode her easily all the days of our journey. And now you ride and walk with no more help than your stick."

Menetopalis chuckled. "I questioned whether it was wise to leave our home and travel so far, but in truth I feared riding a horse again. Now I am glad your mother insisted we come. It is indeed good here."

Brings Dawn followed his gaze along the stream that flowed out of sight around a forested bend to join the larger Muskingum, called *Wakatamothiipi* by their Shawnee neighbors. Some distance south, he knew, it poured into the great Ohio.

All along the well-drained, gently undulating bottomlands of these rivers and their tributaries stretched the towns and villages of many powerful Indian nations. Tamaque's people had settled a short distance off the western end of the Great Path, establishing a town that by now had burgeoned into a major Lenape center called Beaver's Town by the traders after Tamaque's English name.

Many Shawnee, Mingo, Twightwee, and those of other nations were also drawn to its expansive site. Sturdy log cabins stretched far along well-beaten roads winding through what looked like parkland, with fertile fields surrounding it. Brings Dawn, along with the rest of his family, had become fluent enough in several different languages and dialects to carry on the prospering trade he and Menetopalis had developed over the past four years.

Menetopalis's voice held satisfaction as he said, "Here we are free of the English soldiers and settlers."

"But not the traders."

Menetopalis shrugged. "They bring us many goods we need."

"And rum."

Menetopalis bent his head. "It is so. But I promised to never again touch the white man's drink or even visit the traders when your mother swore she would throw everything that belongs to me out of her cabin."

Brings Dawn snickered at his reference to the Lenape custom of divorce. "She will do it too."

"And she will be right in it." A shadow fell across Menetopalis's face. "It is a sickness, one that harms my wife and children the most. I love all of you too much to violate my word." He laid his hand on Brings Dawn's shoulder. "Forgive me, my son, for hurting you as I did. I swear to you I am a better man now."

"I know you are. And I forgave you from the first, my father."

Brings Dawn rose and embraced Menetopalis, reveling in the feel of his father's arms, steady and sure around him again after the bitter winter they had endured. When they drew apart, the darkness had left Menetopalis's face.

He limped over to the creek behind Wulachen's cabin. Earlier that spring, while the sap ran, they had pried long strips from the trunks of young elms and weighted them down with stones in the water to flatten and keep them supple. Now he drew out a thin sheet of red elm bark, holding it up to let it drain before carrying it to Brings Dawn.

They worked with silent concentration, stretching sheets of the bark over the canoe's framework one at a time, with the outside turned inward. Menetopalis held each sheet in place while Brings Dawn cut it to shape and sewed it expertly to the ribbing with lengths of elm-bark bast.

The first years they had spent along the Muskingum were the happiest he had ever known. Only a few months shy of twenty winters, he had reached his adult height, with flowing mahogany locks held back by a woven headband, and piercing hazel eyes. The previous year he had moved out of Wulachen's cabin, as befitted a man, and now lived nearby with Red Squirrel and Wanderer.

The loving ties to his family had not diminished, however. He not only worked closely with his father, but also spent much time at his mother's fire and delighted in the companionship of

290 | Bob Hostetler and J. M. Hochstetler

his younger sisters and brother as much as he did in that of his friends.

Wulachen, sixteen-year-old She Sings, and Moonflower, not yet fourteen, kept them fed with abundant harvests from fields and forest with the help of Bird's Nest, who lived with them now. Brings Dawn supplied ample game, while Contrary Wind, now eleven, fished and minded his traps. The meat, sinew, and bone provided food, tools, and thread for sewing, and the fine pelts of beaver, deer, and other animals bought needed goods from the traders.

In addition, Brings Dawn excelled at building elm-bark canoes of elegant design with beautifully painted symbols on their sides. His mother, sisters, and grandmother wove baskets, rush mats, and hempen bags to trade, while Menetopalis carved ladles, spoons, and stirring paddles. The fine wooden bowls he crafted were as sought after by the people of the surrounding towns as were Brings Dawn's canoes—as well as by the English traders who had begun filtering into the region in greater numbers since the reestablishment of peace.

The traders, however, supplied not only useful goods, but also unlimited quantities of the white man's rum. And two winters earlier everything had fallen into ruin, not only for Brings Dawn's family, but also for many others. Menetopalis had fallen victim to a worse crippling than his physical injury. For more than a year he had wasted all the pelts he and Brings Dawn had taken by trading them to feed his addiction.

During the dark winter just past, the hunger time had stretched out so long that Brings Dawn had begun to wonder if any of them would see the spring. Menetopalis had been incapable of hunting or doing any work at all, and when sober he carried away whatever he could find to trade for liquor, striking anyone who tried to stop him.

Brings Dawn and Contrary Wind had resorted to hiding what little game they took until it could be cooked to feed their family. They lived in fear of Menetopalis's drunken violence, scenes repeated in almost every family they knew, until Wulachen had had enough. Only then, faced with the loss of everything precious to him, Menetopalis finally stopped his self-destructive course.

The canoe's outer skin was finally in place, and Menetopalis got to his feet. Taking a seat on a nearby log, he took up the large bowl he had been working on and with a curved knife began to scrape away the last of the charred wood remaining in its center.

Brings Dawn took a pot filled with a thick, sticky caulk made of finely pounded bast mixed with water and spread it carefully along the vessel's joints using a flat stick. When dried, the coating would be waterproof.

Finished, he rose and stood back to admire the craft. It was long and broad, capable of carrying heavy burdens. Yet its form was also sleek, with a gracefully curved prow and stern. He had built many such craft since settling on the Muskingum and did not need to try it on the river to know that it would glide as lightly on the water's currents as a gull.

He looked up to see Menetopalis watching him with open pride. "It is the best one you have made. Your skill grows with each one."

Grinning, Brings Dawn turned to see Mehíttuk approaching along the path. His eyes brightened at the sight of the canoe.

"I shall be proud to own this one!" He clasped Brings Dawn's hand. "You know the designs I want painted on it?"

"Yes, of course. It will be ready for you tomorrow."

Menetopalis put down his knife. "When my son is finished, it will be worth many beaver skins."

"And I have agreed to pay a great many for it," Mehíttuk replied, wincing, and they all laughed.

✦┄┄┄✦

THE LAST EMBERS of the setting sun tinted the sky above the western trees in brilliant hues as Brings Dawn listened to Tamaque's somber voice. "We marked our names on Brother Onas's treaty, pledging that we would not only return all those of their flesh and blood, but also that we would persuade our brothers and uncles to do so. If other tribes return those born among the Whites and we do not, it will be a shame to our people."

Brings Dawn fixed his gaze on Bird's Nest, who faced her brothers like an embattled sparrow. "You *men* gave your word, not we women, my brother. Is it not true that among our people the children belong to their mothers? Or did something change while I slept?"

Tamaque exchanged a chastened glance with Shingas, who spread his hands in a conciliatory gesture. "Nothing has changed, my sister, but all of us knew the terms of the treaty we put our marks to at Easton. Brings Dawn was my captive, and I—"

"He is *my* son," Wulachen spat. "I did not steal him from you, Uncle. You freely gave him to me."

Brings Dawn sucked in a breath at his mother's impudence. He had never seen her treat anyone with such rudeness, least of all her uncles, who were respected sachems.

The muscles in Shingas's jaw tensed. "Brother Onas's messenger, this man Post, made clear that if we do not return those born among the English, we break the treaty."

"You told us the English would not bother us here," Wulachen returned with venom. "But it appears that the place of the sun's setting is not far enough for them to drive our people."

"Their words are hollow." Bird's Nest glared at her brothers. "Are you not the ones who sent the message to the man Post in the Deep Snow Moon, asking to counsel with Brother Onas?"

Tamaque sighed. "What you say is true, my sister. What other course can we follow? We have no choice but to abide by the treaty if we wish to live in peace."

"They will never leave us in peace! They will not stop until they drive us from the face of the earth!"

Contrary Wind pressed against Brings Dawn's shoulder. He drew the boy close as he glanced surreptitiously from Bird's Nest to Menetopalis.

His father sat behind Wulachen, with She Sings and Moonflower leaning against him on each side. The hazy, pink light of sunset blurred the edges of forest and cabin but could not conceal the anguish in their eyes.

Her face a mask of anger, Bird's Nest demanded, "You go with Post to this treaty then?"

Tamaque hesitated, and when he answered it sounded to Brings Dawn as though he chose his words with care. "Who is to know? It is true that Shingas and I called for this treaty, but Manitou has not yet made clear which course will be the most advantageous to our people."

As he spoke, Shingas stared through the surrounding trees toward the sunset's fading light. Brings Dawn sensed his uneasiness. It occurred to him that Tamaque spoke diplomatically, and that the real reason they delayed in committing to council with the governor after having requested it was that Shingas feared English reprisals against him because of the depredations he had wrought during the war.

Menetopalis pounded his fist into his palm. "If I could fight—"

"Even if you were able," Shingas cut him off harshly, "even if all of us took up the hatchet and struck them without pity, they would rise against us like a flood and wash all of us away."

"Few of our people listen to you and Tamaque and those who counsel peace any longer," Menetopalis returned, his voice flat. "Our Seneca brothers call for war, and many of our young warriors are listening. Neolin also says the Master of Life is displeased with us because we have allowed the white man to come into our lands."

Brings Dawn shifted uncomfortably. The previous year, the Lenape prophet, Neolin, had claimed that in a vision the Master of Life revealed to him that he was greatly displeased with his people for becoming drunk and indulging in the evils of witchcraft, disputes, polygamy, and sexual promiscuity. Worse than even these offenses, however, was their toleration of white men in the lands the Master of Life had given the Lenape.

It was only by following the narrow path that one would find happiness and reach paradise, Neolin counseled. The people must throw out the white man and return to the traditions of their ancestors: abstain from the white man's drink, take only one wife, dress in animal hides, and hunt and war using bow and arrow alone.

This new religion was sweeping through all the native communities in the Ohio region, gaining numerous adherents. When Wulachen threatened to divorce Menetopalis, he had eagerly joined Neolin's disciples and begun to follow the prophet's precepts. Morning and evening Menetopalis recited the prayer Neolin had received from the Master of Life carved on a stick. He had even gone so far as to exchange one buckskin for another called the Great Book of Writing, on which Neolin had inscribed the path that led to heaven and the ones that were blocked by the vices introduced by the Whites.

Shingas responded with a shrug. "The teachings of Neolin's Master of Life have much in common with Post's teachings of the white man's Father in Heaven. How is one to know which is the true path?"

Brings Dawn had to admit Menetopalis had found strength to stop drinking through Neolin's teaching. But the prophet's Master of Life seemed to Brings Dawn, as it evidently did to Shingas, a mixture of the Christian God and man's ideas, thus ultimately as vain as the Lenape's false gods.

Tamaque waved his hand. "Indeed, Post returned with this youth named Heckewelder to teach our people more about his Father in Heaven, as he promised to do last summer when he built a cabin among us. But he also told us that during the winter Brother Onas charged him to summon us to another council. If we do not go and bring back more captives, then we and all our people will be shamed. The English will not remain patient until the end of days."

"I am determined to return those I adopted into my family." Shingas spoke softly, and to Brings Dawn it seemed that the warrior aged before his eyes. "I gave my word, and I will keep it for the good of our people."

Tamaque stared into the fire. "And I will return those belonging to me."

Silence fell. Brings Dawn covered his face with his hands.

Could he return . . . but to what? This was his home, these his people. Everything he loved was here, not behind the mists that shrouded the past. Those he had been born among no longer lived in his heart. For all he knew, they might no longer live in this world. To think of returning to a distant place that seemed no more to him than vague shadows felt like stepping off a high cliff into a black void.

"If I could speak to Post—"

"No! If he sees you, he will try to tear you away from us."

He took Wulachen's hand and held it. "I am a man now—"

"It is so. But I am your mother who loves you." Tears streamed down her face. "Have you changed your mind? Would you leave us now after all?"

"I will never change my mind, nor will I return to the Whites, my mother. But they will continue to demand this of us, and we must find a reasonable solution. I would ask Post whether he truly believes Father in Heaven takes pleasure in tearing families apart. I cannot believe this is His will, for Father in Heaven is a God of love and mercy."

Everyone stared at him.

"You speak as a man who makes good sense, my nephew," Tamaque said, frowning. "And also as one who believes in this God—this white man's Father in Heaven Post talks about."

Brings Dawn cringed. How many winters had come and gone since he had called out to Jesus and received his vision? How many times had he meant to tell the truth of his experience? How often had he failed? He had compromised by only participating in ceremonies and festivals as much as his conscience would allow, holding back from clearly idolatrous practices while praying to the God Who had answered his prayer.

A hot tide of shame rolled over him, burning his cheeks. He drew himself up and met the others' doubtful gazes, gripped by the conviction that he must set things right whatever the consequences.

"I believe in Him and in His Son, Jesus." He hesitated before rushing ahead. "It was to Jesus I prayed when I sought my vision—not to Wsinkhoalican or Manitou or any of the *manitowuks*." He explained the circumstances in detail before concluding, "Wsinkhoalican and Manitou and the other gods have never done anything that I can see. But Jesus took the fear from my heart and warmed it like the sun. He sent the great buck to me who gave me this as a token that He is the True One."

He took the piece of antler from the pouch around his neck and held it up in the firelight. When Contrary Wind reached to stroke it and his sisters crowded eagerly around, Brings Dawn allowed each of them to cup it in their hands, gazing at it in awe, before he returned it to his pouch.

"Why did you not tell us this when you recited the vision?"

Brings Dawn dropped his gaze from Wulachen's astonished one. "I meant to, my mother, but then everyone began to speak of the man-name I would choose, and *Nóhum* told it to me." He nodded to Bird's Nest. "I've wished to tell it to you all this time, but I could not find the words."

He glanced at Menetopalis, then quickly away, a deep pain piercing him. For the first time since he had been made Lenape he saw disappointment in his father's eyes.

"Forgive me. I was wrong to keep this from you."

Silence settled over the twilit clearing once more. Brings Dawn pulled his blanket tightly around his shoulders.

"Perhaps this Jesus held your tongue silent until now," Shingas said quietly. "It may be the time has come for us to hear these words. Post says tomorrow he will speak of this Father in Heaven to those of our people who are willing to listen."

"I will go to listen to him then," Wulachen said, her voice shaking. "But a god who would take a son from his mother is not a worthy god!"

Chapter Thirty-five

PLANTING MOON
Saturday, May 22, 1762

As the Shad Moon gave way to the Planting Moon, Brings Dawn grew increasingly troubled. The tide of war had again begun to rise. White settlers and soldiers pushed ever farther into the Ohio lands despite the warnings of such sachems as Tamaque and Shingas. At last some of the Seneca warriors began to carry the war belt to tribes throughout the region.

Though the dangers mounted, the Moravian missionary, Post, continued to preach regularly, standing on the porch of his cabin. Only a few townspeople came, including Wulachen and occasionally Menetopalis. Both repeatedly questioned Brings Dawn about his vision, what he could remember of the teachings he had learned in his first life, and Post's sermons. His answers led only to disagreements between his parents, whom he had never before heard argue.

"Father in Heaven says we are to love our enemies and not fight them," Menetopalis scoffed that morning. "It seems to me that these are nothing but English lies by which they would enslave us. The Master of Life told Neolin what our people must do to regain his favor and—"

"He says we must cast the white men out of our lands." Kneeling at the hearth, Wulachen stirred the steaming contents of the kettle so hard that some slopped over the side. "But who can believe we will be more successful now than before? Always with you men it is war and death. And always the women and children and elders suffer and die with you." She gestured angrily toward his crippled leg. "Shingas was right. They are too numerous and their weapons are too strong for us to conquer them."

"If we obey the Master of Life, he will make our weapons more powerful than theirs."

"How?" Brings Dawn demanded, distressed by their conflict and by his younger brother and sisters, who crept silently past him and out of the cabin, eyes averted. "It has never happened, my father. What proof is there that this time will be different?"

"I suppose this Father in Heaven spoke to—" Menetopalis stopped abruptly, his gaze unwillingly drawn to the pouch hanging from Brings Dawn's neck.

Brings Dawn held his tongue, but Wulachen rocked back on her heels and said, "He did speak to Brings Dawn."

Menetopalis pushed to his feet. When Brings Dawn rose to take his arm, Menetopalis waved him away. Leaning on his walking stick, he limped to the door and went outside.

THAT NIGHT THEY AGAIN went to hear Post speak. Menetopalis listened with undisguised skepticism, arms folded and posture rigid. Brings Dawn knew his father's mind remained firmly set against the Moravian's teachings, but he could tell that the thought of a God of love moved Wulachen deeply even though she feared where such beliefs might lead.

Wulachen allowed the younger children to attend, but Brings Dawn was forbidden to sit in the yard with them. He stood in the shadows of the trees surrounding Post's cabin, listening intently to every word the Moravian spoke. When his assistant, the sturdy youth named Heckewelder, read passages from Scripture, the long-forgotten words poured over Brings Dawn like water from a clear, flowing stream.

Shingas and Tamaque also sat in the audience, as they had almost every evening Post preached the gospel. And Brings Dawn noted that they listened attentively. The warm relationship between his great-uncles and Post and the mutual respect they shared impressed Brings Dawn.

Post spoke to his audience about peace with Father in Heaven through His Son, Jesus Christ. He explained that true peace with God—and man—could come only through Jesus, whose sacrifice on the cross blazed a trail by which all could have access to the Father by one Spirit.

The missionary's words were never more gentle, Brings Dawn thought, but also powerful. He looked around to see all eyes fixed on the preacher. Some in the audience leaned forward as though held in thrall. Even Shingas—especially Shingas—seemed to be moved like never before by Post's sermon.

The Moravian read from the Bible: " 'And the inhabitants of one city shall go to another, saying, "Let us go speedily to pray before the LORD, and to seek the LORD of hosts: I will go also." ' " Looking up, he placed his hand atop the page and repeated, "Let us go speedily to pray before the LORD, and to seek the LORD of hosts: I will go also."

Post closed the book and bowed his head. Brings Dawn watched with brimming eyes as Heckewelder concluded the service with a prayer. While the others hurried away to the night's dances, Tamaque and Shingas lingered. Brings Dawn watched from the shadows as they lit their pipes at the fire in front of the cabin and sat with Post and Heckewelder.

The two sachems leisurely questioned Post about the scriptures he had preached on. Brings Dawn strained to hear as the Moravian answered and his uncles listened thoughtfully, smoke from their pipes spiraling heavenward. A few moments of silence ensued, after which Post reminded them of the coming treaty and asked whether they were ready to go with him and return their captives.

Shingas met Post's gaze with a steady one. "Once the English offered a great reward for my head. If I continue to meet with them, will the day come when they carry out their intent and hang me?"

Post's expression softened, and it seemed to Brings Dawn that the Moravian must truly love his great uncle. "My brother, does this still trouble you? Both of you have met with the English several times over the past winters without any hurt."

Shingas studied Post intently. "You know, Brother, that I never thought to revenge myself but was always very kind to the prisoners brought to me. Indeed, those I took as my children eat from the same dish as the sons born to me."

Brings Dawn felt a lump form in his throat at the memory of that cold night during the wrenching journey to Presque Isle when Shingas had spread his blanket over him. He had been a boy then. A boy named Joseph.

"You have impressed them by your sincerity of heart," Post was saying. "They know that your people suffer much because of the evil deeds of those who seek to steal your lands."

Shingas nodded gravely. "I assured Brother Onas that, on our side, my brothers and I would be strong to put this peace on a firm foundation. I only wish I could be certain that the English are also sincere and will place strong stones on their side as well."

"My brother, when you put your mark on Brother Onas's treaty, the past was all wiped away and forgiven, just as Father in Heaven forgives us of our sins against Him when we come to Him with a sincere heart."

Tamaque placed his hand on Shingas's arm. "We will go with you to this treaty, Brother," he said to Post. "And we will bring with us those who are your people's flesh and blood as the seal that we trust the English to make right what was done wrong and to do our people good from this time on."

◆⸺◆

BRINGS DAWN WORKED on the canoe, while Shingas sat silent, alternately watching him and staring off into the forest. He tried to concentrate on his work but couldn't help wondering what his uncle wanted to say.

"The words Brother Post spoke the other day have pierced my heart, my nephew," Shingas said at length. "I committed a grave offense against you the day I took you from your first life."

304 | Bob Hostetler and J. M. Hochstetler

The memories Brings Dawn had long repressed rushed back. He thought he had released the hurt. In his mind he had made peace with what had happened. He was fully Lenape now and glad of it.

But he had also been convicted by Post's sermon. His humble teaching reminded Brings Dawn of those he had received as a child among the Amish. And now the conviction struck him painfully that he still harbored a grudge deep in his heart against Shingas.

He kept working, keeping his expression neutral. "The war party you led set the home of my first life and everything we had to the torch," he said evenly. "Had we not escaped before the house broke through, we also would have burned."

He raised his eyes to meet Shingas's pained gaze. "My brother and little sister died at the hands of your warriors. It was by your own hand that my mother died. Yet we had done no wrong to you. The Amish do not ever fight or kill, and my white father would not allow my brothers and me to take up our guns against you." His last words came out clipped, and for a fleeting moment he savored the bitterness in them.

To his surprise the warrior dropped his gaze to the ground. "I was in the wrong, my nephew. What I did was evil. It may be that you cannot forgive my sin, but I ask it though it is a very great thing."

Brings Dawn let his breath out slowly. "It *is* a very great thing and beyond my power to release. Yet I do forgive you—not from my own heart, for the murder of a brother and sister and mother seems impossible for a man to put aside. But I forgive you from the heart of my Father in Heaven for whom nothing is impossible."

Seated on the log, Shingas leaned forward, his hands gripping his knees. "It is from these people called Ah-mish to whom you were born that you have learned about Father in Heaven?"

"They taught me that the Great God who made all life considers the taking of life sin. I also have chosen the path of peace like my uncle Tamaque and would teach our people to do so as well."

Shingas regarded him earnestly for a long moment. "Then you do well, my nephew. I also seek to walk this path, but it is a hard one for a warrior. I cannot promise that I will always keep to it. Yet your forgiveness for my offense calls me to do better than I have done."

Chapter Thirty-six

STRAWBERRY MOON
Thursday, July 8, 1762

B RINGS DAWN STIFFENED as Wulachen wrung her hands. "In two sleeps they will leave for the place called Lan-cas-ter, taking with them all those born among the Whites. Tamaque says I must send Brings Dawn too."

Before he could protest, She Sings recounted the woe of her closest friend, from whose cabin she had just returned. "Evening Rain must go with them. She does not want to, but she is given no choice. She and her mother and father cannot stop weeping, and Speaks Truth says he will never leave her and their baby even if he must live among the Whites." Sitting disconsolately on the cabin's hearth, she poked at the fire with a stick, blinking back tears.

"They will kill him," Menetopalis said grimly. "And since she married one of our people, it will not go well with her. They will never accept her and her child."

Contrary Wind had been listening with growing agitation. Brings Dawn pulled the boy against his chest, wishing he could shelter him against the world that seemed to be crashing in on them all. As Contrary Wind clung tightly to him, Brings Dawn felt him tremble.

"I do not know what I would do if I had to leave Sees Far," She Sings whispered, referring to the young warrior who courted her.

Her face was a mask of misery, and kneeling beside her, Moonflower gathered her in her arms, while Bird's Nest stroked She Sings' bent head.

Brings Dawn released Contrary Wind and sprang up from his stool to pace the narrow room's length. "Evening Rain told me before we came to this place that no one of her first family remains alive. What will become of her when no one claims her?"

Birds Nest's wrinkled face hardened. "I have heard talk that in such cases they are bound as slaves to rich masters who abuse them."

Fighting back panic, Brings Dawn stared, unseeing, through the open door into the hot afternoon sunshine. Would that also be his fate if he was forced to go back? Even if anyone from his first family was still alive, did they desire his return after all this time? Would they accept him now that he was Lenape? Did they still live . . . where? He could not remember the name of the place that had been his home.

"I have been speaking with Mehíttuk and Smoke in Sky," Menetopalis said, his gaze fixed on Wulachen. "Before the sun awakens in the morning, they travel downriver by canoe to Wapatomick at the Forks. They plan to go up the White Woman River to the villages of the Shawnee and Mingo and Twightwee, where some of Smoke in Sky's relatives live. Game is abundant in that region, and they plan to stay until the Corn Moon to hunt while the deer wear their fine red summer coat. Mehíttuk told me the traders there pay the highest prices, and our baskets and bowls and other goods would be in great demand as well."

He glanced in Brings Dawn's direction. "Wanderer goes with them."

Brings Dawn's heart leaped. Wanderer's childhood name had been Wildcat. Brings Dawn remembered that the same night Evening Rain told them that none of her relations from her first life still lived, his friend had also confided his first father's abuse and his determination never to return to the Whites.

Both Wulachen and Bird's Nest beamed. "Aiee!" Wulachen exclaimed. "Then you must take advantage of this opportunity to make a good profit, my husband. We have baskets ready to trade, and with your bowls and the good pelts you will take there on the hunt, you will be able to bring back enough supplies to carry us through the winter."

Menetopalis stroked his chin and glanced at Brings Dawn as though to gauge his reaction. "Brings Dawn must come with me. I will need his help."

Bird's Nest clasped her hands. "You cannot do without him! And Contrary Wind too. It is time he learns to hunt and trade." A triumphant glance passed between her and Wulachen.

The boy let out a whoop and ran to Brings Dawn, almost bowling him over in his excitement. Brings Dawn's laughter matched those of the others.

"Come, little brother! The sun will soon sleep. We have no time to waste before he awakens again. Let us gather all the things we must take on our journey now so the others do not launch their canoes before us in the morning."

He urged Contrary Wind ahead of him, eagerly following his little brother out the door. At the back of his mind nagged the thought that he ought to seek the path Father in Heaven would have him walk, but he thrust it from him that he might follow his own.

Chapter Thirty-seven

Friday, August 13, 1762

JAKOB PEERED over Christian Frederick Post's shoulder. "Be sure to tell the governor that Chief Custaloga holds one of my sons."

The Moravian looked up from the paper on which he was writing. "I've already done it," he assured Jakob with a wry smile. He pointed to the line in the petition that noted the information about Custaloga. "You are as jealous as the Indians about what one writes in English, Brother Jakob."

Jakob bowed his head at the reproof, but his stomach remained knotted.

He felt much older than his fifty years. A year earlier, in spite of his uncertain health and his children's objections, he had made the two-day journey northeast to the conference at Easton, at the confluence of the Lehigh and Delaware rivers. The hope that the Indians would finally return Joseph and Christian had buoyed him then, but he had been disappointed once again.

This time, on learning that Governor James Hamilton would hold another conference with the tribes involved in the war, Jakob had traveled an almost equal distance south to Lancaster, with Johannes accompanying him. He felt as though he was being repeatedly dragged from pillar to post.

"I'm sorry for it. It's been five years since my boys were taken, and—" Jakob began to cough. Hastily pulling out his handkerchief, he covered his mouth until the spell passed, then cleared his throat and continued, "Yet still all I know is that Custaloga holds one of my boys. I do not even know which one."

Post pushed back from the table and stood up. "I met briefly with Custaloga at his town in the spring of 1758, before that peace was concluded. I saw white children there, but I was not allowed anywhere near them."

"When I was at Easton last year, I talked to a British scout by the name of Patterson who'd stopped by Custaloga's Town with another scout in the fall of '59 during a heavy rain. He told me they counted thirty white captives, many German, while they were there. He also thought my son might be among them." Jakob pulled another folded paper from his pocket and held it out. "Two years ago I talked to a man at Philadelphia who had some business with George Croghan."

Post regarded Jakob keenly as he took the paper. "Sir William Johnson's deputy superintendent of Indian affairs?"

"I've talked to everyone who will listen. According to this man, he was accompanying Croghan to a council with a number of the tribes at Venango. I told him about Joseph and Christian, and he wrote their names down and promised to seek information of them." Jakob gestured at the letter. "I got this several months later."

312 | Bob Hostetler and J. M. Hochstetler

Frowning, Post unfolded the page and read it slowly aloud. " 'Mr. Hustetter, as promised, I enquired about your sons Joseph and Christian. Our interpreter at the conference, Andrew Montour, recollected a captured German boy named something like Huster who was brought to Custaloga's town in late 1757. I am sorry I can tell you nothing further. I wish you the best in finding both your sons.' It's signed James Young." He looked up. "This information will certainly help establish your case."

"It's my hope. But time and again the Indians promised to turn back all the captives they hold, and they haven't done it." Frustration overcame Jakob, and he waved his arms. "Why didn't Custaloga give my boy over at the Easton conference last year? Why hasn't the other been returned? How long can it take to bring them down? We keep getting our hopes up, and then . . . nothing." Another coughing fit wracked him.

Urging him to sit in a chair, Post watched Jakob with concern until he caught his breath. "I'm afraid you're not alone. There are many families waiting for their relations' return. Colonel Weiser's death a couple of years ago greatly complicated negotiations. He lived among the Iroquois as a youth and held the Indians' trust like no other white man. So far there's been no one to replace him."

"*Ya,* I know him, and I was real sorry to hear of his death. He was a trustworthy man." Jakob glanced absently around at the cramped, plainly furnished parlor of the house where Post was staying with several members of the Pennsylvania Assembly. "But what of his sons—Samuel and the others? They also lived among the Indians and speak their languages."

"They don't have their father's years of experience negotiating with the tribes."

"What of you? I've heard you're held in high regard among the Indians."

"I've been given great favor," Post allowed mildly, "and I'll do all I can on your behalf. But we're besieged by petitioners, and the chiefs have no power to force their people to do anything. They can only try to persuade. And since the French surrender, many of their people have dispersed farther west into Ohio Territory or north to Canada."

Jakob slumped back in the chair. "So there's nothing we can do but continue to wait and hope. And pray."

"Prayer is our most powerful weapon, and progress is being made. The western tribes turned over seventy-four captives recently at Fort Pitt, and they've brought fifteen more here to the conference. Governor Hamilton's purpose is to urge them to bring the rest down as soon as possible, and Colonel Bouquet is also making every effort toward that end."

Jakob pushed to his feet. "We must wait on His time for He knows what we do not." The words sounded hollow even as he spoke them. As often as he had said those words, it grew harder every day to take any comfort in them.

"Nothing is impossible for *Gott*." Post handed the letter back to Jakob. "I've not much time left, and I need your signature on this." Taking the petition from his desk, he read it aloud.

To the Honorable James Hamilton, Esq. Lieutenant Governor of Pennsylvania, etc. The Humble Petition of Jacob Hockstetler of Berks County. Humbly Sheweth:

That about five years ago your petitioner with two children were taken prisoners and his wife and two other children were killed by the Indians, that one of said children who is still prisoner is named Joseph, is about eighteen years old, and Christian is about sixteen years and a half old, That his house and improvements were totally ruined and destroyed.

That your petitioner understands that neither of his children are brought down, but the ambassador of King Custaloga, who has one of his children, is now here.

That your petitioner most humbly prays your honor to interpose in this matter that his children may be restored to him, or that he may be put into such a method as may be effectual for that purpose.

After Jakob had scratched an X where Post indicated, he sprinkled sand across the fresh ink and shook it off. The door opened and Isaac Stille, the Delaware interpreter who brought Jakob to Post on his arrival at the treaty site, stepped into the room, nodded, then silently withdrew.

Post folded the paper and slipped it into his pocket. "Today's sessions are about to begin, and I'm needed to help translate. The most important business is the captives' return, and I'll give the governor this petition as soon as he's free. Considering all the necessary formalities, it's likely the conference will last at least a fortnight, and then the sachems and headmen will have to return to their towns to search for those still held among them. I'm afraid by the time they're found, it'll be winter. I doubt many more will be returned yet this year."

JOHANNES WAS WAITING in front of the house with the horses when his father came out alone and clearly downcast. "No news again?"

Daat shook his head. "Post said the Indians turned seventy-four captives over at Fort Pitt on their way here. Neither of your brothers was with them—at least no one who fit their age and description or answered to their names."

"You said the children held captive at Buckaloons seemed to forget their families and even their language in just a few months and became like the Indians," Johannes reminded him. "It's been so long now maybe they've forgotten their names and how to speak German."

Daat mounted, and Johannes hurried to do the same. Neither spoke as they reined their horses around, urging them to a walk along the street.

After several moments Johannes said tentatively, "Daat . . . maybe it's not God's will to bring them back."

He saw a dark flush rise to his father's face. "Do you believe it's *Gott's* will to leave your brothers among the heathen? I don't, and I'll keep looking for them until *Gott* brings them home. Where's your faith?"

The reprimand stung, and Johannes bit back a sharp response. When they reached the town's outskirts he ventured a sidelong glance at his father.

Daat sat stiffly, his face tensed as though every joint pained him. He pulled out his handkerchief, covered his mouth, and coughed, wheezing with every convulsion.

Pity constricted Johannes's throat. Suffering had dramatically aged his father. His hair, once abundant and black, had thinned and turned completely white.

Before the attack he had been a tireless worker, one who made up his mind quickly and always sought to do what was right. Now his shoulders hunched, deep lines creased his weathered face, and his steps were sometimes unsteady. He had summoned enough strength to help with the farm work again this spring, but a day's work exhausted him.

Yet in spite of Johannes's and Barbara's objections, he insisted on going anywhere he thought he might uncover some information about Joseph and Christian, no matter how many miles he had to travel. He was only fifty years old. God willing, he still had many years before him. Yet to Johannes's eyes this man on whose strength and steadiness he had relied all his life looked worn and frail, like an old man.

He is an old man.

Johannes bit his lip hard to hold back a wave of emotion, wondering whether, having lost so many loved ones, he would soon lose his father as well. He wasn't ready for that—would never be ready—though it was the normal course of life. He fixed his blurred gaze on the road ahead of them.

The encampment of Indian representatives to the conference sprawled across a pasture to their left. A small cluster of sachems paused at the side of the road to let them pass.

Johannes heard his father draw in a sharp breath and saw that he stared hard at one of them, his face draining of color. He spurred his horse forward.

Johannes urged his own horse to a trot and caught up to him. "Do you know that chief?"

"*Ya.*"

When he said no more, Johannes asked, "Who is he?"

Daat stared straight ahead. "His name is Shingas. He's the one who killed your Maam."

Chapter Thirty-eight

Sunday, August 17, 1762

BARBARA EASED ONTO a chair in the *Küche,* her hand on her rounded belly. "It must be *guud* to be back home after such a long time away."

Anna Blanck looked up from the small crocks of preserves, apple butter, and pickles she was gathering onto a wooden tray and returned Barbara's smile. "Maam's glad to have another set of hands to help with the chores. Your Mattie and Anna do real good with their younger brothers and sisters now—and so do your Jacob and John," she added, nodding at Katie, who bustled across the room carrying dishes to Aunt Katrina at the dry sink.

Katie winked at her over her shoulder. "The boys are usually mindful, but there's a good bit of mischief in them yet."

Barbara chuckled. "Ach, that's true of all young ones—us too when we were little."

The Northkill congregation had gathered at Uncle Crist Buerki's home that morning for church services. Many of those who had moved away during the worst of the attacks had returned, and the house had been bursting at the seams for the dinner that followed worship in the well-swept upper level of Uncle Crist's bank barn.

Now, late in the afternoon, the rest of the church members had gone, leaving only Barbara's extended family and the Blancks. Anna's younger brother and sisters were playing a game outdoors with the other children, and it was unusually quiet inside.

Barbara shifted in the chair. With her pregnancy so far along, it was difficult to find a comfortable position.

"I know your folks needed you back, and our older ones can help out more with those younger now. But Katie and I sure do miss having you with us all the time. It's like we've become sisters."

A becoming blush warmed Anna's cheeks as Katie came to sit with them. "I don't feel any closer to my own family than I do to you."

They fell silent, all thinking the same thing, Barbara knew: If Joseph had not been captured, they would be family by now.

Anna looked down at her hands folded in her lap. "Maam told me yesterday that she and Daat think it isn't good for me to keep holding onto hope that Joseph will come back. She thinks David Beiler's sweet on me and I ought to let him court me."

"David's a nice young man," Katie said, her tone sounding a little too cheerful. She dabbed the perspiration from her brow with the edge of her apron and tucked a wisp of her light brown hair back into her *Haube.* "He'd make a good husband."

"*Ya,* and I like him. But . . ."

Barbara reached out awkwardly to clasp Anna's hands in hers. "All your friends are marrying. It's been five years now and no sign the boys are ever going to be turned over. Maybe you need to go on with your life."

"I can't seem to, no matter how hard I try." Anna bent her head. "How do I know if this feeling that I need to wait is my own desire or from God?"

Barbara released Anna and stretched, her hands pressed to her back. "How do any of us know? All we can do is keep on praying and listen for the Holy Spirit's voice. And be willing to obey."

The sound of coughing drew her attention to the circle of men in front of the settle, where Daat sat to get as close as possible to the fire. The men stopped their conversation to wait until his coughing eased.

Barbara pushed awkwardly to her feet and crossed the room. "Daat, you're running yourself ragged. Your cough isn't getting any better, and if you keep on like this, you're going to drive yourself into an early grave. That trip to Lancaster didn't do you any good—just like Johannes and I said. I wish you'd listen to us for once."

"This time I petitioned the governor and—"

"*Ya,* that ought to do as much good as everything else you tried." When Daat stiffened, she softened her tone. "Maybe you better come back over and stay with us for a while again instead of trying to help Johannes farm. It'll be a worry off Katie's mind, too, not to have to nurse you."

"Ach, he's no bother," Katie said as she joined them, with Anna and Aunt Katrina hovering behind her. "He's just been working too hard. Johannes and the boys can do most of the work, Daat. You need to take it easier."

Daat cocked his head. "So I've become the *Kind* now and you're the parents."

Johannes lifted baby Annali, his and Katie's youngest, patting her back as she laid her head on his shoulder. "You know we don't mean that. Joseph and Christian haven't been brought down in all this time. And like Brother Post told you, it's not likely any more prisoners will be released yet this winter. All of us have to find some peace over this."

Daat clenched his jaw. "That's easy enough to say, but how am I to find peace while my boys are missing? They're alone among the heathen. How can they stand fast in the faith when they're so young? Isn't my responsibility as a father to care for my children's souls?"

Barbara wrung her apron between shaking hands. "Johannes and I are every bit as concerned about Joseph and Christli as you, but what benefit is it for us to get our father back if you only worry yourself to death over them? All of us have to live the life God puts before us as long as He lets us stay on this earth."

She saw everyone's raised eyebrows and sidelong looks, but the long pent-up worry and frustration boiled over. "This is all we talk about anymore. It's all you talk about, Daat! Maybe Joseph and Christli will never come home. Maybe they're not meant to come home. How can we know what God's will is?"

Uncle Jakob Buerki sat back in his rocking chair, thoughtfully stroking his beard. "We humans tend to put our will ahead of *Gott's*. But that never works out so *guud*."

Barbara saw her father flinch. Color rushed into his face and he thrust his chin in the air. "This man Post who wrote the petition to the governor for me has considerable influence. *Gott* willing, he'll persuade Governor Hamilton to put pressure on the Indians to bring them down." He pressed his handkerchief against his mouth, every breath rattling.

Fighting back tears, Barbara said, "We're your *Kinder* too, Daat, and your grandchildren are here. We need you! But anymore it seems like we're nowhere near as important as the ones who are missing."

Crist looked up from bouncing two-year-old Jacob on his knee. *"Liebe—"*

"Well, it's true!"

Daat opened his mouth to speak, but Hans Blanck, who had been listening silently, cut him off. "Maybe by working so hard to bring your boys home instead of trusting Him, you might get in the way of *Gott's* perfect plan, Jakob. And something terrible might happen as a result."

Daat stared at his friend as though stricken. Then he stood abruptly and without another word made his way outside with faltering steps.

Barbara started to follow, but Crist caught her hand, stopping her. When she looked down to meet his gaze, he shook his head.

❖━━━━❖

THE MONOTONOUS DRONE of cicadas pulsated on the air, drowning out the rasp of grasshoppers and whisper of wind that tugged at Jakob's hair and clothing. It was late afternoon by the time they returned home from Barbara and Crist's, and Jakob had gone immediately to walk the fields alone.

Now he dropped to his knees beside the graves of his wife and children. It had been five years, yet the memories still assaulted him, as piercing as on that early autumn day when war cries rang through the valley.

He saw it now: Barbara and Johannes and the others were right. They had seen what he had not. He had been blind!

The realization crushed him. From the moment he and his boys had been carried away from that ruined plantation, he had striven against God. He had determined that this tragedy—which God had allowed—would not break him, that he would restore by the sheer force of his will what remained of his shattered family. No matter the cost.

He had not stopped to consider what God's purpose might have been in allowing the attack and its aftermath, nor what His will might be even now. Instead he had forged ahead in his stubborn self-will every step of the way.

But maybe God had a different end in mind! A better plan than Jakob's own, one he could not see—perhaps never would in this life.

He lay prone on the ground and clawed at the grass and dirt with work-roughened hands, silent sobs shaking him. How was he to give up the desperate longing to clasp his boys again to his bosom? Would that not be to abandon them?

Yet there was no choice. He knew that too. And that this was one thing he could not do in his own strength.

"Your will, *mein Gott*—Your will, not mine!" he cried through tears. "I surrender to You. If You see fit to bring my boys back to me, I will praise You. And if I never . . . if I never see their faces again here on this earth . . . I will still praise you. Change my heart so it is all Thine own."

Agony seared through him, and he could only whisper, weeping, "Only . . . ach, *Gott,* if only it could be Your will that I should hold my boys in my arms again! If only . . ." He drew a shuddering breath. "Yet still I will trust You!"

How long he lay there in anguish, head buried in his arms, he did not know. But by degrees a deep quietness settled in his soul for the first time since that day of destruction.

✦ ⋯ ✦

THE DREAM HAD NOT COME to him since his return home. But that night, lying on his narrow bed in the small *Kammer* he and Johannes and Crist had added onto the back of Johannes's *Stube,* he dreamed that he stood once more on that high hill in the greening spring before the altar. To the east, the rising sun cast long, golden fingers across the land and brightened a cloudless azure sky.

The lamb bound on the wood piled atop the hard grey stones held his attention this time. Its white fleece rippled softly in the breath of the cool wind, and its calm eye held Jakob in a steady, piercing look. Although the lamb made no sound to break the quiet of that morn, a still, clear voice rang in Jakob's ears.

Jakob! Why do you strive with Me? You think that you must make atonement by your works, but only I can atone for sin. Do I not see your children where they are? Do I not hold them in my hand? I have not forgotten them—or you. I have heard your prayers and I will answer.

The voice ceased and the lamb looked away, down the hill. Jakob turned to follow its gaze and saw that two young men walked toward him up the slope. Both were clad in Indian dress, with long hair ruffled by the wind, and as they drew nearer, recognition flooded over Jakob with a shock that took his breath away.

They did not look as they had at his last sight of them. They were taller, lean and muscular, and their faces bore the angular contours of men. But he knew them at once, knew the elder's intense hazel eyes and the younger's, as clear a blue as the sky, and such joy flooded over him that he could not contain it.

He tried to run to embrace them, but his feet would not move, while they continued to climb the hill, silent, gazing up at him in expectation. And when they stopped before him in front of the altar, at last, at last his arms were around them and theirs around him. And together, tears mingling, they fell to their knees before the altar in wonder and gratitude, bowing before the Lamb.

The dream slowly dissolved into the delicate light of early dawn. Jakob came to himself, tears still coursing down his cheeks, his heart too full for utterance.

Chapter Thirty-nine

FALLING LEAF MOON
Thursday, October 14, 1762

B RINGS DAWN PLIED his oar in strong, regular strokes that
matched those of Menetopalis and Red Squirrel. Mehíttuk,
Smoke in Sky, and Wanderer followed closely in the second canoe as they swept around a bend in the Muskingum and
the first scattered cabins of Tamaque's Town came into view
ahead of them.

"You row like women!" Brings Dawn shouted, grinning at
Contrary Wind's laughter behind him and Menetopalis's derisive
snort.

Wanderer taunted, "You'd better let Contrary Wind take your
oar. He can row twice as fast as you."

"And more smoothly too," jeered Mehíttuk. "Your canoe
bucks like a horse."

All day they had traded jests and insults as they raced the heavily laden canoes up the Muskingum. Brings Dawn had designed
both vessels, and they slipped with equal smoothness through the
water, skimming on the current's crest with each stroke of the oar
in spite of the burden of trade goods they bore.

They redoubled their efforts as they approached the town. Contrary Wind shouted encouragement and Brings Dawn, Red Squirrel, and Menetopalis surged ahead to bring their canoe to shore in a swirl of water a forearm's length ahead of the other.

Three moons had passed since they pushed their canoes off for their journey down the Muskingum and far up the White Woman River, with Red Squirrel and Smoke in Sky joining them at the last minute. Now the vibrant crimsons, russet, limes, and golds of the Falling Leaf Moon flamed through the forest, interspersed here and there with the pines' brooding green. On their return along the placid waterways, Brings Dawn had marveled at the glowing tunnel of brilliantly colored branches they slipped through, with only the whisper of current and breeze and splash of oars breaking the hush.

Contrary Wind scrambled onto the riverbank after Brings Dawn, and both steadied Menetopalis as he clambered out. While the others pulled the vessels up onto the landing place, Brings Dawn filled his lungs with the sharp tannin of oak leaves, the acrid scent of wood smoke, and the mouth-watering aroma of cooking meat, corn, and beans that mingled on the cool, dry air. His stomach growled, and he was glad it was almost time for the late afternoon meal.

Many of the townspeople came down to the river to meet them. Brings Dawn saw that a number of them moved slowly, appearing weak and feverish. More troubling, most scowled and turned away when they recognized him and his companions, among them Evening Rain's parents.

Speaks Truth was with them, and Brings Dawn reached out to clasp his friend's hand. But Speaks Truth turned abruptly, face blank, eyes unreadable, and walked off, his movements tentative and uncertain like one who is lost and does not see where he goes. Brings Dawn watched, chastened, as Evening Rain's father went to walk with his daughter's husband, his arm around the younger man's bowed shoulders.

Brings Dawn became aware that Wanderer hesitated beside him, and that both of them were the focus of darkly resentful looks. When Menetopalis greeted their neighbors, the majority turned their backs on him as well and stalked off. Wanderer's parents, who hurried to lead him away, received the same treatment.

Evening Rain's mother stood amid a cluster of villagers. "Wulachen did not give back her son, while we were robbed of our daughter and granddaughter," she said, loudly enough for Brings Dawn to hear. "Even her uncles Tamaque and Shingas gave back their children. Why was she allowed to send Brings Dawn away so he could not be taken from her? Does she not have a younger son to comfort her? But we have no one, and Speaks Truth will never get over his grief." She broke down, weeping, and her friends led her away.

As Brings Dawn turned, stricken, he saw his mother and sisters approaching. Wulachen held her head high and ignored the accusing stares of the others, but his sisters moved furtively, with downcast faces. And all three appeared gaunt and haggard as though they also had recently recovered from some illness.

A few of the townspeople spoke to them as they passed, but none who had been forced to send a child or wife back to the

English. In spite of Wulachen's proud bearing, her lips were pressed into a tight line, her eyes dark with pain.

While they unloaded the trade goods they had purchased and carried them to the cabin, she told them that a deadly sickness had swept the Muskingum Valley during their absence—the same malady Brings Dawn and his party had encountered on the upper White Woman River. Many of the townspeople had died, as had others from villages all around them. Wulachen and her daughters had fallen ill as well, and Bird's Nest had only begun to recover.

When Brings Dawn hurried into the cabin after Menetopalis, he saw that a lingering fever still flushed his grandmother's withered cheeks. The tide of illness had begun to recede from the region, Wulachen assured them, and they were all at last on the mend, though still weak.

Contrary Wind ran outside to find his friends, and Wulachen shooed She Sings and Moonflower off to gather nuts in the forest. While Wulachen sorted through the trade goods they had brought and stowed the packages away, Menetopalis asked about their neighbors' refusal to greet them.

"Let Tamaque and the others be angry," Wulachen snapped. "They made their choice as I made mine. I have both my sons with me and I will not be sorry for that. They could have refused to send their children or wives away too." She met Brings Dawn's gaze, but quickly glanced away. "What they think is nothing to me."

He heard the sorrow and uncertainty in her voice, however. Despite her denials, he knew that the rejection of her people

330 | Bob Hostetler and J. M. Hochstetler

wounded her deeply and feared it would, over time, eat like a canker into her soul.

"What of Shingas and Tamaque?" Menetopalis persisted. "Did they say nothing?"

Wulachen only shrugged.

From her pallet by the fire Bird's Nest answered weakly, "They kept silent, though they took their own children along with the rest." She pursed her lips, deepening the wrinkles around her toothless mouth. "They did not come back after the treaty. Those who returned say my brothers travel far to talk peace to our people and uncles and brothers."

Wulachen waved her hand. "Brother Onas gave out rich gifts at the treaty, unlike this General Amherst, who only sneers at us. But despite Brother Onas's fine words, white settlers already cover our lands like the mosquitoes in summer."

"Our Seneca brothers are for striking the English," Bird's Nest quavered. "They say this General Amherst gave away our lands to the white settlers and has a mind to cut us off from the face of the earth. Their warriors carry the war belt from town to town as they did a winter ago, and now many of our northern kin have taken it in their hands. Our Turkey Division holds back because of my brothers, but even here Neolin's teachings are a whirlwind fanning anger against the Whites."

"We could smell the fear of the Moravian youth called Hec-ke-wel-der." Contempt tinged Wulachen's voice. "Only a few sleeps after the man Post returned from the treaty, the boy rode hurriedly away to seek safety among his people."

"What of Post?"

Wulachen glanced at Brings Dawn, then frowned down at the length of trade cloth she was folding. "That one seems to feel no fear, my son. He rides to all the towns along the Muskingum, urging the people to hold Brother Onas in their bosoms and cast down the war belt." Her voice softened as she added, "He returns often to tell us that his Father in Heaven loves us and would do us much kindness if we followed His ways."

Brings Dawn leaned toward her. "Do you go to hear him speak?"

Wulachen exchanged a glance with Bird's Nest before nodding sadly. "That one respects our people. He speaks many good words from the writings he calls Bi-ble. It comforts me to hear them. But few of our people will listen to him now. More than once our warriors have threatened him with death, but I ask Manitou to spare his life."

Brings Dawn held his tongue, but his curiosity about the Moravian sharpened.

Menetopalis grunted. "These people who call themselves Christians talk much about peace and the way of this man called Jesus. But it seems to me that they expect our people to follow His path, while they do not follow it themselves. They say: Do not steal. But their settlers steal our lands and their traders cheat us. They say: Do not fight. But they kill us. They say: Speak truth. But their tongues are crooked. We put our marks on their treaties and hold to their terms, but they break every one."

"It is so, my father," Brings Dawn agreed. "There are men among the Whites who claim to believe in Father in Heaven but violate His teachings. Those who truly follow Jesus don't act in such ways. The people I was born among have not done these things, nor have these Moravians, and there are others as well. There are bad people among us, too, who speak fine words but do evil."

"Neolin speaks the words of Manitou," Menetopalis growled. "Post's Father in Heaven belongs to the white man, not to the red man. The Master of Life will give us favor and protection when we cast the English out of the lands he has given us. Only then will we have peace."

They were interrupted by Contrary Wind, who entered the cabin, slunk to the fireplace, and squatted on the hearth with his back to them. Wulachen bent and smoothed his hair, then cupped his chin in her hand and lifted his head.

"What troubles you, my son?"

Contrary Wind scowled and crossed his arms over his chest. "My friends will not play with me. They say you disgraced our people by sending Brings Dawn away to hide him, while everyone else had to give children and wives back to the Whites."

Tears rolled down his cheeks. Brings Dawn looked from him to the others, and the anguish he saw in their features tore through his heart like a lance thrust.

Chapter Forty

First Snow Moon

Saturday, November 20, 1762

WULACHEN FACED POST, who stood on his cabin steps. "How can you call Father in Heaven a God of love? Such a God would never tear a son from his mother."

Across the yard, Brings Dawn stepped farther back into the shadows. A wind stirred the last dry leaves that clung to the branches overhead, even as restlessness stirred his soul.

He had accompanied Wulachen to Post's cabin that evening to hear the Moravian preach about a long-lost son who returned to his father. A scattering of the town's matrons and elders and a few children also attended, listening to Post's words with blank expressions before slipping away as soon as he finished his sermon. Wulachen, however, lingered until everyone had gone, stepping forward when the Moravian beckoned her with a smile.

Patiently, gently, Post answered, "Did not Shingas and Tamaque take children from their mothers? Have you yourself not kept a son from the mother who bore him—and from his father and brothers and sisters? I have written petitions to Brother Onas for many such families and seen their tears. Is their grief not as great as your own?"

His chest tightening, Brings Dawn kept his gaze fixed on Wulachen.

She stared at the Moravian for a long moment, then lifted her chin. "The English bring their cattle into our lands and cut down our trees to build their houses—these people who say they believe in Father in Heaven. They sell the drink that drives our people out of their minds, then take lands that belong to us and kill us or throw us out. Are we not justified in defending our homes and families?"

"It is so, my sister. But your warriors also attacked and slaughtered many families who bought lands legally purchased from the tribes who owned them, and carried away their children. They had done you no wrong. If one does evil and the one offended responds with equal evil, can any good result? Are not both still evil?"

Wulachen bowed her head and buried her face in her hands.

"My sister, none of us is without sin. It is the mark of the Father's love that He calls all of us to repentance that He may forgive and restore us to one another and to Him."

She bent like a broken reed and fell to her knees in the dust at the Moravian's feet, rocking back and forth, keening. "How can I send my son away? I cannot tear him from my heart! Father in Heaven, if you are a good God, you will not require this!"

Post knelt beside her, but she would not be comforted.

Brings Dawn spun around and stumbled away, fighting back his own tears. *Father, what would you have me do? My heart is bound to theirs, and if we are torn from one another, how can we live?*

Striding out of the town, he wandered through the surrounding forest. *Tell me what to do! Give me a sign.* But the depths of his heart still harbored the plea: *Let me stay!*

❖┄┄❖

BRINGS DAWN AND HIS FRIENDS finished their dance and moved off toward the far side of the council house yard. Three days had passed, bringing no answers and no peace for Brings Dawn's troubled soul.

His gaze fell on a matron standing in the flickering firelight at the edge of the crowd with three young women he took to be her daughters—one about his age and two younger. Something about them seemed familiar, but he couldn't bring to mind where or when they might have met.

He hurried to join his friends, but his attention was repeatedly drawn to the oldest of the woman's daughters, a lithe maiden garbed in beaded doeskin. Spots of rich red and black were painted on her cheeks and eyelids, and her long, glossy, dark hair, wrapped in a ribbon-laced cloth, cascaded down her back.

He studied her while making a show of adjusting his turkey feather mantle around his shoulders. She seemed to take no notice of him, but when he had given up hope of attracting her attention, unexpectedly she lifted her gaze and returned his with a blush and a shy smile.

His heart leaped as the memory rushed back of their last meeting before he and his family had left Sauconk for the Muskingum—and the keen disappointment that had twisted his heart when she told him she and her family were also moving away, but far north instead. She was more beautiful than he remembered. During the past winters she had grown a little taller and more womanly in shape, and he stood as though frozen, taking her in.

Beside him, Mehíttuk nodded her direction. "See there—it is Many Leaves, with her sisters and mother, First Snow! Have they come to live among us again?"

Their companions all turned to look and murmured their surprise and pleasure. Those standing around First Snow and her daughters were welcoming them with laughter and happy embraces. Mehíttuk wasted no time in striding over to them, leaving Brings Dawn to watch enviously as his friend engaged Many Leaves in conversation.

Red Squirrel nudged him, grinning broadly. "Will you not also greet her, or will you concede the contest to Mehíttuk?"

Brings Dawn shrugged. "No doubt we will meet later. There are many who come to greet them now."

Red Squirrel gave him a sly look. "Let Mehíttuk have her then. I can see her return is nothing to you . . . or perhaps it is that your arrows have no points."

Brings Dawn elbowed Red Squirrel. "It is easy for a man to speak boldly. But a maiden, like a deer, is won slowly, with stealth and skill, not by loud boasts."

"We all know your great stealth and skill when it comes to the maidens, my friend."

"And yours when it comes to White Dove."

The jab struck its mark, and Red Squirrel winced. "In truth, both of us have much to learn about women."

They joined in laughter.

It seemed an eternity to Brings Dawn before the fires were finally extinguished and the dancers began to disperse into the starlit night. Leaning back against the peeling trunk of a tall sycamore whose bare branches laced the sky above him, he studied the constellations arrayed in the indigo bowl of the heavens and estimated that it must be well past midnight.

His family and friends headed off to their cabins, and only a few people lingered on the yard, clustered around First Snow and her daughters. They would make their beds that night in the nearby cabin reserved for guests, he saw.

Although Mehíttuk had clung to Many Leaves' side all evening like a burr, she had from time to time darted uncertain glances toward Brings Dawn. He had no wish to openly challenge his friend, but he grew impatient. At last Mehíttuk and the others took their leave, however, and Brings Dawn straightened and took a step toward the cabin.

Without a glance in his direction, Many Leaves turned her back and followed her mother and sisters into the cabin, closing the door firmly behind her.

✦ ┈┈ ✦

BRINGS DAWN SMILED down at Many Leaves. "I'm glad you and your family will make your home here."

He had tracked her all that day as he would stalk a shy deer, at last managing to cross her path while she was alone. Now he leaned closer, hand propped against the trunk of the tree they stood beneath. Pleased that she did not move away, he gazed into the depths of her dark eyes, feeling as though the ground shifted under his feet.

"Because we can play *pahsahëman* in the spring again?" she asked, her expression sweet, her tone mocking.

"*Pahsahëman?*"

"The last time we talked, you told me you would miss playing against me."

Heat rose to his face. "No—I mean . . . yes! You are a worthy opponent, and I took great pleasure in our contests. I hope you did as well. But that isn't what I meant . . . " He ducked his head, humiliation leaving him at a loss for words.

She touched his hand, and he grasped hers, amazed and encouraged when she wove her fingers between his. He looked down to find her beaming up at him, and his heart leaped at the warmth in her eyes.

"I knew what you meant. I was sad because I feared I would never see you again."

Strangely, he was no longer standing on solid ground. It seemed as though their separation had never been, as though he floated off his feet and it was only her hand that held him firmly to the earth.

"You go to the dance tonight?"

She nodded, smiling, and squeezed his hand. Surely there was no greater happiness than what filled him in that moment.

It was the sign he had sought from Father in Heaven, he assured himself. His future was here with his people after all. And with her.

＋－－－－＋

BRINGS DAWN DREW on his pipe and released a thin stream of tobacco smoke toward the ceiling of Tamaque's cabin. He cast a tentative glance toward his great-uncle and his wife, noting the silver that threaded more thickly than before through the dark hair of both.

"It has been many sleeps since your return, my uncle. My mother and grandmother have missed you and my aunt at our fire, and my uncle Shingas as well."

Tamaque gave him a level look. "We returned many of the white men's flesh and blood at the treaty, my nephew. But Brother Onas reminded us that we did not keep our word to bring all of them. Thus we were disgraced."

For some moments only the crack and pop of the fire broke the silence.

"It is not the fault of your sister and niece that I did not go with you. I am a man, and it was for me alone to make this decision." Brings Dawn struck his chest. "I am Lenape! Here are my people, and I would stay among you. I have little memory of those I was born to. Why should I leave the ones I love and go far away to a people who will consider me as a stranger and an Indian who is no longer welcome in their midst?"

"I am proud of you, my nephew. If it were in my hand, you would stay. All our children would have stayed. But it is not for me to decide this thing. Much evil was done on both sides in that war that brought you to us, and if we do not keep the terms the English set, much more evil will be added to it. You know there is again talk among our Seneca brothers of war against the Whites, and some of our own people begin to hold with them."

Brings Dawn glanced toward Tamaque's wife. Encouraged by her sympathetic nod, he turned back to Tamaque.

"I overheard one of the Seneca warriors talking with two of our own men on my way here. This very night, while everyone is dancing and he is alone, they plan to kill the man Post."

Tamaque stiffened. "I carry Post in my bosom, and this shall not be done. Tell me who these men are."

Brings Dawn complied, and Tamaque took him immediately to speak to men he trusted.

It was a blustery day, with thick clouds streaming across a grey sky and a fine, chilling mist blowing out of the north. Few people were about as their party hurried to Post's cabin by a circuitous route to avoid the men Brings Dawn had named.

Well before midday he and his uncle accompanied the small party out of the town with the Moravian in their midst, moving stealthily. When they had gone some distance the men mounted, whipped their horses to a gallop, and were quickly out of sight.

Brings Dawn and Tamaque returned to the town, deliberately passing the cabin where the men had plotted Post's death. They found them lounging in the yard with bottles of rum in hand, already drunk.

As they strode back to Tamaque's cabin, backs hunched against wind and rain, his uncle's hand rested affectionately on Brings Dawn's shoulder. The few people they passed greeted Tamaque with respect, while keeping their faces turned away from Brings Dawn.

That he had unexpectedly been given the opportunity to protect his uncle's honored friend softened the sting of their rejection, however. For by this deed his place among his people had surely been confirmed by a second sign that he was to stay.

Chapter Forty-one

STRAWBERRY MOON
Saturday, June 18, 1763

STAR CATCHER RAN, crouching, behind the line of warriors, rifle in one hand, two bulging rawhide pouches clutched in the other. Panting, he dodged the bullets that pelted the dawn-gilded branches above his head like hail, scattering torn leaves and broken twigs to the wind, and dropped to his knees behind the tangled windfall where Raven Eye crouched next to Black Fox. Raven Eye acknowledged him with a quick nod before sighting his rifle and firing.

War cries echoed through the forest raising the hair on Star Catcher's neck. A fierce thrill coursed through his veins as flaming arrows sliced the air, impaling the fort's palisade wall and the roofs of the buildings inside.

Fort Le Boeuf stood at a fork of French Creek north of Custaloga's Town. Surrounded on three sides by water, it guarded the southern end of the portage road that led to Lake Erie. Star Catcher had a vague memory of stopping here overnight on the journey to Presque Isle with his captors six winters earlier.

The French had burned the fort when they retreated from the area during the past war, and the British had built a smaller, less imposing structure on the same site. According to a Seneca warrior who had been inside it, the garrison consisted of only a dozen men with no cannon, making it the perfect object for a raid.

A willowy maiden, Draws the Bow, stood a few yards away, fearlessly erect amid the clouds of gunsmoke partially obscuring the warriors who roiled along the windfall to either side. As Star Catcher watched, she nocked a flaming arrow to her bowstring, drew the bow into a graceful curve, and released it to fly in a high, true arc.

It buried its head in the fort's gate with a solid thunk, and immediately flames sprang upward along the tinder-dry wood. Without pausing Draws the Bow took another blazing arrow from her friend, Grey Goose, and sent it after the first.

Raven Eye also watched the maiden with undisguised admiration. "Is Draws the Bow not a warrior second to none, though she is a maiden?"

Star Catcher grunted his agreement. A little older than he, she had become a close friend to him and his older brother. She increasingly occupied Star Catcher's thoughts, as she clearly did Raven Eye's.

Another volley of lead exploded through the leaves, and Star Catcher dropped flat into the dust. Black Fox squinted down the barrel of his rifle, scowling, pulled the trigger, then hastily reloaded, emptying the last of the powder and ball in his pouches.

Early that spring Seneca warriors had brought to Custaloga's Town the war belt sent by the great Ottawa chieftain Pontiac to tribes throughout the lands of the Ohio and the Great Lakes. Custaloga's anger had simmered for some time over the encroachment of British soldiers and forts into the land west of the Allegheny Mountains in violation of their treaty, and this time he had taken up the war belt.

Raven Eye, Black Fox, and many other young men had immediately shaved their heads, leaving only a scalp lock they adorned with turkey feathers and silver brooches. They eagerly accompanied the mixed parties of Seneca and Lenape warriors that soon issued from the town on raids, and each time returned jubilant, bringing scalps and captives.

Only two days earlier a party had attacked Fort Venango downriver where French Creek flowed into the Ohio. Raven Eye confided to Star Catcher that the entire twelve-man garrison had been killed, with their commander kept alive only long enough to write down their grievances before the Seneca warriors burned him at the stake.

The descriptions of the raids aroused painful, long-supressed memories for Star Catcher. He was thankful that at seventeen winters he was not yet the age of a warrior, and also that each man was free to decide whether he would fight. But the longing to prove himself and claim his full place among his people continued to nag at him until he at last decided to test himself by joining the next raid.

His opportunity had come more quickly than he anticipated. He was assigned to carry supplies and guard the horses, along with several other youths of his age and a few of the young women. And fighting back misgivings, he had shaved his head into a scalp lock and painted his face and body in vivid slashes of red and black like the warriors.

"Give me more ammunition!"

Raven Eye's urgent demand wrested Star Catcher back to the present, and he held out the pouches clutched in his hand. Raven Eye snatched them and swiftly reloaded, while Black Fox rose onto his knees, sighted his weapon, and pulled the trigger. Flame and smoke erupted from the barrel with a deafening report as gunfire roared all around them. Black Fox instantly dropped back into cover and snatched the pouches from Raven Eye.

Cautiously Star Catcher raised his head until he could see across the battlefield. "Draws the Bow's arrows set the gate aflame. It totters on its hinges."

A high, warbling cry chorused through the forest, and the line of warriors surged over and around the windfall with shrill, triumphant screams. Raven Eye and Black Fox leaped up to follow them.

Raven Eye waved Star Catcher back. "Guard the horses!"

Star Catcher scrambled to his feet, rifle in hand. "I go with you!"

Standing Stone appeared beside him and shoved him toward the rear. "Do as your brother says!" He ran forward as the fort's gates collapsed in a shower of sparks.

As Star Catcher hesitated more warriors surged around him, sweeping him forward in their wake. They rounded the side of the palisade in a tight pack. Directly ahead of them he saw several soldiers forcing their way through a gap and scrambling into the underbrush.

With the others he closed at full flight, gasping for breath, blood pounding in his ears. The soldiers turned, rifles raised, and bullets whined around him like hornets, a sharp pain searing the length of his arm.

He stumbled to a halt, rifle to his shoulder, sighting his shot with shaking hands. Gunfire exploded on both sides and his finger jerked reflexively on the trigger.

The rifle recoiled with startling force. Squinting down the barrel's length he saw two soldiers fall, while the rest scattered out of sight among the trees.

He stood stock still, staring at the bodies sprawled bleeding on the ground as the battle raged on around him.

❖ • • • ❖

A MAN CANNOT KILL ANOTHER *without having his heart scarred by it.*

The words had resounded in Star Catcher's mind since the previous day, from the moment he fired his rifle at the fleeing soldiers. He absently clamped his hand over the raw furrow a bullet had plowed the length of his arm and fixed his gaze on Custaloga, who stood at the head of the council. Although the sachem's lips moved, Star Catcher could not hear his voice.

Who had said those words? They came to him from long ago. From his white life. Only by slow degrees did the identity of the speaker emerge from the past.

An older brother. Jake. He had been telling him and the other one, whose name he could not remember, about something their father—Daat—had said at another fort, one that had a strange-sounding name. North. North . . . kill.

Did I kill one of those soldiers?

Many warriors had fired, some at the same time, others just before or after he did. The soldiers had fallen together, one dead with a bullet through his head, the other writhing on the ground with blood pulsing from his breast until one of the warriors dispatched him with a tomahawk and scalped him.

Most of the fort's garrison had managed to escape downstream, but those the warriors captured had also been killed and scalped. Although Star Catcher had kept his distance, he had seen enough—too much—the bloody images etched into his mind.

More memories returned with appalling vividness: an inferno in a cabin, cries and screams, terror that made him lightheaded. His white father refusing to let him and his brother shoot at their attackers.

Joseph. The name formed with the images, and he could feel again the scorching heat, the smoke choking his lungs.

As though it came from far away, Custaloga's voice sounded through the roaring in Star Catcher's ears. Head thrown back proudly, the sachem waved his arm toward the fresh scalps hanging on poles at the front of the council house. He spoke of how Neolin's prophecies were coming true, assuring the gathered assembly that the Master of Life would grant them his favor once they had thrown the white settlers and traders entirely out of the lands he had given to them alone. Approving murmurs rippled through the council house.

So many deaths, Star Catcher thought numbly. *On both sides. So much loss. And for what?*

Raven Eye nudged him with his elbow. "You did well in the battle, my brother."

Black Fox added his agreement, and Draws the Bow leaned forward from her seat behind them to whisper, "You brought honor to our people."

Star Catcher forced a smile. He should have been proud, especially at Draws the Bow's praise. He should have been happy.

Instead his heart lay silent as a stone.

Chapter Forty-two

FIRST SNOW MOON
Tuesday, November 15, 1763

S TAR CATCHER STEPPED outside the wigewa he and Raven
Eye had built two springs ago, when Deep Water gave birth
to another son. He gathered his blanket more tightly and
drew in a breath of the crisp, still air as he surveyed the town in
the clear dawn light.

For the last time. The evening before he had gone alone to
visit Nútemau's grave and renewed his pledge to always remain
with the Lenape. Today he and Raven Eye and his family would
join a large party from Custaloga's Town and Cussewago on a
journey many miles southwest to the great native towns along
the upper reaches of the Muskingum.

Late in the summer, when it became clear that the English
would not be dislodged from the Ohio Territory that year, many
families had gone before them to avoid reprisals. With the last of
a poor crop harvested, more townspeople were leaving before the
winter storms made the journey difficult. Some of the men were
staying behind, however. And already many Seneca and Shawnee
warriors had moved into the town to bolster their numbers.

A delicate film of frost coated rooftops and bare branches, and thin ribbons of smoke twined from each chimney and outdoor fire pit into the hazy, pink sky. Always before the sight had brought Star Catcher peace and pleasure. Since the raid four moons earlier, however, a dark foreboding had crouched in his heart like a panther waiting to pounce.

Eight of the smaller British forts had fallen to Pontiac's allies that spring and summer. A combined force of Seneca, Ottawa, and Ojibwa warriors had also dealt a crushing defeat to the British along the Niagara Falls portage, so far the bloodiest engagement of the war. The besieged garrison at Fort Pitt, however, had doggedly held out until a strong force under Colonel Henry Bouquet fought through an ambush at Bushy Run to relieve them.

Now word had reached the town that Fort Detroit, which Pontiac had besieged since the spring, remained undefeated. With all hope of French assistance in their war against the English shattered and many of the tribes deserting him, the Ottawa leader had withdrawn west to the Maumee River to rebuild his alliances.

Raven Eye stepped out of the wigewa, and they walked together to the fire pit in front of his mother's cabin several yards away, where they shared the morning meal.

"I long to see the towns of the Muskingum." Star Catcher wiped his bowl clean with a fragment of corn cake. "Will it not be good to live where the English cannot bother us?"

Raven Eye snorted. "Let the French give the entire upper country to the English in their Paris Treaty if they will. This summer we have shown them that we are not bound by their papers, and in the spring we will finally clear our lands of them."

"The English have many soldiers and much ammunition," Star Catcher pointed out.

Standing Stone looked up from his bowl. "The Master of Life will give us the power to cast them out if we keep the commandments he gave to Neolin."

Raven Eye indicated the buckskin he and Star Catcher wore. "*We* have already cast off the traders' goods, my father." He glanced pointedly at his mother's and sisters' stroud clothing.

"So now you will only hunt and fight with the bow?" Deep Water fed a bite of corn and bean stew to two-year-old Hopping Frog, who squirmed on her lap.

"I have pledged to cast off my rifle when we reach the Muskingum."

Sixteen-year-old Good Road smirked. "Such a thing is easier to say than to do, my brother."

Their neighbors on either side were packing bundles onto horses and travois. Moments later, Black Fox's and Draws the Bow's families passed by, leading their laden horses, on the way to the Big House, where they were to gather.

Black Fox shouted at Raven Eye and Star Catcher, mocking their laziness. They answered his jibes but hurried to help Standing Stone load their own horses, while Deep Water and her daughters extinguished the fire and cleared away the remains of the meal.

At last the cabin stood empty. Star Catcher took the reins of his horse and, joining Raven Eye and Standing Stone at the head of their small party, he strode down the path with a light heart.

Chapter Forty-three

PLANTING MOON
Monday, May 21, 1764

B RINGS DAWN RACED down the field in all-out flight. He tore free of the young women who clawed at him from beside and behind, causing one to tumble onto the ground as she lost hold of his shirt. He could feel the fabric rip but reached the *pahsahikàn* before any of the women could intercept it.

It was the beginning of the corn planting ceremony and the first game of *pahsahëman* for the season, and Brings Dawn exulted in the physical contest. He kicked the oblong deerskin ball hard, spurting it toward Mehíttuk and Red Squirrel, who kept pace with him along the field's outer boundary. The two youths shouted hoarse encouragement at the men who maneuvered to stay between the women players and the *pahsahikàn*.

The ball hit a tuft of grass and bounced high. Before Smoke in Sky could reach it, Many Leaves appeared out of nowhere and dove for it, sliding across the muddy ground. Before Brings Dawn' disbelieving eyes, she rolled several times, then was on her feet, clothing streaked with mud but with the *pahsahikàn* clutched to her breast as she fled back toward the women's goal at the opposite end of the broad field.

He raced down the field. "Stop her!"

Everyone abruptly changed direction, the women now fighting to hold back the men. Gasping for breath and hard on Many Leaves' heels, Brings Dawn passed Red Squirrel, Mehíttuk, and Bear Claw and expertly feinted his way through the melee of screaming women.

Her gleaming black braid swung mockingly from side to side as she ran, and he was momentarily tempted to grab it. Instead he grasped the back of her shirt just as she reached the goal line and threw herself over it, dragging him with her. As he fell hard on top of her, he heard the grunt of her breath expelling from her lungs.

Behind them the women's shouts of victory were answered by the men's loud objections. But Brings Dawn was conscious only of the supple contours of Many Leaves' body as she writhed beneath him, fighting to break free.

Other players surrounded them. He slid off Many Leaves and bent anxiously over her, while she rolled on the muddy ground, chest heaving with the struggle to suck in air.

First Snow and Wulachen pushed through the crowd to kneel beside them, and an instant later Mehíttuk appeared. Shouldering past Brings Dawn, he knelt and gathered Many Leaves into his arms.

She took a shuddering breath, let it out, then turned her head to give Brings Dawn a weak smile. The pace of his heart slowed, but his chest still felt as though it were squeezed in a vise.

"She only lost her breath," Mehíttuk reassured First Snow. "See, she will be well. I will carry her to your cabin."

As he and the women rose, Brings Dawn sprang to his feet, his gaze still fixed on Many Leaves.

Mehíttuk scowled at him. "You are too rough with the women. Next time be more careful. She could have been badly hurt."

Brings Dawn watched Mehíttuk carry Many Leaves off the field, followed by First Snow. He looked around to find Menetopalis and saw him leaning on his walking stick at the field's edge with thirteen-year-old Contrary Wind. The boy ran to Brings Dawn and eagerly accompanied him back to their father, chattering about how he would soon be old enough to join in the rough-and-tumble game and help the men overcome the women.

Menetopalis tipped his head toward Mehittuk and Many Leaves. "That one thinks Many Leaves favors him. But I see her look at you."

Brings Dawn wiped the sweat from his face with his bare arm. "He is right. I could have hurt her."

"But you did not." Menetopalis paused. "Perhaps if you took her to wife. She is willing, and—"

"That would only make things worse. And where would we go?"

"To Chalahgawtha among the Shawnee? The river bottoms at the mouth of the Scioto are good for planting, and our brothers do not care about this matter. They have refused to give back those they took as their own."

"Their hands are also strong in this war, and you know I am opposed to it. Even if I left, it would not change the women's anger against you and my mother."

Menetopalis shrugged but made no reply. They returned to Wulachen's cabin, where Bird's Nest lay on her pallet by the fire as she had since her illness two winters earlier. Brings Dawn knelt and joked with her in an effort to conceal his concern. She seemed to grow weaker and more shrunken with each passing day.

Wulachen soon joined them, with eighteen-year-old She Sings and fifteen-year-old Moonflower. Both maidens gloated over the women's win, but they had been pointedly excluded from the games, and their words sounded hollow.

Wulachen's form had grown gaunt over the past two winters, and white streaked her hair now. Her cheekbones stood out more prominently, and the sadness never left her eyes.

The censure of those who had given children or wives back to the English or had lost husbands and sons in the war showed no sign of softening. The women's scorn had finally driven Wanderer's family to leave Tamaque's Town for Wapatomica, the Shawnee's principal town at the juncture of the White Woman River and the Muskingum. It fell on First Snow and her daughters and the few other women who remained loyal to Wulachen as well. Although she refused to be driven away, the women's rejection was clearly taking a toll.

That many of the men also turned their backs on her husband and sons added to Wulachen's pain. Tamaque and Shingas would not enter her cabin. She and Menetopalis had been excluded from any formal role in the Lenape ceremonials. Worst of all, the preceding autumn, neither of them had been invited to take part in the Big House Ceremony. And the food Wulachen brought was eaten only by her immediate family and friends.

The men had thus far raised no opposition to Brings Dawn's participation in the games—because of his prowess, he reckoned. But as soon as play ended, all except his closest friends scattered as though he was covered with the stink of skunks.

Many Leaves repeatedly sought him out, but he found himself pulling back, afraid that the women would isolate her even more if they saw them together. His withdrawal wounded her deeply, he knew, but he could think of no solution.

The corn planting was to begin the following day, and his stomach clenched at thought of it. Evening Rain's mother had again been chosen by the women to oversee the work, as she had the previous spring, and she had assigned no part in either the planting or the celebration that accompanied it to Wulachen, her daughters, and those who remained their friends.

❖┄┄┄❖

THE NEXT DAY BRINGS DAWN watched his mother and her small party cluster at the fringe of the field, pretending indifference while the rest of the women took turns planting the rows of corn with songs and laughter. When they departed for the feasting and dancing, Wulachen and her daughters and friends planted the last rows of the farthest field, knowing that when harvest came, none of the others would touch their crops. The sun hung at the western treetops by the time they finished and returned home, passing the townspeople celebrating on the council house yard.

Wulachen and Brings Dawn's sisters were subdued as they prepared the evening meal, and then fed Bird's Nest the few bites she could eat. But none of them seemed to have any appetite. Brings Dawn forced down his meal, while averting his gaze from the others.

We're being . . . shunned.

He choked on a fragment of fried shad. It was a thing he had forgotten, but now an incident that had happened in his Amish community during his childhood rose starkly to his mind.

A family had done something—what, he could not remember—and everyone had turned their backs to them. No one would eat with them or talk to them more than necessary. No one visited them or accepted their visits or help with the field work. When they attended worship services, they sat alone at the back, then hurriedly left before the meal to escape further humiliation.

He remembered, too, their confession before the church. The forgiveness that had followed. And the restoration of fellowship.

What the Moravian, Post, had once said to Wulachen returned to him: *None of us is without sin. It is the mark of the Father's love that He calls all of us to repentance that He may forgive and restore us to one another and to Him.*

Feeling sick, he put down his bowl. Only one choice was left to him if his family was ever to be accepted by their people again.

◆ ⋯⋯ ◆

BRINGS DAWN SAT FACING Wulachen on the ground by the fire pit, their knees touching. She searched his eyes, her face taut.

He bent his head and reached for her hands. "I will go," he said past the hard lump in his throat. "As long as I stay, our people will hold you to blame and your uncles will be angry."

Wulachen freed one hand to dash the tears from her eyes, then raised her chin, her expression fierce. "No, my son. Why should you suffer separation from our people?"

"I already do. As do you and my father."

"It will pass! They will forget in time. I will endure their scorn until then."

"I cannot let you do that, my mother! A root of bitterness has grown up among our people that will only continue to grow. I see how they look at you. To live as a castout is a worse shame than any other. They will only forgive you if I return to the people I was born to."

"But the signs you were given—"

"I was wrong! It was my desire, not that of Father in Heaven. I must seek the future He has for me. And so must you."

She covered her face with her hands, tears trickling between her fingers. "How am I to live without both my sons by my side?"

"I would have to leave anyway if I took a wife. I would have to go to her clan, and our children would belong to her."

"But your sisters' children will need their uncle to teach and guide them."

"They have Contrary Wind. Soon he will seek his vision and become a man. And he will be a worthy one."

She nodded, eyes red rimmed. "He will, for you have been a good example to him. But if you went to one of the other towns, I would still see you and your children from time to time."

"There will be no peace between you and my uncles and the others even if I go to another town."

It was the hardest thing he had ever done, but he forced himself to say steadily, "I will go back to the people I was born among so that our people will accept my mother again and so you can live at peace with my uncles."

Seeing the despairing surrender in her eyes, he pulled her into his embrace, held her while she shook with sobs and their tears mingled. And he did not know whether he wept more for her loss or for his.

❖━━━❖

BRINGS DAWN DIDN'T NEED to tell Menetopalis of his decision. He knew his father had sensed it coming, and his silent grief wrenched Brings Dawn's heart as much as Wulachen's tears.

They met with Tamaque and Shingas. After they had smoked their pipes in silence for a long time, Tamaque said quietly, "It is a hard thing you do, my nephew. But my heart tells me you do what is right."

Brings Dawn stared down at his clenched hands, throat too tight for speech, unable to meet the older man's sympathetic gaze.

Gruffly Menetopalis said, "Where can we safely go to take my son back to his white family? Our own warriors, along with those of our brothers the Mingo and Shawnee, have made many raids already this spring. It is said the English gather an army at Fort Pitt to attack us, and to go there—" He broke off with a shake of his head.

Shingas's dark eyes sparked with rage. "Should we not take revenge for those of our people who held to the way of the

Moravians and were slaughtered? It was known they had no weapons and would not go to war, but these men from a place called Paxton took no pity even on the women and children. They killed and scalped all of them and burned their bodies."

Brings Dawn swallowed the bile that rose in his throat, fighting back a tide of burning anger. The news of the massacres that winter had flown through the Muskingum communities, causing many who had held back to take up the war hatchet, vowing revenge. He had found himself without words to oppose his friends when they joined with the warriors.

Tamaque's jaw tensed, but he did not reply to his brother. Using the Mohawk name for Sir William Johnson, the British Superintendant for Indian Affairs in the northern district, he said, "Warraghiyagey calls the Six Nations and those of the Lakes to a treaty at Fort Niagara in less than two moons' time. You will find safety among our brothers there, and Warraghiyagey can be trusted to arrange this matter. Go north and travel along the lake toward the sun's rising. You will find shelter in the towns of our brothers and uncles on your way, but take care to avoid English forts until you reach Niagara."

◆┄┄◆

PREPARATIONS FOR THE LONG journey took much less time than Brings Dawn wished, but he was grateful that his entire family insisted on accompanying him, with the exception of She Sings. Wanting Brings Dawn to share her joy before his departure, she took Grey Wolf, the young warrior who had courted her for several months, as her husband.

Already Brings Dawn saw evidence that his painful decision had been the right one. Tamaque and Shingas and their wives finally entered Wulachen's cabin again and shared a meal with them.

Several days before their departure Bird's Nest died, adding immeasurably to everyone's sadness. All else was put aside until her death rites and burial were complete. The entire town attended, another sign to Brings Dawn that his leaving would bring healing and restoration to his family.

It was near the Strawberry Moon before they finally loaded the supplies for the journey and gifts for Brings Dawn's white family onto their horses. They embraced and kissed She Sings, Shingas, and Tamaque and all their friends.

Many Leaves stood apart from the others, with Mehíttuk hovering nearby while she embraced Wulachen and Moonflower and clasped the hands of Menetopalis and Contrary Wind, blinking back tears. Before mounting his horse, Brings Dawn went hesitantly to take her hand. She did not meet his gaze, but fixed hers on their entwined fingers.

"I am sorry. You know I must go for my mother's sake."

She swallowed, nodded, finally raised her head. Seeing that her eyes brimmed with tears, he almost lost his resolution.

Gripping her hand more tightly, he looked from her to Mehíttuk and back again, hardly able to speak. "He loves you," he said hoarsely. "He would be a good husband, were you to choose him."

Again she nodded, mute.

"May Father in Heaven bless you," he whispered, and let her go.

He turned, strode blindly to his horse, and climbed into the saddle. The rest of his family were already astride, and he jerked the reins and kicked his heels into his mount's sides, urging the stallion onto the path at the rear of the small, forlorn party.

Before they followed the path's curve beyond where the trees blocked their view, he turned once more to see Tamaque and Shingas, She Sings and Grey Wolf, Red Squirrel, Smoke in Sky, and Bear Claw and their families sorrowfully watching them go. First Snow stood with her arm around Many Leaves, whose tears fell unchecked. Mehíttuk had joined them, and he waved to Brings Dawn, his face etched with both sadness and well wishes.

Brings Dawn raised his arm to return his friend's wave. Then his horse passed among the trees, and his home and the ones he loved were gone.

Chapter Forty-four

Thursday, August 23, 1764

"JOSEPH AND CHRISTIAN Hochstetler," Jakob said, speaking slowly and distinctly for the benefit of the lean, dark-haired militia soldier in Indian garb sitting at the writing desk. Grateful that the man was fluent enough in German to understand him, he continued, "Joseph would be—he'd just have turned twenty-two, and Christian, eighteen, back in February."

"Location?"

"Northkill Creek in Berks County, Pennsylvania."

Without looking up, Sir William Johnson's aide, Charles Read, thumbed through the thick sheaves of paper on the desk. Jakob looked idly around at the spacious room lined with shelves of leather-bound books, then down at his twelve-year-old grandson, Jake, Johannes's oldest son, who waited beside him.

The boy reminded Jakob of Johannes at that age, with his curly black hair and blue eyes, though his face, with its rounded contours, held much of the sweetness of Katie's. Jake slipped his hand into Jakob's calloused one, and Jakob squeezed it, glad he had brought the boy along at Johannes and Katie's suggestion.

Jakob's petition at the Easton treaty a couple of years earlier had borne no fruit. They had heard nothing at all about his missing boys, yet he clung to God's promise to Isaiah: "I will bring thy seed from the east, and gather thee from the west; I will say to the north, 'Give up'; and to the south, 'Keep not back: bring My sons from far, and My daughters from the ends of the earth . . . ' "

Word of the treaty meeting at Fort Niagara had not reached the Northkill community until late July. Over Barbara's and Johannes's objections to his traveling several hundred miles over rugged terrain, Jakob had left within a couple of days in the hope of personally speaking to Sir William Johnson. He refused Johannes's offer to come along, not wanting to hinder the work of the plantation any more than his own absence would cause, but gladly took young Jake with him.

As Johannes had predicted, the treaty had concluded by the time they reached Niagara, but Jakob reasoned that as long as they had gone this far they might as well go farther. They had continued north to Johnson Hall, Sir William's estate just outside the small village of John's Town several miles from the Mohawk River in the colony of New York. Jakob knew many captives had been returned there.

Bright sunshine slanted through the windows onto the plank floor. Through the wavy glass panes he caught glimpses of the Indian encampment that sprawled around the imposing Georgian manor with its two stone blockhouses just off the building's rear corners.

One of my boys could be out there. Or both of them, Gott *willing*

"Ah, here it is." Read picked up a page and scrutinized it. "There's one here who's Lenape—that's what the Delaware call themselves. He was taken by a warrior named Shingas—"

"Shingas led the war party that attacked us!"

"Well, he ended up with the boy, and his sister's daughter adopted him. His name is Brings Dawn, and his Indian family brought him all the way up from the Muskingum several weeks ago. They stopped at Fort Niagara first like you did, but Sir William didn't have time to talk to 'em with the treaty going on, so he sent the young man here to be enrolled.

"Says he has twenty-two winters—that's how they reckon years—and near as he can remember he came from a place called Northkill. He wasn't sure about his last name but thought it was something like Hoster or Hostler. He gave his first name as Joseph."

"It's him!" Jake bounced on his toes.

"*Ya,* I think so." Jakob squeezed his grandson's hand tighter. "Me and my boys were the only ones taken from the Northkill area, so it has to be my Joseph. Was there another? We heard a Delaware chief named Custaloga holds one of them, so he must have Christian."

Read shook his head. "No mention of Custaloga or his people bringing in any captives recently. Most brought here are held by one of the Iroquois or Great Lakes tribes. This is the only one I could find who meets your description."

"Any named Specht? I had a friend who was taken with his children, a boy and a girl. He died, but if I can find the children—"

The aide leafed through his papers rapidly, but at last shook his head and laid them down. "I'm afraid not."

He got to his feet and came around the table. "Now don't go thinking your son's going to be glad to see you or eager to go back home. Except for the ones used as slaves, none of the captives who've been held any length of time want to go back to their white kin. In their minds they're Indians, and many of 'em even try to get away and back to their Indian families. They mostly haul 'em back here, but from time to time an escaped captive simply disappears."

Jakob stared at Read, taken aback. "You said . . . his Indian family brought him in. Are they still here?"

Read nodded. "Most of 'em want to see the people they're returning their adopted children or wives to so they can make sure they'll be well treated. Many even give gifts to the white parents."

"We'll get to meet them?"

Read chuckled softly as he met Jake's excited gaze. "You will indeed, young man." Looking up, he said to Jakob, "Follow me, and we'll see if your son's in the camp. Sir William provides as much food for the Indians as he can, but it's often necessary for 'em to go hunting for their meat."

Stunned, Jakob stood frozen, his emotions in turmoil, while the aide took his hat from a peg by the door and handed Jakob and his grandson theirs. He had never imagined that he might meet the people who had held his sons captive.

He started when Jake eagerly tugged his hand. Straining to return the boy's smile, he forced his feet to carry him out the door.

✦ ⋯⋯ ✦

"WE DON'T KNOW if a message has been sent out," Brings Dawn told Wulachen. "Perhaps no one comes because they do not know I am here."

Her face fell. She bent her head over the reed mat she was weaving for the wigewa they had built on their arrival, while Moonflower sewed beside her.

During the weeks of the journey, while they gave careful berth to English forts, detachments of soldiers, and prowling war parties, the same thought had circled ceaselessly in Brings Dawn's mind like fish trapped in a weir: *What if no one comes to claim me?*

He had no way of knowing whether his younger brother and father had ever returned home, or even if they still lived. Neither did he know whether his older brother and sister and their families had survived the war. Even if they had, might they not have fled to find safety far away from the raids? Was he leaving his adopted people, whom he loved, only to return to . . . nothing? What would become of him then?

And more fearful still: If any did come to claim him, could they accept that he was not one of them any more, but Lenape? His people were at war with the English again. If he returned, would he not be hated by the Whites and cast out? If that happened, would those who had scorned his mother welcome him if he returned to Tamaque's Town?

He could find no answer.

As though she read his thoughts, Wulachen said, "If no one comes, my son, then what can you do but come home with us?"

Moonflower looked up from her sewing. "You cannot stay here, my brother. You belong to us, not to these Whites." She turned a scornful look on the servants who crossed back and forth between the manor and various outbuildings.

Brings Dawn poked the fire's seething embers with a charred stick. "If I return, will my uncles accept my mother? And the women—will their hearts not remain hard?"

Wulachen and Moonflower concentrated on their tasks, and a tense silence fell between them. When Menetopalis and Contrary Wind approached from the direction of the meadow Brings Dawn sprang to his feet to greet them, his heart aching at the realization of how deeply he would miss all of them if he was taken away.

✦━━━✦

THE DAY WAS ALREADY oppressively hot though the sun glaring dully through a thin haze had not yet reached its zenith. Jakob mopped his face repeatedly with his handkerchief as he and young Jake followed Read through the large Indian encampment, leading their horses.

Sir William had carved a vast tract of land out of the forest and filled it with gardens, barns, mills, a smithy and Indian store, houses for slaves and servants, and the formidable stone block-houses that reminded visitors of his power. Jakob could hear the shrill cry of children at play on the broad meadow along the encampment's far side and smelled savory aromas rising from steaming kettles and roasting haunches of meat.

368 | Bob Hostetler and J. M. Hochstetler

Many of the women and girls lolling on woven mats in front of the wigewas and tents wore nothing more than short petticoats, and their bare skin glistened with sweat. Jakob responded to the boy's astonished questions by saying only, "It's their way, not ours."

He noted that many of the native men they passed had the shaven heads and scalp locks of warriors. Judging from their dress and ornaments, he guessed that a variety of nations were represented. He recognized the garb of Mingo-Seneca here and there, and some he guessed to be Shawnee, but none that he could identify as Lenape.

His breathing grew more labored with every step. Would he recognize Joseph? Would he be much altered in appearance, transformed by all he had experienced? Had he learned to worship the Indians' pagan gods?

Over the past seven years his boy had surely grown into a man. But Jakob's heart clung to the image of Joseph as he looked the last time Jakob held him in his arms at Presque Isle. He remembered the boy's fear—and anger. Did Joseph still harbor bitterness toward him?

Read switched from one language to another as he queried the passing men, a skill that impressed Jakob. Finally the aide led the way to a canvas-covered wigewa at the far edge of the encampment. Jakob could see several people in front of it, and, shaking now, he stumbled after Read and Jake, who hurried ahead of him.

A woman and girl in trade-cloth petticoats sat by the fire, their sleeveless white shirts painted with spots of red and black, as were their faces. Two men and a youth stood nearby, the older man supporting himself with a walking stick.

Jakob's sight was too blurred to make out their faces, but as he and his companions drew closer, the older of the two men looked toward them. His expression darkened, causing the boy to turn quickly and the woman and her daughter to rise, dismay coming into their faces.

The younger man turned more slowly to follow his companions' gazes. He was slightly taller than Jakob, deeply tanned and garbed in breechcloth, leggings, and moccasins. Like the older man's, his face and body were painted white, streaked with red and black swirls. Hard muscles rippled across his lean chest, and a band woven of many colors, with two turkey feathers protruding from it at the back of his head, encircled his brow, while gleaming mahogany hair cascaded down his back.

Read strode to them. Jakob followed, but his mind protested that surely this fantastically painted Indian could not be his son. The aide spoke to the older man and woman, then introduced them and their children to Jakob.

He stood speechless. Memories of the attack, the punishing journeys to Fort Presque Isle and Buckaloons, and the abuse he had suffered there drove the breath from his lungs and caused his hands to clench.

He had not wanted this meeting. All he could see in the people standing before him was those responsible for the destruction of his home and family, the ripping away of all that was precious to him.

He wiped the moisture from his eyes as Read drew the younger man forward. As their gazes locked, Jakob knew instantly the piercing hazel eyes that warily took his measure.

"*Ich bin Jakob Hochstetler,*" he said hoarsely. "*Bist du . . . Joseph?*"

No emotion showed on the young man's face. When Read translated, he dropped his gaze to the ground and answered in a muffled voice.

"He says, 'I am that one.' "

The woman began to wail like one who mourns the dead. The girl immediately joined in while the older man leaned on his young son, shoulders hunched as though against a blow.

Jakob could bear it no longer. He reached out to touch his boy, hands shaking, and then at last did what he bitterly regretted not doing all those years ago at Presque Isle. He caught Joseph into his arms and drew him to his chest, tears flowing, head thrown back.

"*Mein Sohn, mein Sohn! Ach, Vater, ich lobe Ihnen. Er lebt!*" My son, my son! Ah, Father, I praise You! He lives!"

He could feel Joseph trembling against him and drew back to scan his face, desperately seeking a response he did not find. "Have you forgotten your family, Joseph, in the years these people have held you prisoner?"

The instant the aide translated, Joseph recoiled and tore out of Jakob's embrace. He spat incomprehensible words.

Read shrugged apologetically. "He says he's not their prisoner. He's their son, and they're his family."

Jakob sucked in his breath. He had longed so intensely for this moment, and disappointment and anger seared through him. How dare these people teach his son to despise his father, his dead mother, his brothers and sisters?

The woman—Wulachen—had calmed, though tears still spilled down her cheeks. Before Jakob could speak she took her husband's hand, and with Read translating, said, "The one you call Joseph is named Brings Dawn, and he is as dear a son to us as this one born of our bodies." She indicated her younger son with a light touch before continuing, "He has brought to us the dawn light of Father in Heaven. His path is a hard one for our people to follow, but I . . . I seek to know Him." She nodded toward the others. "And I pray these will too."

Her words, though spoken humbly, struck Jakob like a blow. A lump formed in his throat as he struggled to see past the outlandish garb, the paint, and the silver and copper ornaments to the individuals who wore them.

For the first time he noted the anguish on their faces. It occurred to him that they also loved the son he loved, this young man, so strong and healthy. And handsome, beneath the paint. Perhaps God had placed him where he could flourish during his captivity, even as He had the patriarch Joseph in Egypt, keeping him faithful through his time of trial.

Shame burned his face, and he faltered, "Please . . . forgive me. All these years my eyes have longed to see my son, and I—I spoke hastily. I see that you love him and that he loves you. I am . . . grateful for all your goodness to him."

As Read translated, the woman and her family met Jakob's eyes directly, a tentative hope easing the fear on their faces.

Joseph's expression also softened, though he bit his lip and looked quickly away.

Wulachen motioned to her husband—Menetopalis, Read had called him—and they went into the wigewa. They reappeared a moment later, carrying several bundles.

Menetopalis presented them to Jakob. "By these gifts we ask your forgiveness for the wrong we have done to you and to Brings Dawn in keeping him from you." His voice choked as he spoke.

Jakob laid the bundles on the ground. He and young Jake opened them to find a large carved bowl and ladle polished as smooth as glass, a woven basket, a red clay pot painted with intricate black designs, and a supple buckskin shirt, fringed and decorated with colorful beads and quills.

Jakob got up, cleared his throat, and fumbled for the couple's hands. "Thank you for these gifts. I forgive you, as *Gott* forgives you. I also ask your forgiveness. I harbored resentment toward you though I did not know you. I do now, and I pledge before *Gott* that I will keep you always in my prayers. And I will nevermore bear a grudge against you or your people, nor against those who . . . who took the lives of my wife and children and bore away me and my sons."

✦┄┄┄✦

THE NEXT MOMENTS passed far too quickly for Brings Dawn. His white father had brought a horse for him, apparently the one the boy had ridden. But it looked like a poor thing compared to the stallion he had traded many beaver skins for and had trained and cared for like a child. Wulachen and Menetopalis insisted that he take the stallion, and he gathered the reins in his hand, grateful that one thing at least would remain to him of the life he must now leave behind forever.

He could see that Wulachen was determined not to weep for his sake, though her eyes brimmed with tears. He also kept his emotions under tight control, whispering his love for them as he embraced her and Menetopalis, who clutched him tightly before releasing him. Then Brings Dawn embraced Contrary Wind and Moonflower, whose tears overflowed.

At last he turned and followed his white father, the boy, and Read back through the camp, feeling that something inside him had shattered. He dared not look around for fear he would bolt back to those dear ones he had left sadly clustered together by the wigewa.

I am Lenape! his soul cried. *How can I be White again?*

When they came around the front of the mansion, Read said something to the man, who glanced anxiously at Brings Dawn. Read turned to him and said in Lenape, "With this war going on, it isn't safe for Indians to travel where you're going. It's best if you take off your Indian garb and put on the clothes your father brought for you."

Brings Dawn jerked back his head and gave the man a hard stare. Jaw clenched, he swung into the saddle and kicked the stallion's sides, urging him forward.

THEY RODE IN SILENCE for much of the day before stopping along the bank of a creek, where a rocky outcrop surrounded by trees afforded shelter. The man—Daat, Brings Dawn reminded himself—had taken the lead along the southwesterly trail, while Jake held his horse beside Bring Dawn's.

The boy seemed eager to talk and occasionally pointed out to Brings Dawn something that caught his interest. Then he spoke slowly and clearly in his strange tongue, gesturing to indicate what he meant.

Brings Dawn responded with only a shake of his head or an indifferent glance to where Jake pointed. The memory of his younger brother and sisters teaching him the Lenape tongue aroused a turmoil of emotions, all the more wrenching because young Jake was close in age to Contrary Wind. As the day passed, however, the meaning of some words and the cadences of the language began to come back to him, and he practiced them with silent reluctance.

When they dismounted Brings Dawn turned his back on the others and led his stallion down to the creek. He waded out into the shallows and stared upstream while the animal drank, his throat so tight he could not swallow, feeling that he would suffocate in the still, humid air.

He wanted to be anywhere but there. With anyone but these strangers.

Not strangers, he corrected himself. He saw much in young Jake that reminded him of the little boy he had delighted in playing with all those years earlier. Jake's happy, open acceptance of him continually brought Contrary Wind to mind, which made their separation both easier and harder to bear.

He glanced at his white father. Memories began to take shape, and Brings Dawn saw how he had aged since . . . before. His once black, curly hair was now thinner and frosted, as with snow. His face was lined and hollowed, and he did not move with the sureness he once had.

Brings Dawn remembered being often angry with him, though he had no recollection of why he should have felt that way. The man's bearing was gentle and humble, and he spoke only when it was important to do so, qualities greatly admired by the Lenape in their leaders.

The sound of water splashing behind him drew Brings Dawn around. Jake waded to his side and tugged at his hand, laughing and gesturing toward the water. He had already shed his clothes on the grassy slope, and he dove into the stream, eagerly beckoning to Brings Dawn and calling out in German. Brings Dawn caught the word *wasser*. Water.

The man—Daat—strode down to them, laughing at Jake's antics. Then he did a surprising thing, something Brings Dawn did not expect. He pulled off boots and hose and breeches and waded out into the creek clad only in shirt and drawers. Sinking chest deep into the water near Jake, he called Brings Dawn to join them.

Except he called him Joseph.

He had lost his name once and had been given another. Only to lose it now again.

Yet if he was to do this thing that Father in Heaven called him to, he must somehow learn to do it with a whole heart even though he did not want to.

Fighting back tears, he led his stallion back up the bank and tethered him beside the other horses. Then he walked back down to the creek. He stepped out of his moccasins, unlaced his leggings and dropped them and his breechcloth to the ground. Then he strode into the water a short distance from the others and bathed the paint from his body.

At last he stood there trembling and looked up to the heavens in supplication. *I cannot do it! Help me, my Father!*

He felt Daat's arms enfold him then. The years fell away until it seemed he was a boy again, and he turned into Daat's embrace and wept.

Chapter Forty-five

Sunday, September 9, 1764

J AKOB SAW THAT JOSEPH began to take greater interest in the land they passed through as they followed the long, hazy bulk of the Blue Mountain on their left. Jakob had spent much time praying, not rushing the journey so Joseph would have time to work out this great change in his mind.

They had spoken little. A subtle tension hung between them, but that was to be expected, Jakob assured himself. He found encouragement in the easy fellowship Joseph and young Jake had begun to forge on the long journey through the wilderness.

The day before, Joseph had asked, with awkward signs and broken words, whether Christian had returned. He had not concealed his concern on learning that his younger brother was still missing. Jakob took comfort in that too.

Healing took time. But by God's grace it would happen.

Love him.

He smiled as the small, still voice rang in his mind. His first impulse was always to admonish his children to make sure they stayed in the faith. He was learning how foolish that was. God loved them and held them in the palm of His hand, and He alone could keep them safe. Jakob's part was to love his children with a love like God's and to trust that He would carry out His good will for them.

It was mid afternoon when they rode down the familiar curving wagon lane. Joseph straightened and looked around, apprehension showing on his face. As they turned their horses at the branch to Johannes's house, Jake rose in his stirrups, waving his hand.

"We're home, *Onkel* Joseph!"

From behind him Jakob heard his son catch his breath. He didn't turn but pressed forward, riding out from between the trees in the lead.

He saw Bishop Hertzler's carriage by the barn along with several others and realized that it was Sunday and that the church had met there today. The bishop, Johannes, Crist and his brothers, along with Katie's brothers, were on their way to the carriages, the little boys trailing behind.

Jakob looked toward the house and saw Barbara step outside. She glanced toward him and half turned to say something over her shoulder to Katie and her mother in the doorway behind her.

He urged his mount into the yard, heard Jake and Joseph's horses follow. Barbara swung back around.

She stiffened, and then her hands flew up to cover her mouth.

Chapter Forty-six

CORN MOON
Tuesday, September 11, 1764

STAR CATCHER SPIED Raven Eye running toward him, garbed, as was he, in his finest regalia for the evening dance. He sat next to Star Catcher at the fire in front of the cabin they shared with Black Fox and Runs Far, a handsome, young, half-French Shawnee man who had become a close friend since their arrival on the Muskingum.

"Tonight the maidens dance with us, my brother! Those who wish to take a husband will accept the hand of the one they choose. When Draws the Bow passes behind me, I intend to claim her, and—"

"How do you know she will reach for your hand?" Star Catcher frowned down at the small trade mirror he held and concentrated on adding black lines to the red he had streaked across the white clay coating his face. "Perhaps she prefers another."

Raven Eye grinned. "Has she not made clear to me that she is willing?"

Star Catcher said nothing, but his eager anticipation of the night's dances evaporated like the morning mist.

It had been almost a year since Custaloga and his people had come to the area. By now the village of scattered log cabins and wigewas they initially built had turned into a thriving town where Lenape, Wyandot, Miami, Shawnee, and Mingo-Seneca residents mingled. During that time Star Catcher's friendship with Draws the Bow had become so close that they were rarely apart from one another. They engaged in friendly rivalry at *pahsahëman* and other games, and Draws the Bow always sought him out at ceremonials and evening dances. She occupied his thoughts so often lately that his friends had started to notice his preoccupation, though he kept its object well concealed.

She was close friends with Raven Eye, too, though, and the three of them were almost always together. Now Star Catcher concluded that one of them was mistaken about whom she favored, and the apprehension was sinking in that it was him.

"We will live in that wigewa we built when we first came here," Raven Eye said, "and I will build her a cabin before the winter." He put his arm around Star Catcher's shoulders. "Do not be sad! You also will take a wife one day. Besides, will we not always be brothers?"

Star Catcher forced a smile. "Of course—no matter whom Draws the Bow chooses for a husband."

Raven Eye regarded him smugly. "Tonight you will see."

That evening when the unmarried men gathered on the council house yard, the unmarried women in their festive garments formed a circle inside the men's, both facing outward. To the low throb of the drums, the chatter of rattles, and the dancers' chants, women and men circled in opposite directions.

Star Catcher glanced back repeatedly, searching for Draws the Bow, while both lines moved back and forth, periodically changing direction. He and Raven Eye were separated by several dancers, and he could not tell whether Draws the Bow hesitated behind his friend when their paths converged.

The dance drew near its end. Several of the older maidens had already taken the hand of the man they chose and slipped away with him into the shadows, while the remaining dancers closed seamlessly behind them. Several times Draws the Bow had passed behind Star Catcher but without pausing. He watched as the women circled around again, and his breath caught.

Draws the Bow stepped close behind Raven Eye. Neither looked at anyone else, and Star Catcher watched him lead her out of the swaying line. Together they vanished into the night.

◆ • • • ◆

HER FRIENDSHIP WAS NEVER *for my sake, but because she wanted Raven Eye.*

Star Catcher felt like a fool. Surely the signs had been clear to everyone, and he should have seen them too. But he had been blinded by her laughing eyes, sweet face, and appealing nature.

And her unvarying kindness to him. Her thoughtfulness. The interest she showed in him and her sensitivity to the emotions he often struggled with.

But once again, he had been left behind. Was he always to wander, never finding home?

He had lain awake for a long time that night, unable to sleep. He prayed the *Unser Vater* prayer again and found in it a measure of comfort and peace. At last he drifted off to sleep, only to awaken at first light feeling even more deeply the pain of crushed hopes.

He rolled over and saw that Black Fox and Runs Far had gone out, leaving him to face his disappointment alone. He got up and pulled on his clothing, wondering bleakly what his future held. All the doubt and fear and longing pushed to the back of his mind during the move to the Muskingum flooded back over him.

Since the last treaty, Custaloga had surrendered a number of those taken in raids during that earlier war, Fire Keeper among them. Star Catcher remembered vividly the young woman's devastation as she followed Custaloga away with the others, her grief wrenching his heart.

Rumors had been swirling through Custaloga's Town and the villages in the vicinity that the English were gathering an army at Fort Pitt to invade the Ohio lands, perhaps as far west as the Muskingum. Star Catcher could not help wondering whether, if they succeeded, he would also be caught up in their net and forced to return to a people and way of life that existed in his memory only as vague shadows.

Just then Runs Far and Black Fox burst into the cabin and dropped onto the sleeping platform. "Now I know why your brother held back when I pressed him to go with me to the Scioto to visit my mother at Chalahgawtha," Runs Far said with a rueful laugh.

Black Fox snorted. "That one is drunk with love. Many times I saw him and Draws the Bow look at each other like a buck and a doe circling each other at mating season. But I never believed he would bind himself to a wife so soon."

"What is to hold us back now?" Runs Far demanded. "There are many more women—and more desirable ones too—at Chalah-gawtha. The journey is only a few sleeps, but it is far enough from the English that they will not soon come to bother us there. My mother and sisters will receive you with great pleasure!"

Star Catcher looked from one to the other. He loved his brother but had no desire to watch Raven Eye and Draws the Bow's happiness grow over the coming moons, while feeling himself cut off from both. "I will go."

Black Fox echoed the sentiment. Of one accord they began eagerly to gather the supplies they would need for the journey.

Chapter Forty-seven

Wednesday, September 12, 1764

A ROBIN'S SONG WOKE Joseph, as it had the previous two mornings. He rolled over, careful to make no sound.

His pallet lay against the wall opposite Daat's narrow bed in the small *Kammer* added at the back of the *Stube* during his absence. Through the panes of the single window, he could see the sky faintly brightening while the robin's trill poured forth as though in praise of the coming day.

But praise was a long way from what he felt.

One by one more sounds joined the robin's chorus: the cheerful twitter of other birds; Katie and Johannes's muted stirrings as they rustled about in the *Küche*, building up the fire and preparing breakfast; the footfalls of the older children creaking on the stairs; their giggles and chatter and Johannes's low, gentle voice in response.

Daat rolled over with a grunt, sat up, levered to his feet, and began to dress. Joseph considered pretending to be asleep, but he was wide awake now. He waited until Daat left the room before rising and reluctantly pulling on Johannes's worn shirt and breeches that Barbara and Katie had hastily let out to fit him.

After two days the garments still felt uncomfortable and restrictive. Ignoring the stockings and shoes beside his pallet, he slipped on his moccasins as a gesture of defiance, then pulled his headband out of his pack. For a moment he fingered it, holding close the image of Wulachen lovingly weaving it for him from the brightly colored yarns she had gotten from a trader. He took a deep breath, raked his fingers through his long hair to work out the tangles, and tied the band around his head.

He steeled himself for the day. Chores waited to be done. Not that Daat or the others had so far pressed him to help with the work, but he knew he would eventually be expected to fit into the rhythms of plantation and family and community as though he had never been absent.

Among my people, what these men do is women's work.

He sat on his pallet again. These were his people too. Their ways had to be his ways now. He sighed and—once more—prayed for patience and strength to bend his will to Father-in-Heaven's.

Every nerve urged him to bolt outside through the side *Stube* door, but he rose and went out into the firelit *Küche*. Daat and Johannes sat at the table drinking steaming tea and eating slices of bread and butter with the children gathered around them, their happy chatter mingling with the grown-ups' voices.

Joseph returned the men's greetings with a curt nod, but when the older children ran to him, he squatted and gathered them into his arms, delighting in the feel of their arms clutching for him and their rosy cheeks pressed against his. He laughed in spite of himself. Their joyful welcome had done much to ease his anguish at losing Contrary Wind and his sisters and the overwhelming feeling of strangeness, of distance from this long-forgotten world.

When he rose, Daat looked up from three-year-old Annali on his lap and smiled. Seven-year-old Frany, who was obviously a little mother to the younger children, took his hand and led him to a seat at the table next to Johannes, then carefully delivered the cup of tea Katie poured for him.

"Danke," he said softly.

Katie straightened from the hearth, belly rounded with pregnancy, and pressed her hand against her back. *"Morgen."* Morning.

"Morgen," he echoed.

Johannes sent Jake and ten-year-old John to drive the cows up from the pasture for milking, then pushed the bread and butter over to Joseph. He yawned as he helped himself to a thick slice. The Lenape always danced long into the night and rose late, not having chores to attend to. This was yet another change he would have to make.

He took a bite of the buttered bread, the flavor bringing back memories of how he had eagerly devoured Maam's bread as a child. It tasted as good, though he missed Wulachen's savory corn cakes seasoned with wild onion. He had to swallow the bite past a lump in his throat, and gulped some of the hot tea to wash it down, almost choking.

Johannes rested his hand on Joseph's shoulder and spoke— asking whether he had slept well, Joseph guessed. He nodded.

But he hadn't. Ever since leaving Johnson Hall he had found it hard to quiet his mind enough for slumber. And the pallet, though thin, was softer than the sleeping platform he was used to. He could not get comfortable on it.

The greatest strain, however, was the struggle to understand what the others said. The children had begun to make a game of teaching him words in their Amish dialect, and the language was coming back a word or two at a time. But there was still much he had to relearn just in order to make it through each day.

How long would it take before he began to think in German again? When that happened he would truly have lost forever the Lenape man he had been, the unfettered way of life, and all his loved ones back on the Muskingum. Would he then forget them too?

When they had ridden into the yard two days earlier, everyone had immediately crowded around him, exclaiming loudly and speaking so rapidly that panic threatened to suffocate him. They clearly expected him to recognize each one, to understand what they were saying, to be delighted to be home. But none of it was so, and he had come very close to reining his stallion around and fleeing.

He was grateful that Barbara and Katie had quickly realized how overwhelmed he was. They had quieted the children and tactfully shooed their visitors home. The kindness of the two women had repeatedly helped to relieve Joseph's tension since then.

Crist, Johannes, and Daat had thus far been careful to place no demands on him, though they seemed to welcome his company eagerly. Even so, Joseph found it hard to let down his guard, to conceive of entering again into their world, walled about with strictly enforced boundaries unlike that of the Lenape.

Returning was much harder than he had expected.

Jakob surreptitiously studied Joseph across the table. The past couple of days had been as much a strain to everyone's nerves as they clearly were to Joseph's.

The journey from Johnson Hall had gone surprisingly well, but now that they were home Jakob felt as though he wasn't doing anything right. Whenever he tried to reach out to the boy, he pulled back. He had not allowed Jakob to embrace him since that evening at the river.

He had sensed Joseph's panic on finding so many people gathered when they arrived home. Jakob was grateful that Hertzlers and Stutzmans seemed to understand that his boy was going to need considerable time to find his way again. They had heeded his request to advise neighbors and friends to wait for a while before calling to welcome Joseph home. With the corn harvest just beginning, most of the church members would be too busy for visiting anyway.

Jakob drained his cup and set it down. "We better get to the milking or Crist will be here before we're done."

Johannes rose and stretched, yawning. "*Ya,* and we won't have time to eat that *guud* breakfast my Katie's cooking."

Bending over the dutch oven on the hearth, she smiled up at him. "There'll be enough for Crist too."

"You don't know how hungry we are." He winked at her, then, sobering, added, "And we can't waste time if we want to get Daat's cornfield harvested by the end of the day."

Jakob, Johannes, and young Jake had spent the much of past two days at Barbara and Crist's plantation cutting the ripe corn and binding the stalks into shocks to finish drying. Jakob had invited Joseph to go along, and although he had shied from it, he accompanied Katie and the younger children later in the morning when they came to help Barbara prepare food for the men.

Yesterday he had agreed to Johannes's suggestion that he take several of his little nieces and nephews fishing at nearby Northkill Creek while the others finished Crist's fields. To everyone's delight, Joseph and the children had brought back a bounty of trout for the evening meal.

That Joseph seemed to take pleasure in the children's company encouraged Jakob too. But when Joseph swallowed his last bite of bread, pushed away from the table, and went outside without speaking, Jakob fought back his disappointment.

He had been so anxious to bring his boys home and be a father to them again, to somehow make up for the great tragedy that befell them because of the decision he had made. But Joseph didn't seem to want that.

It weighed on Jakob that he had torn Joseph away from the Indian family he loved as the war party had once torn him from this family. And he couldn't help thinking that Christian's return would force him to endure the same arduous journey from the life he now knew to the one he had left behind years ago.

AN OVERWHELMING NEED to escape drove Joseph to the barn. He would go down to the pasture and take his stallion out for a ride, he decided.

The air was fresh, with a hint of chill. Dawn bloomed in the eastern sky, the sun's first rays sparkling like jewels in the dew and casting long, mysterious shadows from each building and tree.

Rounding the barn's lower level, he found Jake and John already driving the cows up the lane toward him, their lantern winking in the shadows of the overhanging trees. Their happy calls and the once-familiar scene drew him after them as they swung open the heavy plank doors. He had avoided entering it until now, and he did so hesitantly at the boys' playful urging.

Lantern light rippled across the huge, ax-hewn beams overhead and the thick pillars that supported the barn's upper floor. The mewling barn cats scattered before the cows that plodded to their places between the stanchions. Their bawling and the pungent scents of beast and muck and hay assailed Joseph's senses, evoking the tide of memories he had feared.

Jake moved between the cows, washing their teats. But Joseph saw another boy named Jake in his mind's eye, and himself instead of Johannes's John carrying shovelfuls of muck outside to the dung heap.

Daat and Johannes entered the barn and Johannes came over. He put one hand reassuringly on Joseph's back and with the other motioned toward the cows and the wooden milk buckets.

"Do you want to try milking, Joseph? You never forget how. It'll come back to you."

Trembling, Joseph shook his head and fled outside, avoiding Daat's worried gaze.

JAKOB TURNED FROM CRIST to Barbara and the children, who were helping Katie clear the last of the breakfast dishes from the table. "That field's going to take us all day, and we're already late starting. We likely won't have time for dinner."

Crist raked his fingers through his hair. "One of my cows was ailing this morning, and I had to take care of her. I can't afford to lose her."

"Nobody's blaming you for that," Johannes said.

Crist transferred his gaze to Joseph. "Maybe you could help," he said tentatively. "We can use all the hands we can get right now."

Joseph raised his chin, his jaw tensing. "It is women's work among my people. I go hunting."

At a loss, Jakob watched Joseph grab rifle, powder horn, and bullet bag, his face set.

"That may be true for the Indians, Joseph, but *we're* your people and all our men are expected to help with the farm work."

Jakob held up his hand to cut off Barbara's protest. *Gott, what should I do?*

Love him.

The answer formed in his mind, as clear and unmistakable as on the journey back from Johnson Hall. With it came the memory of how the Seneca children had made the forest and fields their playground and work a game. And how he had rejoiced when granted freedom to hunt on his own.

He went to Joseph and placed his arm around his shoulders, ignoring his stiffening. "That sounds like a good idea, Joseph. When I lived with the Seneca they sent me out to hunt sometimes. It was the only time I got some freedom. I haven't been out in the forest for too long, and I miss the cool air and the trees and how the wet ground smells. A man gets tired of tending fields after a while." He hesitated, then asked, "Would it be all right if I went hunting with you?"

Joseph stood thunderstruck, remembering angry confrontations between them during his childhood. He had always sensed Daat's disapproval and resented his severity. But this was a different man, one who had experienced some of the things he had.

He searched the eyes of this man who was his first father and finally nodded. "It is good."

Barbara threw her hands up in frustration. "Ach, Daat, if the two of you go hunting, that puts more on Crist and Johannes."

Johannes shrugged. "We can get it done."

"I think the two of you ought to go with us. Jake too. It'll do us good to spend the day out in the woods." Daat turned back to Joseph. "If you don't mind."

"If you waste the whole day—"

Daat laughed. "My *Kinder* are more important than work, Barbli. The corn will still be there tomorrow, *Gott* willing. Right now today is all we have, and I'd not waste it. *Bitte,* fix us a lunch to take along."

His use of her childhood nickname brought a smile to Barbara's face. "You, know, a venison roast for dinner would taste real *guud.*"

"I wouldn't mind turkey either," Katie chimed in.

Johannes and Crist exchanged grins, then hurried to fetch rifles and powder horns, Jake on their heels.

Joseph felt his chest expand with something akin to elation, and what seemed like shackles fell from him. He turned to Daat with a broad smile.

"It is very good."

Chapter Forty-eight

Sunday, September 16, 1764

B ARBARA CLASPED Anna's hands. "I thought maybe you'd come for a visit sooner, but I suppose you've been as busy harvesting corn as we have."

"*Ya,* even Maam and all us girls helped out. And we heard you asked everybody to put off visits for a while to let Joseph settle in some, so we didn't want to come over too soon. We were just so relieved to hear he'd finally come home!"

It was mid afternoon on the Sunday between church services. Johannes and his family, with Daat and Joseph, and uncles Jakob and Crist Buerki and their families had gathered for dinner at Barbara and Crist's house. They had just finished the meal when the Blancks' carriage turned into the lane.

Katie hurriedly dried the last dish and shooed her girls outside to play before coming to join the other women. Anna greeted her, then glanced toward the men gathered just inside the *Stube* doorway around Joseph.

A blush rose to her cheeks. "He looks so *guud,*" she murmured. "How's he doing?"

Barbara followed her gaze to Joseph, who was listening to

the men's conversation, his expression unreadable. "Ach, Anna, he's having a hard time of it."

"I expect he is. It's only been a week since he's been home, after all."

Katie sighed. "It's going to take a long while for him to get over all this."

"I'm not so sure you can just get over this kind of thing." Anna frowned down at her clasped hands.

Maudlin's wizened face tightened. "I can't understand why he isn't happy to be rid of those people and be home with his own kin. After what they did to your folks—"

"The ones who adopted him didn't take part in the attack."

Katie's sharp response caused Maudlin to flush, and Barbara said quickly, "From what Daat told us they were real *guud* to him."

The men moved out of the *Stube* doorway. Chair legs scraped across the plank floor, and the muted hum of conversation resumed.

Anna kept darting shy glances in Joseph's direction. He was seated just inside the room, and Barbara could tell she strained to hear what he said when the men questioned him.

Seeing that her mother, Mattie, watched her with concern, Barbara drew the women's attention and ushered everyone to the table. Once they were seated she related briefly how Daat had found Joseph at Johnson Hall and met his Delaware family.

Katie described the gifts Wulachen and Menetopalis had offered and repeated what Wulachen said about Joseph bringing the dawn light of God to them. "They both asked Daat's forgiveness for having kept Joseph from us."

A murmur passed around the circle of women.

"To think that we were afraid the boys would turn away from God and take up the Indians' pagan religion!" Barbara exclaimed, "That especially worried Daat."

Aunt Katrina patted her hand. "There's been such a change in your Daat. He never talked much about it, but after he came back we could see that his worries ate away at him. But now he says it was all foolish when we've seen so many proofs of God's faithfulness over the years."

"He keeps reminding us that God was with Joseph even among the Indians and that we can trust Him to watch over Christli too. That's a lesson I'm trying to learn." Barbara shook her head. "But it'll be a lot easier when my Christli walks in that door."

JOSEPH SAT TENSELY on the edge of his chair, feeling the sidelong looks the men directed toward him.

The day they had gone hunting had done much to ease the pain that had gripped his chest ever since he'd known he would have to leave the Lenape. They had brought back plenty of game for both families and even got back in time to do the evening chores. Believing that Father in Heaven willed for him to fit in with his white family, Joseph had volunteered to help, though painful memories of Jake made it impossible for him to yet take part in the milking. But what he could do he had done with feigned cheerfulness.

Several times Barbara and Johannes and Daat had gently suggested the wisdom of cutting his long hair and setting aside the colorful woven band he wore around his head. Crist had related bitter talk he had heard among some of their English neighbors and even from a few church members about Joseph bringing his Indian ways home with him. Joseph's stomach clenched every time the subject arose, no matter how delicately phrased.

He listened to the men's talk now, straining to understand what they said and to answer their questions in their awkward tongue. He had met Crist's brothers, Hans and Jakob, earlier in the week when the men worked together during the corn harvest and had quickly recognized them and their mother, Maudlin. But he had only a vague memory of Hans and Mattie Blanck and their daughters, and none at all of their son, John, who was several years younger than he was.

He was glad that as usual young Jake clung to his side instead of going out to play, as though sensing that his nearness made things easier for Joseph. The boy seemed to have an instinct for what Joseph struggled to say and quickly supplied the right words, which he carefully fixed in his mind. His comprehension grew daily, though he still lacked the confidence to speak more than absolutely necessary.

The men's conversation trailed off. Joseph looked up to see a young woman enter the room, clothed in a plain brown *Halsduch* and petticoat that did little to conceal the appealing, womanly curves of her slender figure. He had barely noticed her among the Blancks' other daughters in the confusion of their arrival.

She nodded to the other men before stopping in front of him. "Do you remember me? I'm Hans and Mattie's daughter, Anna."

He sprang to his feet, almost knocking over his chair, and took the hand she extended to him. The sweetness of her voice and the light in her green eyes left him strangely breathless.

Anna!

"*Y-ya*, I . . . I remember you," he stuttered, feeling the heat climb to his face at the men's chuckles.

In appearance she could not have provided a greater contrast to tall, lithe Many Leaves. Although Anna had grown taller in his absence, he still towered over her.

A few wisps of blonde hair had worked free of her demure white cap to curl in front of her ear, and the unexpected impulse to touch the glossy strands made him hurriedly drop his gaze to her hand, still clutched in his. It was small and delicate, but the strength of her grip surprised him.

He recalled feeling as a boy that he had never beheld anyone so pretty. He felt so now.

His chest tightened at the memory of their last encounter in the orchard that long-ago evening of the *apfelschnitzen*. They had been wrenched apart from each other just as his boyish admiration had begun to ripen into the feelings of a man for a woman.

When he raised his eyes he found her studying him intently. Could it be that she hadn't married though so many years had passed? She had come with her parents. Surely if she had a husband, he would be with her.

He hastily released her hand. "How . . . how have you been?"

"I've been fine." She laughed up at him the way she used to, her cheeks turning rosy. She sobered then and added, "We all missed you, of course—and Christli too. It was such a relief when your Daat made it home, and now you. We hope and pray Christli will also come back before too much longer."

When the men returned to their conversation, she suggested they go out into the *Küche* to talk. He followed her, feeling so awkward he was afraid he would trip over his own feet.

All the women looked up as they stepped into the room, and Joseph's flush deepened. Laughing, Barbara shooed them out the door, saying that they were talking of women's affairs and didn't need an audience.

Outside, the children were shouting and running around the barnyard a little distance away, playing games. He walked with Anna to the shade of the trees at the garden's edge, almost in panic at the prospect of carrying on a conversation with her.

She swung around and studied him earnestly. "I'm so sorry for all you've had to go through. I can't imagine how awfully hard it must be to come back here after making a life with the Indians. But you know all of us will do anything we can to help."

He looked away. "Not everyone feels that way."

"The ones who matter do."

"They see me as Lenape. And I am. That isn't going to change because of where I live." Anger and resentment edged his words, but to his surprise she did not flinch or drop her gaze.

She placed her hand on his arm. "I know. An experience like that changes you, and you'll always carry it with you. You'll always carry *them* with you, Joseph. But don't let that keep you from making a life here with us."

"Father in Heaven—God—has called me to do this thing. I will do it with His help."

She smiled and her green eyes held his. "I've been praying for you. Ever since you were taken away. And I won't stop now that you've come home."

He drew back slightly. The word *home* evoked images of his cabin on the Muskingum and his Lenape family. He gritted his teeth and forced himself to nod.

Anna must have read on his features the war that raged in his heart. She took both of his hands in hers.

"If you ever need to talk, I'll be glad to listen. I promise I won't judge you. I want to hear about your life with your Indian family and anything else you'd like to share."

As he looked down at her, his tension melted away. Eight years ago she had been the first to stir his heart. He had been a boy then, and she just a girl.

Both of them had changed in the years since then. If it could ever be possible for them to find their way back to that moment of promise, they would have to find new ground to walk on.

He found himself wanting to try.

"Ya," he blurted out. "I'd like that."

Chapter Forty-nine

Friday, October 12, 1764

JOSEPH WINCED as Barbara daubed the seeping scrape above his eye with a wet towel, her hand shaking.

"Did they shoot at you?"

He shrugged. "*Nay.* I was riding fast beneath the trees to get away from them and caught a branch across my face."

"Hold still." She held his chin with one hand as she flattened a leaf of lamb's ear steeped in hot water across the wound. When it stuck firmly to the skin, she stepped away.

"Bear's grease works better."

Their childhood banter was slowly returning to him. He was pleased to see her smile, though it was a weak one.

"I don't have any of that right now. Maybe you can hunt up a bear for me sometime."

He grinned. "The meat is very good."

He glanced cautiously at Daat, who leaned against the mantel, smoking his pipe, with Johannes beside him.

The door opened and Crist ushered the tearful children in ahead of him. "They rode off."

The children ran to Barbara, who bent to wipe their tears away with her apron.

Daat removed the pipe from his mouth. "What happened?"

"I meant to take the road over here, but it is a fine day and I rode through the woods instead. I didn't hear those men coming until they were almost on me."

"They were most likely lying in wait for you then," Johannes said, "or you'd have heard them sooner."

"*Ya.* I thought so too."

"Go on." Daat clamped his teeth over the pipe stem.

"They moved to come around me, but I pulled the stallion back toward the road and put some trees between us. They cursed me and said Indians are vermin and if I love them so much, I should go back to them and leave decent people alone. When I started to ride off, they called me an Amish Indian and a coward." Joseph dropped his gaze. "The rest are not words to repeat."

The children had calmed, and Crist motioned them back outside with a stern look. "There are chores to be done." When they looked up at him fearfully, he gently steered them to the door. "Those men took off, and they're not coming back. Everything's going to be all right. Go get your work done."

The children scattered, but Joseph noted that the adults seemed more doubtful about Crist's assurances.

"If we hadn't already been here—"

"I doubt they left because of us since *die Englishe* know we don't fight," Daat cut Johannes off quietly. "Most likely it was *die Kinder.* There's something about the innocent ones that makes a man ashamed of the evil he means to do."

Barbara propped her fists on her hips and rounded on Joseph. "It's that long hair! You can't go riding around here looking like an Indian and expect that those who lost homes and loved ones in the raids won't be mad."

"Maybe you are too." The bitter words were out before Joseph could bite them back.

Her eyes filled with tears. "It's just past seven years since the attack, and every single day I've missed Maam and Jake and Annali—"

Joseph sprang to his feet, upending the chair. "You think I don't? You think my life was not torn apart on that day?"

She swung away, her hand pressed over her mouth. Daat came over, gripped Joseph's shoulder, and drew Barbara around to face them. He put her hand in Joseph's.

"Barbli, Joseph has taken the better part, which is to forgive. And to love. It's *Gott's* way, the only way good can come out of evil. If we're to serve Him, it must be our way too."

Barbara nodded, head down. "I know, Daat. I know. I want to be obedient. Most of the time I can put the pain away, but sometimes it hurts too much."

Joseph squeezed her hand, thinking how much she reminded him of Maam. Anguish, anger, and regret surged through him in equal measure. His emotions still careened wildly from one pole to the other over the slightest matter, and he could not seem to control them.

He pulled her roughly into his embrace. "I cannot find the path through this wilderness. Perhaps there is none. I am sorry—"

She drew back to look into his eyes. "It isn't your fault. I know that. You couldn't help what happened. You were just a boy, and you did the best you could. I don't blame you for any of it."

Johannes came over to them. "Barbara's right that your hair needs to get cut, though. And you need to put off your headband and moccasins. We're all sorry for it, and if it was up to us, we'd let it go. But it's causing talk among our English neighbors and even in the church. Just the other day I heard one of the men say he was surprised you didn't show up with your face painted."

Barbara flinched. "One of the women wondered whether you're an idol worshiper since you hold back during church."

"I do not worship idols!" Pushing away from her, Joseph strode across the room and back, waving his arms. "I serve Father —God—as you do."

"We know that, but looking like an Indian is a danger to you. And to us and the children. None of us can live just for ourselves. We have to take others into account too."

Crist's words struck Joseph like a blow. For a tense moment he hesitated, looking from one sober face to another, knowing they were right. He had wrestled with this lesson as a boy, but living among the Lenape had taught him the value of it.

Finally he conceded a wry smile. Reaching behind his head, he untied and removed his headband, and shoved it into the pocket of his breeches.

"Cut it then. But is it not foolishness to try to make a Lenape man into an Amish one?"

They regarded him doubtfully, clearly taken aback. Then Daat chuckled, and after a moment the others did too. When Joseph grinned, they all laughed.

Barbara winked at him. "I'll make you into a *guud* one." She placed her hands on his shoulders, pushed him back down into the chair, and bustled off to fetch her scissors.

While the men went outside to check on the children, Barbara swathed Joseph in a sheet and set to work. In minutes long strands of mahogany hair covered the floor around him. He watched them fall, outwardly submitting but inwardly grieving.

Finally Barbara stepped back to admire her handiwork. Joseph stood up and ran his hand down his now shoulder-length hair. He felt naked.

He glanced down at his clothing. The day following his return, Barbara and Katie had managed to alter one of Johannes's shirts and breeches enough for Joseph to wear during the week so he wouldn't have to resort to leggings and breechcloth. By now they had almost completed a fine linen shirt and a black suit for Sunday wear.

He was grateful for their efforts, but trying to fit into the Amish way of life again after the freedom he had experienced for so many years seemed to him an exercise in frustration and futility. He was far from certain it was even possible.

It was the rules he remembered most. Arbitrary demands for obedience to strictures whose purpose he could not fathom.

He touched the bulge of the small pouch concealed under his shirt, the one that held the length of the buck's antler. He might have to wear Amish clothes, put away his headband and moccasins, and let his hair be cut. But this he would never give up, for it kept alive in his memory those in that other world whom he had lost yet would forever love.

Chapter Fifty

Sunday, April 21, 1765

J OSEPH CREPT UP the rise behind the Blancks' barn and ducked
between the budding trees, certain he had made no sound
to betray his approach. Before he reached her, however,
Anna turned and smiled at him.

He closed the distance between them. "You wouldn't hear
me if I was wearing moccasins."

"That may be so, but I knew you'd come, so I'd have spotted
you anyway."

It was a glorious spring day. Delicate shades of green softened the branches of trees and underbrush, and a breeze drove
a scattering of clouds across the azure sky, whipping Anna's black
shawl and petticoats around her slender form and tugging at
Joseph's coat. He glanced back through the trees toward the
barn and the house beyond, where the church members were
preparing to leave after the lunch that followed worship.

Grinning, he captured her hand. "Among the Lenape the
young people conceal their courtship too."

She laughed softly. "Are we courting, then?"

The look he turned on her brought a blush to her cheeks.

Hastily she said, "I've missed our talks. Everyone's too busy plowing and planting to get together except for church."

He shoved his fingers through his wind-blown hair. "I forgot how much work there is to do on a plantation in the spring . . . and summer and fall." He drew out the words, eliciting her giggle.

"Are you getting used to doing women's work again?"

He grimaced. "I don't have much choice. They need every hand to help." He filled his lungs with the fresh air and turned his face to the sky. "But I like being outside again and smelling the earth and feeling the sun after being cooped up all winter. Daat makes sure we take off time to go hunting or fishing whenever we can. That helps too."

He drew her to a fallen tree, and they sat side by side on the decaying trunk. "You don't know how much I appreciate that you listen and don't tell me what I ought to feel and do like some in the church." He tilted his head toward the departing carriages beyond the barn.

"It's unfair for sure. But do you remember how you felt when you were first with the Indians—how they couldn't understand your ways and the people you came from? You had to learn to live and think the way they did if you were going to make it through. Well, those in the church can't understand the way the Indians think or feel either. They've never lived with them like you have."

"You're right. I'm judging them the same way they judge me." He studied her for a moment. "Daat's changed from how I remembered him, though. I've told him more about what happened with me than I have Johannes and Barbara and Crist, and he seems to understand."

"He hasn't said much about his time with the Seneca."

"He won't talk much about that, even to me. I wish he would."

"He'll tell you when he's ready, just like you do with me." She squeezed his hand. "Time brings healing."

Slipping his arm around her shoulders, he drew her close. "I've told you more than anyone."

She smiled up at him. "I'm glad you trust me that much."

"You remember when I went with Daat to Carlisle last fall? He was so sure Christli would be with the captives Colonel Bouquet brought back from the Muskingum. When he wasn't, it was really hard for him to accept, but he kept saying God's going to bring him home."

He dropped his gaze to their intertwined fingers. "Would you think it bad of me if I told you I was glad Christli didn't come back then . . . and that part of me hopes he never does?"

With her free hand she turned his head until he met her searching gaze. "Why?"

"It isn't because I don't want him back with us—I do! But I don't want him to have to lose his adopted family like I have. He was so young when he was taken away, Anna. Being forced to come back is going to be even harder for him than for me. I don't want him to suffer that way."

"Maybe he doesn't have the same kind of situation you did. Wulachen and Menetopalis treated you kindly. You had a brother and sisters, and you made good friends too. It might be different for him. Maybe he isn't happy. Maybe he wants to come home."

"That worries me just as much." Releasing her, he leaned forward, head bent, hands clasped between his knees. "The worst part is not knowing."

"All we can do is keep praying. Don't forget that if he comes home, he'll have you to help him. And your Daat—your whole family. That will make things easier for him."

He looked up. "And I'll make it up to him for being so mean when we were boys."

She hesitated before asking softly, "We're having communion Sunday after next, and I've been wondering . . . have you resolved things in your mind enough that you can think about whether you might join church? Some day, I mean."

"I know if I don't there can't be anything between us—"

"*Nay,* Joseph, you mustn't think of doing it because of me! It has to be because the Holy Spirit draws you and you choose it for yourself."

"*Ya,* I know."

A moment of silence passed between them before she said, "And I don't want you feeling like you have any obligation to me. I waited for you because I believed that was what God wanted me to do, but I don't want you to feel trapped by my decision."

He straightened and turned to cup her cheek in his hand. "I keep wondering why God sent such a good woman to me when I don't deserve her. Anna, all those years I thought I'd forgotten you. For a while I even felt like I was in love with Many Leaves. But I always carried you in my heart. It wasn't until I saw you again that day last fall that I knew it."

When she beamed up at him, he said quickly, "But things are still unsettled in me. Not what I feel for you, but everything else. And maybe it'll always be that way. Living among the Lenape— becoming one of them—changed me in ways I can't undo."

"What I experienced while we were apart changed me too, *ya?*"

Her face was turned up to his, and giving in to turmoil and need he brushed his lips against hers. Her immediate response shook him, and he slid his hand down the curve of her back and drew her to him, kissing her as he had once imagined, before they had been torn away from each other.

At last he pulled back and rested his cheek against the crown of her head. Emotions beyond words welled up in him: gratitude and wonder—and something he had never felt before.

"I love you," he whispered. "I want you for my wife if you could take a man like me for a husband."

She slipped her arms around his neck, laughing. "You goose, would I have waited all this time only to say *nay* if you asked me? The things around us may change, but love doesn't when it's meant to be."

He touched his forehead to hers. "I want to be a good husband to you. To hold nothing back. If only I could forget . . . "

"I know you still miss them, and I don't blame you. I can't imagine what it's like to lose two families."

He let out a low groan. "I wish I could let go of them and get married and settle down and live like everybody else! But I keep wondering whether Wulachen and Menetopalis and the children got home safe, whether they're happy and doing well, whether they've forgotten me . . . "

He pulled away and jumped up to pace between the trees. "They're part of who I am, and I'll always carry them with me. There'll always be this hole in me where they used to be. You have to understand and accept that before we can ever marry. You have to be able to choose the man I am now, not the boy you remember."

"I have some idea of who that man is. He's shared his heart with me, and I've come to love him even more than I loved the boy I used to know."

He strode over and pulled her to her feet and into his arms. "My family knows my struggles, but they expect that I'll get over it pretty soon and take up where I left off. Even Daat. But his experience was different from mine, and I don't know if that's possible for me. There are times when I feel like it never will be."

She nestled against his chest. "I love you enough to want you to find God's way for you and follow where He leads, even if that means we can't be together. He can't bless you if you don't."

What she didn't say cut through him: That she had been baptized and joined church during his absence. That if he never joined the church, marrying him would mean breaking her vow and losing her family, who would have no choice but to shun her.

That would never happen, he knew. As much as she loved him, she loved God more.

Above all else, it was her purity that drew him to her. And broke his heart.

Chapter Fifty-one

Tuesday, April 30, 1765

"I'VE COME TO REALIZE that so much of your rebellion as a boy was because of my attitude. Too often I was stubborn and harsh." Jakob's brow furrowed as he finished rubbing down the mare. "The Bible says, 'Ye fathers provoke not your children to wrath: but bring them up in the nurture and admonition of the Lord.' How can we parents teach our children that *Gott* is gracious and loving unless we model His grace before them? If *Gott* had to let me suffer to learn that, then I count everything I endured well worth it."

It was late afternoon. He and Joseph had been working in the barn currying the Belgians when Joseph asked him to relate what he had endured as a captive of the Seneca and during his escape. He had recounted no more than the basic facts to the rest of the family but, recognizing that Joseph needed to hear it, had finally given in.

"Daat . . . it wasn't your fault," Joseph said gruffly. "It was mine. You were a good father. I was just rebellious, that's all."

"I'm the parent. I'm responsible for my actions."

"I misjudged you because I was ignorant. And when you needed me most, I ran away."

Jakob stared at Joseph, puzzled. After a moment understanding dawned.

"Ach, *nay!* I wanted you to get away—all of you. If I could have—"

"You did everything you could to save us, Daat! And when we were taken away, you escaped and found your way home over all those miles of wilderness in such danger, almost starving, just because you loved Christli and me so much you wanted to find us and bring us home."

Jakob cleared his throat and bent to run his hand down the mare's foreleg, checking for the sore spot he had noticed the previous day.

"Can you understand that I found a home and family among the Lenape that I came to love, and how much it hurts to lose them? It's going to be the same for Christian."

Jakob straightened and ran his hand along the mare's gleaming flank, fighting to keep his emotions under control. "I can now. Before I met Menetopalis and Wulachen and their children, all I saw was an enemy. And then *Gott* convicted me that He loves them as much as He loves us. Ever since, I've been wrestling with whether I did the right thing in taking you away from them. And whether I should keep trying to find Christian now."

He turned to face Joseph again. "I don't know what the answer is, Joseph, just that I'm so thankful you're home. And I long to see my Christli safe home too."

414 | Bob Hostetler and J. M. Hochstetler

Joseph dropped his curry brush into the bucket, searching for answers. Finally, leaning back against the stall's stanchion, he described what had happened to Wulachen and her family because of him, and why he had decided he must leave for their sake.

Daat studied him intently. "We can't see yet what the end of all these things is, and maybe we never will. We can only trust that *Gott* is working out His good purpose, and that He'll bless us and your Indian family too—and Christian's if he comes home. There'll be peace again once these treaty conferences at Fort Pitt and at Johnson Hall are concluded—"

"For this Colonel Bouquet to bring an army into the Ohio lands—right to their towns!—must have broken my people's spirit." Joseph cast Daat a despairing look. "Menetopalis put all his hopes in Neolin's vision and teachings. I worry about how he feels now that everything's fallen apart and the man he believed in so strongly has been shown to be a false prophet."

Daat led the mare into her stall and released her. "Do you think he might seek Jesus like Wulachen was doing?"

"She was close, Daat, but if there's no one to teach her the truth, how will she ever be able to take hold of it? And if Menetopalis goes back to drinking—"

"We'll pray about that." Closing the stall door, Daat came back to take the gelding's bridle. "What about that Moravian, Brother Post? Once it's safe maybe he'll go back to the mission he started out there."

"I hope he will."

Daat led the gelding to his stall. "I'm going over to Heidelberg after the planting's done and talk to Samuel Weiser—

Colonel Weiser's son. I want to see if he'll write a petition to Johnson to find out whether Custaloga finally brought Christian down. If he didn't, it can't hurt to remind Johnson of it."

"I'll go with you."

Joseph hurried to fill the Belgians' feed boxes with a measure of oats. Working in quiet harmony, they wiped down the harnesses and hung them on their hooks, then put away the curry brushes and rags and other equipment. Finished, they headed outside.

At the door Daat stopped. "Do you remember how the patriarch Joseph was carried away because of his brothers' evil actions? He made a new home and family among the Egyptians, but *Gott* restored his father and brothers to him. And He blessed the Egyptians, too, because of him."

"That Joseph's father was also named Jacob."

His voice thickening, Daat said, "And his Joseph was dear to him, the way my Joseph is to me."

Joseph reached out, and Daat caught him into his arms in a fierce embrace. It was their first since that moment in the river on the journey from New York, though Daat often reached out to touch him, a thing Joseph did not remember him doing before.

He was reminded of the feel of Menetopalis's arms around him, assuring him that all would be well and that he was loved. And he dared to believe it now too.

Chapter Fifty-two

D AAT STOPPED JOSEPH when the children and unbaptized youths rose to leave before the communion service. "If you want to stay, sit on the bench back by the door. No one will say anything to you."

Joseph glanced uneasily toward Bishop Hertzler, who stood at the head of the room. To his surprise, the older man met his gaze and nodded.

Something strangely akin to panic possessed him. He'd had every intention of escaping outside, but that plain wooden bench rose up to block his way. It stood well out of the path to the outer door, yet he could not pass it by. It drew him like a magnet and he sank onto it, leaning forward, arms propped on his knees, head bowed, feeling as though a great weight pressed him down and held him there.

To his relief, no one appeared to notice that he stayed. And so for the next hours he listened and watched as the congregation sang hymns and the bishop and ministers preached what they called the Golden Path through the Scriptures, from the patriarchs through the prophets and into the Gospels.

When the break for lunch came the members of the congregation greeted him as though he belonged there. The women made sure his plate was filled. Men beckoned him to join them in conversation. A nod here. A smile there. A hand gently squeezing his shoulder. A sense of acceptance and love and well-wishes expressed without words. And he was keenly aware of how often Anna smiled warmly at him from across the *Küche,* though she kept her distance.

After the simple meal he sat down again on the back bench, blinking away the tears that welled into his eyes. Soon he was wiping them from his cheeks as the fourth minister preached on the suffering of Christ. Just as a grain of wheat dies, he said, and is then raised to new life by sunshine and rain, so should our Christian life be: the dying off of the old man and the growth of the new man in Christ.

At mid afternoon the bread and wine were served. Then the passage of scripture on foot-washing was read and another hymn sung. Two deacons brought in basins and towels for foot washing.

The beautiful simplicity of the service struck Joseph: the symbols of the bread and wine, the humility of each believer kneeling to wash another's feet, the heart-deep knowing that every word spoken, each movement, every whispered prayer and slowly chanted hymn was true and sacred and holy. Finally, while all the members knelt, heads bowed, and the final prayer was spoken, Joseph looked up to find the bishop's kind gaze on him.

"If there be any here today who need to follow the Lord in baptism and who would freely join our faith and our fellowship, let him come forward."

A battle raged in Joseph's soul. These people were flawed. Some of them hadn't shown him the love and grace Jesus called them to. In some things they rebelled against Jesus' commands.

They were imperfect, stubborn, rebellious. Just like him. But over the past months there had been changes in their hearts. And in his.

Together they were God's church, the Body of Christ, and the Father loved them and showed grace to them in their weakness. As He had to Joseph.

Daat's words on that night of terror long ago came back to him: *We cannot be halfhearted and expect the Lord's favor. The only way of obedience is . . . obedience.*

Back then Joseph had not heard the anguish in those words. He had railed against his father's stubborn refusal to fight, to save his family, all for a God none could see or hear. But now, through the lives of these plain people—through his father's life—Joseph saw with his own eyes and heard with his own ears this great God.

He was on his feet, then, stumbling forward, to fall to his knees before the bishop, his hands covering his face, tears of release flowing between his fingers as Bishop Hertzler bent to lay his hand on his head.

Daat knelt beside him, and Johannes and Katie, Barbara and Crist, Anna, too, along with other members of the congregation who came forward to surround him as soft murmurs of *"Gelobt sei Gott!"*—God be praised!—filled the room.

Chapter Fifty-three

Tuesday, June 4, 1765

NEITHER RAVEN EYE or Draws the Bow would meet Star Catcher's gaze.

"I am sorry to see you, my brother," Raven Eye said somberly. "I had hoped you would stay away for some time yet—at least until next winter."

Star Catcher's heart fell. He had put his disappointment behind him and hoped that Draws the Bow and Raven Eye had not guessed the reason for his abrupt departure for the Shawnee towns far south on the Scioto River. But evidently he had been wrong.

Before he could speak, Raven Eye gripped his shoulder. "We would rejoice at your return, for we have longed to see you! But—" he glanced at Draws the Bow "—everything has changed. You heard that the English colonel called Bouquet brought his army here during the Falling Leaf Moon?"

Star Catcher nodded, feeling numb. "I could not believe our warriors did not stop them!"

Draws the Bow wrung her hands. "The soldiers were too many for us. They built a town at the Forks and summoned our sachems and captains. Bouquet demanded that they put their marks on his paper and deliver up to him all those of white birth still living among us."

Frowning, Star Catcher lowered to a stool beside the hearth in the snug cabin. "We heard that many were brought in and that Bouquet then returned to Fort Pitt—"

"Both Tamaque and Custaloga had very few they could bring in," Raven Eye broke in. "And when they explained that the rest were too far away to come back until the spring, Bouquet said they must return them at the conferences that are now taking place at Fort Pitt and Johnson Hall or the English would not honor the treaty. Everyone left among us born of the Whites has to be returned now if the English are not to make war on us again. Many have already been carried away."

Draws the Bow sat down beside Star Catcher. "Custaloga has given no one any choice. He even sent messengers to Chalahgawtha in the Frog Moon to bring you back, but you were not there."

"I went west with Runs Far and the others to their hunting camp. We did not return until the Shad Moon."

Raven Eye joined them, sitting on Star Catcher's other side. "Would that you had not come back!"

The words were hardly out of his mouth when Custaloga stepped through the door. All three of them sprang to their feet.

Stern lines etched the sachem's face. "I heard that you had returned."

He flicked a cold glance at Raven Eye and Draws the Bow. Two warriors stepped into the cabin behind the sachem, and Custaloga indicated the older of the two.

"Killbuck of the Wolf division has come on his way to Johnson Hall. Warraghiyagey has given us forty days to bring the last of our people born of the Whites to him. Killbuck leaves tomorrow with those Tamaque has sent." He fixed his gaze on Star Catcher. "You must go with him."

"I will not! I swore to my father, Nútemau, that I would not leave my people, and I will not break my vow!"

Custaloga's face hardened. He motioned to the warriors, who pushed Raven Eye and Draws the Bow aside and gripped Star Catcher's arms. They were larger and stronger than he, and his struggle to break free availed nothing.

"Wait!" Raven Eye stepped between Star Catcher and Custaloga. "Let us at least give my brother provisions for the journey and wish him well."

Custaloga turned his back and strode out the door, and the two warriors dragged Star Catcher after him.

Chapter Fifty-four

Monday, July 8, 1765

S TAR CATCHER SAT across a table from a soldier in the shade
of a great elm tree. His gaze traveled to the imposing façade
of Johnson Hall, then to the other prisoners who milled
across the lawn, faces as blank as his.

He was weary and footsore. Killbuck and the other warrior
had left their party at Fort Pitt, where a guard of English soldiers had driven them like cattle for hundreds of miles until they
reached the estate belonging to William Johnson.

On the night of his taking Star Catcher had heard the voices
of Raven Eye and Draws the Bow and later Deep Water and Standing Stone outside the cabin where he was held. Hope had stirred
in his breast, but he had not been allowed to see them, though
he had been given the provisions they brought for him. Sleep
had not come for hours, and then he had been prodded awake
before first light the next morning and herded with the others
onto the path east.

The journey had been one of misery for all those, like him,
being forcibly returned. He had not been allowed to take his
horse, weapons, or even his dog, Bear—because, he suspected,

they feared he would attempt to escape if he had them. Several times someone in the party tried to get away, but each time they were caught and driven back with blows, bound, and again marched onward.

Little of the journey remained in his memory now except anger and grief—along with Killbuck's curt words at Fort Pitt: "Do not try to return to us. If you do, we will carry you back to the Whites, and they will surely beat you for trying to escape. You are no longer one with our people. Go back to those who gave you birth and do not trouble us any longer."

For a brief instant Star Catcher had thought he saw moisture shimmering in Killbuck's eyes. But the warrior quickly turned and strode away without a backward glance.

"What's your name—your white name?"

The soldier's voice wrested Star Catcher from his reverie. He tried to swallow, but his mouth had gone dry. All he could do was shake his head.

"You don't remember?"

Star Catcher held his silence.

"What of your father's name?"

Star Catcher cast a longing look at the woods that bordered the estate. There were too many soldiers; he would never reach it. He searched his memory.

"Jak . . . Jak-ob."

The man dipped his pen in the pot of ink and wrote on the paper in front of him. "Last name?"

Star Catcher shrugged. "Hess . . . no, Huss . . . Huss-er?"

The pen scratched on the paper. "Anything else you remember?"

The words of the Father-in-Heaven prayer that he recited each night occurred to Star Catcher. But he shook his head.

He was taken to the sprawling Indian camp behind the mansion, to a tent with three other youths. Lounging on their blankets, they regarded him sympathetically when he entered. He grunted a response to their greetings. Spreading out his blanket in an open space, he dropped his pack onto it and sat cross-legged, shoulders drooping, head bowed.

There was no place he belonged now. His entire identity had been stripped away.

He was no longer Lenape and could not go back to his people. Yet neither was he White. He did not know whether his first family still lived, or where, or whether they would welcome his return.

He had nowhere else to go, however. He could not stay in this place. If no one claimed him, he would be sold as something the English called an indenture. Those who had told him this said it was akin to slow torture.

Teeth clenched, he looked out through the tent's opening to the dark line of forest that stretched along the cleared land bordering house and outbuildings.

The other youths rose, and the oldest one beckoned him to come with them. "It is time for the evening meal. Come with us and eat."

Star Catcher fixed his gaze on the ground until he heard them leave. He could smell the savory aromas from the cooking fires, but they only made his stomach lurch.

He sat motionless for some time, thinking. At last it came to him that there had been a river—no, a creek—and a mountain down which those clear waters tumbled. The name emerged slowly: the Blue Mountain. Kittatinny. And then Northkill—the creek and the place where his first family had lived.

When the other youths returned, he asked gruffly, "Do you know a place called Northkill? It lies by the Kittatinny Mountain on the side of the sun's rising."

They exchanged glances. "We do not know such a place," the oldest answered, "but there are elders here who may. Come and we will ask them."

Star Catcher followed them out of the tent. With dread. But a tentative hope lay beneath.

Chapter Fifty-five

Thursday, August 29, 1765

THROUGH THE OPEN DOOR, Jakob saw the carriage drive up the lane and pull to a halt in front of the house as he washed up for the noon meal.

Johannes went outside to greet the visitors and soon ushered Hans Blanck, Mattie, and Anna inside. After directing her daughters to set the food back to keep warm, Katie offered their guests seats at the table.

Jakob dried his hands and joined them, leaving Joseph at the sink to finish washing. "What brings you folks this way in the middle of the week?"

Blanck gave him a keen look. "We may have some good news for you, Jakob. It looks like that petition Samuel Weiser wrote to Johnson for you might have yielded fruit."

Johannes pulled out a chair and sat. "What do you mean?"

"While I was at Reading on business yesterday, I picked up a copy of *Der Wochentliche Philadelphische Staatsbote*."

Finished with their tasks, the girls hurried to the table. Joseph came to stand behind Anna as her father pulled the folded newspaper out of his pocket and opened it.

Everyone bent to scrutinize the page, while Blanck read aloud: " 'Sir William Johnson, Bart. gives this public notice that in consequence of his treaty in May last with the Senecas and Delawares of the Susquehanna, the following twenty-five persons have been sent to him, who will be delivered to their relations on application.' The notice is dated July 4." He pointed to a line and looked up triumphantly. "It says here: Jacob Husser's son, about eighteen or twenty years old."

Jakob sat back in his chair, frowning. "Jacob Husser?"

"Don't you see, Jakob? Christian has been with the Delaware so long that he likely doesn't remember his last name exactly. And it doesn't give a first name, which means he probably doesn't know it either."

"It's true, Daat. I remembered my first name, but only part of my last. It makes sense that Christian would forget too. He's been with the Lenape longer than I was."

Jakob regarded Joseph thoughtfully before turning back to Blanck. "Christian would be nineteen, so this boy is the right age. He's held at Johnson Hall?"

Mattie leaned forward and tapped the paper. "He's been there at least since July 4."

"It's the end of August now. Do you think he'd still be there?"

Joseph placed his hand on Anna's shoulder. "They hold those who are returned until someone claims them, Daat. If no one does, after several months they sell them as indentures."

Jakob started to his feet. "There isn't time to waste then. It'll be day after tomorrow before I can get enough provisions together to go so far—"

Johannes held up his hand. "You know Barbara's going to object to your going all that way again, and so do I. You've been working too hard, and you're tired all the time. It'll take a fortnight or more to get to Johnson Hall and—"

"I remember the journey." Sinking back into his chair, Jakob looked up at Joseph. "You'll go with me, *ya?* I'll need you to translate for us."

"*Ya*, sure," Joseph said eagerly He came around the table to Jakob. "I'll start getting things ready right after dinner."

Katie got up and motioned her daughters back to the worktable. "Ach, *nay,* let Johannes go with Joseph. And our Jacob too. It's too much for you, Daat."

❖ • • • • ❖

WHILE THE ARGUMENT CONTINUED, Joseph caught Anna's eye and tipped his head toward the door. She pushed back from the table and slipped across the room to the door without attracting notice. Joseph waited a few moments before following her.

She waited just outside the door, and he caught her hand and drew her after him. They ran to the line of trees bordering the kitchen yard. The day was hot and muggy, and sweat beaded his brow by the time they came to a halt in the shade, standing close together, hands clasped, breathless and laughing.

She turned a radiant smile up at him, color flaming in her cheeks—whether from the day's heat or the success of their escape, he couldn't tell. "We didn't have a chance to talk Sunday, and I wanted to tell you that I felt light as air to see you baptized."

He chuckled. "So did I. With all the farm work to be done, it seemed like it took a long time to get through Instruction, especially the part about our *Ordnung*. But I learned so much that my head and heart are still full with it."

"Bishop Hertzler is a good teacher, *ya?*"

"He's patient, that's for sure. I suspect my questions made his head spin."

Both of them sobered. Hesitantly Anna asked, "Do you think Christli really has been brought back after all this time?"

"I hope so though I dread it, too, for his sake. There's only one way to know, though."

"You'll leave day after tomorrow?"

"We're going to be busy getting things together so fast." He stared out across the fields. "If it is Christli, he's going to need me to help him through this."

"I know. And no one can help him make peace with coming home better than you."

"But our wedding—"

She touched her fingers to his lips. "I've waited this long. I can wait a while longer."

He drew her into his arms and closed his eyes, reveling in the feel of her body against his. "Sometimes I think you're stronger than me. I can't wait to be your husband."

She laid her cheek against his chest. "I've been thinking about something, but I've been afraid to mention it to you." Peering up anxiously, she met his questioning gaze. "Do you think that maybe . . . that God wants you to go visit your Lenape family? Didn't Wulachen say you brought the dawn light of the Father to them? Maybe you could help her find Him, and Menetopalis and their children too."

Releasing her, he stepped back and studied her for a long moment. Then he clasped her hands in his.

It had seemed an intractable dilemma: To have one family, he must give up the other. But could there be another possibility? Might he, after all, be able to keep both and do a good work at the same time?

"Do you . . . do you truly think it would be all right to go back and see them from time to time?"

She chewed her lip. "I'm afraid of what might happen. There are dangers, *ya*. But I can't stop thinking that it's what you're meant to do."

An exuberant smile spread across his face. "I'd have to wait until Christli comes home and gets settled, but maybe next spring . . ." He let the words trail off, his mind whirling with possibilities. "Daat and the others—they won't like it. They'll worry—"

"Talk to them! You might be surprised. If it's God's will, He'll open the doors. He may not make it easy but He can make it possible."

He caught her into his arms and swung her in a circle, both of them laughing. "You amaze me, Anna! But you're truly willing for me to go?"

"So long as you come back."

She spoke lightly, but he heard the worry that lay beneath her words. Setting her back on her feet he cupped her face in his hands and gazed deeply into her eyes, so close his lips almost touched hers. Engulfing her in his arms, he kissed her.

"How could I not come back," he murmured against her cheek, "when I'll have you waiting for me?"

Chapter Fifty-six

Friday, August 30, 1765

STAR CATCHER STEPPED onto the rocky ledge where overhanging trees and thick undergrowth gave way to limitless space. The sun had begun the slow descent from its zenith in a cloudless azure sky, while below his feet the great valley of the Susquehanna and Schuylkill rivers spread out into the vast, hazy distance.

Moments before, grizzled Sergeant Geiger and the greyhaired Mohawk elder, Wise Counselor, had led Star Catcher through the narrow, rocky gap in the ridge. He had waited almost a moon from his arrival at Johnson Hall until he could bear the uncertainty no longer. Twelve sleeps earlier he and his companions had slipped away. They had covered uncounted miles, yet he felt no gladness at reaching their journey's end.

With the back of his hand he wiped away the sweat beading his brow. The sun beat relentlessly down on them, and he lifted his face gratefully to the cooling breeze that swept across the ridge top before focusing his gaze again on the land below him.

Between the dark swaths of forest that cloaked the undulating hills, he made out a patchwork of fields and pastures bounded by winding lines of hedgerows and rail fences, where the tiny figures of cattle and horses grazed. Barns and outbuildings dotted the land, and between them lay log houses with smoke twining lazily upward from their chimneys.

"Look familiar?" the Pennsylvania militia sergeant said gruffly in the Lenape tongue.

Star Catcher did not answer or turn. He had stood here once, long ago. He knew it with piercing clarity. Everything had changed that day he was carried away from his first life. Now his second life was ending, and his future felt as uncertain and daunting as it had then.

"That's the headwaters of the Northkill." Geiger indicated a stream that trickled downward from the rocks at the summit. "When you mentioned it, I figured you had to be the boy taken from that Amish family. What was their name . . . let's see . . . Hochstetler?"

Star Catcher stiffened and Geiger grinned. "I reckon that was it. Their settlement is there, down below."

Wise Counselor stepped to Star Catcher's side and shaded his eyes with his hand, appearing to measure the sun's decline. "This thing will be hard to do, my son, but you must bear it, for we cannot delay. If I do not return quickly, Warraghiyagey will send soldiers to look for me."

"And I need to get back to my regiment." Geiger cocked his eye at Star Catcher. "Go. Make a new life."

Star Catcher did not move. He felt as though he was trapped between two worlds and could not go to either.

"Do not run away from them." Wise Counselor gave him a stern look. "You have no weapons for hunting or protection. The Whites hate the red man, and they will kill you."

"These people don't fight or kill," Geiger protested. "You'll be safe among them."

Star Catcher continued to gaze out over the valley. Dark clouds were building along the southern horizon, presaging a storm.

"This water will take me there. I will go alone from here."

"You sure?"

Star Catcher nodded at Geiger and clasped Wise Counselor's hand. Then he strode down the trail, following the stream's winding course.

✦ • • ✦

JAKOB LINGERED over the midday meal, hoping that the food and a short rest would replenish his energy. He and Joseph had to finish packing the supplies needed for their trip by evening or they would get a late start. Rubbing his sore shoulder, he gave little Kateli and Frany a quick smile as they helped their mother clear the dishes from the table.

"I'm glad you men got that hog butchered for Anna Lehman Wednesday since you're leaving for Johnson Hall tomorrow," Katie said as she bustled around the *Küche*. "How long has her husband been gone now?"

"Three years." Jakob clamped his mouth shut, chiding himself for speaking too quickly.

"Seems like you've been spending considerable time over there lately."

Hearing the teasing tone in her voice, Jakob returned stiffly, "It's the church's responsibility to take care of widows and orphans."

434 | Bob Hostetler and J. M. Hochstetler

"I'm glad for it too. Anna's such a help to us women, and what she says always lifts you up." Katie raised her voice above the clatter of pots. "It's a shame she has no children to help her out. I'm sure she gets real lonely at times."

As he set down his knife and fork a shadow fell over him and he looked up from his plate. A man stood in the open doorway, blocking the sunlight that streamed in around him, casting him in shadow.

Jakob started to rise, but the man swung hastily away and strode back out of sight. Jakob turned to Katie and the girls over by the dry sink washing dishes in the large basin.

"Did you see that man?"

Katie set down the plate she was wiping. "*Ya,* but I couldn't tell who it was."

"He looked like an Indian," eight-year-old Frany said.

Katie dried her hands. "There haven't been any Indians hereabouts in a long time. Should I get Johannes and Joseph from the barn?"

"I'll go. Maybe they saw him come by."

Jakob went outside. A south wind had sprung up, moisture-laden, stirring the trees and cooling the air. A rainstorm was brewing.

The stranger was sitting on the stump of a tree at the edge of the barnyard. Jakob noted that he was a young man, tanned and bare chested, garbed in leggings, breechcloth, and moccasins. At the back of his head a couple of turkey feathers stuck out of the colorful band that held back his hair. Shoulders hunched, he sat with his arms propped on his knees, staring at the ground.

As Jakob approached, the young man turned his back to him. Jakob saw that the long hair the wind teased around his shoulders and down his back was not black, as he had expected, but a light brown.

He was not an Indian.

Jakob's heart began to pound. He walked slowly to the young man and lightly placed his hand on his back. He did not look up.

"Is there anything you need?" Receiving no reply, Jakob gestured toward the house. "Will you come inside and eat? You are welcome here."

The muscles under his hand tensed. The young man began to stammer words Jakob understood though they were clumsily pronounced.

"Unser Vater in Himmel . . . dein Wille auf Erden . . . täglich Brot gib uns . . . vergib unsere Schulden . . . "

Jakob fell to his knees and gently turned the young man's face to his own. The boy did not resist, and when he looked up, Jakob sucked in a sharp breath.

He gazed into eyes as blue as the sky.

THE RAIN'S POUNDING on the roof had at last ceased. Star Catcher tried vainly to still his limbs' trembling. He glanced apprehensively at Joseph, who leaned against the great hearth's mantel, watching him with palpable warmth.

It seemed to Star Catcher as if the only thing he and Daat and Johannes wanted to do was to gaze at him. Indeed, Daat had not released his hand until Barbara and Katie put a meal on the table. The unfamiliar food had stuck in Star Catcher's throat, and when he tried to choke it down he had hardly been able to swallow a mouthful though his stomach cramped with hunger.

Barbara kept saying the same thing, voice breaking, each time she passed by, reaching to touch his arm or shoulder or head. "My little Christli, all grown up now." Each time they called him by that name, it took a moment for Star Catcher to realize that they spoke to him.

He had the clear sense that Joseph—Brings Dawn, he had told Star Catcher—understood his overwhelming impulse to flee the cabin's smothering confines for the gathering twilight outside. If he had not been there to translate and reassure him, Star Catcher would certainly have broken away as soon as this dimly remembered family began to gather around him.

When he had first heard Joseph speak—in a different dialect than his own, but one he could understand by listening carefully—a surge of relief had swept through him. There had been time only for this brother to relate the barest outlines of his own story and Daat's, but he had promised that they would speak at length after Star Catcher had eaten and rested.

He was glad of the rain's ending for he was still not certain he could bear to stay the night. The interior of the house seemed both strange and familiar, and he studied his surroundings, feeling lost and fearful.

Jake and Annali were missing, he thought, throat tightening painfully. And Maam. Most of all her. His heart wrenched at the memory that had never left him of his mother's tenderness and laughter. And of her death.

With the memories, images of a scorching fire rose to his mind. Not this house, but the other. The one that lay beyond the road in the dark shadow he had given wide berth to on his way to Johannes's house. The place where Star Catcher could never go because, although he could not remember why, the evil that had happened there had been his fault.

As though sensing his increasing distress, Joseph pushed away from the fireplace and said something to the others. A worried look came over Daat's face, and his reply made Joseph frown and shake his head.

He crossed the room to Star Catcher. In a low voice, he said in Lenape, "Our father worries that you will run away and asked me to keep you close, for if you were lost to him again, he could not bear it. If we go outside, will you stay with me for his sake?"

Relieved, Star Catcher quickly gave his assent, and Joseph beckoned for him to follow. He bolted after his brother, grateful to get outside away from the others, from the tormenting memories, into the cool, rain-misted night where he could breathe.

Chapter Fifty-seven

Saturday, March 15, 1766

CHRISTIAN BROUGHT his mount to a halt beside Joseph's. The first delicate tinge of green lay across the land, and a keen spring wind teased the horses' manes.

Throughout the fall and winter Christian had wrestled mightily with a turmoil that drove his emotions back and forth like wind-tossed trees in a storm. Had it not been for this brother, he knew, he could not have stayed among this people.

Joseph, who had pushed him away in their childhood, had turned out to be his anchor and guide back into their Amish community, his translator and tutor, his protector and advocate. And, in a way, his savior. He seemed to sense when anguish or frustration overwhelmed Christian. At such times, Joseph would say in the Lenape tongue, "Brother, let us go hunting." Or fishing. Or riding across the fields, as on this day.

"Soon you go to the Muskingum?"

Joseph met Christian's gaze. "It is Anna who suggested it. She thinks Father in Heaven might wish me to speak His words to our people, and I feel it too." He grinned. "And I will get there in time to play *pahsahëman.*"

Christian chuckled, then slowly sobered. "But will you come back?"

"I will. My home is here now, with Anna—and with you and our father and the rest. But Wulachen and Menetopalis and their children will always be my kindred too. I cannot think of never seeing them again, never knowing whether it goes well with them and whether they choose to follow Father in Heaven. I only worry that my absence will make more work for everyone since I must be gone during planting."

"Women's work." Christian's tone was deliberately disdainful, and they laughed together. "I will not let Johannes and our father do the work alone." He turned a longing gaze to the horizon. "I miss so much of our lives among our people."

"Then why do you not go back to visit Raven Eye and the others?"

"I cannot. I was told that if I return, they will bind me and carry me back to the English."

"Things have changed. Our people have made peace with the English. It is not only the traders who go into the Ohio lands now."

Christian's mount tossed her head and sidestepped, and he tightened the reins. "If I go back to the Lenape, my brother," he said grimly, "I'll not return."

"You have as much to hold you here as—"

"I've not told you all." Avoiding Joseph's gaze, Christian recounted the raid at Fort Le Boeuf, concluding, "The man I aimed at fell."

"Ah, my brother." Dismay and pity edged Joseph's voice.

"None could tell whether he died at my hand or that of one of those who fired with me. Yet this thing will not leave my mind."

"Speak to our father—"

"No—do not tell him of this! He was right in not taking up weapons against those who attacked us, and he will hate me—"

"He will not! All he has suffered has changed him." Joseph broke off and regarded him silently for a long moment. Finally he said, "I will keep your confidence, my brother. This matter is yours to tell, not mine. But you will feel no peace until you seek Father in Heaven's forgiveness."

Christian gave him a defiant look. "I do not know whether I believe in this God. I go to church because Daat wishes me to, but my heart is not in it."

"Do you believe in Manitou, the *manitowuks,* Misinghalikun?"

Pressing his lips together, Christian looked away. "For a long time I did, and when I sought a vision from Manitou, I was given one. But it has done me no good. How can I even tell that it came from him? I do not know what to believe."

He curbed his restive mount before turning back to Joseph. "You will take a wife in the Falling Leaf Moon, and soon you will have children to bind you to this place. That I do not have. I must seek what there is for me, whether here or elsewhere—if I can find it."

"You will not find it, my brother. It will find you."

Christian jerked the reins and brought his horse around in a circle. "Leave me for a while. I would be alone." Seeing the concern in Joseph's eyes, he added, "I will not run away. I have nowhere else to go. I only want to think."

"I will see you at home then." Joseph drew his stallion around and after a quick glance over his shoulder at Christian urged him back the way they had come.

Home.

Christian watched him ride away, the bitter taste of hopelessness on his tongue. As his bond with this family strengthened, his life among the Lenape increasingly faded into the recesses of memory. Yet a large share of his heart and sinew and bones still belonged to that other land and to those loved ones who forever lay out of reach.

He did not know how to bridge those opposing worlds, how to give up one and hold to the other. He knew only that his guilt stood between him and the home he had lost. And he could not tell whether it was the one on the Muskingum or the one on the Northkill.

Or both. Or neither.

It will find you, Joseph had said.

His hand shaking, Christian drew the small pouch he wore around his neck from its concealment under his shirt. He rubbed the soft leather between his fingers, his heart painfully wrenched by the vivid memory of Nútemau giving it to him when he first came to the Lenape, and of the old man's wisdom and kindness and love.

Slowly he drew the rawhide thong over his head. Loosening the pouch's neck, he let the small cluster of crystals tumble out onto his palm. Fiery rainbows of light sparkled in the pale sunlight as he turned it.

He tried to swallow past the hard lump in his throat. Had the vision he cherished been deception after all?

It came to him that to return to the Lenape would be to return to vain idols and the temptation to violence. If his sin was ever to be atoned for, he could not go back.

He took a deep breath and, clenching his fingers around the crystals, drew back his arm. With all his strength he flung the cluster in a high arc into the woods at the edge of the field and watched as it struck a tree trunk, rebounded, and fell into a drift of leaves. For a long moment he stared after it, the pouch clutched in his other hand, held motionless by the sharp clarity of the images that filled his mind, of Nútemau, Raven Eye, Deep Water, Standing Stone, and all the others.

He held out his arm, then, feeling as though he tore open the fragile scab that had only just begun to close over a great, gaping wound. And averting his gaze, he opened his hand and let the small rectangle of leather fall from his fingers to the muddy ground.

Kicking his heels into his mare's flanks, he urged her forward along the path toward home.

Chapter Fifty-eight

SHAD MOON
Wednesday, April 23, 1766

J OSEPH HEARD THE THROB of drums and clamor of excited voices
before the first scattered cabins and wigewas came into view
at the turning of the path. He urged his stallion forward,
holding him alongside Red Squirrel's as his friend's father, Long
Mountain, led the way into the town, with Smoke in Sky and Grey
Wolf closing ranks behind them.

Red Squirrel grinned broadly. "Everyone waits to greet you,
Brings Dawn! They cannot believe you have returned."

Joseph laughed. "I am eager to see them, too, but especially
my mother and father."

He had encountered his three friends unexpectedly at Fort Pitt,
where they had come to trade. Mutual astonishment had quickly
given way to joyful embraces, and the next day they had struck out
on the Great Path along the same route they and their families had
followed from Sauconk to the Muskingum years earlier.

As they neared their destination Red Squirrel had hurried
ahead to announce Joseph's arrival, while he stayed behind with

Smoke in Sky and Grey Wolf to garb himself in the clothing Wulachen had given him many moons ago at Johnson Hall. After dressing his hair in a roach adorned with a tuft of deer fur, he carefully painted his face.

If only Bishop Hertzler could see me now!

His laughter prompted his companions to demand the reason for it, and he soon had them doubled over in mirth.

In a short time Red Squirrel had returned with Long Mountain to conduct them in. Now as they advanced onto the council house yard, the deafening drumbeats and chanting were joined by the crack of rifle fire.

The entire town appeared to have turned out to welcome him, but it was Wulachen and Menetopalis he looked for first. They stood next to Tamaque at the head of the dancing crowd, tears coursing down their cheeks.

Wulachen reached for him the moment he dismounted and clasped him to her bosom. "You have come to stay, my son?"

He held her tightly before pulling back to look into her beloved face. "Only one moon, my mother—for now. But I will come again as often as I can. And I bring many gifts to you from my white father and brothers and sister."

He turned to Menetopalis, rejoicing in the feel of the older man's strong arms around him and his heartfelt welcome. Then, laughing and weeping, Joseph embraced in turn lithe, muscular Contrary Wind—who quickly informed Joseph that his man-name was He Makes Peace—then Moonflower, and She Sings, who carried her and Grey Wolf's little daughter. Cuddling the fat, laughing child in his arms, he admired the roundness of

She Sings' belly with the child to come and marveled at how tall and handsome Contrary Wind had grown.

Mehíttuk and Many Leaves, with their small son and infant daughter, came forward to embrace him, followed by all Joseph's other friends. He exulted that none of them had forgotten him and that they all considered him still one of their own. He was grateful most of all for the evidence that Wulachen had been re-instated to full fellowship with the women of the community.

After some moments she turned to survey those who crowded around them, her head held high. "My son, Brings Dawn, who was lost to us, has come back to bring us gifts from his first family. It is according to the vision the great Creator, Father in Heaven, gave to my younger son when he received his new name: He Makes Peace."

Amid the swelling crowd and babble of eager voices, Joseph tried to call to memory his arrival at Sauconk all those years ago when he had been an angry, rebellious, terrified youth. But he could not.

The intervening years had washed away all the pain and hurt. What remained was home and kindred, no less here than on the Northkill.

JOSEPH TREASURED each moment in the weeks that followed, even as he dreaded leaving the Muskingum again. He found it deeply gratifying to renew friendships, join in the Lenape's games and hunts, observe the evening dances, and join in every aspect of the communal life of Tamaque's Town.

He and Menetopalis and Wulachen engaged in many earnest talks about his white life and all he had felt and learned, always returning to the subject of Father in Heaven. The story of He Makes Peace's vision of a brilliant man clothed in white who told him to follow Father in Heaven's way of peace had thrilled Joseph, as did Menetopalis's new openness to hearing about this God. Although Joseph felt unequal to the task, the time spent studying with Bishop Hertzler during Instruction—as well as discussions with Daat, Johannes, and others—bore surprising fruit in their discussions.

Most surprising of all, however, was the eagerness he felt as the time of his departure approached. He missed Daat and his brothers, sister, and their extended family more than he had expected. He yearned to find out how Christian had gotten along in his absence. Most of all, he hungered to hold Anna in his arms again and to at last make firm plans for their wedding and a home of their own.

The knowledge that he would see his Lenape kindred again often and that God had brought his life full circle and would make him fruitful filled him with eagerness and joy for the days to come.

Chapter Fifty-nine

Thursday, June 12, 1766

S EATED BESIDE DAAT on the wagon's bench, Christian looked around with growing interest as the Belgians plodded along the rutted road winding along the Northkill toward its confluence with the Tulpehocken River. He took in the well-kept plantations coming into view around each hill and fold of the valley, feeling for the first time as though the fog of loss and uncertainty that had enveloped him for so long was finally lifting.

His bonds with Daat and the rest of his family had strengthened over the past months as the memories of his life among the Lenape continued to blur. And it struck Christian that it was because of Joseph's absence that he had been forced to increasingly let down his defenses.

He had finally found the courage to confess to Daat what had happened at Fort Le Boeuf. Despite initial shock and dismay, he had shown unexpected grace and offered such comfort and wise counsel that a great burden had lifted from Christian's shoulders. As a result he found himself cautiously considering whether he might find a future in this place after all.

Daat patted his knee now as though sensing his thoughts, and Christian looked up to return his smile. He welcomed the press of Daat's shoulder against his as they rode in companionable silence.

A short distance farther along they saw a man walking from his house to the large barn across a broad yard, with several young sons skipping before him. They all turned to wave at Christian and Daat, and they lifted their hands in return.

Noting their plain dress and the man's beard, unadorned with a mustache, Christian asked, "Are these people Amish too?"

Daat shook the reins across the Belgian's backs. "Their church is called the Church of the Brethren. Some call them German Baptists or Tunkers. Or just Brethren. Like us, they dress plain and hold to believers' baptism and nonresistance."

Christian frowned. "Then why aren't they Amish?"

Daat glanced at him, one eyebrow raised, and chuckled. "It makes you wonder, doesn't it? They're believers just like we are, but where we live our faith before the unbelievers so they may see our good works and praise Gott, the Brethren believe in going out and gathering them in by their preaching. And they hold other differences of doctrine. But Gott gives each person understanding according to His will, and He calls all His children to live in peace with one another."

Christian had expected a long, impossible to understand diatribe on why the Amish were right and everyone else was wrong, arguments he had heard from some in the Northkill church since his return. But he was discovering that Joseph was right: The years following the attack had changed their father, even as they had changed him and Joseph.

"Joseph should be home any day now." Daat turned the Belgians into the yard of a large grist mill, wheels creaking as the heavily laden wagon jounced through the ruts.

"*Ya,* he thought he'd be back in time to help harvest the oats and rye." Christian sat up straighter, suddenly eager to have his brother home.

Along the tall building's far side, facing the millrace that branched off from the creek, the huge water wheel turned in slow rhythm, water spilling across its paddles to cascade into the race's lower level. A bewhiskered, plainly dressed man appeared from inside as Daat brought the wagon to a halt at the building's loading dock. Daat introduced him as Reichardt Umbenhauer, the owner of the mill.

Umbenhauer welcomed them with hearty handshakes as soon as they climbed down from the wagon, and they went inside. In short order the mill's workers unloaded the large sacks of wheat from the wagon, and Christian watched with keen interest as they transferred the sacks to the mill's upper floor by means of a hoist.

"I haven't seen you here before."

Startled, he swung around to meet the smiling gaze of a slender young woman who had seemingly materialized at his side. She stood tall enough that she lifted her head only slightly to look into his eyes. Her unadorned dark-grey clothing was similar to that worn by the women of his Amish community, though the white linen cap that covered her brown hair had a different shape. Although her face was plain, her features were pleasant and regular, and her blue eyes sparkled with good humor.

"*Y-ya.* I haven't been here before—*nay,* I came a few times when I was little, but—" He broke off in confusion.

She seemed to take no notice. "That would have been before I came to live with the Umbenhauers. I'm Barbara Rupp. You're Christian, aren't you—Jakob Hochstetler's youngest son, the one who came back from the Indians last fall?"

"I suppose everybody talks about me and my brother Joseph—the Amish Indians."

His caustic tone caused her to blush. "Nay, I only know about you from your Daat. He and your older brother, Johannes, told us about your return last fall when they brought the corn in for grinding. We'd already heard Joseph was home."

Christian glanced toward Daat, who stood several yards away, deep in conversation with Umbenhauer. "You work here?"

"I'm good at figures, and I help out by keeping the mill's accounts. Would you like me to show you around?"

He accepted and they climbed the steep stairway along one wall to the building's third floor, where they found workers emptying sacks into a bin. Dust motes danced thickly in the sunlight that slanted through the high windows, and far below Christian could hear the rumble of the millstones grinding the grain.

While Barbara explained how the grain was cleaned, ground, and sifted, Christian bent over the railing to look down the dizzying channel formed by the thick timbers of the mill's stairway all the way to the dark, stone-walled basement that housed the immense millstones. She came to stand beside him, and he turned around and leaned against the railing, arms folded across his chest.

"How did you come to work here?"

She clenched her hands over the railing and looked down below. "My Maam died when I was just nine, and three years later my Daat was killed in an accident. I went to live with my Maam's brother, but he and his wife already had six children and a new baby, and she didn't want another to care for. So the Umbenhauers took me in."

When he remained silent, she looked up. "Were you happy living with the Indians?"

"I was."

"We heard that many captives didn't want to come back."

"I didn't. Plenty of those who were dragged back with me fought to get away. I would have, but I knew I wouldn't last long in the wilderness without a horse and weapons." He dropped his gaze to his shoes. "I still don't feel like I belong here. If it hadn't been for Joseph, I wouldn't have stayed this long."

She lightly touched his hand. "You probably don't think I understand, but I do. I've felt that way for so long that I've forgotten what it's like to really belong someplace." When Christian looked up in surprise, she continued, "I'm not saying that the Umbenhauers haven't been good to me. They always treat me the same as their own children, and I love them for it."

"Daat and the rest of my family have been good to me too. It's just—" He stopped, searching for the right words.

Dimples formed in her cheeks. "We've had some of the same struggles, *ya?*"

He returned her smile. *"Ya."* Wondering why he felt compelled to share with her feelings that were so personal, he burst out,

"The Lenape dance and sing and take real joy in each day, and I miss that. The Amish way seems so dry and colorless in comparison."

She laid her hand on his arm. "Maybe you should try coming to my church. We're having evangelistic services all week, and our preachers sure aren't dry and colorless."

"You're one of the Brethren?"

Her dimples deepened. "That's right."

He looked her deliberately up and down. "You don't look like a Brethren to me."

Her laugh sounded like music. Blushing, she said, "I don't mean to try to take you away from the Amish, but—"

"I haven't joined church. I know my Daat wants me to, and I try to fit in. But I don't feel like I do—or ever will."

"Maybe God's leading you someplace else then. Elder Klein is such a good preacher. For the first time in my life I know that my true home is in heaven, and it doesn't matter if I don't have one here." When he hesitated, she said, "Truly, won't you come? It might make a difference."

Gazing down into her deep blue eyes, he felt suddenly breathless. Her hand still rested on his arm, and he realized that he liked having it there.

Had he thought her plain? When she gazed up at him with such warmth, it seemed to him as though he, too, caught a glimpse of something that felt like home.

He laid his hand over hers, smiling down at her. "I just might do that."

Chapter Sixty

Wednesday, October 22, 1766

AFTER THEY FINISHED the repairs to Widow Lehman's small house, Christian helped to load the large toolbox into the back of the wagon. He waited with Johannes and Joseph, while Daat leaned against the sideboard, talking to the diminutive, fifty-year-old widow. With her spritely manner and brown bodice and petticoat, she reminded Christian of a sparrow.

She thanked them profusely before turning to Christian. "I haven't seen you at church for a while. You haven't been sick, I hope."

He flushed. "*Nay*, it's just . . . I've . . . been attending services at the Northkill Brethren Church."

"Oh." A slight frown creased her brow, then her expression cleared. "I have a good friend who attends there, and she sings the praises of Elder Klein."

"He's a good preacher, that's for sure."

Not looking at Christian, Daat set his hat carefully on his head. "We'd better get going, Anna. We've yet the evening chores to do."

Johannes grinned. "Ach, Daat, the boys are old enough to take care of the milking if—"

"*Nay*, there's plenty of work for all of us, and we've taken enough of Anna's time."

The widow protested, but Daat was already climbing onto the wagon. Relieved that the attention had shifted away from him, Christian jumped in the back with his brothers. He noted that Daat returned Anna's wave with a nod and a smile as the wagon rolled forward.

Christian kept his expression sober as a funeral all the way home, studiously avoiding the glances Joseph and Johannes repeatedly cast in his direction. He knew that if he looked at them, he would snicker, and Daat would surely hear.

After the Belgians and the wagon had been put away, Daat and Johannes headed toward the house. Joseph grabbed Christian's arm before he could escape and hauled him back into the barn.

"If you don't talk to Daat now, it's only going to get harder. This is the perfect opportunity! You see how interested he is in Widow Lehman. He's planning to move to that plantation he bought over by Blancks' before winter, and I suspect he has in mind to get married again."

"It is time for him to think about his future now that we're both home again," Christian said, frowning. "With you and your Anna getting married tomorrow—"

"That's what I mean! He'll understand how you feel."

"But my decision isn't just about Barbara and me. *Ya,* we're getting close, but I feel I have a place in the Brethren Church."

"I understand that. So tell Daat. You can't keep putting it off, and more than likely he's figured it out anyway."

While Joseph headed down the lane to help their nephews drive the cows up from the pasture for milking, Christian lingered in the barn considering the matter. At last he drew himself erect, thrust his hands into his pockets, and strode toward the house.

◆ • —— • ◆

JAKOB STUDIED his youngest son silently, his heart heavy. He had suspected what was coming ever since Christian first attended evangelistic services at the Brethren Church. And when he had begun spending an increasing amount of time with Barbara Rupp, premonition had turned into certainty. Jakob had wrestled mightily with the matter, but finally concluded he had to trust God in this too.

"I just feel like . . . like home is where Barbara is," Christian said, head bent, hands clasped between his knees.

"You've been looking for that for a long time, haven't you? Home."

Christian looked up, blinking back tears. "*Ya.* I don't know why, but . . . I can't seem to find it here."

"I know."

"But it's more than that, Daat!" Christian said in a rush. "I used to think I could gain God's favor if I was good. Then when the attack happened, for a long time I thought it was my fault because I hadn't been good enough."

"How could you think that? If it was anybody's fault, it was mine. I should have taken you all to safety when the raids began—"

"You couldn't know what would happen. You did what you thought was best. And after that raid at Fort LeBoeuf, my heart told me you made the right decision that night."

Jakob patted him on the shoulder, at a loss for words.

Christian straightened, and a light came into his eyes. "Last Sunday Elder Klein preached on Jesus' parables about the lost sheep and the prodigal son. He said none of us is worthy of God's forgiveness, but when we come to Him, He forgives us anyway, and it just hit me here." He pressed his hand to his chest. "Daat, He brought me home not because I'm good enough, but because He loves me! I know that now. And I'm going to be baptized and become a member of the church. I know you always wanted your children to be Amish, but deep in my heart I know that God's calling me to do this."

Jakob pulled out his kerchief and wiped his eyes. "*Nay,* Christian. That's where you're wrong. *Ya,* I'm disappointed that you won't be a member of my church. But what I've always wanted is for my children to obey *Gott* rather than man. And if He's calling you to the Brethren, then how can I not rejoice that you're following Him?"

✦ ‒‒‒‒ ✦

CHRISTIAN STARED HARD at the dusky tree line at the western end of the rows of corn shocks. "I had bad dreams for a long time. Sometimes I still do."

Joseph glanced toward Johannes's house, out of sight behind the trees along the lane, and when he turned back Christian caught the glimmer of moisture in his eyes. "*Ya,* me too."

The look that passed between them held understanding. And sorrow.

After talking with Daat, Christian had gone to find Joseph. They had walked toward the road, while Christian related their father's reaction to his decision. Of one accord, without needing to speak of it, they had pushed through the break in the hedgerow where the carriageway to the old homestead had been and turned into the cornfield below.

Joseph lifted his eyes toward the top of the field's long, gentle upward slope. "I haven't been able to go to that place since my return—not alone or with anyone else. I feel darkness there."

Christian followed his gaze, his chest tight. "If we're ever to have peace, we have to face it someday. We could do it together . . . now."

He saw Joseph's jaw harden. After a brief hesitation, he nodded.

Together they crossed the field to where a faint path drew them toward the hazy line of the orchard running along the base of the distant hill. It was hard to make out, but Christian thought the fence had followed the gradual rise on his left. Joseph and Jake had discarded their hats among the bushes there on the day of Barbara's wedding as, in defiance of Daat's orders, they went to track a band of Shawnee crossing their fields. Unknown to them Christian had followed and run into the warriors.

Joseph strode ahead of him. "The cows broke through the fence into the field here and trampled the corn that day I ran off to hunt the fox that was bothering the chickens."

A few more strides up the rise, and both of them made out the slight depression, thickly weed-grown now, all that indicated where the barn's lower level had once cut into the bank. Where he had helped milk the cows with Joseph and Jake.

Christian stumbled after Joseph up the last yards to the level area where the barnyard had been, with the house across from it. Here, too, everything had changed.

Turning slowly, he scanned the drying grasses studded here and there with saplings that clothed the land's gentle undulations, seeking for traces of the smokehouse and other outbuildings, finding none.

It had all been let go to pastureland, the grasses unmown, a few cows and sheep grazing a short distance away. Little by little, the forest was reclaiming it.

With dread he glanced toward the house yard. A scattered pile of blackened stones almost buried in a rank growth of weeds marked the place where the bake oven had been—where the band of Lenape and Shawnee warriors and their French scouts had gathered that night. Where he had laid baby Annali, unconscious, when they escaped from the inferno.

Beyond the stones he noted a small, neatly kept patch of ground with two wooden markers. A crushing sense of loss bowed his shoulders.

He advanced haltingly, Joseph following, until he could make out the front wall of the cellar's blackened ruins. A tangle of weeds and vines obscured the rest of the collapsed walls, filling the cavernous space where they had sought shelter from their attackers.

Sweat broke out on Christian's brow. He could not go any closer, nor did Joseph.

As though it had happened yesterday, Christian was enveloped by the searing heat and heavy, cider-tinged smoke as the house burned down over their heads, felt the exquisite relief of their escape from its hellish confines at daybreak and the terror of the warrior's triumphant war cries as they swept out of the orchard.

A welter of emotions drew Joseph's gaze from the ruins to the now mature trees of the orchard, their branches laden with ripening apples and peaches. The evening of the apfelschnitzen, before the attack, he and Anna had stood among them, with his baby sister, Annali, in her arms. He had thought her the most beautiful and dearest young woman he had ever known and had longed to tell her that he loved her, but had not found the words.

A glint of water where the trickle from the spring wound among the trees caught his eye. Their Indian captors had allowed him and Daat and Christli to bathe their faces and slake their thirst there, and then to gather ripe peaches as provision for the coming journey—a harvest that had saved them from the gauntlet at Shikellamy's Town.

He tried to block consciousness of the steep, wooded hill that loomed just behind the orchard, but he was powerless to turn away. He had fled up its slope in terror, leaving his family to face their attackers. Cowering behind a fallen log, he had watched in horror while the warriors killed and scalped Maam and Jake and Annali and took Daat and Christian prisoner. Fear had pinned him to the earth until the warriors came to take him too.

"I ran away and hid. I should have run for help, but I was so scared I couldn't move."

Christian swung to face him. "Who could have helped us? Daat and I needed you on that journey. It would have been harder for us alone. God knew that. And then He gave you a family so you could tell them about Him."

Joseph stared at Christian, breathless. He turned and strode several yards away, then came back and gripped his younger brother by the shoulders. "Thank you! You don't know what that means to me."

Silently, of one accord, they went to the graves and knelt. At length Christian raised his head, listening. The air was filled with the dry, pulsating rasp of locusts and grasshoppers, the low hum of bees, the silvery hiss of wind through the trees.

"It's peaceful here," he murmured.

"It's strange that I refused to come here for so long," Joseph said. "The darkness I felt over this place is gone."

"The earth has cleansed itself of the evil. It takes back the land as though man was never there."

Joseph pushed to his feet. "Let's go to the Northkill where we crossed that day."

Christian rose and followed him westward along the orchard. They crossed Melchior Detweiler's fields, detouring around hedgerows and climbing over rail fences until they came to the narrow, rushing waters of Northkill Creek, easily waded at this time of year.

Christian looked upstream, to the north, where the creek emerged from the deep forest. Looming above the trees two miles away, the long, misty bulk of the Blue Mountain stretched across the horizon from southwest to northeast, casting its ancient shadow across the land.

Joseph sat down on the grass and pulled off shoes and hose. Rising, he waded through the cool, ankle-deep water, his feet slipping on the mossy rocks of the streambed, until he reached a boulder that protruded above the water. He ran his hands over the rough surface, then straightened and glanced back at Christian.

"Do you remember how I hit my knee on this rock when we crossed? It drew blood, but all trace of it has been washed away."

Christian kicked off his shoes and bent to pull off his stockings. "Last Sunday Elder Klein preached a sermon about the Israelites crossing the Jordan into the Promised Land. God held back the water while the priests stood in the middle of the river so they could cross. Afterward He told Joshua to set up twelve stones right there as a reminder to their descendents of how He had brought them across on dry land."

"Then let'a make this our stone of remembrance!"

Christian waded over to him, and they set to work digging the heavy stone free. The swirling water had eroded the rocky creek bed around it, but both were soaked to the skin and splattered with mud by the time they wrestled the boulder onto the bank and set it on end above the shallow ford.

Wiping his face with the back of his hand, Joseph stepped back to study their work. He turned to Christian and gave a firm nod.

"Let this stone bear witness to God's faithfulness in our time of trial. As long as it stands may we remember all He did for us."

✦ ⋯ ✦

JOSEPH ROSE EARLY the next morning, while it was still dark. He had yearned for this day for so long that sleep had come with difficulty and soon fled.

After washing and brushing his hair, he dressed in his sober black Sunday breeches and waistcoat, hurrying so he would be ready to ride over to Uncle Crist's plantation with the others in time for the service. His hands shook with impatience and excitement.

He reached for his black coat, but feeling the pouch slide across his chest beneath his shirt, he laid his hand over it. He never removed it except when he bathed. But after a moment he pulled the rawhide thong loose and drew it over his head.

The small pouch Menetopalis had given him was worn and frayed at the edges. Joseph opened it and shook the piece of antler into his hand. He had studied it closely many times, but now he looked at it with new eyes.

Within it lay his vision. And his name: Brings Dawn. In it he felt the life of the Lenape, of Wulachen and Menetopalis and their children, Tamaque and Shingas as well. And more, for it had come at a time when he desperately needed comfort and assurance.

He weighed the antler in his hand, remembering Bishop Hertzler's response when he had told him how he received the vision after praying to Jesus. The bishop had considered the matter thoughtfully before saying that God supplies all our needs. God rarely does so ahead of time, he had added, but just when it's needed most. Perhaps He had given Joseph the vision so that he might find favor with his Lenape family, while reminding Joseph that He was always near.

Today Anna would become his wife, and he would take on the responsibilities of being a faithful and loving husband to her. For all time no matter what trials they faced until they both came to their true home.

That spring he had pledged to be a faithful member of the Amish church, but more than that, to bear the name of his Savior. And that was the only name he needed, the one he cherished more than any other.

He slipped the antler back into the pouch and closed his fingers tightly around it. Then he tucked the pouch into the pack that held the clothing and other personal effects he was taking to the Blancks' plantation, where he and Anna would live with her parents.

He listened to the muted voices and activity out in the *Küche,* while he finished dressing. Then he took a last, quick look in his small mirror and smiled. Catching up his coat, he went to join Daat and the others with a light step.

Chapter Sixty-one

Tuesday, August 14, 1770

B ARBARA LINGERED in the *Küche* after the dishes and leftovers from the noon meal had been cleared away. The entire family had gathered at her home that day to welcome Joseph back and hear the news he brought from his latest visit to the Musk-ingum. He had gone right after planting was done so he could be back in time for harvest.

Daat had married Anna Lehman the previous fall, and they lived on the plantation in Heidelberg Township he had purchased shortly before Christian's return. They were seated side by side on the couch in the *Stube,* with Anna leaning on Daat's arm, Christian and his wife, and Barbara's own Crist across from them. Barbara smiled, reflecting on how quickly she had grown to love her new stepmother, whose kindness and joy in life had become a blessing to them all.

Although Anna and Daat lived several miles away, they were close to Joseph and his Anna, who had bought her parents' plantation a year earlier when Hans and Mattie moved to Lancaster County. Christian and his Barbara, expecting their first child, also lived nearby, down the road from the Northkill Brethren

Church. It was where Daat wanted to be, near the two sons God had given back to him for his faithfulness.

Bright sunshine flooded in through the open windows—the protective Indian shutters long since removed. Barbara could hear the voices of the children calling to one another with happy laughter as they played in the yard.

Seeing the entire family gathered, all of them believers and doing so well now after the years of trial and uncertainty, Barbara's heart swelled with joy. She would always miss Maam, Jake, and Annali but took comfort in knowing that they were in heaven and that the day would come when they would all be together again.

Joseph had recounted his visit to Tamaque's Town while they ate. Wulachen and Menetopalis and their children—and grandchildren—were prospering. They sent many thanks for the gifts Joseph had brought and had sent gifts in return, accompanied by their prayers and love.

"I told them about the new town the missionary David Zeisberger helped the Moravian Lenape establish on the Beaver River this spring," Joseph was saying now, still seated at the table beside his Anna, who held their youngest, across from Johannes and Katie, who cradled their latest grandchild in her lap. "I stopped there on my way west. They call it *Friedensstadt,* Town of Peace. Wulachen is determined to move there before winter so they can hear the preaching of the gospel, and Menetopalis and their children are eager to go too. I believe they're not far from the Kingdom. Even Tamaque and Shingas say they want to hear more."

"God's doing a mighty work!" Johannes exclaimed.

Barbara delighted in Joseph's news. It amazed her that she

had come to love Joseph's Lenape family, though she had never met them and likely never would. But they had accepted Joseph as their own and brought him up to be the man he was today. And soon, God willing, they would join the family of faith.

In the *Stube* she could hear Christian—now a tall, lanky man whose devout faith inspired hers, no matter that he had been led to a different church—saying, "I asked my Barbara what she'd say if I told her the Lord was calling me to ministry."

His Barbara leaned forward, her face wreathed in a smile. "I told him, if that's the Lord's leading, then He couldn't choose a better man."

Barbara couldn't help smiling as she watched them. So much had been lost, yet so much had been gained. And miraculously love had grown.

Johannes left the table and came to her side. "It's a good day."

Looking up at him, she said, "Do you remember the day we buried Maam and Jake and little Annali?"

His broad, good-humored face sobered. "*Ya,* like it was yesterday."

"The bishop said in his sermon that what Satan means for evil, God will turn to good, that our children and grandchildren and the generations who follow will see the day of blessing."

"I've thought of it often."

She drew a quick, light breath. "I couldn't believe then that any good could ever come out of such destruction and grief. But today my eyes see it, and I praise God, Who brought it to pass. And I feel it in my heart that there are many more such days to come."

Epilogue

Thursday, November 30, 1775

J AKOB STUMBLED to a halt at the top of the hill. The exertion
of the steep climb had caused his chest to tighten, and he
was panting a little. He pulled off his black beaver-felt hat
and took his handkerchief out of the crown to mop the sweat
from his brow.

He replaced his hat and surveyed the plantation where he
and Anna had lived since their marriage. The look of it, with its
rugged, heavily forested hills sheltering a small spring-watered
valley, pleased him. His eye lingered on the glimpse of the Tulpehocken River winding between the trees and hills along a broader
valley off to the east.

The land was fertile. It had borne good crops, and the house
he had built for his Anna was snug, just big enough for the two of
them. They had been happy there, but last spring they had decided
to move closer to Christian and his family, now living farther west
in Lebanon Township, and Jakob had purchased a parcel of land
from him.

He frowned as he looked down on the peaceful land below
him. Unsettling news of the colonies' great war against England

reached them too frequently. His sons and older grandsons had refused to join the militia, and again the enmity of their English neighbors, whether loyal to the king or to the new Continental Congress, turned against the Amish of the Northkill community.

The wind teased his hair, completely white now, and sent a shiver down his back. The waning day had turned cold, and he chided himself for not heeding Anna's urging to wear his winter coat. The weather had been unseasonably warm for so late in the fall, and he had left it behind.

For some moments he stood, puzzled, hands clenching and unclenching, until the image of his first Anna, lost long ago, dissipated and that of his new wife replaced it. Although the name was common in his community, he felt it strange that he had married two women who bore it. Lately the face of the other Anna would come to him first, momentarily confusing him. Then he had to stop and think hard to fix the right one in his mind.

He shook his head, the thoughts drifting away, as they did often lately, to gratitude and praise. Over the years even the grief for his friend Hans Specht's death and the loss of his children that had troubled Jakob for so long had given way to peace. Christian had told him of little Hannah's death and Franz's loving mother. And now Jakob thought of how the Almighty's grace covered all things, even those beyond a man's understanding.

In spite of his desperate plea God had allowed him and his boys to be separated for a time. But he saw now that his Lord had been faithful, accomplishing so much more in their lives through suffering than he could ever have foreseen. He could not wish to give up the treasures each one of them had gained through the fiery trial.

Gott, *you are good, and I praise you for the blessings you have poured out on me and on my children!*

Suddenly aware that the light had dimmed, he looked up to see that the wind was blowing dark clouds in from the north. The sun hung in the southwest at the tops of the distant hills, its fading glow casting a red light across the valley. He had walked the land for too long, and his Anna would be worrying.

It came to him then as he scanned the western horizon: As in his long-ago dream he stood on a high hill. But this time it was near winter. The grasses were dry and brown, the trees barren, and racing clouds spread across the sky to swallow up the setting sun.

No altar stood before him now. But he knew that, though he could not see it with his physical eyes, it was there. And on it lay his precious Lamb, His blood ever flowing to the foot of the throne high above in the realm of the One who loved him, where his sins were washed away in the sea of His mercy and never more called to mind.

A glimpse of movement drew him around. Two young men approached up the slope, garbed not in Indian dress now, but in the plain dress of their childhood.

His heart leaped, and a strange tightness clenched his chest, spreading out to his limbs and bringing heat to his face. As he struggled to drag air into his lungs, a shock seared through him like a hard blow, and he fell to his knees, clutching his chest, trying to cry out.

But no sound came from his mouth, and he slumped forward as Christian and Joseph raced the last yards up the hill.

✦ • • •✦

BY SLOW DEGREES Jakob became aware that his children gathered around him in his and Anna's *Kammer*. In the next room he could hear his grandchildren's muted voices.

There was something he had forgotten, something he felt great urgency to tell them. But his mind refused to summon the words.

When Johannes sprang from his chair and reached out, Barbara stopped him. "He's not choking. He's crying."

Someone took his hand, the one that lay beside him like a stone. "Does something pain you, Jakob?"

Anna's tender voice. With great effort he managed the slight shake of his head.

Johannes bent over him again, his anxious face coming into Jakob's view. "What troubles you, Daat? What can we do?"

At last the scripture took shape in Jakob's mind: *"Nun aber bleibt Glaube, Hoffnung, Liebe—diese drei; aber die Liebe ist die größte unter ihnen."* And now abides faith, hope, love—these three; but love is the greatest of them.

He had forgotten to tell them once, at another parting. But he would not forget again.

Forcing his eyes to open, he took in each one gathered around his bed. Barbara. Johannes. Joseph. Christian. His dear Anna. He lifted his good hand, and Christian reached to take it, while the others pressed close around him.

Summoning the last of his strength, he whispered, *"Immer . . . hab' ich euch . . . geliebt."* Always I have loved you.

"Ach, Daat." Barbara dabbed away tears with the edge of her apron even as she smiled.

His voice choked, Joseph said, "We've always loved you, too, Daat."

"Always," Christian added firmly, while the others echoed their assent.

There was something else, though not as important as the first, something Jakob wanted them to know but could not form the words: that God was working even in the rebel, that He alone determined the course of each life, that as parents they were called to love their children and to walk beside them in grace even when they rebelled.

For God knew surely how to bring the rebel back to Him again, and He could be trusted to do it. After all, had He not brought Jakob home?

But they would learn this too. In God's time.

A faint smile flickered across his face. It seemed to him that a radiance bathed the *Kammer* as though winter had, by some miracle, given way to spring before its time. And feeling the stir of wind across his cheek, he breathed in the sweet, fresh scent of coming rain.

Glossary

For more extensive information and resources, visit *www.northkill.com.*

NATIVE AMERICAN WORDS AND PHRASES

Ane (a-nay-e): (Lenape) the Milky Way; believed to be the path to heaven

bast: strong, woody fibers obtained from tree bark

beson: (Lenape) medicine; also, poison

Beaver's (Tamaque's) Town: near present-day Bolivar, Ohio

Dë'ëh hi:gë:h?: (Seneca) What is that?

Dë'ëh o'si'?: (Seneca) What did you say?

Father Onontio: (Lenape) the French governor of Canada

Gachene wullet: (Lenape) It is surely good.

gáhowees: (Lenape) mother

Gaji'sashono': (Seneca) false face

Gänä'yasta': (Iroquois) Midwinter Ceremony or White Dog Sacrifice

Gane'onwon: (Seneca) Harvest Thanksgiving Ceremony

Gishela-mukaong: (Lenape) the Great Spirit, the Great Creator

ji:yäh: (Seneca) dog

Manitou: (Lenape) the leader of all gods, the Power that resides in all things in nature

manitowuk: (Lenape) one of many lesser gods below Manitou

Menetopalis: (Lenape) One Who Fights

Mehittuk: (Lenape) Forked Tree

Mingo: a division of the Seneca tribe of the Iroquois Confederacy that moved west into western Pennsylvania and the upper Ohio River region

Muskingum River: considered by the native peoples to include what is today called the Tuscarawas

Nauwaneu: (Seneca) the creator god, the Master of Life

nchutièstuk: friend

Niyawë:(Seneca) Thank you.

nóhum: (Lenape) my grandmother

Nútemau: He Watches

O'dän'kot: (Seneca) Sunshine

Ohi:'i:o': (Seneca) river beautiful; the Ohio River, including the Allegheny, considered by the native peoples to be the headwaters of the Ohio rather than a separate river

ohum: (Lenape) grandmother

o:ne:ka': (Seneca) water

pahsahëman: (Lenape) a ballgame similar to rugby that the men played against the women from early spring until mid June

pahsahikàn: (Lenape) an oblong ball used for playing *pahsahëman* made of leather stuffed with deer fur

Sedékonî?': (Seneca) You come to eat.

Sgëno: (Seneca) a greeting

ti'so:t: (Seneca) grandfather

Twightwee: the Miami Indian tribe

Wakatamothiipi: (Shawnee) Muskingum River

wampum: belts and strings made of variously colored shell or trade beads that the Indians used as money as well as for ornaments

Waano"naogwa:"ciot: (Seneca) corn planting ceremony

White Woman River: Walhonding River

wigewa: a domed dwelling for one family, common among Eastern Woodland Indians, framed with poles and overlaid with bark, woven mats, or animal hides

Wsinkhoalican: (Lenape) a miniature carved head representing a god

Wulachen: (Lenape) Fair Wind

GERMAN WORDS AND PHRASES

Apfelschnitzen: a gathering to cut and prepare ripe apples for drying and cooking

bitte: please

Daat, Daati: dad; daddy

danke: thank you

die: (pronounced dee), the

die Englishe: the English; non-Germans

Freund: friend

Freundschaft: friendship, acquaintance

Gott sei dank!: Thank God!

Gott: God

Grossdaati: grandfather

guud: good

Halsduch: women's triangular neck cloth or cape

Haube, pl. Hauben: prayer covering worn by married women

Hochzeit: wedding

Kind, pl. Kinder: child, children

Kammer: bed chamber

Küche: kitchen

Liebe: love, beloved, dear one

Maam, Maami: mommy; mom

Morgen: morning

mein: my, mine

nay: no

Onkel: uncle

Stube: parlor

Tante: aunt

Wie geht's?: How are you doing?

Vater: father

ya: yes

Appendix

WE ARE DEEPLY INDEBTED to a wealth of historical resources that allowed us to flesh out the known facts of our ancestor Jacob Hochstetler's life into a full-length story. These include contemporary records held in the Pennsylvania Archives and among private papers, such as those of Colonel Henry Bouquet. You will find a full listing on the Resources page on the Northkill website.

Our indispensable resource was the massive genealogy of the Hochstetler family, *Descendents of Jacob Hochstetler,* which includes stories passed down through the family as well as pertinent historical details about their time. Equally critical was Beth Hochstetler Mark's *Our Flesh and Blood, A Documentary History of the Jacob Hochstetler Family During the French and Indian War Period, 1757–1765.* This became the "bible" for our story's timeline and provided exact details of many events portrayed in *The Return,* such as Jacob's escape, detailed in his interrogation by Colonel Bouquet, and his petitions for the return of his sons. Mark has our greatest gratitude for the depth of the research she provided in this fascinating work—and for her gracious endorsement of this series.

The appendix provided in Book 1, *Northkill,* details many of the decisions we made in writing the series. In this volume we faced other questions. It's known that Jacob was held at the Seneca town of Buckaloons on the Allegheny River at present-day Irvine, Pennsylvania, and that one of his sons was held by the Lenape sachem Custaloga. The name of this son is not known, nor where or by which tribe the other was held. Several considerations led us to place Christian with Custaloga in Custaloga's Town at the confluence of the French Creek and North Deer Creek in present-day Mercer County, Pennsylvania. We then placed Joseph with the Lenape warrior Shingas in Sauconk on the Ohio River at present day Beaver, Pennsylvania, near the mouth of Beaver Creek, where important historical events took place.

Since both boys lived among the Indians for a number of years, we had to decide how to refer to Joseph and Christian as they fully assumed new native identities. In the story we refer to them by their given names until they undertake their vision quest. At that point we call them by the Lenape names we chose for them, transitioning back to their given names on their return home.

It is highly likely that Jacob and his sons knew about the work of the Moravian missionaries to the Indians and possibly even encountered some of them. The details of Christian Frederick Post's journey to Fort Du Quesne on behalf of Governor Denny, during which he passed through Sauconk, his speeches and those of several Lenape leaders, and his relationship with Tamaque and Shingas were taken from his journals and are entirely accurate except for any interaction with Joseph and his Lenape family. Post later established a short-lived mission on the Muskingum as portrayed. Another well-known missionary, David Zeisberger, did indeed found a mission settlement on the Beaver River, and later moved to the Muskingum to live among his beloved Lenape people and share their trials until his death.

We count ourselves highly blessed by the faithful witness of our ancestor Jacob and his descendents, who speak to us down through the years of God's enduring love and provision in the deepest trial. May our Lord and Savior Jesus Christ be glorified in this story, and through it may His grace and mercy abound to you.

Made in the USA
Monee, IL
11 June 2023

35614751R00267